序 言

　　「全民英語能力檢定測驗」已逐漸成爲國内各大企業選用人才的篩選標準，因此對於一般大學生而言，在畢業之前，通過「**中高級英語能力檢定測驗**」是勢在必行的。在講求專業認證的社會，擁有英語能力的證書，才能證明你的社會價值，才有足夠的競爭力。

　　根據全民英檢中心所公佈的資料指出，通過中高級英檢的人，英語能力相當於「**大學非英語主修系所畢業**」，也就是說，無論你的學歷如何，通過這個測驗，你的英語能力就有大學生的程度。現在不管是公家機關或是私人企業，在任用人才時，都設立了英語能力的門檻，許多學校在甄選教師時，也規定必須要有通過中高級英檢的證書。英語能力已經隨著時代的進步，而日趨重要了。

　　中高級英檢分爲初試和複試，初試是在每年五月和十月舉辦，測驗内容包含聽力測驗和閱讀測驗。而「**中高級英語模擬試題詳解 ①**」就是專爲中高級英檢初試設計的，書中一共收錄四回完整的試題，每一回都分爲聽力和閱讀兩部份，題型完全仿照全民英檢測驗，準備報考中高級英檢的讀者，一定要擁有且善用這本書。

　　書中所有試題都經專業外籍教師 Laura E. Stewart、及資深英語教師謝靜芳老師、蔡琇瑩老師，以及張碧紋老師審慎校對過，每一道題目都附有詳盡的解説及註釋，讓讀者能一目了然。另外，本書雖經審慎編校，但仍恐有疏漏之處，望各界先進不吝批評指教。

劉 毅

中高級英檢測驗內容

測驗項目	初　　試		複　　試	
測 驗 項 目	聽力測驗	閱讀能力測驗	寫作能力測驗	口說能力測驗
總 題 數	45題	50題	2題	10題
總作答時間	約35分鐘	50分鐘	50分鐘	約20分鐘
測 驗 內 容	問答 簡短對話 簡短談話	詞彙和結構 段落填空 閱讀理解	中譯英 引導寫作	回答問題 看圖敘述 申述題
總測驗時間 （含試前、 試後說明）	兩項一共約需2小時		約需1小時	約需1小時

中高級英檢成績計算及通過標準

初　　試	通過標準	滿分	複　　試	通過標準	滿分
聽力測驗	80	120	寫作能力測驗	80	100
閱讀能力測驗	80	120	口說能力測驗	80	100

註：　根據語言訓練中心所公佈的資料說明，英檢測驗並未針對特定領域
　　　或教材命題，但因測驗包含聽、說、讀、寫四部分，而國內英語教
　　　育偏重讀、寫，因此考生平日須另外加強聽、說訓練，同時多接觸
　　　英語媒體（如報章雜誌、廣播、電視、電影、網站等），以求在測
　　　驗時有較好的表現。

全民英語能力分級檢定測驗
GENERAL ENGLISH PROFICIENCY TEST
中高級聽力測驗
HIGH-INTERMEDIATE LISTENING COMPREHENSION TEST

This listening comprehension test will test your ability to understand spoken English. In this test, each conversation, short talk and question will be spoken JUST ONE TIME. They will not be written out for you. There are three parts to this test. Special instructions will be given to you at the beginning of each part.

Part A

In part A, you will hear 15 questions. After you hear a question, read the four choices in your test book and decide which one is the best answer to the question you have heard.

Example:

<u>You will hear</u>: Mary, can you tell me what time it is?

<u>You will read</u>: A. About two hours ago.

B. I used to be able to, but not now.

C. Sure, it's half past nine.

D. Today is October 22.

The best answer to the question "Mary, can you tell me what time it is?" is C: "Sure, it's half past nine." Therefore, you should choose answer C.

1. A. I'll do my best.
   B. Sorry, I'm dating someone else.
   C. His schedule looks fully booked up.
   D. Never in the future.

2. A. Yes, I have a layover.
   B. I'm flying directly to my destination.
   C. No, I have two departure dates.
   D. I have a confirmed round trip ticket.

3. A. I prefer to pour my own.
   B. I'll give you cream and sugar.
   C. I like mine black.
   D. I love ice cube in mine.

4. A. Of course, making money.
   B. What a ridiculous answer!
   C. I am crazy about both.
   D. Romance can be expensive.

5. A. It smells sweaty.
   B. It's coming from the air vent.
   C. It's a burning odor.
   D. It's going to the toilet.

6. A. Don't answer that question.
   B. You're hoping to catch up on my friends.
   C. She has to lose much weight.
   D. I have to make some bucks.

7. A. Oops. I'm sorry to
   disturb you.
   B. You should try again.
   C. I'm sorry to disagree.
   D. It won't happen again.

8. A. That's not uncomfortable
   to me.
   B. Sorry, I can't borrow it
   from you.
   C. Sorry buddy, absolutely
   not.
   D. We gave credit to his
   story.

9. A. I just saw a funny movie.
   B. I have chronic allergies.
   C. My eyes don't scratch me.
   D. I saw something itchy.

10. A. Only if you are
    sick.
    B. It's unhealthy and
    sanitary.
    C. Of course it is.
    D. No, thank you, not
    today.

11. A. He advised you to
    reconsider.
    B. I suggest that I do.
    C. By all means, yes.
    D. She is so popular.

Please turn to the next page. ▮⇨

12. A. My parents inherited
     it to me.
    B. I work out every
       morning.
    C. I practice exercise
       every month.
    D. It's my lifestyle.

13. A. Sure I can,
       anything for you.
    B. Let me dwell about it.
    C. Sorry, I'm almost
       broke.
    D. I'll think about you
       later.

14. A. If you insist, OK.
    B. We should both
       treat.
    C. I can't let you say
       that.
    D. It's my turn to go
       Dutch.

15. A. I was upset over her
       illness.
    B. Can I tell you why?
    C. I'll feel bad about
       your presence.
    D. I'll be disappointed
       but that's OK.

Part B

In part B, you will hear 15 conversations between a man and a woman. After each conversation, you will hear a question about the conversation. After you hear the question, read the four choices in your test book and choose the best answer to the question you have heard.

Example:

You will hear: (Man)   May I see your driver's license?
              (Woman) Yes, officer. Here it is. Was I speeding?
              (Man)   Yes, ma'am. You were doing sixty in a forty-five-mile-an-hour zone.
              (Woman) No way! I don't believe you.
              (Man)   Well, it is true and here is your ticket.

Question: Why does the man ask for the woman's driver's license?

You will read: A. She was going too fast.
              B. To check its limitations.
              C. To check her age.
              D. She entered a restricted zone.

The best answer to the question "Why does the man ask for the woman's driver's license?" is A: "She was going too fast." Therefore, you should choose answer A.

Please turn to the next page.

16. A. She will go to graduate school.
    B. She doesn't know yet.
    C. She can't tell you later.
    D. She doesn't want to find out.

17. A. Being able to keep his job.
    B. Being unable to finish his workload.
    C. Being too tired to work overtime.
    D. Dying from too much paperwork.

18. A. She's going to be fine.
    B. She's going to be in a traffic jam.
    C. She's going to buy a ticket.
    D. She's going to get a speeding ticket.

19. A. Failing the exam.
    B. Arguing with everyone in the homeroom.
    C. Having a mean homeroom teacher.
    D. Being hit by her teacher.

20. A. The woman is driving dangerously.
    B. The man is too worried.
    C. She missed the correct exit.
    D. He thinks they will get lost.

21. A. Relieved.
    B. Shocked.
    C. Fearful.
    D. Exhausted.

22. A. They both hate movies.
    B. They both hate getting sick.
    C. They both find violent movies disturbing.
    D. They both dislike late movies.

23. A. She's proud of herself.
    B. She's happy about the company.
    C. She feels ready to get promoted.
    D. She is happy for him.

24. A. Was her safety equipment broken?
    B. Was she lucky or forgetful?
    C. Was she going too fast?
    D. Was she careful or careless?

25. A. She dislikes telling secrets.
    B. She hates people who talk too much.
    C. She dislikes gossip.
    D. She hates talking to Her classmates.

26. A. The woman will return her items.
    B. The woman will call the police.
    C. The man will argue with himself.
    D. The woman will get in line and wait.

27. A. At a student orientation.
    B. At a graduation ceremony.
    C. In a hospital emergency room.
    D. On a vacation.

28. A. That she looks terrific.
    B. That she looks terrible.
    C. That the spa is inexpensive.
    D. That the spa is not cheaper.

29. A. He dialed the wrong phone number.
    B. It was his first time calling collect.
    C. He forgot to buy the answering machine.
    D. He forgot to dial a zero first.

30. A. To give sincere appreciation.
    B. To express their sorrow.
    C. To give themselves pity.
    D. To make the deceased feel better.

Please turn to the next page. ⏩

Part C

In part C, you will hear several short talks. After each talk, you will hear 2 to 3 questions about the talk. After you hear each question, read the four choices in your test book and choose the best answer to the question you have heard.

Example:

<u>You will hear</u>:

Thank you for coming to this, the first in a series of seminars on the use of computers in the classroom. As the brochure informed you, there will be a total of five seminars given in this room every Monday morning from 6:00 to 7:30. Our goal will be to show you, the teachers of our schoolchildren, how the changing technology of today can be applied to the unchanging lessons of yesterday to make your students' learning experience more interesting and relevant to the world they live in. By the end of the last seminar, you will not be computer literate, but you will be able to make sense of the hundreds of complex words and technical terms related to the field and be aware of the programs available for use in the classroom.

Question number 1: What is the subject of this seminar series?

<u>You will read</u>: A. Self-improvement.
 B. Using computers to teach.
 C. Technology.
 D. Study habits of today's students.

The best answer to the question "What is the subject of this seminar series?" is B: "Using computers to teach." Therefore, you should choose answer B.

Now listen to another question based on the same talk.

<u>You will hear</u>:

Question number 2: What does the speaker say participants will be able to do after attending the seminars?

<u>You will read</u>: A. Understand today's students.
 B. Understand computer terminology.
 C. Motivate students.
 D. Deal more confidently with people.

The best answer to the question "What does the speaker say participants will be able to do after attending the seminars?" is B: "Understand computer terminology." Therefore, you should choose answer B.

Please turn to the next page. ▯⟹

31. A. A volcanic eruption.
    B. A melting glacier.
    C. Volcanic activity.
    D. An earthquake.

32. A. Ten nations experienced a setback.
    B. Dozens were devastated.
    C. Scores of nations were damaged.
    D. Twelve nations suffered the most damage.

33. A. The International Red Cross.
    B. The World Health Organization.
    C. The United Nations.
    D. The European Economic Union.

34. A. Phone number for return call.
    B. Name of the caller.
    C. A brief message stating purpose of the call.
    D. Time available for returning the call.

35. A. very informal and casual.
    B. happy about the holidays.
    C. both silly and humorous.
    D. very formal and solemn.

36. A. A severe thunderstorm
   is affecting the area.
   B. A serious snowstorm is
   fast approaching.
   C. A dangerous rainstorm
   is moving in fast.
   D. An icy typhoon is moving
   away.

37. A. Check your
   thermometers.
   B. Dress warm and evacuate.
   C. Stay inside, and avoid
   going out.
   D. Illegal drivers will be
   arrested.

38. A. A tour group member.
   B. A friendly airport worker.
   C. A tour operator or ticket
   agent.
   D. A concerned food vendor.

39. A. Losing your
   valuables—getting
   ripped off.
   B. Getting sick from
   the food.
   C. Being careful about
   taking photos.
   D. Spending too much
   money.

40. A. Be frugal with your
   money.
   B. Don't ridicule
   people.
   C. Be alert, aware and
   careful.
   D. Be trusting and
   respectful.

Please turn to the next page. ▯⟹

41. A. The cost of tuition.
    B. Class size.
    C. Teacher qualifications.
    D. Testing methods.

42. A. Acquiring a New York accent.
    B. Fast learning.
    C. Acquiring a learning license.
    D. Computerized testing.

43. A. Selecting job candidates.
    B. Developing serious policies.
    C. Business efficiency.
    D. Improving communication skills.

44. A. Training for the media.
    B. International peace conference.
    C. National security planning.
    D. Emergency training for teachers.

45. A. be secretive and prepared.
    B. be in top physical condition.
    C. be willing to volunteer.
    D. be careful about selections

-The End-

中高級閱讀測驗
HIGH-INTERMEDIATE
READING COMPREHENSION TEST

This test has three parts, with 50 multiple-choice questions (each with four choices) in total. Special directions will be provided for each part. You will have 50 minutes to complete this test.

Part A: Sentence Completion

This part of the test has 15 incomplete sentences. Beneath each sentence, you will see four words or phrases, marked A, B, C and D. You are to choose the word or phrase that best completes the sentences. Then on your answer sheet, find the number of the question and mark your answer.

1. Readers sometimes skip the _____ and go directly to the first chapter of a book.
   A. cover
   B. preface
   C. index
   D. footnotes

Please turn to the next page. ⟹

2. You must wait until the wound _____ completely before you play any more baseball.
   A. heals
   B. injures
   C. swells
   D. corrects

3. When the _____ rate between the NT dollar and the US dollar is favorable, many Taiwanese take the opportunity to go to the United States.
   A. interest
   B. crime
   C. exchange
   D. unemployment

4. Miranda keeps up with all the latest _____ by reading fashion magazines.
   A. flows
   B. streams
   C. tones
   D. trends

5. The old church needs to be _____ because it's one of the most important historical buildings in the city.
   A. served
   B. reserved
   C. preserved
   D. observed

6. If you want to work in Spain, it will be a(n) _____ if you can speak Spanish.
   A. drawback
   B. advantage
   C. explanation
   D. indication

7. The fact that students don't like to wear uniforms is not enough reason to _____ the requirement.
   A. do away with
   B. look up to
   C. take notice of
   D. set eyes on

8. Mr. Roberts used to be _____ our local sales department before he was promoted to regional sales manager.
   A. in view of
   B. in accordance with
   C. in terms of
   D. in charge of

Please turn to the next page.

9. The baseball equipment is designed for boys _____ four and up.
   A. in age
   B. aged
   C. who age
   D. whom ages

10. Though _____ by heavy housework for a year, he still did well in school.
    A. having been distracted
    B. being distracted
    C. distracting
    D. having distracted

11. She _____ the hospital so soon, for she has not yet recovered.
    A. wouldn't have left
    B. shouldn't have left
    C. mustn't have left
    D. hadn't had left

12. Sherry went out with her friends and hadn't come home by midnight, _____ made her parents worry.
    A. that
    B. what
    C. it
    D. which

13. I'm too tired to cook tonight. How about having something
    _____?

    A. deliver

    B. delivered

    C. delivering

    D. delivery

14. This building and its contents are fully insured, _____.

    A. however it happens

    B. whenever it happens

    C. whatever happens

    D. what will happen

15. Mr. Scott said the painting was _____ no value, but I
    think it's a masterpiece of abstract art.

    A. by

    B. under

    C. for

    D. of

Please turn to the next page. ⇨

Part B: Cloze

This part of the test has two passages. Each passage contains seven or eight missing words or phrases. There is a total of 15 missing words or phrases. Beneath each passage, you will see seven or eight items with four choices, marked A, B, C and D. You are to choose the best answer for each missing word or phrase in the two passages. Then, on your answer sheet, find the number of the question and mark your answer.

Questions 16-22

It's miraculous that Italy's leaning tower of Pisa has remained ____(16)____ for over 800 years. The laws of physics state ____(17)____ the tower should come crashing down if it leans more than 5.4 degrees. Yet by 1995, it had reached a dangerous 5.5-degree lean and was still standing.

John Burland, a soil mechanics engineer from England, took on the task of saving this cultural jewel ____(18)____ ruin. Most previous projects to straighten the tower had only worsened its lean, so Burland's team faced constant ____(19)____ . ____(20)____ pipes inserted beneath the tower, the team carefully sucked out 70 tons of soil and then settled the structure into the remaining cavity.

The tower is now straight enough to remain stable ____(21)____
keeping its famous lean. After more than 800 years of gravity,
Pisa's miraculous tower is safe and secure—____(22)____ a few
more centuries, at least.

16. A. standing
    B. stood
    C. to stand
    D. stands

17. A. which
    B. what
    C. when
    D. that

18. A. into
    B. from
    C. about
    D. with

19. A. criticism
    B. entertainment
    C. compliments
    D. dependence

20. A. To use
    B. Used
    C. Using
    D. Used to

21. A. because
    B. while
    C. though
    D. if

22. A. on
    B. with
    C. for
    D. at

Please turn to the next page. ▯⟹

<u>Questions 23-30</u>

One day, when Mr. Smith came home from work he found his wife very ___(23)___ about something. Mr. Smith always thought that he was more sensible than his wife, so he started to give her a lecture ___(24)___ the importance of always remaining calm.

Finally he said, "It's a waste of your strength to get excited ___(25)___ small things. Train yourself to be patient, like me. Now, look at the fly that has just ___(26)___ on my nose. Am I sweeping or waving my arms around? No, I'm not. I'm ___(27)___ calm."

Just ___(28)___ he said this, Mr. Smith started shouting. He jumped ___(29)___ and waved his arms around wildly. He could not talk for some time, but at last he was able to tell his wife: The insect on his nose had not been a fly, ___(30)___ a bee.

23. A. annoy
    B. annoyed
    C. annoying
    D. annoyance

24. A. with
    B. at
    C. on
    D. in

25. A. on
    B. with
    C. about
    D. of

26. A. boarded
    B. landed
    C. fallen
    D. dropped

27. A. vividly
    B. perfectly
    C. simultaneously
    D. enthusiastically

29. A. here and now
    B. far and wide
    C. up and down
    D. back and forth

28. A. although
    B. because
    C. as
    D. if

30. A. but also
    B. instead of
    C. as well as
    D. but

Part C: Reading

In this part of the test, you will read several passages. Each passage is followed by several questions. There is a total of 20 questions. You are to choose the best answer, A, B, C or D, to each question on the basis of what is stated or implied in the passage. Then on your answer sheet, find the number of the question and mark your answer.

<u>Questions 31-33</u>

The government of Afghanistan is initiating a war upon women. Since the Taliban took power in 1996, women have lived in fear of their lives for any slight misbehavior. Women are not allowed to work or go out in public without a male relative. Professional women have been forced from their jobs

Please turn to the next page. ⟹

and stuffed into homes. Homes where a woman is present must have their windows painted so that outsiders can never see her. Women must wear silent shoes so that they are never heard.

Because they cannot work, those without male relatives or husbands are either starving to death or begging on the street, even if they hold Ph.D.'s. Therefore, depression is becoming so widespread that it has reached emergency levels. Without proper medication and treatment for severe depression, more and more women would rather take their lives than live in such conditions. It is at the point where the term "human rights violations" has become an understatement. Husbands have the power of life and death over their female relatives, especially their wives, but an angry mob has just as much right to stone or beat a woman, often to death, for exposing an inch of flesh or offending them in the slightest way.

31. Women in Afghanistan _____.
    A. work outside if they hold degrees
    B. can be stoned to death for exposing an arm
    C. are not allowed to wear silent shoes
    D. are better off without any male relatives

32. What is the best title for the article?
    A. Women's Liberation Movement
    B. Extraordinary Inhumanity
    C. Tyrannical Women in Afghanistan
    D. Women's Revolution

33. What does "human rights violations has become an understatement" mean?
    A. "Human rights violations" is strong enough to describe their situation.
    B. Women are treated badly to the point of extreme brutality.
    C. People take human rights violations lightly.
    D. It is stated that a violation of human rights is against the law.

Questions 34-36

Olaf Stapledon wrote a book called *Last and First Men*, in which he looked millions of years ahead. He told of different men and of strange civilizations, broken up by long "dark ages" in between. In his view, what is called the present time is no more than a moment in human history and we are just the First Men. In 2,000,000,000 years there will be the Eighteenth or Last Men.

However, most of our ideas about the future are really very shortsighted. Perhaps we can see some possibilities for the next fifty years. But the next hundred? The next thousand? The next million? That's much more difficult.

When men and women lived by hunting 50,000 years ago, how could they even begin to picture modern life? Yet to men

Please turn to the next page. ⇨

of 50,000 years from now, we may seem as primitive in our ideas as the Stone-Age hunters do to us. Perhaps they will spend their days *gollocking* to make new *spundels*, or struggling with their *ballalators* through the *cribe*. These words, which I have just made up, stand for things and ideas that we simply can't imagine.

So why bother even to try imagining life far in the future? Here are two reasons. First, unless we remember how short our own lives are compared with the whole of human history, we are likely to think our own interests are much more important than they really are. If we make the earth a poor place to live in because we are careless or greedy or quarrelsome, our grandchildren will not bother to think of excuses for us.

Second, by trying to escape from present interests and imagining life far in the future, we may arrive at quite fresh ideas that we can use ourselves. For example, if we imagine that in the future men may give up farming, we can think of trying it now. So set your imagination free when you think about the future.

34. The particular mention made of Stapledon's book in the opening paragraph _____.
    A. serves as a description of human history
    B. serves as an introduction to the discussion
    C. shows a disagreement of views
    D. shows the popularity of the book

R

35. *Spundels* and *ballalators* are used in the text to refer to
    _____.
    A. tools used in farming
    B. ideas about modern life
    C. unknown things in the future
    D. hunting skills in the Stone Age

36. According to the writer of the text, imagining the future
    will _____.
    A. serve the interests of the present and future generations
    B. enable us to better understand human history
    C. help us to improve farming
    D. make life worth living

Questions 37-39

Dentists think that women can put up with more pain than men. Michael is a dentist and he says, "Women are more aware of what pain is than men." Men do not seem to expect any pain and are surprised when the drilling hurts. Pain researchers think that men don't prepare for pain. A dental patient says, "I think men just try to fight the pain head-on."

There is the pain only a mother can know. Stephanie says, "I thought to myself when I had a child, 'My husband could never go through this.'" Bruce was working out at the gym

Please turn to the next page. ⎯⟹

when he said, "I think it's a big cover-up; men grunt and groan and scream at the gym more than women do. Women are much more stoic."

Some people wonder how pain tolerance is figured out. One weight lifter said, "How do you measure how much pain you feel as compared to someone else? I think we need a pain-o-meter before we can do this really right."

How about for those who've lived through years of pain? John says, "I think women endure pain better than men do but complain more often about it." Park says he complained to his wife for years about his stomach problems. What about her ability to cope with pain? He says, "She can take it. I don't know how she can take it. When she goes to the dentist, she feels nothing."

In the end, we all have to grin and bear it.

37. A pain-o-meter would be something that is used to
_____.
A. cause people to feel pain
B. help a dentist drill teeth
C. reduce patients' pain
D. measure people's tolerance for pain

38. Stephanie thinks that men can't stand as much pain as women because _____.
    A. men feel pain more often
    B. men wouldn't be able to stand the pain of childbirth
    C. women are tougher than men spiritually
    D. men are more stoic than women in many ways

39. In the last sentence the author suggests that _____.
    A. pain should make us happy
    B. pain can be cured with a smile
    C. pain is unavoidable so we have to tolerate it
    D. pain will end when one grins

Questions 40-41

Pascal says that the greatest compliment that can be paid to a book, even to a thought, is the exclamation, "I could have written that!" or "I could have said that!" In fact, the author whom we admire most is the one who writes a book that we "could" have written ourselves. And we say "bravo" when a philosopher gives us a thought of our own, only better expressed than we could have said it, or when he confirms an opinion that we already hold ourselves.

40. Pascal thinks a good book is one which _____.
    A. teaches a lesson   B. is truly interesting
    C. reads easily   D. confirms our thoughts

Please turn to the next page. ▯⟹

41. According to Pascal, a philosopher would NOT be characterized as one who _____.
    A. compliments our thoughts
    B. better expresses our thoughts
    C. confirms our opinions
    D. gives us a thought of our own

Questions 42-46

GET YOUR DEGREE AT HOME!

Have you ever wondered what a degree might be worth to you in your job or career? A lot of Americans with an associate degree average nearly $10,000 more in yearly earnings than those with just a high school diploma.

Harcourt Learning Direct offers you a way to get a specialized associate degree in 11 of today's growing fields without having to go to college full-time. With Harcourt, you study at home in your spare time, so you don't have to give up your present job while you train for a better one. Choose from exciting majors like Business Management, Accounting, Dressmaking & Design, Bookkeeping, Photography, Computer Science, Engineering, and more!

Your training includes everything you need!

Books, lessons, learning aids, even professional quality tools and equipment—everything you need to master your training and move ahead to a new career is included in your low tuition.

Your education is nationally recognized!

Nearly 2,000 American companies, including General Electric, IBM, Mobil, General Motors, Ford, and many others, have used our training for their employees. If companies like these recognize the value of our training, you can be sure that employers in your area will, too!

Earn your degree in as little as two years! Get a career diploma in just six months!

The career of your dreams is closer than your think! Even if you have no experience, you can learn valuable job skills in today's hottest fields! Step-by-step lessons make learning easy. Prepare for promotions, pay raises, and even a business of your own.

Send today for FREE information about Harcourt at-home training!

Simply fill in your name and address on the coupon above. Then, write in the name and number of the one program you're most interested in, and mail it today. We'll rush you free information about how you can take advantage of the opportunities in the field you've chosen.

Act today! Mail your coupon today!

Or call the number below:

1-800-372-1589 Call anytime, 24 hours a day, 7 days a week.

www.harcourt-learning.com

E-mail: harcourt@learning.com

Please turn to the next page. ▮⇨

42. What kind of people will probably answer this advertisement?
    A. College students preparing to work in big companies.
    B. College students preparing to study for a degree.
    C. High school graduates who want to take at-home training.
    D. High school graduates preparing for college entrance examinations.

43. Which major is NOT mentioned in the advertisement?
    A. Photography.
    B. Physiology.
    C. Accounting.
    D. Bookkeeping.

44. Through Harcourt, people can get a specialized associate degree by _____.
    A. studying full-time at school
    B. working in some big famous companies
    C. studying in their spare time
    D. studying abroad for two years

45. Harcourt training has NOT been used by _____ for its employees.
    A. General Motors
    B. Harvard University
    C. General Electric
    D. Mobil

46. How can you contact Harcourt Learning Direct?

    A. By e-mail.

    B. By visiting the office on weekdays.

    C. By making a call on weekdays only.

    D. By sending a letter no later than today.

Questions 47-50

The easy way out isn't always easiest. I learned that lesson when I decided to treat Doug, my husband of one month, to a special meal. I glanced through my cookbook and chose a menu which included homemade bread. Knowing the bread would take time, I started on it as soon as Doug left for work. As I was not experienced in cooking, I thought if a dozen was good, two dozen would be better, so I doubled everything. As Doug loved oranges, I also opened a can of oranges and poured it all into the bowl. Soon there was a sticky dough covered with ugly yellowish marks.

Realizing I had been defeated, I put the dough in the rubbish bin outside so I wouldn't have to face Doug laughing at my work. I went on preparing the rest of the meal, and, when Doug got home, we sat down to Cornish chicken with rice.

Please turn to the next page. ▯⟹

He tried to enjoy the meal but seemed disturbed. Twice he got up and went outside, saying he thought he heard a noise. The third time he left, I went to the window to see what he was doing.

Looking out, I saw Doug standing about three feet from the rubbish bin, holding the lid up with a stick and looking into the container. When I came out of the house, he dropped the stick and explained that there was something alive in our rubbish bin. Picking up the stick again, he held the lid up enough for me to see. I felt cold. But I stepped closer and looked harder. Without doubt it was my work. The hot sun had caused the dough to double in size and the fermenting yeast made the surface shake and sigh as though it were breathing. It looked like some unknown being from outer space. I could see why Doug was so shaken. I had to admit what the "living thing" was and why it was there. I don't know who was more embarrassed by the whole thing—Doug or me.

47. The writer's purpose in writing this story is _____.
   A. to share an interesting experience
   B. to show the easiest way out of a difficulty
   C. to describe the trouble facing a newly married woman
   D. to explain the difficulty of learning to cook from books

R

48. Why did the woman's attempt at making bread turn out to be unsuccessful?
   A. The canned oranges had gone bad.
   B. She didn't use the right kind of flour.
   C. The cookbook was hard to understand.
   D. She did not follow the directions closely.

49. What made the dough in the bin look frightening?
   A. The rising and falling movement.
   B. The strange-looking marks.
   C. Its shape.
   D. Its size.

50. When Doug went out the third time, the woman looked out of the window because she was
   A. surprised at his being interested in the bin.
   B. afraid that he would discover her secret.
   C. unhappy that he didn't enjoy the meal.
   D. curious to know what disturbed him.

-The End-

中高級聽力測驗詳解 ①

🎧 PART A

1. (**A**) Can you schedule me for an appointment?

   A. I'll do my best.

   B. Sorry, I'm dating someone else.

   C. His schedule looks fully booked up.

   D. Never in the future.

   * schedule〔'skɛdʒʊl〕v. 安排 n. 時間表
   appointment〔ə'pɔɪntmənt〕n. 約會
   do one's best 盡某人之力   date〔det〕v. 和~約會
   booked up （某人）時間已排滿

2. (**B**) Are you flying non-stop?

   A. Yes, I have a layover.

   B. I'm flying directly to my destination.

   C. No, I have two departure dates.

   D. I have a confirmed round trip ticket.

   * non-stop〔'nɑn'stɑp〕adv. 中途不停地；直達地
   layover〔'le,ovə〕n. 臨時滯留
   directly〔də'rɛktlɪ〕adv. 直接地
   destination〔,dɛstə'neʃən〕n. 目的地
   departure〔dɪ'partʃə〕n.（飛機）起飛；出發
   confirmed〔kən'fɝmd〕adj. 確認過的
   round trip ticket 來回票

3. (**C**) How do you like your coffee?

A. I prefer to pour my own.

B. I'll give you cream and sugar.

C. I like mine black.

D. I love ice cube in mine.

* ***prefer to*** 寧願～   pour〔pur〕v. 倒

black〔blæk〕adj. (咖啡)不加牛奶的

ice cube 冰塊

4. (**C**) Do you prefer romance or adventure novels?

A. Of course, making money.

B. What a ridiculous answer!

C. I am crazy about both.

D. Romance can be expensive.

* romance〔'roməns〕n. 愛情小說

adventure〔əd'vɛntʃɚ〕n. 冒險故事

make money 賺錢

ridiculous〔rɪ'dɪkjələs〕adj. 可笑的；荒謬的

be crazy about 熱衷於～

5. (**B**) Where's that strange smell coming from?

A. It smells sweaty.

B. It's coming from the air vent.

C. It's a burning odor.

D. It's going to the toilet.

* strange〔strendʒ〕adj. 奇怪的

sweaty〔'swɛtɪ〕adj. 有汗臭的   vent〔vɛnt〕n. 通風孔

odor〔'odɚ〕n. 味道   toilet〔'tɔɪlɪt〕n. 廁所

6. (**D**) What are your summer plans?

    A. Don't answer that question.

    B. You're hoping to catch up on my friends.

    C. She has to lose much weight.

    D. I have to make some bucks.

    * **catch up** 趕上　　*lose weight* 減輕體重

    buck〔bʌk〕*n.* 美元　　*make some bucks* 賺點錢

7. (**A**) Sorry, you have dialed the wrong number.

    A. Oops. I'm sorry to disturb you.

    B. You should try again.

    C. I'm sorry to disagree.

    D. It won't happen again.

    * dial〔'daɪəl〕*v.* 撥電話號碼　　oops〔ups〕*interj.* 糟糕；對不起

    disturb〔dɪ'stɜb〕*v.* 打擾

    disagree〔,dɪsə'gri〕*v.* 不一致　　happen〔'hæpən〕*v.* 發生

8. (**C**) Can I borrow your credit card?

    A. That's not uncomfortable to me.

    B. Sorry, I can't borrow it from you.

    C. Sorry buddy, absolutely not.

    D. We gave credit to his story.

    * borrow〔'baro〕*v.* 借（入）　　*credit card* 信用卡

    uncomfortable〔ʌn'kʌmfətəbl̩〕*adj.* 不舒服的

    buddy〔'bʌdɪ〕*n.* 好朋友

    absolutely〔'æbsə,lutlɪ〕*adv.* 絕對地

    give credit to 相信～

9. (**B**) Why are your eyes all red?

    A. I just saw a funny movie.

    B. I have chronic allergies.

    C. My eyes don't scratch me.

    D. I saw something itchy.

    * chronic (ˈkrɑnɪk) *adj.* 慢性的

    allergy (ˈælɚdʒɪ) *n.* 過敏

    scratch (skrætʃ) *v.* 使發癢　itchy (ˈɪtʃɪ) *adj.* 癢的

10. (**C**) Do you think it's rude to spit?

    A. Only if you are sick.

    B. It's unhealthy and sanitary.

    C. Of course it is.

    D. No, thank you, not today.

    * rude (rud) *adj.* 粗魯的　　spit (spɪt) *v.* 吐痰

    unhealthy (ʌnˈhɛlθɪ) *adj.* 不健康的

    sanitary (ˈsænə͵tɛrɪ) *adj.* 合乎衛生的

11. (**C**) Should we invite her to join us?

    A. He advised you to reconsider.

    B. I suggest that I do.

    C. By all means, yes.

    D. She is so popular.

    * invite (ɪnˈvaɪt) *v.* 邀請　　advise (ədˈvaɪz) *v.* 建議

    reconsider (͵rikənˈsɪdɚ) *v.* 再考慮

    suggest (səˈdʒɛst) *v.* 建議　　***by all means*** 一定

    popular (ˈpɑpjələ) *adj.* 受歡迎的

12. (**B**) How do you stay in such good shape?

    A.　My parents inherited it to me.

    B.　I work out every morning.

    C.　I practice exercise every month.

    D.　It's my lifestyle.

    * **stay in shape** 保持良好的健康狀態

        inherit〔ɪnˈhɛrɪt〕v. 繼承　　**work out** 運動

        lifestyle〔ˈlaɪfˌstaɪl〕n. 生活方式

13. (**A**) Could you do me a super big favor?

    A.　Sure I can, anything for you.

    B.　Let me dwell about it.

    C.　Sorry, I'm almost broke.

    D.　I'll think about you later.

    * **do** sb. **a favor** 幫忙某人

        dwell〔dwɛl〕v. 思索

        broke〔brok〕adj. 破產的　　**think about** 考慮

14. (**A**) Don't argue. It's on me.

    A.　If you insist, OK.

    B.　We should both treat.

    C.　I can't let you say that.

    D.　It's my turn to go Dutch.

    * argue〔ˈargju〕v. 爭吵　　on〔an〕prep. 由～支付

        insist〔ɪnˈsɪst〕v. 堅持　　treat〔trit〕v. 請客

        it's one's **turn** 輪到某人　　**go Dutch** 各付各的

15. (**D**) Would you mind if I didn't attend?

    A. I was upset over her illness.

    B. Can I tell you why?

    C. I'll feel bad about your presence.

    D. I'll be disappointed but that's OK.

    * attend〔ə'tɛnd〕*v.* 出席   upset〔ʌp'sɛt〕*adj.* 心煩的
      illness〔'ɪlnɪs〕*n.* 疾病   presence〔'prɛzns〕*n.* 出席
      disappointed〔,dɪsə'pɔɪntɪd〕*adj.* 失望的

📑 PART **B**.

16. (**B**) M: Are you going to grad school after you graduate?

    W: If I'm lucky, no. I have other plans.

    M: Are you trying for a scholarship or an internship?

    W: I've applied to be a student ambassador at an overseas consulate.

    M: Wow! I'm impressed. Good luck!

    Question: What is the woman going to do next year?

    A. She will go to graduate school.

    B. She doesn't know yet.

    C. She can't tell you later.

    D. She doesn't want to find out.

    * ***grad school*** 研究所 (= *graduate school*)
      graduate〔'grædʒu,et〕*v.* 畢業   ***try for*** 爭取
      scholarship〔'skalə,ʃɪp〕*n.* 獎學金
      internship〔'ɪntɜn,ʃɪp〕*n.* 實習   ***apply to*** 向～申請
      ambassador〔æm'bæsədə〕*n.* 大使
      overseas〔'ovə'siz〕*adj.* 國外的
      consulate〔'kanslɪt〕*n.* 領事館
      impress〔ɪm'prɛs〕*v.* 使印象深刻；使感動   ***find out*** 發現

17. (**B**) W：It's lunchtime. Let's grab a bite.

M：Sorry, I'm buried in paperwork here.

W：Come on, a short break won't kill you.

M：I really can't today. I don't want to be here all night.

W：I understand. Hang in there, buddy!

Question：What is the man probably worried about?

A. Being able to keep his job.

B. Being unable to finish his workload.

C. Being too tired to work overtime.

D. Dying from too much paperwork.

* **grab a bite** 吃東西　　**be buried in** 埋首於～

paperwork〔'pepə‚wɜk〕n. 文書工作

hang in (**there**) 堅持下去；不要氣餒

workload〔'wɜk‚lod〕n. 工作量

overtime〔'ovə‚taɪm〕adv. 超過時間地

die from 死於～

18. (**D**) M：Miss, may I see your license, please?

W：What seems to be the problem, officer?

M：You were doing sixty in a twenty-five mile per hour school zone!

W：But today's Sunday, school is out, officer.

M：We enforce speed limits seven days a week, ma'am.

Question：What is going to happen to the woman?

A. She's going to be fine.

B. She's going to be in a traffic jam.

C. She's going to buy a ticket.

D. She's going to get a speeding ticket.

* license〔'laɪsn̩s〕*n.* (駕駛) 執照　　do〔du〕*v.* 行駛
  per〔pɝ〕*prep.* 每　　zone〔zon〕*n.* 地區
  School is out. 學校不上課。
  enforce〔ɪn'fors〕*v.* 推行；實施　　***speed limit*** 速度限制
  ma'am〔mæm〕*n.* 女士 (= *madam*)
  ticket〔'tɪkɪt〕*n.* 罰單；票
  fine〔faɪn〕*adj.* 極好的【在此若要作「罰款」解，須用 fined】
  traffic jam 塞車　　speeding〔'spidɪŋ〕*adj.* 超速的

19. (**C**) W: There's our new homeroom teacher.

M: What a serious face! She looks strict!

W: This could be a long, tough year ahead.

M: Relax. You can't judge a book by its cover.

W: I hope you're right.

Question: What is the girl worried about?

A. Failing the exam.

B. Arguing with everyone in the homeroom.

C. Having a mean homeroom teacher.

D. Being hit by her teacher.

* homeroom〔'hom,rum〕*n.* 班級教室
  homeroom teacher 導師　　serious〔'sɪrɪəs〕*adj.* 嚴肅的
  strict〔strɪkt〕*adj.* 嚴格的　　tough〔tʌf〕*adj.* 艱難的
  judge a book by its cover 以貌取人
  fail〔fel〕*v.* 不及格　　argue〔'ɑrgju〕*v.* 爭吵
  mean〔min〕*adj.* 卑鄙的；脾氣暴躁的

20. (**A**) M：Slow down! Our exit is coming up.

W：Don't shout. You make me nervous.

M：Why are you accelerating?

W：I have to get ahead of that truck.

M：You drive like a maniac!

Question：Why is the man uncomfortable?

A. The woman is driving dangerously.

B. The man is too worried.

C. She missed the correct exit.

D. He thinks they will get lost.

* ***slow down*** 減速　　exit (ˈɛksɪt) *n.* 出口

come up 出現；前來　　accelerate (ækˈsɛləˌret) *v.* 加速

get ahead of 超過　　maniac (ˈmenɪˌæk) *n.* 瘋子

dangerously (ˈdendʒərəslɪ) *adv.* 危險地　　***get lost*** 迷路

21. (**A**) W：Is that an ambulance or a fire truck?

M：Neither. It's an air raid siren.

W：What? Are we being attacked?

M：No, silly. It's just a practice drill.

W：Thank God, I'm too young to die!

Question：How does the woman feel?

A. Relieved.　　　　B. Shocked.

C. Fearful.　　　　D. Exhausted.

* ambulance (ˈæmbjələns) *n.* 救護車　　***fire truck*** 消防車

neither (ˈniðɚ) *adv.* 兩者皆非　　***air raid*** 空襲

siren (ˈsaɪrən) *n.* 警報器　　attack (əˈtæk) *v.* 攻擊

silly (ˈsɪlɪ) *n.* 傻瓜　　drill (drɪl) *n.* 演習

relieved (rɪˈlivd) *adj.* 放心的

shocked (ʃɑkt) *adj.* 震驚的　　fearful (ˈfɪrfəl) *adj.* 害怕的

exhausted (ɪgˈzɔstɪd) *adj.* 精疲力竭的

22. (**C**) M : How was the movie last night?

W : Very disturbing.　It was too violent.

M : All blood and guts huh?

W : Yes, it was sickening.

M : I hate movies like that, too.

Question : What do they agree on?

A.　They both hate movies.

B.　They both hate getting sick.

C.　They both find violent movies disturbing.

D.　They both dislike late movies.

* disturbing〔dɪsˋtɝbɪŋ〕 *adj.* 使人心神不寧的
　violent〔ˋvaɪələnt〕 *adj.* 暴力的
　guts〔gʌts〕 *n. pl.* 內臟　　***blood and guts*** 殘酷的內容
　huh〔hʌ〕 *interj.*（表輕蔑、生氣等感嘆）哼；嘿
　sickening〔ˋsɪkənɪŋ〕 *adj.* 令人噁心的
　agree〔əˋgri〕 *v.* 意見一致　　　late〔let〕 *adj.* 深夜的

23. (**D**) W : Congratulations!　I heard you got promoted.

M : Well, actually I got a contract extension.

W : Great!　That's a vote of confidence.　Any other perks?

M : I received some stock options, too.

W : You deserve it.　Let's celebrate.

Question : How does the woman feel about the man?

A.　She's proud of herself.

B.　She's happy about the company.

C.　She feels ready to get promoted.

D.　She is happy for him.

* congratulations〔kən͵grætʃə'leʃənz〕n. pl. 恭喜

promote〔prə'mot〕v. 升遷

contract〔'kɑntrækt〕n. 契約

extension〔ɪk'stɛnʃən〕n. 延期　　vote〔vot〕n. 投票

confidence〔'kɑnfədəns〕n. 信心

a vote of confidence 信任票；支持　　perk〔pɝk〕n. 津貼

stock〔stɑk〕n. 股票　　option〔'ɑpʃən〕n. 買賣的特權

deserve〔dɪ'zɝv〕v. 應得　　celebrate〔'sɛlə͵bret〕v. 慶祝

proud〔praʊd〕adj. 感到光榮的

happy〔'hæpɪ〕adj. 感到滿足的 < *about* >

24.（ **D** ）M：Why are you wearing a cast?

W：I broke my wrist yesterday.

M：You poor thing. What happened?

W：I was rollerblading, lost control and wiped out!

M：Weren't you wearing safety gloves and wrist guards?

Question：What does the man want to know?

A. Was her safety equipment broken?

B. Was she lucky or forgetful?

C. Was she going too fast?

D. Was she careful or careless?

* cast〔kæst〕n. 石膏　　wrist〔rɪst〕n. 手腕

rollerblade〔'rolɚ͵bled〕v. 溜直排輪

wipe out （溜直排輪時）翻跌下來

safety〔'seftɪ〕adj. 保障安全的　　glove〔glʌv〕n. 手套

guard〔gɑrd〕n. 防護物　　*wrist guard* 護腕

equipment〔ɪ'kwɪpmənt〕n. 裝備

broken〔'brokən〕adj. 壞掉的

25. (**C**) W: Please don't gossip about our classmates.

　　　M: I'm not.

　　　W: Yes, you are.　You're spreading rumors.

　　　M: That's not my intention.

　　　W: I know.　Just don't exaggerate, OK?

　　Question: What does the girl dislike?

　　A.　She dislikes telling secrets.

　　B.　She hates people who talk too much.

　　C.　She dislikes gossip.

　　D.　She hates talking to her classmates.

　　* gossip〔'gɑsəp〕v. 閒聊；傳播流言蜚語　n. 閒聊；流言蜚語
　　　spread〔sprɛd〕v. 散佈（動詞三態為：spread-spread-spread）
　　　rumor〔'rumɚ〕n. 謠言
　　　intention〔ɪn'tɛnʃən〕n. 意圖；目的
　　　exaggerate〔ɪg'zædʒəˌret〕v. 誇張　　secret〔'sikrɪt〕n. 秘密

26. (**D**) M: Excuse me, Miss, the line is over here.

　　　W: But I just have one item.

　　　M: I only have three.

　　　W: But I'm in a real hurry.

　　　M: Sorry, I won't let you cut in line.

　　Question: What will probably happen next?

　　A.　The woman will return her items.

　　B.　The woman will call the police.

　　C.　The man will argue with himself.

　　D.　The woman will get in line and wait.

　　* item〔'aɪtəm〕n. 物品　　***in a hurry*** 匆匆忙忙
　　　cut in line 插隊　　return〔rɪ't3n〕v. 退還
　　　call the police 報警

27. (**B**) W: Please keep in touch.

M: I promise; I'll drop you a line.

W: Thanks, kiddo; I'll miss you.

M: Ditto that, I feel the same.

W: Thanks for all the great memories.

Question: Where might this conversation be taking place?

A. At a student orientation.

B. At a graduation ceremony.

C. In a hospital emergency room.

D. On a vacation.

* **keep in touch** 保持聯絡 (= *stay in touch*)

promise ('pramɪs) v. 答應;允諾

drop sb. **a line** 寫封短信給某人

kiddo ('kɪdo) n. 老兄;老姐 (一種表示親暱的稱呼)

ditto ('dɪto) v. 表示同意   same (sem) adj. 相同的

memory ('mɛmərɪ) n. 回憶   **take place** 發生

orientation (,orɪɛn'teʃən) n. 新生訓練

graduation (,grædʒʊ'eʃən) n. 畢業

ceremony ('sɛrə,monɪ) n. 典禮

hospital ('haspɪtḷ) adj. 醫院的

emergency (ɪ'mɝdʒənsɪ) n. 緊急情況

emergency room 急診室

vacation (ve'keʃən) n. 休假

on a vacation 度假中;休假中

28. (**A**) M : Wow! You look gorgeous! What did you do to
yourself?

W : I got a makeover at the spa.

M : What does that include?

W : I got a perm, a facial and they dyed my hair.

M : I bet you spent a fortune.

Question : What does the man think?

A. That she looks terrific.

B. That she looks terrible.

C. That the spa is inexpensive.

D. That the spa is not cheaper.

* gorgeous〔'gɔrdʒəs〕 *adj.* 極好的
makeover〔'mekovə〕 *n.* 美容
spa〔spɑ〕 *n.* 溫泉勝地 (在此指的是美容中心)
include〔ɪn'klud〕 *v.* 包括　　perm〔pɝm〕 *n.* 燙髮
facial〔'feʃəl〕 *n.* 臉部按摩；美容　　dye〔daɪ〕 *v.* 染
bet〔bɛt〕 *v.* 打賭；確信　　fortune〔'fɔrtʃən〕 *n.* 大筆錢
terrific〔tə'rɪfɪk〕 *adj.* 極好的　　terrible〔'tɛrəbl〕 *adj.* 可怕的
inexpensive〔ˌɪnɪk'spɛnsɪv〕 *adj.* 便宜的
cheaper〔'tʃipə〕 *adj.* 比較便宜的

29. (**D**) W : Bell Telephone, this is the operator. How may I help
you?

M : I'm having trouble making a collect call.

W : Did you dial a zero before the area code and the
number?

M : Oh, I totally forgot. That's the reason for sure.

W : Do you need any further assistance?

Question : What was the man's problem?

A. He dialed the wrong phone number.

B. It was his first time calling collect.

C. He forgot to buy the answering machine.

D. He forgot to dial a zero first.

* operator〔ˈɑpəˌretə〕n. 總機

have trouble + V-ing 做～有困難

collect〔kəˈlɛkt〕adj. , adv. 由對方付費的（地）

dial〔ˈdaɪəl〕v. 撥電話　　**area code** 區域號碼

reason〔ˈriznˌ〕n. 理由　　**for sure** 一定

further〔ˈfɝðə〕adj. 更進一步的

assistance〔əˈsɪstəns〕n. 幫助

answering machine 電話答錄機

30. (**B**) M：Did you hear that Tom's grandmother passed away?

W：Oh, what a shame!

M：Yeah, she was a sweet lady.

W：What can we do for Tom's family?

M：Let's write a sympathy card to offer our condolences.

Question：Why do people write sympathy cards?

A. To give sincere appreciation.

B. To express their sorrow.

C. To give themselves pity.

D. To make the deceased feel better.

* **pass away** 去世　　shame〔ʃem〕n. 令人遺憾之事

sympathy〔ˈsɪmpəθɪ〕n. 慰問　　offer〔ˈɔfə〕v. 給予

condolences〔kənˈdolənsɪz〕n. pl. 慰問的話

sincere〔sɪnˈsɪr〕adj. 眞誠的

appreciation〔əˌpriʃɪˈeʃən〕n. 感激

express〔ɪkˈsprɛs〕v. 表達　　sorrow〔ˈsɑro〕n. 悲傷

pity〔ˈpɪtɪ〕n. 同情　　**the deceased** 死者

📁 PART C.

Questions 31-33 refer to the following information.

A tsunami is a very large ocean wave caused by an earthquake or a volcanic eruption. At the end of 2004, a devastating tsunami hit South East Asia, leaving millions homeless and over 200,000 people missing or dead. Twelve Asian nations were in a state of emergency and required immediate assistance. Experts said the killer tsunami had set these nations back at least ten years. Since the tragedy, the United Nations has mobilized many disaster relief agencies. There has been a great deal of worldwide cooperation. Billions of dollars have been donated to help ease the plight of the millions of victims.

💻 Vocabulary.

tsunami〔tsuˈnɑmi〕*n.* 海嘯　　wave〔wev〕*n.* 海浪
cause〔kɔz〕*v.* 引起　　earthquake〔ˈɝθ͵kwek〕*n.* 地震
volcanic〔vɑlˈkænɪk〕*adj.* 火山的
eruption〔ɪˈrʌpʃən〕*n.* (火山) 爆發
devastating〔ˈdɛvəs͵tetɪŋ〕*adj.* 破壞性極大的
hit〔hɪt〕*v.* 襲擊　　***South East Asia*** 東南亞
leave〔liv〕*v.* 使～處於某種狀態
homeless〔ˈhomlɪs〕*adj.* 無家可歸的

missing﹝'mɪsɪŋ﹞ adj. 失蹤的

emergency﹝ɪ'mɝdʒənsɪ﹞ n. 緊急情況

state of emergency 緊急狀態　　require﹝rɪ'kwaɪr﹞ v. 需要

immediate﹝ɪ'midɪɪt﹞ adj. 立即的　　expert﹝'ɛkspɝt﹞ n. 專家

killer﹝'kɪlə﹞ adj. 致命的　　**set~back** 使（進步等）退後

at least 至少　　tragedy﹝'trædʒədɪ﹞ n. 悲劇

the United Nations 聯合國　　mobilize﹝'mobḷ,aɪz﹞ v. 動員

disaster﹝dɪ'zæstə﹞ n. 災難　　relief﹝rɪ'lif﹞ n. 救濟

agency﹝'edʒənsɪ﹞ n. 機構　　**a great deal** 許多；大量的

cooperation﹝ko,ɑpə'reʃən﹞ n. 合作

donate﹝'donet﹞ v. 捐獻　　ease﹝iz﹞ v. 減輕；減緩

plight﹝plaɪt﹞ n. 困境　　victim﹝'vɪktɪm﹞ n. 受害者

31. (**B**) Which of the following does not cause a tsunami?

　　A. A volcanic eruption.

　　B. A melting glacier.

　　C. Volcanic activity.

　　D. An earthquake.

　　* melt﹝mɛlt﹞ v. 融化　　glacier﹝'gleʃə﹞ n. 冰河

32. (**D**) How many nations were seriously affected?

　　A. Ten nations experienced a setback.

　　B. Dozens were devastated.

　　C. Scores of nations were damaged.

　　D. Twelve nations suffered the most damage.

　　* affect﹝ə'fɛkt﹞ v. 影響　　experience﹝ɪk'spɪrɪəns﹞ v. 經歷

　　setback﹝'sɛt,bæk﹞ n. 挫敗；倒退

　　dozen﹝'dʌzṇ﹞ n. 打；十二個

　　devastate﹝'dɛvəs,tet﹞ v. 破壞　　**scores of** 多數的

　　damage﹝'dæmɪdʒ﹞ v. 損壞　　n. 損害

　　suffer﹝'sʌfə﹞ v. 受損；遭受

33. (**C**) Who helped organize assistance?
    A. The International Red Cross.
    B. The World Health Organization.
    C. The United Nations.
    D. The European Economic Union.
    * organize〔ˈɔrgənˌaɪz〕v. 組織
      the International Red Cross 國際紅十字會
      the World Health Organization 世界衛生組織
      the European Economic Union 歐洲經濟聯盟

Questions 34-35 refer to the following recording.

> Hello, you have reached the residence of John and Mary Washington. We are sorry, but we are unable to come to the phone right now. Please feel free to leave your name, phone number, and a brief message after the beep. We'll do our best to get back to you as soon as possible. Thanks for calling. We look forward to talking with you. Happy Holidays!

💻 Vocabulary

recording〔rɪˈkɔrdɪŋ〕n. 錄音
reach〔ritʃ〕v. 與～取得聯繫   residence〔ˈrɛzədəns〕n. 住所
come to the phone 接電話   *right now* 現在
feel free 覺得自在   brief〔brif〕adj. 簡短的
message〔ˈmɛsɪdʒ〕n. 訊息   beep〔bip〕n. 嗶聲
get back to sb. 在電話用語中指「晚點再跟某人聯絡」。
as soon as possible 儘快   *look forward to* 期待

34. (**D**) What information is not requested when leaving a message?

    A. Phone number for return call.

    B. Name of the caller.

    C. A brief message stating purpose of the call.

    D. Time available for returning the call.

    * information〔͵ɪnfɚˋmeʃən〕 *n.* 資訊；消息

       request（rɪˋkwɛst）*v.* 要求

       return〔rɪˋtɝn〕 *adj.* 回答的　*v.* 回覆

       return call 回電　　state〔stet〕 *v.* 陳述

       purpose（ˋpɝpəs）*n.* 目的

       available〔əˋveləbḷ〕 *adj.* 有空的

35. (**A**) The tone of this recording can best be described as

    A. very informal and casual.

    B. happy about the holidays.

    C. both silly and humorous.

    D. very formal and solemn.

    * tone〔ton〕 *n.* 語調

       describe（dɪˋskraɪb）*v.* 描述

       informal〔ɪnˋfɔrmḷ〕 *adj.* 不正式的

       casual（ˋkæʒuəl）*adj.* 隨便的

       silly（ˋsɪlɪ）*adj.* 愚蠢的

       humorous〔ˋhjumərəs〕 *adj.* 幽默的

       formal（ˋfɔrmḷ）*adj.* 正式的

       solemn（ˋsɑləm）*adj.* 嚴肅的

Questions 36-37 are based on the following emergency broadcast.

Ladies and gentlemen, we are sorry for the inconvenience. We'd like to interrupt tonight's regularly scheduled program to give you this brief news bulletin. The National Weather Bureau has issued an extreme storm warning for the northeast region tonight. Estimated snow accumulation is expected to be between 20 to 30 inches in the next 24 hours. Temperatures will be dropping to sub zero levels. It is strongly advised that all residents in the northeast region stay inside and avoid any unnecessary activities. Extreme caution is advised. Stay safe by staying indoors and stay tuned to this station for further updates. Now back to our scheduled program.

Vocabulary

emergency〔ɪˋmɝdʒənsɪ〕*adj.* 緊急的
broadcast〔ˋbrɔdˏkæst〕*n.* 廣播
inconvenience〔ˏɪnkənˋvinjəns〕*n.* 不便
would like 想要　　interrupt〔ˏɪntəˋrʌpt〕*v.* 中斷
regularly〔ˋrɛgjələlɪ〕*adv.* 如期地；照常地
scheduled〔ˋskɛdʒuld〕*adj.* 按時刻表的；預定的
bulletin〔ˋbulətɪn〕*n.* 快報　　bureau〔ˋbjuro〕*n.* 政府機關
issue〔ˋɪʃju〕*v.* 發出　　extreme〔ɪkˋstrim〕*adj.* 最大的
storm〔storm〕*n.* 暴風雨　　warning〔ˋwɔrnɪŋ〕*n.* 警告
region〔ˋridʒən〕*n.* 地區　　estimated〔ˋɛstəˏmetɪd〕*adj.* 估計的
accumulation〔əˏkjumjəˋleʃən〕*n.* 累積

expect〔ɪk'spɛkt〕v. 預期　　inch〔ɪtʃ〕n. 吋

temperature〔'tɛmprətʃɚ〕n. 溫度

drop〔drɑp〕v. 下降；降低　　sub〔sʌb〕prep. 在…之下

advise〔əd'vaɪz〕v. 勸告；建議　　resident〔'rɛzədənt〕n. 居民

avoid〔ə'vɔɪd〕v. 避免　　unnecessary〔ʌn'nɛsə,sɛrɪ〕adj. 不必要的

caution〔'kɔʃən〕n. 警告；小心　　safe〔sef〕adj. 安全的

stay〔ste〕v. 保持（…的狀態）；停留

tuned〔tjund〕adj. 調好（廣播電台、電視台）的

further〔'fɝðɚ〕adj. 進一步的　　update〔ʌp'det〕n. 最新資料

36. (**B**) What is happening in the northeast region?

    A. A severe thunderstorm is affecting the area.

    B. A serious snowstorm is fast approaching.

    C. A dangerous rainstorm is moving in fast.

    D. An icy typhoon is moving away.

    * severe〔sə'vɪr〕adj. 劇烈的

    thunderstorm〔'θʌndɚ,stɔrm〕n. 雷雨

    snowstorm〔'sno,stɔrm〕n. 暴風雪

    approach〔ə'protʃ〕v. 接近

    rainstorm〔'ren,stɔrm〕n. 暴風雨　　***move in*** 襲擊

    icy〔'aɪsɪ〕adj. 冰冷的

37. (**C**) What does the National Weather Bureau recommend?

    A. Check your thermometers.

    B. Dress warm and evacuate.

    C. Stay inside, and avoid going out.

    D. Illegal drivers will be arrested.

    * recommend〔,rɛkə'mɛnd〕v. 建議　　check〔tʃɛk〕v. 查看

    thermometer〔θɚ'mɑmətɚ〕n. 溫度計

    evacuate〔ɪ'vækju,et〕v. 撤離

    illegal〔ɪ'lig!〕adj. 非法的　　arrest〔ə'rɛst〕v. 逮捕

Questions 38-40 refer to the following advice.

Here are some valuable tips for Third World travel. Be very careful when touring in a Third World country as caution is the key. Watch out for pickpockets, scam artists and thieves. Keep an eye on your belongings at all times. Never leave your stuff unattended. Also, avoid food sold on the streets. Eat only packaged and properly prepared food. Drink only bottled water or name brand beverages. Never travel alone. Stick with a partner or the group. Also, be sensitive about taking photos. Respect the people and the culture. Don't embarrass anyone. Finally, use traveler's checks, keep your passport locked in the hotel safe and just have an unforgettable experience.

Vocabulary

valuable (ˋvæljuəbḷ) *adj.* 寶貴的　　tip (tɪp) *n.* 秘訣
the Third World 第三世界 (泛指全球未開發或開發中國家)
tour (tur) *v.* 旅行　　key (ki) *n.* 關鍵　　***watch out*** 小心
pickpocket (ˋpɪkˏpɑkɪt) *n.* 扒手　　scam (skæm) *n.* 詐騙
scam artist 詐財的騙子　　thief (θif) *n.* 賊；小偷
keep an eye on 注意　　belongings (bəˋlɔŋɪŋz) *n. pl.* 財產；所有物
at all times 隨時　　stuff (stʌf) *n.* 東西
unattended (ˏʌnəˋtɛndɪd) *adj.* 未被注意的
packaged (ˋpækɪdʒd) *adj.* 包裝的　　properly (ˋprɑpɚˏli) *adv.* 適當地
bottled (ˋbɑtḷd) *adj.* 瓶裝的　　***name brand*** 知名品牌
beverage (ˋbɛvərɪdʒ) *n.* 飲料　　***stick with*** 緊跟著
sensitive (ˋsɛnsətɪv) *adj.* 敏感的　　respect (rɪˋspɛkt) *v.* 尊敬
embarrass (ɪmˋbærəs) *v.* 使尷尬　　***traveler's check*** 旅行支票
passport (ˋpæsˏport) *n.* 護照　　locked (lɑkt) *adj.* 上鎖的
safe (sef) *n.* 保險箱　　experience (ɪkˋspɪrɪəns) *n.* 經歷

38. (**C**) Who is probably giving this advice?

    A. A tour group member.

    B. A friendly airport worker.

    C. A tour operator or ticket agent.

    D. A concerned food vendor.

    * ***tour group*** 旅行團   member〔ˈmɛmbɚ〕 *n.* 成員
    tour operator 旅行社   agent〔ˈedʒənt〕 *n.* 代理商
    concerned〔kənˈsɝnd〕 *adj.* 擔憂的
    vender〔ˈvɛndɚ〕 *n.* 小販

39. (**D**) Which of the following dangers is not mentioned?

    A. Losing your valuables—getting ripped off.

    B. Getting sick from the food.

    C. Being careful about taking photos.

    D. Spending too much money.

    * danger〔ˈdendʒɚ〕 *n.* 危險   mention〔ˈmɛnʃən〕 *v.* 提及
    valuables〔ˈvæljuəblz〕 *n. pl.* 財產   ***rip off*** 偷竊

40. (**C**) What is the main idea of this passage?

    A. Be frugal with your money.

    B. Don't ridicule people.

    C. Be alert, aware and careful.

    D. Be trusting and respectful.

    * ***main idea*** 主旨   passage〔ˈpæsɪdʒ〕 *n.* 文章
    frugal〔ˈfrugl̩〕 *adj.* 節儉的
    ridicule〔ˈrɪdɪˌkjul〕 *v.* 嘲笑   alert〔əˈlɝt〕 *adj.* 警覺的
    aware〔əˈwɛr〕 *adj.* 察覺到的
    trusting〔ˈtrʌstɪŋ〕 *adj.* 信任的
    respectful〔rɪˈspɛktfəl〕 *adj.* 有禮貌的

Questions 41-42 refer to the following advertisement.

Master English in just a few months! Be fluent and bilingual in no time at all! At the New York Language Institute you can learn to speak like a native speaker. We offer top quality, intensive language training by the most experienced instructors in Asia. Small classes, computerized testing and efficient methods are just a few of the advantages we offer. All of our teachers are licensed experts. Stop procrastinating and start learning. Join us at New York English Institute right now!

Vocabulary

advertisement (ˌædvɚˈtaɪzmənt) *n.* 廣告
master (ˈmæstɚ) *v.* 精通　　fluent (ˈfluənt) *adj.* (說話) 流利的
bilingual (baɪˈlɪŋgwəl) *adj.* (能說) 兩種語言者的
in no time (at all) 立刻　　institute (ˈɪnstəˌtjut) *n.* 協會
native (ˈnetɪv) *adj.* 本國的　　top (tɑp) *adj.* 最高的
quality (ˈkwɑlətɪ) *n.* 品質　　intensive (ɪnˈtɛnsɪv) *adj.* 密集的
experienced (ɪkˈspɪrɪənst) *adj.* 經驗豐富的
instructor (ɪnˈstrʌktɚ) *n.* 教師
computerize (kəmˈpjutəˌraɪz) *v.* 電腦化
efficient (ɪˈfɪʃənt) *adj.* 有效率的　　method (ˈmɛθəd) *n.* 方法
advantage (ədˈvæntɪdʒ) *n.* 好處
licensed (ˈlaɪsn̩st) *adj.* 有執照的
procrastinate (proˈkræstəˌnet) *v.* 延遲

41. (**A**) What is not mentioned in this article?
      A. The cost of tuition.   B. Class size.
      C. Teacher qualifications.   D. Testing methods.

      * tuition〔tju'ıʃən〕 *n.* 學費
        qualifications〔,kwɑləfə'keʃənz〕 *n. pl.* 資格

42. (**B**) What is the major claim of this ad?
      A. Acquiring a New York accent.
      B. Fast learning.
      C. Acquiring a learning license.
      D. Computerized testing.

      * major〔'medʒɚ〕 *adj.* 主要的   claim〔klem〕 *n.* 要求；主張
        acquire〔ə'kwaır〕 *v.* 獲得   accent〔'æksənt〕 *n.* 口音

Questions 43-45 refer to the following statement.

    Ladies and gentlemen, welcome to this Emergency Anti-Terrorism Seminar, and good luck! Each one of you has been carefully selected to participate in this vital conference for our nations' safety. For the next week, you will be challenged ten hours a day in group discussions and activities. Mandatory attendance is expected. Every attendee must be on time. All students must be thoroughly prepared each day. You will be writing strategy reports and giving oral presentations, too. No recording devices are allowed here. No one is allowed to talk to the media or the press. This is a code red—top secret conference. Once again, good luck and remember your country is depending on you.

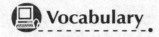 **Vocabulary**

anti-terrorism〔ˌæntɪˈtɛrəˌrɪzəm 〕*n.* 反恐怖活動（主義）
seminar〔ˈsɛməˌnɑr 〕*n.* 研討會　　select〔 səˈlɛkt 〕*v.* 挑選
participate〔 pɑrˈtɪsəˌpet 〕*v.* 參加　　vital〔ˈvaɪtl̩ 〕*adj.* 重要的
conference〔ˈkɑnfərəns 〕*n.* 會議
challenge〔ˈtʃælɪndʒ 〕*v.* 要求　　***group discussion*** 團體討論
mandatory〔ˈmændəˌtorɪ 〕*adj.* 強制的
attendance〔 əˈtɛndəns 〕*n.* 出席　　attendee〔 əˈtɛndi 〕*n.* 出席者
on time 準時　　thoroughly〔ˈθɜolɪ 〕*adv.* 徹底地
strategy〔ˈstrætədʒɪ 〕*n.* 策略　　oral〔ˈorəl 〕*adj.* 口述的
presentation〔ˌprɛznˈteʃən 〕*n.* 發表；介紹
device〔 dɪˈvaɪs 〕*n.* 設備；儀器　　allow〔 əˈlaʊ 〕*v.* 允許
media〔ˈmidɪə 〕*n. pl.* 媒體　　***the press*** 新聞界
code〔 kod 〕*n.* 代碼　　***code red*** 紅色警戒（表示極為緊急）
depend on 信賴；依靠

43. (**B**) What is the purpose of this seminar?

　　A. Selecting job candidates.

　　B. Developing serious policies.

　　C. Business efficiency.

　　D. Improving communication skills.

　　* candidate〔ˈkændəˌdet 〕*n.* 候選人
　　　develop〔 dɪˈvɛləp 〕*v.* 制定；研發
　　　serious〔ˈsɪrɪəs 〕*adj.* 重要的　　policy〔ˈpɑləsɪ 〕*n.* 政策
　　　efficiency〔 ɪˈfɪʃənsɪ 〕*n.* 效率
　　　improve〔 ɪmˈpruv 〕*v.* 改善
　　　communication〔 kəˌmjunəˈkeʃən 〕*n.* 溝通
　　　skill〔 skɪl 〕*n.* 技巧

44. (**C**) What kind of seminar is this?

    A. Training for the media.

    B. International peace conference.

    C. National security planning.

    D. Emergency training for teachers.

   * training〔'trenɪŋ〕n. 訓練

    international〔,ɪntɚ'næʃənḷ〕adj. 國際的

    peace〔pis〕n. 和平   national〔'næʃənḷ〕adj. 國家的

    security〔sɪ'kjurətɪ〕n. 安全

    planning〔'plænɪŋ〕n. 計畫

45. (**A**) All participants are reminded to

    A. be secretive and prepared.

    B. be in top physical condition.

    C. be willing to volunteer.

    D. be careful about selections.

   * participant〔par'tɪsəpənt〕n. 參加者

    remind〔rɪ'maɪnd〕v. 提醒

    secretive〔sɪ'kritɪv〕adj. 守口如瓶的

    prepared〔prɪ'pɛrd〕adj. 準備好的

    top〔tɑp〕adj. 最大的；最優良的

    physical〔'fɪzɪkḷ〕adj. 身體的

    condition〔kən'dɪʃən〕n. 狀況

    be willing to 願意   volunteer〔,vɑlən'tɪr〕v. 自願

    careful〔'kɛrfəl〕adj. 謹慎的

    selection〔sə'lɛkʃən〕n. 挑選

中高級閱讀測驗詳解 ①

🖱 PART A：Sentence Completion

1. (**B**) Readers sometimes skip the <u>preface</u> and go directly to the first chapter of a book.
讀者有時會略過書的<u>序言</u>，直接閱讀書的第一章。
   (A) cover〔'kʌvɚ〕 *n.* 封面　(B) *preface*〔'prɛfɪs〕 *n.* 序言
   (C) index〔'ɪndɛks〕 *n.* 索引
   (D) footnote〔'fʊt͵not〕 *n.* (書頁下欄的) 註腳；註釋
   * skip〔skɪp〕 *v.* 略過　chapter〔'tʃæptɚ〕 *n.* 章

2. (**A**) You must wait until the wound <u>heals</u> completely before you play any more baseball.
你必須等到傷口完全<u>復原</u>，才能再打棒球。
   (A) *heal*〔hil〕 *v.* 復原；痊癒
   (B) injure〔'ɪndʒɚ〕 *v.* 傷害　(C) swell〔swɛl〕 *v.* 腫起來
   (D) correct〔kə'rɛkt〕 *v.* 改正　*adj.* 正確的
   * wound〔wund〕 *n.* 傷口

3. (**C**) When the <u>exchange</u> rate between the NT dollar and the US dollar is favorable, many Taiwanese take the opportunity to go to the United States. 當新台幣對美金的<u>匯</u>率有盈差時，許多台灣人就會趁機去美國玩。
   (A) interest〔'ɪntrɪst〕 *n.* 利息
   (B) crime〔kraɪm〕 *n.* 犯罪；罪
   (C) *exchange*〔ɪks'tʃendʒ〕 *n.* 交換；兌換
   (D) unemployment〔͵ʌnɪm'plɔɪmənt〕 *n.* 失業
   * rate〔ret〕 *n.* 比率；率　favorable〔'fevərəbḷ〕 *adj.* 有利的
   opportunity〔͵ɑpɚ'tjunətɪ〕 *n.* 機會

4. (**D**) Miranda keeps up with all the latest <u>trends</u> by reading fashion magazines.

米蘭達藉由閱讀流行雜誌，以趕上最新的流行。

(A) flow〔flo〕*n., v.* 流動

(B) stream〔strim〕*n.* 水流；溪流

(C) tone〔ton〕*n.* 語氣；語調

(D) ***trend***〔trɛnd〕*n.* 趨勢；流行 (= *fashion*)

* ***keep up with*** 趕上　　latest〔'letɪst〕*adj.* 最新的

5. (**C**) The old church needs to be <u>preserved</u> because it's one of the most important historical buildings in the city.

那棟老教堂需要好好維護，因為那是本市最重要的歷史建築之一。

(A) serve〔sɝv〕*v.* 服務

(B) reserve〔rɪ'zɝv〕*v.* 預訂；保留

(C) ***preserve***〔prɪ'zɝv〕*v.* 維護；保存

(D) observe〔əb'zɝv〕*v.* 觀察；遵守

* historical〔hɪs'tɔrɪkḷ〕*adj.* 歷史的

6. (**B**) If you want to work in Spain, it will be an <u>advantage</u> if you can speak Spanish.

如果你想去西班牙工作，會說西班牙語是個優勢。

(A) drawback〔'drɔ,bæk〕*n.* 缺點

(B) ***advantage***〔əd'væntɪdʒ〕*n.* 優點；優勢

(C) explanation〔,ɛksplə'neʃən〕*n.* 說明；解釋

(D) indication〔,ɪndə'keʃən〕*n.* 指示；徵兆；指標

* Spain〔spen〕*n.* 西班牙
  Spanish〔'spænɪʃ〕*n.* 西班牙語

7. (**A**) The fact that students don't like to wear uniforms is not enough reason to <u>do away with</u> the requirement.

學生其實不喜歡穿制服，但這並不是<u>廢除</u>這項要求的充分理由。

(A) ***do away with*** 廢除 (= *abolish* 〔ə'bɑlɪʃ 〕)

(B) look up to 尊敬 (= *respect*)

   (↔ look down upon 輕視；瞧不起)

(C) take notice of 注意 (= *pay attention to*)

(D) set eyes on 看見 (= *lay eyes on* = *see*)

* uniform 〔'junə,fɔrm 〕 *n.* 制服

   requirement 〔 rɪ'kwaɪrmənt 〕 *n.* 要求

8. (**D**) Mr. Roberts used to be <u>in charge of</u> our local sales department before he was promoted to regional sales manager. 羅伯茲先生在升任爲區域銷售經理之前，曾經<u>負責</u>我們當地的銷售部門。

(A) in view of 有鑒於；由於～的緣故

(B) in accordance with 依據；依照 (= *according to*)

(C) in terms of 以～觀點來看；就～而言

(D) ***in charge of*** 負責；管理

* ***used to V.*** 以前…　　local 〔'lokḷ 〕 *adj.* 當地的

   department 〔 dɪ'pɑrtmənt 〕 *n.* 部門

   promote 〔 prə'mot 〕 *v.* 升遷

   regional 〔'ridʒənḷ 〕 *adj.* 區域的

9. (**B**) The baseball equipment is designed for boys <u>aged</u> four and up. 這個棒球裝備是設計給四<u>歲</u>以上的男生使用的。

* 「***aged*** + 歲數」表「～歲」。

   boys ***aged*** four = boys of age four 四歲的男生

10. (**A**) Though <u>having been distracted</u> by heavy housework for a year, he still did well in school.

雖然一年來他因爲繁忙的家務而<u>分心</u>，但他在學校的功課仍然很好。

 * 由 for a year 可知，這裡須用完成式，且依句意爲被動，故選 (A)。本句是由：Though he had been distracted 省略主詞，轉化而來。

 distract 〔 dɪ'strækt 〕 v. 使分心　heavy 〔 'hɛvɪ 〕 adj. 大量的
 housework 〔 'haʊs,wɝk 〕 n. 家事　***do well*** 表現好；功課好

11. (**B**) She <u>shouldn't have left</u> the hospital so soon, for she has not yet recovered.

她當初<u>不應該</u>那麼早出院，因爲她還沒完全康復。

 $\begin{cases} \textit{\textbf{should have}} + \textit{\textbf{p.p.}} \ 表「過去應做而未做」 \\ \textit{\textbf{shouldn't have}} + \textit{\textbf{p.p.}} \ 表「過去不應做而做」 \end{cases}$

 * ***not yet*** 尚未　recover 〔 rɪ'kʌvɚ 〕 v. 恢復（健康）

12. (**D**) Sherry went out with her friends and hadn't come home by midnight, <u>which</u> made her parents worry.

雪莉和她的朋友出去，到半夜都還沒回家，讓她父母很擔心。

 * 關係代名詞 which 可代替前面一整句話，引導補述用法的形容詞子句。補述用法的形容詞子句不可用 that 引導，要用 which，而且前面必須有逗點。

13. (**B**) I'm too tired to cook tonight. How about having something <u>delivered</u>? 我今晚累的不想煮飯。我們叫<u>外送</u>好不好？

 $\textit{\textbf{have}} + \textit{\textbf{O}}. + \begin{cases} \textit{\textbf{V}}. \ 表「主動」 \\ \textit{\textbf{p.p.}} \ 表「被動」 \end{cases}$ 依句意爲被動，故選 (B)。

14. (**C**) This building and its contents are fully insured, <u>whatever</u> <u>happens</u>. 無論發生什麼事，這棟建築物及其內容物都有投保。

* whatever 除引導副詞子句外，在子句中有代名詞的作用，做 happen 的主詞。whatever 等於 no matter what。

contents〔'kɑntɛnts〕*n. pl.* 所容納的東西；所含之物

insure〔ɪn'ʃur〕*v.* 將~投保

15. (**D**) Mr. Scott said the painting was <u>of</u> no value, but I think it's a masterpiece of abstract art.
史考特先生說這幅畫沒什麼價值，但我卻認爲它是抽象藝術中的傑作。

* *of no value*「沒有價值的」(= *valueless*)。「*of* + 抽象名詞」等於形容詞，例如：a man *of courage*「有勇氣的人」(= a *courageous* man)，a man *of importance*「重要的人」(= an *important* man)。

masterpiece〔'mæstɚ,pis〕*n.* 傑作

abstract〔æb'strækt〕*adj.* 抽象的

📄 PART B：Cloze

Questions 16-22

It's miraculous that Italy's leaning tower of Pisa has remained <u>standing</u> for over 800 years. The laws of physics state <u>that</u> the
16   17
tower should come crashing down if it leans more than 5.4 degrees. Yet by 1995, it had reached a dangerous 5.5-degree lean and was still standing.

義大利的比薩斜塔已經屹立了八百多年，真是不可思議。物理學的定理說，如果這座塔的傾斜度超過五點四度，它就會轟然倒下。可是在一九九五年時，比薩斜塔的傾斜度就達到危險的五點五度了，但它卻仍然屹立著。

miraculous〔məˈrækjələs〕adj. 不可思議的
lean〔lin〕v. n. 傾斜　　tower〔ˈtaʊɚ〕n. 塔
remain〔rɪˈmen〕v. 仍然是　　law〔lɔ〕n. 定理
physics〔ˈfɪzɪks〕n. 物理學　　state〔stet〕v. 說明
come down 倒下來　　crash〔kræʃ〕v. 轟隆一聲地倒塌
degree〔dɪˈgri〕n. 度

16. (**A**) 由於 remain（仍然是）之後須接名詞、形容詞，或分詞做補語，故選 (A) *standing*。

17. (**D**) *that* 引導名詞子句，做 state 的受詞，故選 (D)。

　　John Burland, a soil mechanics engineer from England, took on the task of saving this cultural jewel <u>from</u> ruin. Most previous
18
projects to straighten the tower had only worsened its lean, so Burland's team faced constant <u>criticism</u>. <u>Using</u> pipes inserted
19　　　　　　　20
beneath the tower, the team carefully sucked out 70 tons of soil and then settled the structure into the remaining cavity.

　　約翰・伯蘭是英國的土壤力學工程師，他承擔了拯救這個文化瑰寶免於毀滅的任務。之前大多數要把塔扶正的計劃，都只是使它的傾斜程度惡化，所以伯蘭的小組，面臨了持續不斷的批評。後來這個小組把管子插入塔的下方，小心地吸出七十噸的泥土，然後再把這座塔放進剩下的洞裡。

soil〔sɔɪl〕*n.* 土壤

mechanics〔məˈkænɪks〕*n.* 力學

engineer〔ˌɛndʒəˈnɪr〕*n.* 工程師

take on 承擔；開始進行

task〔tæsk〕*n.* 任務　　save〔sev〕*v.* 拯救

jewel〔ˈdʒuəl〕*n.* 瑰寶　　ruin〔ˈruɪn〕*n.* 毀滅

previous〔ˈprivɪəs〕*adj.* 先前的

project〔ˈprɑdʒɛkt〕*n.* 計劃

straighten〔ˈstretn̩〕*v.* 把…弄正

worsen〔ˈwɜsn̩〕*v.* 使惡化　　face〔fes〕*v.* 面臨

constant〔ˈkɑnstənt〕*adj.* 持續不斷的

pipe〔paɪp〕*n.* 管子　　insert〔ɪnˈsɜt〕*v.* 插入

beneath〔bɪˈniθ〕*prep.* 在…之下　　suck〔sʌk〕*v.* 吸出

ton〔tʌn〕*n.* 噸　　settle〔ˈsɛtl̩〕*v.* 放置

structure〔ˈstrʌktʃə〕*n.* 建築物

remaining〔rɪˈmenɪŋ〕*adj.* 剩下的　　cavity〔ˈkævətɪ〕*n.* 洞

18. (**B**) ***save*** A ***from*** B 拯救 A，使它免於 B

19. (**A**) (A) ***criticism***〔ˈkrɪtəˌsɪzəm〕*n.* 批評

　　　　(B) entertainment〔ˌɛntəˈtenmənt〕*n.* 娛樂

　　　　(C) compliment〔ˈkɑmpləmənt〕*n.* 稱讚

　　　　(D) dependence〔dɪˈpɛndəns〕*n.* 依賴

20. (**C**) 本句是由副詞子句：When the team used…簡化而來的分詞

　　　構句。副詞子句改為分詞構句有三個步驟：①去連接詞

　　　（ When 去掉），②主詞相同可省略（ the team 省略），

　　　③動詞改為現在分詞（ used 改成 using ），故選 (C) ***Using***。

The tower is now straight enough to remain stable <u>while</u>
                                                        21
keeping its famous lean. After more than 800 years of gravity,
Pisa's miraculous tower is safe and secure—<u>for</u> a few more
                                               22
centuries, at least.

比薩斜塔現在夠直了，它可以在保持穩定的狀態下，仍然保有著名
的傾斜。在八百多年的地心引力作用之下，不可思議的比薩斜塔仍舊安
全而穩固——而且至少可以再維持幾個世紀。

> straight〔stret〕adj. 直的   stable〔'stebḷ〕adj. 穩定的
> gravity〔'grævətɪ〕n. 地心引力   secure〔sɪ'kjur〕adj. 穩固的
> century〔'sɛntʃərɪ〕n. 世紀   **at least** 至少

21. (**B**) 依句意，選 (B) **while**「當…的時候；同時（= *at the same
      time*）」。而(A) 因為，(C) 雖然，(D) 如果，均不合句意。

22. (**C**) 表「持續（多久）」，介系詞用 **for**，選 (C)。

Questions 23-30

One day, when Mr. Smith came home from work he found his
wife very <u>annoyed</u> about something. Mr. Smith always thought
             23
that he was more sensible than his wife, so he started to give her a
lecture <u>on</u> the importance of always remaining calm.
        24
有一天史密斯先生下班回到家時，發現他太太在煩惱某件事。史密斯
先生總覺得自己比太太明智，所以他開始教訓他太太，告訴她永遠保持冷
靜的重要。

> sensible〔'sɛnsəbḷ〕adj. 明智的   lecture〔'lɛktʃə〕n. 訓話
> calm〔kɑm〕adj. 冷靜的

23. (**B**) 情感動詞，現在分詞修飾事物，過去分詞修飾人，依句意，選
(B) *annoyed* 〔əˋnɔɪd〕 *adj.* 心煩的；生氣的。而 (A) annoy
〔əˋnɔɪ〕 *v.* 使心煩，(C) annoying 〔əˋnɔɪɪŋ〕 *adj.* 令人心煩的，
(D) annoyance 〔əˋnɔɪəns〕 *n.* 令人心煩的事物，均不合句意。

24. (**C**) 表「關於」，介系詞用 *on* (= *about*)，選 (C)。

Finally he said, "It's a waste of your strength to get excited
<u>about</u> small things. Train yourself to be patient, like me. Now,
25
look at the fly that has just <u>landed</u> on my nose. Am I sweeping or
26
waving my arms around? No, I'm not. I'm <u>perfectly</u> calm."
27

最後他說：「為了小事而激動是浪費力氣。要訓練自己，像我一樣
有耐心。現在，看著剛停在我鼻子上的蒼蠅。我有揮舞手臂來趕走牠
嗎？不，我沒有。我非常冷靜。」

waste 〔 west 〕 *n.* 浪費　　strength 〔 strɛŋθ 〕 *n.* 力氣
excited 〔 ɪkˋsaɪtɪd 〕 *adj.* 激動的　　train 〔 tren 〕 *v.* 訓練
patient 〔ˋpeʃənt 〕 *adj.* 有耐心的　　fly 〔 flaɪ 〕 *n.* 蒼蠅
sweep 〔 swip 〕 *v.* 揮掉　　wave 〔 wev 〕 *v.* 揮動

25. (**C**) *be excited about* 對…感到興奮；對…感到激動

26. (**B**) 依句意，選 (B) *land* 〔 lænd 〕 *v.* 停在…上面 < on >。而 (A)
board 〔 bord 〕 *v.* 上 (車、船、飛機)，(C) fall「掉落」，
(D) drop「掉落」，均不合句意。

27. (**B**)　(A)　vividly〔ˈvɪvɪdlɪ〕*adv.* 生動地

　　　　　(B)　***perfectly***〔ˈpɝfɪktlɪ〕*adv.* 非常

　　　　　(C)　simultaneously〔ˌsaɪmḷˈtenɪəslɪ〕*adv.* 同時地

　　　　　(D)　enthusiastically〔ɪnˌθjuzɪˈæstɪkḷɪ〕*adv.* 熱衷地

　　　　Just <u>as</u> he said this, Mr. Smith started shouting.　He jumped
　　　　　　　28

<u>up and down</u> and waved his arms around wildly.　He could not
　　　　29

talk for some time, but at last he was able to tell his wife: The

insect on his nose had not been a fly, <u>but</u> a bee.
　　　　　　　　　　　　　　　　　30

　　　就在史密斯先生說這句話的時候,他開始大叫。他跳來跳去,並瘋
狂地到處揮動手臂。他有一陣子說不出話來,最後他才告訴他太太說:
「在他鼻子上的昆蟲,不是蒼蠅,而是蜜蜂。」

　　　　　shout〔ʃaut〕*v.* 大叫　　　wildly〔ˈwaɪldlɪ〕*adv.* 瘋狂地
　　　　　insect〔ˈɪnsɛkt〕*n.* 昆蟲　　bee〔bi〕*n.* 蜜蜂

28. (**C**)　表「當…時候」,連接詞用 ***as***(= *when*),選 (C)。

29. (**C**)　(A)　here and now 在此時此地;立刻

　　　　　(B)　far and wide 到處

　　　　　(C)　***up and down*** 上下地

　　　　　(D)　back and forth 來回地

30. (**D**)　依句意,選 (D) ***not*** A ***but*** B「不是 A,而是 B」。而 (A) 須用
　　　　　於 not only A but also B「不僅 A,而且 B」,在此不合;
　　　　　(B) instead of「而不是」,(C) as well as「以及」,則不合
　　　　　句意。

📁 PART C：Reading

Questions 31-33

The government of Afghanistan is initiating a war upon women. Since the Taliban took power in 1996, women have lived in fear of their lives for any slight misbehavior. Women are not allowed to work or go out in public without a male relative.

阿富汗政府正向女性開戰。自從塔利班政權在一九九六年掌權之後，女性就活在恐懼之下，她們害怕自己會因為任何輕微的不當舉止而送命。女人不准工作，而且沒有男性親屬的陪同，就不能到公共場所去。

Afghanistan〔æf'gænə,stæn〕n. 阿富汗
initiate〔ɪ'nɪʃɪ,et〕v. 開始；發起　　***take power*** 掌權
in fear of 擔憂…的安全　　slight〔slaɪt〕adj. 輕微的
misbehavior〔,mɪsbɪ'hevjɚ〕n. 不當的舉止
allow〔ə'laʊ〕v. 准許　　***in public*** 公開地
male〔mel〕adj. 男性的　　relative〔'rɛlətɪv〕n. 親屬

Professional women have been forced from their jobs and stuffed into homes. Homes where a woman is present must have their windows painted so that outsiders can never see her. Women must wear silent shoes so that they are never heard.

職業婦女都被迫離開工作崗位，然後被塞進家裡。有女性成員的家庭，窗戶就要上油漆，好讓外人永遠看不到她們。女人必須穿無聲的鞋子，這樣別人就永遠聽不到她們走路的聲音。

professional〔prə'fɛʃənl〕adj. 職業的
be forced from 被迫離開　　stuff〔stʌf〕v. 塞入
present〔'prɛznt〕adj. 存在的　　paint〔pent〕v. 油漆
silent〔'saɪlənt〕adj. 無聲的

Because they cannot work, those without male relatives or husbands are either starving to death or begging on the street, even if they hold Ph.D.'s. Therefore, depression is becoming so widespread that it has reached emergency levels. Without proper medication and treatment for severe depression, more and more women would rather take their lives than live in such conditions. It is at the point where the term "human rights violations" has become an understatement. Husbands have the power of life and death over their female relatives, especially their wives, but an angry mob has just as much right to stone or beat a woman, often to death, for exposing an inch of flesh or offending them in the slightest way.

因為不能工作，所以沒有男性親屬或丈夫的女人，不是快餓死，就是在街上乞討，即使有博士學位也一樣。因此，憂鬱症變得非常普遍，而且已經到達緊急的程度。有愈來愈多患有重度憂鬱症的女性，因為缺乏適當的藥物和治療，所以寧願自殺，也不願活在這樣的環境下。情況已經到了用「違反人權」這個名詞來描述，都算是輕描淡寫的程度。丈夫掌控女性親屬的生殺大權，尤其是太太的生死，但是一群憤怒的暴民，也同樣有用石頭丟一個女人，或打她的權利，而且常常是把她打死，理由是她暴露了一吋肌膚，或是因為她稍微冒犯到他們。

starve〔stɑrv〕v. 餓死　　beg〔bɛg〕v. 乞討
even if 即使　　hold〔hold〕v. 擁有
Ph.D. 博士學位（= *Doctor of Philosophy*）【複數為 Ph.D.'s】
depression〔dɪ'prɛʃən〕n. 沮喪；憂鬱症
widespread〔'waɪd,sprɛd〕adj. 普遍的
emergency〔ɪ'mɝdʒənsɪ〕adj. 緊急的
proper〔'prɑpɚ〕adj. 適當的
medication〔,mɛdɪ'keʃən〕n. 藥物
treatment〔'tritmənt〕n. 治療　　severe〔sə'vɪr〕adj. 嚴重的

would rather A ***than*** B 寧願 A 也不願 B

take *one's* ***life*** 自殺　　conditions〔kən'dɪʃənz〕*n. pl.* 環境

point〔pɔɪnt〕*n.* 階段；程度　　term〔tɜm〕*n.* 名詞；說法

violation〔ˌvaɪə'leʃən〕*n.* 違反

understatement〔'ʌndɚˌstetmənt〕*n.* 輕描淡寫

female〔'fimel〕*adj.* 女性的

especially〔ə'spɛʃəlɪ〕*adv.* 尤其是

mob〔mɑb〕*n.* 暴民【集合名詞】

as much 一樣多　　stone〔ston〕*v.* 向…丟石頭

beat〔bit〕*v.* 打　　expose〔ɪk'spoz〕*v.* 暴露

inch〔ɪntʃ〕*n.* 吋　　flesh〔flɛʃ〕*n.* 肌膚

offend〔ə'fɛnd〕*v.* 冒犯

31. (**B**) 阿富汗的婦女 ＿＿＿＿＿＿＿＿ 。

　　(A) 如果有學位，就可以外出工作

　　(B) 可能會因為露出手臂，而被人用石頭打死

　　(C) 不准穿無聲的鞋子

　　(D) 沒有任何男性親屬的話，情況會比較好

　　* degree〔dɪ'gri〕*n.* 學位　　***better off*** 情況比較好

32. (**B**) 本文最好的標題是什麼？

　　(A) 婦女解放運動　　　(B) 非常不人道的行為

　　(C) 阿富汗的殘暴婦女　　(D) 女性革命

　　* liberation〔ˌlɪbə'reʃən〕*n.* 解放

　　movement〔'muvmənt〕*n.* 運動

　　extraordinary〔ɪk'strɔrdṇˌɛrɪ〕*adj.* 非常的

　　inhumanity〔ˌɪnhju'mænətɪ〕*n.* 不人道的行為

　　tyrannical〔tɪ'rænɪkḷ〕*adj.* 殘暴的

　　revolution〔ˌrɛvə'luʃən〕*n.* 革命

33. (**B**) 『「違反人權」已經變成是種輕描淡寫的說法』是什麼意思？

(A) 「違反人權」已經強烈到足以描述他們的情況。

(B) 婦女被虐待到極端殘忍的程度。

(C) 人們對於違反人權這件事掉以輕心。

(D) 大家都說違法人權是違法的。

* describe 〔 dɪˈskraɪb 〕 v. 描述
  situation 〔 ˌsɪtʃuˈeʃən 〕 n. 情況
  treat 〔 trit 〕 v. 對待
  extreme 〔 ɪkˈstrim 〕 adj. 極端的
  brutality 〔 bruˈtælətɪ 〕 n. 殘忍
  take…lightly 對…掉以輕心
  It is stated that… 大家都說…
  against the law 違法

Questions 34-36

Olaf Stapledon wrote a book called *Last and First Men*, in which he looked millions of years ahead. He told of different men and of strange civilizations, broken up by long "dark ages" in between.

史塔普列頓寫了一本叫作「人之始末」的書，在那本書中，他看到了幾百萬年以後的未來。他談到了不同時期的人類，以及被中間的黑暗時代所打斷的奇特文明。

million 〔ˈmɪljən〕 n. 百萬　　ahead 〔 əˈhɛd 〕 adv. 往後；將來
different 〔ˈdɪfərənt〕 adj. 不同的　　man 〔 mæn 〕 n. 人類
strange 〔 strendʒ 〕 adj. 奇特的
civilization 〔ˌsɪvl̩əˈzeʃən〕 n. 文明　　break 〔 brek 〕 v. 中斷
dark ages 黑暗時代　　*in between* 在中間

In his view, what is called the present time is no more than a moment in human history and we are just the First Men. In 2,000,000,000 years there will be the Eighteenth or Last Men.

照他看來，所謂的現在，在人類史上只不過是一瞬間，我們只是最初的人類。在二十億年後，就是第十八代的人類，也就是最後的人類。

> ***what is called***… 所謂的…   present〔'prɛzn̩t〕*adj.* 現在的
> ***no more than*** 只…   moment〔'momənt〕*n.* 片刻；瞬間

However, most of our ideas about the future are really very shortsighted. Perhaps we can see some possibilities for the next fifty years. But the next hundred? The next thousand? The next million? That's much more difficult.

但是，我們對於未來的看法，大多非常短視。也許我們在接下來的五十年裡，可以看到一些可能性。但是一百年後呢？一千年後呢？一百萬年後呢？那就困難多了。

> shortsighted〔'ʃɔrt'saɪtɪd〕*adj.* 近視的
> possibility〔ˌpɑsə'bɪlətɪ〕*n.* 可能性

When men and women lived by hunting 50,000 years ago, how could they even begin to picture modern life? Yet to men of 50,000 years from now, we may seem as primitive in our ideas as the Stone-Age hunters do to us.

五萬年前，人們以打獵為生，他們甚至不知道怎麼開始想像現代生活。但是，我們對五萬年之後的人們來說，就跟石器時代的獵人對我們來說一樣原始。

> hunting〔'hʌntɪŋ〕*n.* 狩獵   picture〔'pɪktʃə〕*v.* 想像
> modern〔'mɑdən〕*adj.* 現在的   yet〔jɛt〕*conj.* 但是
> primitive〔'prɪmətɪv〕*adj.* 原始的
> ***Stone-Age*** *adj.* 石器時代的   hunter〔'hʌntə〕*n.* 獵人

Perhaps they will spend their days *gollocking* to make new *spundels*, or struggling with their *ballalators* through the *cribe*. These words, which I have just made up, stand for things and ideas that we simply can't imagine.

也許他們一輩子都在 *gollocking*，以製造新的 *spundels*，或是用 *cribe* 來和他們的 *ballalators* 搏鬥。這些字都是我捏造的，它們代表我們完全無法想像的事物和想法。

> perhaps〔pɚˋhæps〕*adv.* 或許　days〔dez〕*n. pl.* 人的一生
> ***spend** one's days* 用一生的時間來…
> struggle〔ˋstrʌɡḷ〕*v.* 搏鬥　***make up*** 捏造
> ***stand for*** 代表　simply〔ˋsɪmplɪ〕*adv.* 全然
> imagine〔ɪˋmædʒɪn〕*v.* 想像
> unless〔ʌnˋlɛs〕*conj.* 除非

So why bother even to try imagining life far in the future? Here are two reasons. First, unless we remember how short our own lives are compared with the whole of human history, we are likely to think our own interests are much more important than they really are.

所以我們為什麼要費心去試著想像遙遠的未來生活呢？有兩個理由。首先，除非我們知道，和人類整個歷史相較之下，自己的人生有多短暫，否則我們很有可能把自身的利益，看得比實際上來得重要許多。

> bother〔ˋbaðɚ〕*v.* 費勁　unless〔ənˋlɛs〕*conj.* 除非
> compare〔kəmˋpɛr〕*v.* 比較
> whole〔hol〕*adj.* 整個的
> interest〔ˋɪntrɪst〕*n.* 利益

If we make the earth a poor place to live in because we are careless or greedy or quarrelsome, our grandchildren will not bother to think of excuses for us.

如果我們因為粗心、貪心，或愛吵架，而把地球變成很糟糕的居住地點，那麼我們的子孫，將不會費心為我們找藉口。

> poor〔pʊr〕*adj.* 糟糕的　careless〔ˋkɛrlɪs〕*adj.* 粗心的
> greedy〔ˋgridɪ〕*adj.* 貪心的
> quarrelsome〔ˋkwɔrəlsəm〕*adj.* 愛爭吵的
> grandchildren〔ˋgrænd͵tʃɪldrən〕*n. pl.* 子孫
> excuse〔ɪkˋskjus〕*n.* 藉口

Second, by trying to escape from present interests and imagining life far in the future, we may arrive at quite fresh ideas that we can use ourselves. For example, if we imagine that in the future men may give up farming, we can think of trying it now. So set your imagination free when you think about the future.

第二，藉由擺脫眼前的利益，並想像久遠之後的生活，我們可能會得到一些自己可以運用的嶄新想法。舉例來說，如果我們想像未來人們將會放棄農耕，那麼我們可以考慮現在就試試看。所以當你想到未來時，要讓你的想像力自由發揮。

> escape〔əˋskep〕*v.* 擺脫
> arrive〔əˋraɪv〕*v.* 獲得
> quite〔kwaɪt〕*adv.* 非常
> fresh〔frɛʃ〕*adj.* 新的　*give up* 放棄
> farming〔ˋfɑrmɪŋ〕*n.* 農耕　*set free* 釋放
> imagination〔ɪ͵mædʒəˋneʃən〕*n.* 想像力

34. (**B**) 作者第一段特別提到史塔普列頓的書是要 ＿＿＿＿＿＿＿＿＿＿。

(A) 用來描述人類歷史

(B) 作爲討論的前言

(C) 表達不同的看法

(D) 表達這本書受歡迎的程度

* mention〔ˋmɛnʃən〕n. 提到　　*make mention of* 提到
opening〔ˋopənɪŋ〕adj. 開頭的　　serve〔sɝv〕v. 用作
description〔dɪˋskrɪpʃən〕n. 描述
introduction〔͵ɪntrəˋdʌkʃən〕n. 前言
disagreement〔͵dɪsəˋgrimənt〕n. 意見的不同
popularity〔͵pɑpjəˋlærətɪ〕n. 廣受歡迎

35. (**C**) 在本文中，*spundels* 和 *ballalators* 是用來指 ＿＿＿＿＿＿＿＿＿＿。

(A) 農耕用具

(B) 關於現代生活的看法

(C) 未來不可知的事物

(D) 石器時代的打獵技巧

* text〔tɛkst〕n. 本文　　refer〔rɪˋfɝ〕v. 是指
tool〔tul〕n. 工具　　unknown〔ʌnˋnon〕adj. 未知的

36. (**A**) 根據本文的作者，想像未來會 ＿＿＿＿＿＿＿＿＿＿。

(A) 對現在及往後的世代有利

(B) 使我們更了解人類史

(C) 有助於改善農耕

(D) 使人生更有意義

* generation〔͵dʒɛnəˋreʃən〕n. 世代
improve〔ɪmˋpruv〕v. 改善　　*worth living* 更有意義

Questions 37-39

Dentists think that women can put up with more pain than men. Michael is a dentist and he says, "Women are more aware of what pain is than men." Men do not seem to expect any pain and are surprised when the drilling hurts. Pain researchers think that men don't prepare for pain. A dental patient says, "I think men just try to fight the pain head-on."

牙醫認為女性比男性更能忍受痛苦。麥克是牙醫,他說:「女人比男人更了解疼痛。」男人似乎無法預期任何疼痛,所以當鑽孔造成疼痛時,他們會感到很驚訝。疼痛研究人員認為,男性不會為疼痛作準備。一名牙醫患者說:「我認為男人只是想要直接對抗疼痛。」

dentist (ˈdɛntɪst) *n.* 牙醫　　　***put up with*** 忍受
be aware of 知道;察覺到　　　expect (ɪkˈspɛkt) *v.* 預期
drilling (ˈdrɪlɪŋ) *n.* 鑽孔　　　researcher (rɪˈsɝtʃɚ) *n.* 研究員
patient (ˈpeʃənt) *n.* 病患　　　head-on (ˈhɛdˈɑn) *adv.* 直接地

There is the pain only a mother can know. Stephanie says, "I thought to myself when I had a child, 'My husband could never go through this.'" Bruce was working out at the gym when he said, "I think it's a big cover-up; men grunt and groan and scream at the gym more than women do. Women are much more stoic."

有一種痛,只有母親能了解。史蒂芬妮說:「我生小孩時,對自己說:『我的丈夫絕對無法忍受這個過程。』」布魯斯在健身房運動時說:「我認為男人很會掩飾;男人比女人更常在健身房喃喃抱怨、呻吟,和尖叫。女人冷靜多了。」

think to oneself 在心中想　　　***have a child*** 生小孩
go through 對…忍受到底　　　***work out*** 運動
gym (dʒɪm) *n.* 健身房　　　cover-up (ˈkʌvɚˌʌp) *n.* 掩飾
grunt (grʌnt) *v.* 發出哼聲;喃喃抱怨　　　groan (gron) *v.* 呻吟
scream (skrim) *v.* 尖叫　　　stoic (ˈsto·ɪk) *adj.* 冷靜的;堅忍的

Some people wonder how pain tolerance is figured out. One weight lifter said, "How do you measure how much pain you feel as compared to someone else? I think we need a pain-o-meter before we can do this really right."

有些人想知道，忍痛能力是如何計算出來的。一名舉重選手說：「你如何測量出和別人相較之下，你感受到多少疼痛？我想我們需要一個疼痛計，才能很正確地測量疼痛。」

> wonder〔'wʌndɚ〕v. 想知道
> tolerance〔'talərəns〕n. 忍受能力
> **figure out** 計算出來　　**weight lifter** 舉重選手
> measure〔'mɛʒɚ〕v. 測量
> pain-o-meter〔pen'amətɚ〕n. 疼痛計

How about for those who've lived through years of pain? John says, "I think women endure pain better than men do but complain more often about it." Park says he complained to his wife for years about his stomach problems.

那麼對那些長期忍受疼痛而活著的人來說，又是如何呢？約翰說：「我認為女人比男人更能忍受疼痛，但是也比較常抱怨。」派克說，他多年來，都一直向太太抱怨他的胃有問題。

> **live through** 活過；熬過　　endure〔ɪn'djur〕v. 忍受
> complain〔kəm'plen〕v. 抱怨　　stomach〔'stʌmək〕n. 胃

What about her ability to cope with pain? He says, "She can take it. I don't know how she can take it. When she goes to the dentist, she feels nothing."

In the end, we all have to grin and bear it.

那他太太應付疼痛的能力又如何呢？他說：「她可以忍受疼痛。我不知道她是怎麼忍下來的。當她去看牙醫時，她覺得沒什麼」。

我們大家終究都必須苦笑著忍受。

cope〔kop〕*v.* 應付　***take it*** 忍耐
grin and bear it 苦笑著忍受；逆來順受

37. (**D**) 疼痛計是用來 ＿＿＿＿＿＿＿＿。

(A) 使人們覺得疼痛　　(B) 協助牙醫在牙齒上鑽孔
(C) 減輕病患的疼痛　　(D) 測量人們忍受疼痛的能力

* drill〔drɪl〕*v.* 鑽孔　　reduce〔rɪˈdjus〕*v.* 減輕

38. (**B**) 史蒂芬妮認為，男人無法像女人那麼能忍受疼痛，因為

＿＿＿＿＿＿＿＿。

(A) 男人比較常覺得痛
(B) 男人無法忍受生小孩的痛
(C) 女人在精神上比男人更堅強
(D) 男人在許多方面都比女人冷靜

* childbirth〔ˈtʃaɪldˌbɝθ〕*n.* 分娩　　tough〔tʌf〕*adj.* 堅強的
spiritually〔ˈspɪrɪtʃʊəlɪ〕*adv.* 在精神上

39. (**C**) 在最後一句，作者暗示 ＿＿＿＿＿＿＿＿。

(A) 疼痛應該會讓我們開心
(B) 微笑可以治療疼痛
(C) 疼痛是無法避免的，所以我們必須忍受
(D) 當一個人咬緊牙關時，就會停止疼痛

* author〔ˈɔθɚ〕*n.* 作者　　cure〔kjur〕*v.* 治療
unavoidable〔ˌʌnəˈvɔɪdəbḷ〕*adj.* 無法避免的
tolerate〔ˈtɑləˌret〕*v.* 忍受
grin〔grɪn〕*v.* 露齒而笑；咬緊牙關

Questions 40-41

　　Pascal says that the greatest compliment that can be paid to a book, even to a thought, is the exclamation, "I could have written that!" or "I could have said that!" In fact, the author whom we admire most is the one who writes a book that we "could" have written ourselves.

　　帕司卡說，對一本書，或甚至是一個想法最大的讚美，就是大叫：「我本來可以寫出那本書的！」或是「我本來可以說出那個想法的！」事實上，我們最敬佩的作家，就是寫出我們「原本可以」寫出來的書的那個人。

> Pascal〔'pæskḷ〕n. 帕司卡【1623-62，法國數學家、物理學家及哲學家】
> compliment〔'kɑmpləmənt〕n. 讚美
> ***pay a compliment to*** 稱讚　　thought〔θɔt〕n. 想法
> exclamation〔͵ɛksklə'meʃən〕n. 大叫
> ***could have + p.p.*** 原本可以⋯　　admire〔əd'maɪr〕v. 欽佩

　　And we say "bravo" when a philosopher gives us a thought of our own, only better expressed than we could have said it, or when he confirms an opinion that we already hold ourselves.

　　當一位哲學家說出我們心中的想法，而且表達得比我們更好時，或是當他肯定我們心中所持的意見時，我們就會說「太棒了」。

> bravo〔'bravo〕interj. 太棒了
> philosopher〔fə'lɑsəfɚ〕n. 哲學家　　give〔gɪv〕v. 告訴；說
> express〔ɪk'sprɛs〕v. 表達　　confirm〔kən'fɝm〕v. 肯定
> opinion〔ə'pɪnjən〕n. 意見　　hold〔hold〕v. 擁有

40.(**D**) 帕司卡認為一本好書是 ＿＿＿＿＿＿＿＿。
　　(A) 給人教訓　　　　(B) 令人覺得真的很有趣
　　(C) 容易讀的　　　　(D) 肯定我們的想法的
　　* teach a lesson 給人教訓

41. (**A**) 根據帕司卡的說法，哲學家不能被形容成是會 ＿＿＿＿＿＿＿。

(A) 稱讚我們的想法　　(B) 以更好的方式來表達我們的想法

(C) 肯定我們的意見　　(D) 說出我們心中的想法

＊ *be characterized as* 被視為；被形容成是

compliment〔ˈkɑmpləˌmɛnt〕v. 稱讚

Questions 42-46

GET YOUR DEGREE AT HOME!

Have you ever wondered what a degree might be worth to you in your job or career? A lot of Americans with an associate degree average nearly $10,000 more in yearly earnings than those with just a high school diploma.

Harcourt Learning Direct offers you a way to get a specialized associate degree in 11 of today's growing fields without having to go to college full-time. With Harcourt, you study at home in your spare time, so you don't have to give up your present job while you train for a better one. Choose from exciting majors like Business Management, Accounting, Dressmaking & Design, Bookkeeping, Photography, Computer Science, Engineering, and more!

Your training includes everything you need!

Books, lessons, learning aids, even professional quality tools and equipment—everything you need to master your training and move ahead to a new career is included in your low tuition.

Your education is nationally recognized!

Nearly 2,000 American companies, including General Electric, IBM, Mobil, General Motors, Ford, and many others, have used our training for their employees. If companies like these recognize the value of our training, you can be sure that employers in your area will, too!

Earn your degree in as little as two years! Get a career diploma in just six months!

The career of your dreams is closer than your think! Even if you have no experience, you can learn valuable job skills in today's hottest fields! Step-by-step lessons make learning easy. Prepare for promotions, pay raises, and even a business of your own.

Send today for FREE information about Harcourt at-home training!

Simply fill in your name and address on the coupon above. Then, write in the name and number of the one program you're most interested in, and mail it today. We'll rush you free information about how you can take advantage of the opportunities in the field you've chosen.

Act today! Mail your coupon today!

Or call the number below:

1-800-372-1589　Call anytime, 24 hours a day, 7 days a week.

www.harcourt-learning.com

E-mail: harcourt@learning.com

在家就可以取得學位！

你是否曾想知道，學位對你的工作或事業可能有多少價值？許多擁有準學士學位的美國人，年薪平均比只有高中文憑的人，多了快一萬元。

Harcourt Learning Direct 提供一個途徑，讓你不必整天到大學聽課，就能拿到現在正在發展的十一個領域的專業準學士學位。有了 Harcourt，你可以利用空閒時間在家學習，所以不必放棄現有的工作，就能同時接受訓練，以找到更好的工作。選一個令人興奮的主修科目，像是企管、會計、服裝設計、簿記、攝影、電腦科學、工程等！

你的訓練課程包括你所需要的一切！

書本、課程、輔助學習的器具，甚至是具有專業品質的用具和設備——你在精通訓練課程和進入新行業時所需的一切，都包括在低廉的學費裡。

你所受的教育是全國認可的！

有將近兩千家美國公司，包括通用電氣、IBM 電腦、Mobil 石油公司、通用汽車公司、福特汽車，還有許多其他公司，都是採用我們的訓練課程，來做員工訓練。如果這些公司都認可我們的訓練課程的價值，那麼你就可以確定，你那個領域的雇主，也會認可！

你可以在短短兩年內取得學位！並在六個月內就取得專業認證！

你夢想中的職業比你想像的更靠近你！即使沒有經驗，你也可以學到目前最熱門的領域的珍貴工作技能！循序漸進的課程讓你能輕鬆地學習。要做好升遷、加薪，甚至是自行創業的準備。

今天就來函索取免費的 Harcourt 函授課程資料！

　　只要把你的姓名和住址填入上面的優惠券裡。然後寫上你最有興趣的課程名稱和號碼，今天就把它寄出去。我們會儘快把免費的資料寄給你，讓你知道如何在你選擇的領域裡，善用機會。

　　今天就行動！今天就把優惠券寄過來！

　　或是打以下的電話：

　　1-800-372-1589　任何時候都可以打，一星期七天，一天二十四小時。

　　www.harcourt-learning.com

　　電子信箱：harcourt@learning.com

---

degree〔dɪ'gri〕n. 學位　　worth〔wɝθ〕adj. 有…價值的

career〔kə'rɪr〕n. 職業　　adj. 專業的

associate〔ə'soʃɪ,et〕adj. 準…的

associate degree 【唸兩年短大而得到的】準學士學位；專科學位

earnings〔'ɝnɪŋz〕n.pl. 薪水

diploma〔dɪ'plomə〕n. 文憑；證書

offer〔'ɔfɚ〕v. 提供　　specialized〔'spɛʃəl,aɪzd〕adj. 專業的

growing〔'groɪŋ〕adj. 發展中的　　field〔fild〕n. 領域

full-time〔'fʊl'taɪm〕adv. 整天地　　spare〔spɛr〕adj. 空閒的

train〔tren〕v. 接受訓練　　major〔'medʒɚ〕n. 主修科目

management〔'mænɪdʒmənt〕n. 管理

accounting〔ə'kaʊntɪŋ〕n. 會計

dressmaking〔'drɛs,mekɪŋ〕n. 女裝裁縫

design〔dɪ'zaɪn〕n. 設計

bookkeeping〔'bʊk,kipɪŋ〕n. 簿記

photography〔fə'tɑgrəfɪ〕n. 攝影

engineering〔,ɛndʒə'nɪrɪŋ〕n. 工程學　　aid〔ed〕n. 輔助器具

professional〔prə'fɛʃənḷ〕adj. 專業的

quality〔'kwɑlətɪ〕*n.* 品質　　equipment〔ɪ'kwɪpmənt〕*n.* 設備

master〔'mæstɚ〕*v.* 精通　　training〔'trenɪŋ〕*n.* 訓練課程

move ahead to 往前進　　tuition〔tju'ɪʃən〕*n.* 學費

nationally〔'næʃənḷɪ〕*adv.* 全國地

recognize〔'rɛkəg,naɪz〕*v.* 認可；承認

employee〔,ɛmplɔɪ'i〕*n.* 員工　　value〔'vælju〕*n.* 價值

employer〔ɪm'plɔɪɚ〕*n.* 雇主　　area〔'ɛrɪə〕*n.* 領域

earn〔ɜn〕*v.* 努力獲得　　***even if*** 即使

valuable〔'væljuəbḷ〕*adj.* 珍貴的

step-by-step *adj.* 逐步的；循序漸進的

promotion〔prə'moʃən〕*n.* 升遷　　pay〔pe〕*n.* 薪水

raise〔rez〕*n.* 增加　　***a business for*** *one's own* 自行創業

at-home〔ət'hom〕*adj.* 在家裡進行的

at-home training 函授課程　　simply〔'sɪmplɪ〕*adv.* 只要

fill in 填寫　　address〔ə'drɛs〕*n.* 地址

coupon〔'kupɑn〕*n.* 優待券　　program〔'progræm〕*n.* 課程

rush〔rʌʃ〕*v.* 趕緊發送　　***take advantage of*** 利用

42.(**C**) 哪一種人可能會回覆這則廣告？

　　(A) 準備要到大公司工作的大學生。

　　(B) 準備要研讀學位的大學生。

　　(C) 想上函授課程的高中畢業生。

　　(D) 要準備大學入學考試的高中畢業生。

　　* answer〔'ænsɚ〕*v.* 回覆

　　　advertisement〔,ædvɚ'taɪzmənt〕*n.* 廣告

　　　graduate〔'grædʒu,et〕*n.* 畢業生

　　　entrance〔'ɛntrəns〕*n.* 入學

43.(**B**) 這則廣告中，沒有提到哪個主修課程？

　　(A) 攝影。　　　　　(B) 生理學。

　　(C) 會計。　　　　　(D) 簿記。

　　* physiology〔,fɪzɪ'ɑlədʒɪ〕*n.* 生理學

44. (**C**) 透過 Harcourt，人們可以藉由 ＿＿＿＿＿＿＿＿ 得到準學士學位。

    (A) 整天在學校唸書   (B) 在某些有名的大公司工作

    (C) 在空閒時間唸書   (D) 出國唸兩年的書

    * abroad〔ə'brɔd〕adv. 到國外

45. (**B**) Harcourt 訓練課程並沒有被何者採用，作為員工訓練課程？

    (A) 通用汽車公司   (B) 哈佛大學

    (C) 通用電氣   (D) Mobil 汽油公司

    * university〔ˌjunə'vɝsətɪ〕n. 大學

46. (**A**) 你要如何和 Harcourt Learning Direct 取得連絡？

    (A) 用電子郵件。   (B) 平日去辦公室拜訪。

    (C) 只能在平日打電話過去。

    (D) 最慢要在今天寄信過去。

    * contact〔kɑn'tækt〕v. 連絡

    weekday〔'wik,de〕n. 平日   ***no later than*** 最遲

Questions 47-50

    The easy way out isn't always easiest. I learned that lesson when I decided to treat Doug, my husband of one month, to a special meal. I glanced through my cookbook and chose a menu which included homemade bread.

    簡單的解決方法不一定很容易。我從決定請新婚一個月的丈夫道格吃一頓大餐這件事當中，學到這個教訓。我瀏覽了食譜之後，選了包括自製麵包的菜單。

    not always 不一定   treat〔trit〕v. 款待；宴請

    treat sb. ***to*** sth. 請某人吃某物   meal〔mil〕n. 一餐

    glance〔glæns〕v. 瀏覽   cookbook〔'kʊk,bʊk〕n. 食譜

    menu〔'mɛnju〕n. 菜單   homemade〔'hom'med〕adj. 自製的

Knowing the bread would take time, I started on it as soon as Doug left for work. As I was not experienced in cooking, I thought if a dozen was good, two dozen would be better, so I doubled everything.

我知道做麵包很花時間，所以道格一出門上班，我就開始做。因爲我沒什麼烹飪經驗，所以我以爲如果一打是剛好，那麼兩打就會更好，所以我把每樣東西都加倍。

take〔tek〕v. 花費　　**as soon as** 一…就…
as〔əz〕conj. 因爲　　experienced〔ɪk'spɪrɪənst〕adj. 有經驗的
dozen〔'dʌzn̩〕n. 一打　　double〔'dʌbl̩〕v. 使加倍

As Doug loved oranges, I also opened a can of oranges and poured it all into the bowl. Soon there was a sticky dough covered with ugly yellowish marks.

因爲道格喜歡柳橙，所以我還開了一罐柳橙，然後全部倒進碗裡。不久就出現一塊黏呼呼的麵糰，上面還佈滿醜陋的黃色斑點。

can〔kæn〕n. 罐　　pour〔pur〕v. 傾倒
bowl〔bol〕n. 碗　　sticky〔'stɪkɪ〕adj. 黏黏的
dough〔do〕n. 麵糰
cover〔'kʌvɚ〕v. 覆蓋…的表面；佈滿於
ugly〔'ʌglɪ〕adj. 醜的
yellowish〔'jɛlo·ɪʃ〕adj. 略帶黃色的　　mark〔mark〕n. 斑點

Realizing I had been defeated, I put the dough in the rubbish bin outside so I wouldn't have to face Doug laughing at my work. I went on preparing the rest of the meal, and, when Doug got home, we sat down to Cornish chicken with rice.

我知道自己失敗了之後，就把那個麵糰丟到外面的垃圾桶，這樣我就不必面對道格對失敗作品的嘲笑。我繼續準備其餘的餐點，當道格回到家後，我們坐下來吃春雞飯。

> defeat〔dɪˋfit〕v. 使失敗　　rubbish〔ˋrʌbɪʃ〕n. 垃圾
> **rubbish bin** 垃圾桶　　face〔fes〕v. 面對
> **laugh at** 嘲笑　　work〔wɝk〕n. 作品
> **go on** 繼續　　rest〔rɛst〕n. 其餘的東西
> **sit down to** 入席；坐下來吃　　**Cornish chicken** 春雞

He tried to enjoy the meal but seemed disturbed. Twice he got up and went outside, saying he thought he heard a noise. The third time he left, I went to the window to see what he was doing.

他試圖要好好享用這頓飯，但似乎心神不寧。他站起來兩次，並走到外面去，他說他覺得自己聽到奇怪的聲音。他第三次離開座位時，我到窗邊去看他在幹嘛。

> disturbed〔dɪˋstɝbd〕adj. 心神不寧的　　**get up** 站起來
> noise〔nɔɪz〕n. 奇怪的聲音　　time〔taɪm〕n. 次

Looking out, I saw Doug standing about three feet from the rubbish bin, holding the lid up with a stick and looking into the container. When I came out of the house, he dropped the stick and explained that there was something alive in our rubbish bin.

　　當我往外看，我看到道格站在離垃圾桶三呎遠的地方，用棍子把蓋子掀起來，然後往垃圾桶裡看。當我走出屋子，他丟下棍子，並且解釋說，垃圾桶裡有活的東西。

> feet〔fit〕n. pl. 呎　　lid〔lɪd〕n. 蓋子　　stick〔stɪk〕n. 棍子
> container〔kənˋtenɚ〕n. 容器　　drop〔drɑp〕v. 丟下
> explain〔ɪkˋsplen〕v. 解釋　　alive〔əˋlaɪv〕adj. 活的

Picking up the stick again, he held the lid up enough for me to see. I felt cold. But I stepped closer and looked harder. Without doubt it was my work. The hot sun had caused the dough to double in size and the fermenting yeast made the surface shake and sigh as though it were breathing.

他又把棍子撿起來，然後把垃圾桶蓋掀高一點，好讓我看到。我覺得很恐怖。但是我走近一點，並目不轉睛地看。無疑地，那是我的作品。炎熱的太陽把麵糰變成兩倍大，而發酵的酵母菌使麵糰的表面抖動，並發出像呼吸的嘆息聲。

pick up 撿起　　cold〔kold〕*adj.* 使人顫慄的
step〔stɛp〕*v.* 踏出一步；走　　hard〔hɑrd〕*adv.* 認眞地
without doubt 無疑地　　fermenting〔fəˈmɛntɪŋ〕*adj.* 發酵的
yeast〔jist〕*n.* 酵母菌　　surface〔ˈsɝfɪs〕*n.* 表面
shake〔ʃek〕*v.* 搖動　　sigh〔saɪ〕*v.* 嘆息
as though 好像…的　　breathe〔brið〕*v.* 呼吸

It looked like some unknown being from outer space. I could see why Doug was so shaken. I had to admit what the "living thing" was and why it was there. I don't know who was more embarrassed by the whole thing—Doug or me.

那看起來就像某種未知的外太空生物。我可以了解道格爲何如此震驚。我必須坦承那個「生物」是什麼，還有它爲什麼會在那裡。我不知道誰會因爲這整件事而比較尷尬──是道格還是我。

being〔ˈbiɪŋ〕*n.* 生物　　**outer space** 外太空
see〔si〕*v.* 了解　　shaken〔ˈʃekən〕*adj.* 震驚的
admit〔ədˈmɪt〕*v.* 承認　　**living thing** 生物
embarrassed〔ɪmˈbærəst〕*adj.* 尷尬的
by〔baɪ〕*prep.* 因爲

47. (**A**) 作者寫這個故事的目的是 _____ 。

(A) 分享一個有趣的經驗　(B) 說明解決困難最簡單的方法

(C) 描述一名新婚女子所面臨的困難

(D) 說明看書學做菜很難

* purpose〔'pɜpəs〕n. 目的　　share〔ʃɛr〕v. 分享
out of 脫離（…的狀態）　describe〔dɪ'skraɪb〕v. 描述；說明
newly〔'njulɪ〕adv. 新近　　married〔'mærɪd〕adj. 結婚的

48. (**D**) 為何那位女士嘗試做麵包會失敗？

(A) 罐裝柳橙已經壞了。　(B) 她用的麵粉種類不對。

(C) 食譜很難懂。　　　　(D) 她沒有嚴格遵照書中的指示。

* attempt〔ə'tɛmpt〕n. 嘗試
turn out (**to be**) 結果（成為）
unsuccessful〔ˌʌnsək'sɛsfəl〕adj. 失敗的
canned〔kænd〕adj. 罐裝的　　flour〔flaʊr〕n. 麵粉
directions〔də'rɛkʃənz〕n. pl. 指示
closely〔'kloslɪ〕adv. 嚴格地

49. (**A**) 是什麼使得垃圾桶裡的麵糰看起來如此可怕？

(A) 上下的移動。　　　(B) 看起來很怪的斑點。

(C) 麵糰的形狀。　　　(D) 麵糰的大小。

* frightening〔'fraɪtṇɪŋ〕adj. 可怕的
movement〔'muvmənt〕n. 移動；動作　shape〔ʃep〕n. 形狀

50. (**D**) 當道格第三次走出去時，那位女士往窗外看，因為她

(A) 對於道格對垃圾桶有興趣感到很驚訝。

(B) 害怕他會發現她的祕密。

(C) 對道格不喜歡餐點這件事感到不快。

(D) 很好奇地想知道，是什麼使他不安。

* discover〔dɪ'skʌvə〕v. 發現　　secret〔'sikrɪt〕n. 祕密
curious〔'kjurɪəs〕adj. 好奇的　　disturb〔dɪ'stɜb〕v. 使不安

全民英語能力分級檢定測驗
GENERAL ENGLISH PROFICIENCY TEST
中高級聽力測驗
HIGH-INTERMEDIATE LISTENING COMPREHENSION TEST

This listening comprehension test will test your ability to understand spoken English. In this test, each conversation, short talk and question will be spoken JUST ONE TIME. They will not be written out for you. There are three parts to this test. Special instructions will be given to you at the beginning of each part.

Part A

In part A, you will hear 15 questions. After you hear a question, read the four choices in your test book and decide which one is the best answer to the question you have heard.

Example:

You will hear: Mary, can you tell me what time it is?

You will read: A. About two hours ago.
　　　　　　　　B. I used to be able to, but not now.
　　　　　　　　C. Sure, it's half past nine.
　　　　　　　　D. Today is October 22.

The best answer to the question "Mary, can you tell me what time it is?" is C: "Sure, it's half past nine." Therefore, you should choose answer C.

1. A. So far so good.
   B. I really need glasses.
   C. The doctor said I should put ice on it.
   D. I got hit by a baseball.

2. A. Thanks. I guess I got lucky.
   B. Yes, you deserve it.
   C. Thanks for paying me.
   D. You can win my praise, too.

3. A. Yes, it did.
   B. Yes, please don't go.
   C. I always leave it open.
   D. Yes, I did.

4. A. It's a big region.
   B. Exactly fifty.
   C. The continent has five countries.
   D. There were thirteen original colonies.

5. A. I have no idea!
   B. It's a photo ID.
   C. Should I call the police?
   D. Mind your step.

6. A. Yes, I will soon.
   B. No, I'll never order it.
   C. Yes, they are delicious.
   D. No, they're easy to find around here.

7. A. Love is blind.
   B. Don't be shy. Let him know!
   C. Go for it; ask her!
   D. I would if I were you.

8. A. The movement caused big waves.
   B. The earth provides everything.
   C. Falling rocks made a giant wave.
   D. It killed a lot of people.

9. A. I'll make an appointment with the dentist.
   B. They went to the beach.
   C. I haven't a memory.
   D. I relaxed and took it easy.

10. A. Sorry, you are so loud.
    B. Sorry, I'm upset.
    C. I apologize for my silence.
    D. Sorry, I'll be quiet.

Please turn to the next page. ⇨

11. A. They seldom visit me.
　　B. We used to live together.
　　C. About once a month.
　　D. For a month.

12. A. No, they moved to the
　　　suburbs.
　　B. Yes, they live in a
　　　downtown high-rise.
　　C. Yes, they live in another
　　　country.
　　D. No, they don't have
　　　passports.

13. A. I used to own one.
　　B. I think they exaggerate
　　　things.
　　C. I plan to buy a stereo TV.
　　D. Shows today are too
　　　expensive.

14. A. Yes, I love action
　　　movies.
　　B. Yes, I read one
　　　last week.
　　C. No, thank you.
　　D. No, I haven't.

15. A. For two months.
　　B. In six weeks.
　　C. In the U.S.A. for
　　　sure.
　　D. Sometime in the
　　　past.

Part B

In part B, you will hear 15 conversations between a man and a woman. After each conversation, you will hear a question about the conversation. After you hear the question, read the four choices in your test book and choose the best answer to the question you have heard.

Example:

<u>You will hear</u>: (Man)   May I see your driver's license?
(Woman) Yes, officer. Here it is. Was I speeding?
(Man)   Yes, ma'am. You were doing sixty in a forty-five-mile-an-hour zone.
(Woman) No way! I don't believe you.
(Man)   Well, it is true and here is your ticket.

Question: Why does the man ask for the woman's driver's license?

<u>You will read</u>: A. She was going too fast.
B. To check its limitations.
C. To check her age.
D. She entered a restricted zone.

The best answer to the question "Why does the man ask for the woman's driver's license?" is A: "She was going too fast." Therefore, you should choose answer A.

Please turn to the next page. ▯⟹

16. A. Admiring.
    B. Resentful.
    C. Jealous.
    D. Courageous.

17. A. Her grandparents.
    B. A friend of many years.
    C. Her grandpa.
    D. An ex-boyfriend.

18. A. Frustrated by politics.
    B. Too nervous to watch.
    C. Not interested in debates.
    D. Excited about the debate.

19. A. Her computer was stolen.
    B. Her files were damaged.
    C. She got very sick.
    D. She received an infection.

20. A. Encouraging and assisting.
    B. Informing on her.
    C. Registering for the lady.
    D. Giving her the time of day.

21. A. He's working extra for no pay.
    B. He's about to get fired.
    C. He's going to go bankrupt soon.
    D. He's exhausted and broke.

22. A. She's going to be a trainer.
    B. She's going to study muscles.
    C. He's going to pull her body.
    D. He's going to help her exercise.

23. A. To win a gold medal.
    B. To be famous.
    C. To win lots of money.
    D. To join in a top-level competition.

24. A. She can become
    intelligent.
  B. She can also serve
    her country.
  C. She wants him to join
    her.
  D. He volunteered to
    impress her.

25. A. The knowledgeable
    man.
  B. The confused
    woman.
  C. The amazed man.
  D. The intelligent
    woman.

26. A. Take lots of
    vitamins.
  B. Take the oil out of
    the fast food.
  C. Eat right and work
    out.
  D. Bathe several times
    a day.

27. A. She is disappointed.
  B. She is proud of his
    bravery.
  C. She is worried she'll get
    into trouble.
  D. She is shocked and
    surprised.

28. A. No, they aren't
    convinced.
  B. Yes, they both do.
  C. They don't think it
    might be true.
  D. They have no idea.

29. A. Nobody knows yet.
  B. She hopes for a boy.
  C. She wants a healthy girl.
  D. It's up to the doctor.

30. A. They're discussing love.
  B. They're falling in love.
  C. Romance is in the air.
  D. They're trying to define
    a puzzle.

Please turn to the next page. ▯⟹

Part C

In part C, you will hear several short talks. After each talk, you will hear 2 to 3 questions about the talk. After you hear each question, read the four choices in your test book and choose the best answer to the question you have heard.

Example:

<u>You will hear:</u>

> Thank you for coming to this, the first in a series of seminars on the use of computers in the classroom. As the brochure informed you, there will be a total of five seminars given in this room every Monday morning from 6:00 to 7:30. Our goal will be to show you, the teachers of our schoolchildren, how the changing technology of today can be applied to the unchanging lessons of yesterday to make your students' learning experience more interesting and relevant to the world they live in. By the end of the last seminar, you will not be computer literate, but you will be able to make sense of the hundreds of complex words and technical terms related to the field and be aware of the programs available for use in the classroom.
>
> Question number 1: What is the subject of this seminar series?

<u>You will read</u>: A. Self-improvement.
B. Using computers to teach.
C. Technology.
D. Study habits of today's students.

The best answer to the question "What is the subject of this seminar series?" is B: "Using computers to teach." Therefore, you should choose answer B.

Now listen to another question based on the same talk.

<u>You will hear</u>:

Question number 2: What does the speaker say participants will be able to do after attending the seminars?

<u>You will read</u>: A. Understand today's students.
B. Understand computer terminology.
C. Motivate students.
D. Deal more confidently with people.

The best answer to the question "What does the speaker say participants will be able to do after attending the seminars?" is B: "Understand computer terminology." Therefore, you should choose answer B.

Please turn to the next page. ▐⇨

31. A. Over seven hours every week.
    B. It depends on the number of registrants.
    C. Too many popular ones.
    D. Over seventy all summer.

32. A. Adults only.
    B. Students on summer vacation.
    C. Both young people and adults.
    D. Young people only.

33. A. School officials are going on vacation.
    B. A contagious disease is spreading fast.
    C. Animals are spreading sickness.
    D. Many employees are quitting their jobs.

34. A. Yes, but they're advised not to.
    B. No, the police are locking doors.
    C. Only for unnecessary travel.
    D. Everyone is too nervous to go out.

35. A. Public schools.
    B. Government offices.
    C. Departments and agencies of the government.
    D. Hospitals and clinics.

36. A. An older sibling.
    B. A nursery school administrator.
    C. A loving parent.
    D. A child psychologist.

39. A. Wild dinosaur statues.
    B. Excellent hiking trails.
    C. The new penguin house.
    D. The petting zoo area.

37. A. Just about every day.
    B. Several times a month.
    C. Just on the weekends.
    D. Almost all day long.

40. A. Bring a ball to play with.
    B. Don't feed the animals.
    C. Go early and stay long.
    D. Take many photos.

38. A. It's free for everyone.
    B. It's not mentioned in the article.
    C. Entrance is free on weekdays.
    D. The price depends on your age.

41. A. Objective and fair.
    B. Subjective and biased.
    C. Critical and tolerant.
    D. Informative and upset.

Please turn to the next page. ⇨

42. A. About ten.
    B. Over a dozen.
    C. Too many to count.
    D. Two main languages.

43. A. Some bags were stolen.
    B. Some passengers are stowaways.
    C. There was a mix-up with baggage security.
    D. There is mechanical difficulty in the storage section.

44. A. Not more than four hours.
    B. Probably about two hours.
    C. Until the weather clears up.
    D. It depends on the police.

45. A. They'll receive free drinks and snacks.
    B. They'll get free coupons.
    C. A full refund is available.
    D. Free mileage discounts will be offered.

-The End-

中高級閱讀測驗

HIGH-INTERMEDIATE

READING COMPREHENSION TEST

This test has three parts, with 50 multiple-choice questions (each with four choices) in total. Special directions will be provided for each part. You will have 50 minutes to complete this test.

Part A: Sentence Completion

This part of the test has 15 incomplete sentences. Beneath each sentence, you will see four words or phrases, marked A, B, C and D. You are to choose the word or phrase that best completes the sentences. Then on your answer sheet, find the number of the question and mark your answer.

1. The mayor was asked to _____ his speech in order to allow time for his audience to raise questions.
   A. constrain
   B. conduct
   C. condense
   D. contrast

Please turn to the next page. ⇨

2. The morning newspaper says a school bus _____ with a train and the police were sent to the scene immediately.
   A. bumped
   B. collided
   C. crashed
   D. struck

3. Of the thousands of known volcanoes in the world, the _____ majority are inactive.
   A. dogmatic
   B. merciful
   C. impromptu
   D. overwhelming

4. I want to get a _____ so that I can have curly hair.
   A. germ
   B. herb
   C. perm
   D. term

5. He was _____ to steal the money when he saw it lying on the table.
   A. dragged
   B. tempted
   C. inhaled
   D. attracted

6. Although most dreams apparently happen _____, dream
   activity may be provoked by external influences.
   A. spontaneously
   B. simultaneously
   C. contagiously
   D. instantaneously

7. The insurance company paid him $10,000 in _____ after
   his accident.
   A. compensation
   B. comparison
   C. substitution
   D. commission

8. Your excuse that an elephant fell on you and made you late
   is just _____.
   A. inevitable
   B. indispensable
   C. incredible
   D. incurable

Please turn to the next page. ▢⟹

9. Iceland lies far north in the Atlantic, with its northernmost
_____ actually touching the Arctic Circle.
A. oval
B. tip
C. crust
D. dome

10. A window in the kitchen was _____, there was rubbish
everywhere, and the curtains and carpets had been stolen.
A. scattered
B. scraped
C. scratched
D. smashed

11. If you _____ the bottle and cigarettes, you'll be much
healthier.
A. take off
B. keep off
C. put off
D. set off

12. They tossed your thoughts back and forth for over an hour,
but still could not _____ them.
A. make sense of
B. make the most of
C. make light of
D. make fun of

13. Though _____ rich, he was better off than at any other
    period in his life.
    A. by any means
    B. by some means
    C. by all means
    D. by no means

14. A large part of human activity, particularly that in relation
    to the environment, is _____ conditions or events.
    A. in response to
    B. in favor of
    C. in contrast to
    D. in excess of

15. Recycling waste _____ the rate at which we use up the
    Earth's finite resources.
    A. slows down
    B. speeds up
    C. puts away
    D. copes with

Please turn to the next page. ⟹

Part B: Cloze

This part of the test has two passages. Each passage contains seven or eight missing words or phrases. There is a total of 15 missing words or phrases. Beneath each passage, you will see seven or eight items with four choices, marked A, B, C and D. You are to choose the best answer for each missing word or phrase in the two passages. Then, on your answer sheet, find the number of the question and mark your answer.

<u>Questions 16-22</u>

Although interior design has existed since the beginning of architecture, its development ___(16)___ a specialized field is really quite recent. Interior designers have become important partly because of the many facilities that might be ___(17)___ in a single large building.

The importance of interior design becomes evident when we realize how much time we spend surrounded by four ___(18)___. Being indoors so much, we want our surroundings to be as attractive and comfortable as possible. We also expect each place to be appropriate to its use. You would be shocked if your bedroom were suddenly changed to look like the inside of a restaurant. And you wouldn't feel ___(19)___ in an office that had the appearance of a school.

It soon becomes clear that the interior designer's most important and basic concern is the function of the particular space.

For example, a theater with poor lines of sight, poor sound quality, and too few entrances and ___(20)___ will not work for its purpose, no matter how beautifully it might be decorated.

___(21)___ , for any kind of space, the designer has to make many decisions. He or she must coordinate the shape, lighting and decoration of everything from ___(22)___ to floor. In addition, the designer must usually select furniture or design built-in furniture, according to the functions that need to be served.

16. A. into
    B. of
    C. for
    D. with

17. A. consisted
    B. contained
    C. composed
    D. compromised

18. A. pillars
    B. beams
    C. columns
    D. walls

19. A. correct
    B. proper
    C. right
    D. suitable

20. A. exits
    B. exists
    C. axis
    D. matrixes

21. A. On the contrary
    B. Consequently
    C. Nevertheless
    D. Namely

22. A. roof
    B. cabinet
    C. ceiling
    D. cupboard

Please turn to the next page. ▐⟹

Questions 23-30

When Winston Churchill retired for the second time from his post ____(23)____ prime minister of England, he was invited to ____(24)____ the graduating class at Oxford University. Sir Winston was seated at the head table, and was dressed in his formal wear, including his ever-present top hat, cane, and cigar.

After an ____(25)____ and too-lengthy introduction, he walked to the podium. ____(26)____ the lectern in both hands, he paused for a number of seconds and looked at his audience. Then in that Churchillian way that was ____(27)____ his, he looked at them for a full thirty seconds and said, "Never, never, never give up!" Then another long pause, and with even greater emphasis and ____(28)____, he repeated, "Never, never, never give up!" He looked at the audience a few more seconds and sat down.

Undoubtedly, this presentation was the shortest major address in history. It also was one of Churchill's most ____(29)____.

If you do ____(30)____ the advice of Winston Churchill, then I really will see you at the top!

23. A. for
    B. as
    C. on
    D. at

24. A. talk
    B. speak
    C. address
    D. speech

25. A. extension
    B. extensible
    C. extended
    D. extending

26. A. To grab
    B. Grabbed
    C. For grabbing
    D. Grabbing

27. A. universally
    B. uniquely
    C. ultimately
    D. solemnly

28. A. hypocrisy
    B. eloquence
    C. prosperity
    D. vanity

29. A. forgetful
    B. scornful
    C. memorial
    D. memorable

30. A. take
    B. receive
    C. grant
    D. adapt

Part C: Reading

In this part of the test, you will read several passages. Each passage is followed by several questions. There is a total of 20 questions. You are to choose the best answer, A, B, C or D, to each question on the basis of what is stated or implied in the passage. Then on your answer sheet, find the number of the question and mark your answer.

Please turn to the next page. ▯⟹

Questions 31-35

Although "lie detectors" are being used by governments, police departments, and businesses that all want guaranteed ways of detecting the truth, the results are not always accurate. Lie detectors are also called emotion detectors, for their aim is to measure bodily changes that indicate a contradiction in what a person says. The polygraph machine records changes in heart rate, breathing, blood pressure, and the electrical activity of the skin. In the first part of the polygraph test, you are electronically connected to the machine and asked a few neutral questions, like "What's your name?" or "Where do you live?". Your physical reactions serve as the standard for evaluating what comes next. Then you are asked a few critical questions among the neutral ones, like "When did you rob the bank?" The assumption is that if you are guilty, your body will reveal the truth, even if you try to deny it. Your heart rate and respiration will change quickly as you respond to the incriminating questions.

That is the theory, but psychologists have found that lie detectors are simply not reliable. Since most physical changes are the same across all emotions, machines cannot tell whether you are feeling guilty, angry, nervous, or thrilled. Innocent people may be nervous about the whole procedure. They may react greatly to a certain word ("bank") not because they robbed it, but because they recently bounced a check. In either case the machine will record a "lie." Besides, some practiced liars can lie without flinching, and others learn to beat the machine by tensing muscles or thinking about an exciting experience during neutral questions.

31. According to the passage, polygraph tests
    A. record a person's physical reactions.
    B. measure a person's thoughts.
    C. always reveal the truth about a person.
    D. make guilty people angry.

32. According to the passage, what kind of questions are asked on the first part of the polygraph test?
    A. Critical.
    B. Unimportant.
    C. Incriminating.
    D. Emotional.

33. What is the topic of the passage?
    A. Physical reactions reveal guilt.
    B. How lie detectors are used and their reliability.
    C. Lie detectors distinguish different emotions.
    D. Lie detectors make innocent people nervous.

Please turn to the next page. ⟹

34. Which of the following can be inferred from the passage?
    A. Lie detectors are very reliable.
    B. Innocent people are never found guilty.
    C. Psychologists never argue about anything.
    D. Most people can't control their bodily reactions.

35. It can be concluded from the passage that a polygraph test
    A. is the best way to determine a person's guilt.
    B. can read a person's thoughts.
    C. is the only evidence needed in a court of law.
    D. works in principle but not in practice.

Questions 36-37

    One of the most serious respiratory diseases is influenza, for it is able to attack people of all ages throughout the world. Incidence frequently is highest in young adults. It is an example of a disease that has increased in virulence throughout the years, although since 1942 it seems to have become milder again. Influenza periodically has been epidemic in the United States from 1918 to the present time. Several tragic worldwide pandemics have occurred. One of the most dreadful was the 1918-1919 outbreak, in which there were some 20 million cases of influenza and pneumonia and approximately 850,000 deaths occurred.

Influenza is an acute disease of the respiratory tract that affects the whole body. It is characterized by a sudden onset, with chills, a fever of around 102 degrees that may rise to 104 degrees, headache, muscular pains, prostration, sore throat, and cough. Like the common cold, it paves the way for secondary infections such as hemolytic streptococci and pneumonia. Most deaths are due to complications from pneumonia. Recovery is usual in four or five days.

36. Influenza is a disease which
    A. has generally increased in virulence.
    B. was unknown in the United States.
    C. has remained constant in its toxicity.
    D. is not difficult to control.

37. Most deaths from influenza are due to
    A. parainfluenza.
    B. faulty diagnosis.
    C. complications due to pneumonia.
    D. complications leading to hepatitis.

Questions 38-40

Fungi are seen as a diverse group of either single-celled or multicelluar organisms that obtain food by direct absorption of nutrients. The food is dissolved by enzymes that the fungi

Please turn to the next page. ⇨

excrete, is then absorbed through thin cell walls, and is distributed by simple circulation, or streaming, of the protoplasm. Together with bacteria, fungi are responsible for the decay and decomposition of all organic matter and are found wherever other forms of life exist. Some are parasitic on living matter and cause serious plant and animal diseases. The study of fungi is called mycology.

Fungi were traditionally classified as a division in the plant kingdom. They were thought of as plants that have no stems or leaves and that in the course of becoming food absorbers lost the pigment chlorophyll, which is needed for conducting photosynthesis. Most scientists today, however, view them as an entirely separate group that evolved from unpigmented flagellates and place them either in the protist kingdom or in their own kingdom, according to the complexity of organization. Approximately 100,000 species of fungi are known. The more complex groups are believed to have derived from the primitive types, which have flagellated cells at some stage in their life cycle.

38. Which of the following would be the best title for the passage?
   A. The Plant Kingdom
   B. The Bacteria Kingdom
   C. Nature's Decomposer
   D. The Process of Photosynthesis

39. According to the passage, which of the following is correct?
   A. Fungi are plants that use enzymes produced by the food they eat.
   B. Fungi are plants that have no stems or leaves.
   C. Fungi can't absorb food.
   D. Fungi are not plants.

40. Which of the following can be inferred from the passage?
   A. Fungi should be exterminated because they cause serious plant and animal diseases.
   B. Fungi belong to a unique division in the plant kingdom.
   C. The only difference between fungi and plants lies in the pigment chlorophyll, which is needed for conducting photosynthesis.
   D. Fungi depend on plants and animals for their survival.

Questions 41-43

   Alexander, Caesar, Napoleon—they spent their lives fighting wars, defeating nations and building empires. We remember these men because they wanted the world and often came close to winning it. But none came as close as one man—Genghis Khan.

   Genghis Khan had an outgoing personality, but even as a boy he was merciless. It is said that his half-brother Bekhter often stole the food Genghis Khan got by hunting and fishing.

Please turn to the next page. ▯⟶

To repay these insults, Khan and his younger brother killed Bekhter by shooting him with an arrow.

Khan's strategy in gaining followers was straightforward and very effective. First, he realized that the best way to build a skillful army was by rewarding and promoting the most able warriors. Thus his officers gained power not because of which family they belonged to, but because they had served Khan well. Furthermore, to his enemies, Khan gave a very simple choice: Surrender or die.

Thus, Khan, who was not born into greatness or power, through a combination of strong leadership, personal courage and effective discouragement of resistance, was able to build an empire that reached from the Pacific Ocean to the Adriatic Sea.

41. Why did Khan kill his half-brother?
    A. He stole Khan's money.
    B. He challenged Khan for power.
    C. He betrayed Khan.
    D. He stole the food Khan got himself.

42. How were soldiers promoted in Khan's army?
    A. By serving Khan and the army well.
    B. By paying a large amount of money.
    C. By having good family connections.
    D. By defeating Khan in battle.

43. According to the passage, which of the following statements is FALSE?
   A. Khan was next to no one when it came to conquering the world.
   B. For those who were captured by Khan's army, surrendering to Khan was the only way they were able to stay alive.
   C. Though merciless as a boy, Khan was always gentle to the people around him.
   D. Khan did not achieve his greatness on the strength of his family background.

Questions 44-46

Attention
Vintage Volkswagen Enthusiasts

Do you like vintage Volkswagens ("bugs" or vans made before 1970)? The San Jose chapter of the International Volkswagen Fan Club is looking for you. The club is open to all who are interested in old Volkswagens and the era they represent. We welcome owners, previous owners or those who just like to talk about the cars. We meet on the 2nd and 4th Sundays of each month at the Elks Club on Grove Street at noon. Members who have one drive their Volkswagens to the club for everyone to see and take a ride in. Twice a year we organize a cross-country rally of

---

Please turn to the next page. ⇨

over 50 "bugs" and vans. If interested in joining us, call
Harry Anderson at 555-1234 after 5:00 p.m., or Richard
Bailey at 555-4321 after 6:00 p.m. Richard can also be
reached through our website at www.volkswagenclub.com.
Or just stop by the club on Sundays when we're meeting.
You'll find us to be the friendliest people on earth!

44. What is the club looking for?
    A. Old Volkswagens.
    B. Sponsors for their upcoming rally.
    C. New members.
    D. The owner of the club.

45. How often do the club's members get together?
    A. Twice a month.
    B. Twice a year.
    C. Every Sunday.
    D. Once a month.

46. Which of the following is true?
    A. There is a club entry fee.
    B. Only those who own "bugs" are allowed to join
       the club.
    C. The club holds car races twice a year.
    D. Both Harry and Richard can be reached through the
       Internet.

Questions 47-50

OBITUARY

BROWN, Nat Jackson—

Nat Jackson Brown was born in Selma, Alabama, on April 22, 1916. He graduated from the Tuskegee Institute in Tuskegee, Alabama in 1938 with a degree in elementary education. In 1941 Mr. Brown received a master's degree in education administration from Morehouse College in Atlanta, Georgia.

After teaching for several years at George Washington Carver Elementary School in Atlanta, Mr. Brown moved to Savannah, Georgia. There he became an assistant principal at Du Bois Middle School in 1946. Mr. Brown remained assistant principal at Du Bois for eight years until he was promoted to principal, a position he held for the next ten years.

Mr. Brown so impressed the school board that they recommended him to the State Secretary of Education for the job of superintendent of schools for the whole of Harris County, Georgia in 1966.

Mr. Brown remained superintendent for 15 years—the longest in Georgia's history— until he retired in 1981 to Savannah, Georgia. However, he served on the board of education for a local elementary school in Savannah until his death. When asked why he chose to finish his career on the board of an elementary school, Mr. Brown replied, "because that's where it all begins."

Please turn to the next page. ▯⟹

47. What is an obituary?
   A. A written account of a person's education and past employment, used when they're looking for a job.
   B. A report about details of other people's behavior and private lives.
   C. A printed notice of a person's death with a short biographical account.
   D. An exciting news report printed or broadcast before one's competitors can do so.

48. How long was Mr. Brown a principal?
   A. Five years.
   B. Eight years.
   C. Ten years.
   D. Fifteen years.

49. In what field did Mr. Brown receive his master's degree?
   A. Special education.
   B. Elementary education.
   C. Business administration.
   D. Education administration.

50. What was Mr. Brown's job when he died?
   A. Principal.
   B. School board member.
   C. Assistant principal.
   D. Superintendent of schools.

-The End-

中高級聽力測驗詳解 ②

🖱 PART A

1. (**D**) Why is your eye so swollen?
   A. So far so good.
   B. I really need glasses.
   C. The doctor said I should put ice on it.
   D. I got hit by a baseball.

   * swollen〔'swolən〕 *adj.* 浮腫的
     So far so good. 到目前為止還好。

2. (**A**) Congratulations on winning the scholarship!
   A. Thanks. I guess I got lucky.
   B. Yes, you deserve it.
   C. Thanks for paying me.
   D. You can win my praise, too.

   * congratulations〔kənˏgrætʃə'leʃənz〕 *n. pl.* 恭喜
     scholarship〔'skɑlə˖ʃɪp〕 *n.* 獎學金
     deserve〔dɪ'zɝv〕 *v.* 應得　　praise〔prez〕 *n.* 讚美

3. (**D**) You made sure you locked the doors, didn't you?
   A. Yes, it did.
   B. Yes, please don't go.
   C. I always leave it open.
   D. Yes, I did.

   * ***make sure*** 確定　　lock〔lɑk〕 *v.* 鎖上
     leave〔liv〕 *v.* 使處於（某種狀態）

4. (**B**) How many states make up the U.S.A.?

    A.　It's a big region.

    B.　Exactly fifty.

    C.　The continent has five countries.

    D.　There were thirteen original colonies.

    * state〔stet〕*n.*（美國的）州　　***make up*** 組成

    region〔'ridʒən〕*n.* 地區　　exactly〔ɪg'zæktlɪ〕*adv.* 正好

    continent〔'kɑntənənt〕*n.* 洲；大陸

    original〔ə'rɪdʒənḷ〕*adj.* 原本的

    colony〔'kɑlənɪ〕*n.* 殖民地

5. (**A**) How could you lose your ID?

    A.　I have no idea!

    B.　It's a photo ID.

    C.　Should I call the police?

    D.　Mind your step.

    * lose〔luz〕*v.* 遺失　　***ID*** 身分證（＝ *identity card*）

    photo ID 附有相片的身分證（＝ *picture ID*）

    mind〔maɪnd〕*v.* 注意　　step〔stɛp〕*n.* 腳步

6. (**C**) Have you ever tried bagels or pancakes?

    A.　Yes, I will soon.

    B.　No, I'll never order it.

    C.　Yes, they are delicious.

    D.　No, they're easy to find around here.

    * bagel〔'begəl〕*n.* 貝果　　pancake〔'pæn,kek〕*n.* 薄煎餅

    order〔'ɔrdɚ〕*v.* 訂購；點（餐）

    delicious〔dɪ'lɪʃəs〕*adj.* 好吃的

7. (**D**) Should I tell her that I love her?

    A. Love is blind.

    B. Don't be shy. Let him know!

    C. Go for it; ask her!

    D. I would if I were you.

    * blind〔blaɪnd〕*adj.* 盲目的

    Love is blind. 【諺】愛情是盲目的。

    shy〔ʃaɪ〕*adj.* 害羞的　　*go for it* 努力爭取；大膽一試

8. (**A**) Why did the earthquake cause a tsunami?

    A. The movement caused big waves.

    B. The earth provides everything.

    C. Falling rocks made a giant wave.

    D. It killed a lot of people.

    * earthquake〔'ɝθ͵kwek〕*n.* 地震　　cause〔kɔz〕*v.* 導致

    tsunami〔tsu'nɑmɪ〕*n.* 海嘯

    movement〔'muvmənt〕*n.* (板塊) 運動

    wave〔wev〕*n.* 海浪　　provide〔prə'vaɪd〕*v.* 提供

    giant〔'dʒaɪənt〕*adj.* 巨大的　　kill〔kɪl〕*v.* 使喪生

9. (**D**) What did you do over the weekend?

    A. I'll make an appointment with the dentist.

    B. They went to the beach.

    C. I haven't a memory.

    D. I relaxed and took it easy.

    * appointment〔ə'pɔɪntmənt〕*n.* 約會

    dentist〔'dɛntɪst〕*n.* 牙醫

    memory〔'mɛmərɪ〕*n.* 記憶力【可數名詞】

    relax〔rɪ'læks〕*v.* 放鬆　　*take it easy* 放輕鬆

10. (**D**) Could you please keep it down?

   A. Sorry, you are so loud.

   B. Sorry, I'm upset.

   C. I apologize for my silence.

   D. Sorry, I'll be quiet.

   * ***keep down*** 壓低（聲音）
     loud (laʊd) *adj.* 大聲的   upset (ʌp'sɛt) *adj.* 不高興的
     apologize (ə'pɑlə,dʒaɪz) *v.* 道歉
     silence ('saɪləns) *n.* 沉默   quiet ('kwaɪət) *adj.* 安靜的

11. (**C**) How often do you visit your grandparents?

   A. They seldom visit me.

   B. We used to live together.

   C. About once a month.

   D. For a month.

   * seldom ('sɛldəm) *adv.* 很少   ***used to V.*** 以前常常

12. (**A**) Are they still living in the countryside?

   A. No, they moved to the suburbs.

   B. Yes, they live in a downtown high-rise.

   C. Yes, they live in another country.

   D. No, they don't have passports.

   * countryside ('kʌntrɪ,saɪd) *n.* 鄉下
     suburbs ('sʌbɝbz) *n. pl.* 郊區
     downtown ('daʊn'taʊn) *adj.* 商業區的
     high-rise ('haɪ'raɪz) *n.* 高樓
     passport ('pæs,port) *n.* 護照

13. (**B**) What do you think about TV talk shows?

   A. I used to own one.

   B. I think they exaggerate things.

   C. I plan to buy a stereo TV.

   D. Shows today are too expensive.

   * show〔ʃo〕*n.* 表演節目

   talk show 對談節目；（電視上的）脫口秀

   own〔on〕*v.* 擁有

   exaggerate〔ɪgˈzædʒə‚ret〕*v.* 誇大

   stereo〔ˈstɛrɪo〕*adj.* 立體聲的；立體音響的

14. (**D**) Have you seen any good movies lately?

   A. Yes, I love action movies.

   B. Yes, I read one last week.

   C. No, thank you.

   D. No, I haven't.

   * lately〔ˈletlɪ〕*adv.* 最近   ***action movie*** 動作片

15. (**B**) When is their baby due?

   A. For two months.

   B. In six weeks.

   C. In the U.S.A. for sure.

   D. Sometime in the past.

   * due〔dju〕*adj.* 預定的

   in six weeks 再過六個星期   ***for sure*** 一定

   sometime〔ˈsʌm‚taɪm〕*adv.* 某時   ***in the past*** 在過去

📄 PART **B**.

16. (**A**) M：Your cousin is a real knockout!

W：I told you she was a model.

M：Is she a full-time or part-time model?

W：She's a career professional with many clients.

M：Wow! I bet she's really rich!

Question：How does the man feel about the model?

A. Admiring. B. Resentful.

C. Jealous. D. Courageous.

* knockout〔'nɑk͵aut〕*n.* 有吸引力的人或物
 model〔'mɑdḷ〕*n.* 模特兒 full-time〔'ful'taɪm〕*adj.* 全職的
 part-time〔'pɑrt'taɪm〕*adj.* 兼職的
 career〔kə'rɪr〕*adj.* 內行的；專業的
 professional〔prə'fɛʃənḷ〕*n.* 專家
 client〔'klaɪənt〕*n.* 客戶 bet〔bɛt〕*v.* 打賭；斷定
 admiring〔əd'maɪrɪŋ〕*adj.* 佩服的；讚賞的
 resentful〔rɪ'zɛntfḷ〕*adj.* 憤恨的
 jealous〔'dʒɛləs〕*adj.* 忌妒的
 courageous〔kə'redʒəs〕*adj.* 勇敢的

17. (**B**) W：I just received the funniest e-mail.

M：Really? From whom?

W：From an old pal who's coming to town.

Question：Who sent the message?

A. Her grandparents. B. A friend of many years.

C. Her grandpa. D. An ex-boyfriend.

* funny〔'fʌnɪ〕*adj.* 好玩的 pal〔pæl〕*n.* 好友
 ex-boyfriend〔ɛks'bɔɪ͵frɛnd〕*n.* 前男友

18. (**D**)　M：Are you going to watch the presidential debates
　　　　　　　　tonight?

　　　　　W：Are you kidding me?

　　　　　M：No, I'm serious.　It's gonna be like watching
　　　　　　　　fireworks.

　　　　　W：Sorry, politics turns me off.

　　　　　M：But, it's your duty as a citizen.

　　　　　Question：How does the man feel?

　　　　A.　Frustrated by politics.

　　　　B.　Too nervous to watch.

　　　　C.　Not interested in debates.

　　　　D.　Excited about the debate.

　　　　* presidential〔ˌprɛzəˈdɛnʃəl〕*adj.* 總統的
　　　　　 debate〔dɪˈbet〕*n.* 辯論　　　kid〔kɪd〕*v.* 開～玩笑
　　　　　 serious〔ˈsɪrɪəs〕*adj.* 認眞的　　gonna〔ˈgɔnə〕(= *going to*)
　　　　　 firework〔ˈfaɪrˌwɜk〕*n.* 煙火
　　　　　 politics〔ˈpɑləˌtɪks〕*n.* 政治
　　　　　 turn** sb.* ***off 使某人失去興趣
　　　　　 duty〔ˈdjutɪ〕*n.* 責任；義務　　citizen〔ˈsɪtəzn̩〕*n.* 公民
　　　　　 frustrated〔ˈfrʌstretɪd〕*adj.* 受挫的
　　　　　 nervous〔ˈnɜvəs〕*adj.* 緊張的

19. (**B**)　W：What a nightmare of a weekend!

　　　　　M：What the heck happened to you?

　　　　　W：A computer virus ruined all my files.

　　　　　M：Don't you have an anti-virus protection program?

　　　　　W：I was too frugal and pigheaded to buy one.

　　　　　Question：What happened to the woman?

A. Her computer was stolen.

B. Her files were damaged.

C. She got very sick.

D. She received an infection.

* nightmare〔'naɪt,mɛr〕n. 惡夢

　heck〔hɛk〕interj. 究竟；到底　　virus〔'vaɪrəs〕n. 病毒

　ruin〔'ruɪn〕v. 破壞　　file〔faɪl〕n. 檔案

　anti-virus〔,æntɪ'vaɪrəs〕adj. 防毒的

　protection〔prə'tɛkʃən〕n. 保護

　program〔'progræm〕n. 程式　　**too…to~** 太…而不能~

　frugal〔'frugl̩〕adj. 節省的

　pigheaded〔'pɪg'hɛdɪd〕adj. 頑固的

　damage〔'dæmɪdʒ〕v. 損害　　infection〔ɪn'fɛkʃən〕n. 感染

20.（ **A** ）M：I registered for summer classes this afternoon.

W：I totally forgot today was early registration!

M：It's not too late. They're open till nine.

W：I'm on my way. What do I need?

M：Just an ID and a credit card.

Question：What is the man doing?

A. Encouraging and assisting.

B. Informing on her.

C. Registering for the lady.

D. Giving her the time of day.

* register〔'rɛdʒɪstɚ〕v. 登記；註冊　　**register for** 註冊

　totally〔'totl̩ɪ〕adv. 完全地

　registration〔,rɛdʒɪ'streʃən〕n. 登記　　till〔tɪl〕prep. 直到

　encourage〔ɪn'kɝɪdʒ〕v. 鼓勵　　assist〔ə'sɪst〕v. 幫助

　inform on （向警方）密告（某人）

　give the time of day 互相問候

21. (**A**) W : Why all the overtime hours?

M : My boss said it was necessary.

W : Are you being compensated?

M : Not one single penny!

W : You poor guy. That's not fair.

Question : Why does the woman pity the man?

A. He's working extra for no pay.

B. He's about to get fired.

C. He's going to go bankrupt soon.

D. He's exhausted and broke.

* overtime〔'ovɚ,taɪm〕*adj.* 超過時間的

   hours〔aʊrz〕*n. pl.* 工作時間　　***overtime hours*** 加班

   necessary〔'nɛsə,sɛrɪ〕*adj.* 必要的

   compensate〔'kɑmpən,set〕*v.* 補償

   single〔'sɪŋɡl̩〕*adj.* 單一的

   penny〔'pɛnɪ〕*n.* 一文錢　　guy〔gaɪ〕*n.* 人

   fair〔fɛr〕*adj.* 公平的；合理的

   pity〔'pɪtɪ〕*v.* 同情　　extra〔'ɛkstrə〕*adv.* 額外地

   pay〔pe〕*n.* 薪水　　***be about to*** 即將

   get fired 被解僱　　bankrupt〔'bæŋkrʌpt〕*adj.* 破產的

   exhausted〔ɪg'zɔstɪd〕*adj.* 筋疲力竭的

   broke〔brok〕*adj.* 破產的；沒錢的

22. (**D**) M : Welcome to Power Fitness Center.

W : Are you my personal trainer?

M : You got it, baby! My name is Muscles.

W : What a modest name! How should I begin?

M : Let's stretch and warm up.

Question: What's about to happen?

A. She's going to be a trainer.

B. She's going to study muscles.

C. He's going to pull her body.

D. He's going to help her exercise.

* ***fitness center*** 健身中心　　personal〔'pɜsn̩l〕*adj.* 個人的

trainer〔'trenɚ〕*n.* 教練　　***You got it.*** 你答對了。

muscle〔'mʌsl̩〕*n.* 肌肉

modest〔'mɑdɪst〕*adj.* 謙虛的；適度的

stretch〔strɛtʃ〕*v.* 伸展肢體　　***warm up*** 暖身

study〔'stʌdɪ〕*v.* 研究　　　　pull〔pʊl〕*v.* 拉

23. (**C**) W: What's your number one fantasy?

M: Winning an Olympic gold medal and being world-
famous. And you?

W: I want to win the lottery.

M: Nice choice. I like yours better than mine.

W: Yeah, mine is possible; yours is just a dream.

Question: What does the woman want?

A. To win a gold medal.　　B. To be famous.

C. To win lots of money.

D. To join a top-level competition.

* fantasy〔'fæntəsɪ〕*n.* 夢想；幻想

Olympic〔o'lɪmpɪk〕*adj.* 奧林匹克運動會的

gold medal 金牌

world-famous〔'wɜld'feməs〕*adj.* 舉世聞名的

lottery〔'lɑtərɪ〕*n.* 獎券　　choice〔tʃɔɪs〕*n.* 選擇

join〔dʒɔɪn〕*v.* 參加　　top-level〔'tɑp'lɛvl̩〕*adj.* 最高級的

competition〔,kɑmpə'tɪʃən〕*n.* 競賽

24. (**B**) M : I start military training next week.

W : Cool! Did you volunteer or get drafted?

M : I volunteered. I want to be an intelligence officer.

W : Great choice. What a challenge. I envy you.

M : That career path is open to you, too.

Question : What does the man suggest?

A. She can become intelligent.

B. She can also serve her country.

C. She wants him to join her.

D. He volunteered to impress her.

* military (ˈmɪləˌtɛrɪ) *adj.* 軍事的

cool (kul) *adj.* 酷的；很棒的

volunteer (ˌvɑlənˈtɪr) *v.* 自願　　draft (dræft) *v.* 徵召

intelligence (ɪnˈtɛlədʒəns) *n.* 情報

officer (ˈɔfəsɚ) *n.* 官員　　challenge (ˈtʃælɪndʒ) *n.* 挑戰

envy (ˈɛnvɪ) *v.* 羨慕　　career (kəˈrɪr) *adj.* 職業性的

path (pæθ) *n.* 道路　　intelligent (ɪnˈtɛlədʒənt) *adj.* 聰明的

serve (sɜv) *v.* 為 (國家) 服務

impress (ɪmˈprɛs) *v.* 使印象深刻

25. (**A**) W : What's culture shock? Is it like jet lag?

M : No, culture shock is traveler's depression. You
feel stressed or out of place.

W : And jet lag?

M : Jet lag is just being tired from traveling through
different time zones.

W : Thanks for clearing that up.

Question : Who seems to be the experienced traveler?

A. The knowledgeable man.

B. The confused woman.

C. The amazed man.　D. The intelligent woman.

* shock〔ʃɑk〕*n.* 衝擊　　***culture shock*** 文化衝擊
jet lag 時差　　depression〔dɪ'prɛʃən〕*n.* 沮喪
stressed〔strɛst〕*adj.* 緊張的
out of place 不自在的　　***time zone*** 時區
clear up 澄清　　experienced〔ɪk'spɪrɪənst〕*adj.* 有經驗的
knowledgeable〔'nɑlɪdʒəbḷ〕*adj.* 知識淵博的
confused〔kən'fjuzd〕*adj.* 困惑的
amazed〔ə'mezd〕*adj.* 吃驚的

26. (**C**) M：What happened to your beautiful complexion?

W：I guess all that oily junk food went to my face.

M：That's just a theory. Who knows if it's true?

W：How can I clear up my skin?

M：Eat lots of fruits and veggies and exercise daily.

Question：What's the man's advice?

A. Take lots of vitamins.

B. Take the oil out of the fast food.

C. Eat right and work out.

D. Bathe several times a day.

* complexion〔kəm'plɛkʃən〕*n.* 臉色
oily〔'ɔɪlɪ〕*adj.* 油膩的　　***junk food*** 垃圾食物
theory〔'θiərɪ〕*n.* 理論　　***clear up*** 把～弄乾淨；去除～的污點
veggie〔'vɛdʒɪ〕*n.* 蔬菜（ = *vegetable*）
daily〔'delɪ〕*adv.* 每天地　　advice〔əd'vaɪs〕*n.* 勸告
vitamin〔'vaɪtəmɪn〕*n.* 維他命
work out 運動　　bathe〔beð〕*v.* 洗澡

27. (**D**) W：Where is Kenny today?

M：Shh! Can you keep a secret?

W：Sure, I promise on my mother's grave.

M：OK, he's skipping school. He went to Disney World with a cousin.

W：Oh, my God! Is he crazy or brave?

Question：How does the woman react?

A. She is disappointed.

B. She is proud of his bravery.

C. She is worried she'll get into trouble.

D. She is shocked and surprised.

* shh〔ʃ〕*interj.* 噓（命令對方安靜）

   keep a secret 保守秘密　　promise〔'pramɪs〕*v.* 保證

   promise on 以…保證　　grave〔grev〕*n.* 墳墓

   skip〔skɪp〕*v.* 不出席（學校）；翹（課）

   cousin〔'kʌzn̩〕*n.* 堂（表）兄弟姊妹

   brave〔brev〕*adj.* 勇敢的　　react〔rɪ'ækt〕*v.* 反應

   be proud of 以～爲榮　　bravery〔'brevərɪ〕*n.* 勇敢

   get into trouble 惹上麻煩　　shocked〔ʃakt〕*adj.* 震驚的

28. (**B**) M：Do you believe some people have ESP, which stands for extrasensory perception?

W：You mean like a sixth sense?

M：Yes, that's exactly what I mean.

W：Sure, I'm convinced we have this ability.

M：Me too. I'd love to read people's minds.

Question：Do these two believe in ESP?

A.　No, they aren't convinced.

B.　Yes, they both do.

C.　They don't think it might be true.

D.　They have no idea.

* ***ESP*** 第六感（＝ *extrasensory perception* ）　***stand for*** 代表

　　extrasensory〔͵ɛkstrə'sɛnsərɪ〕*adj.* 超感覺的

　　perception〔pə'sɛpʃən〕*n.* 知覺　　***sixth sense*** 第六感

　　exactly〔ɪg'zæktlɪ〕*adv.* 正是

　　convinced〔kən'vɪnst〕*adj.* 確信的

　　believe in 相信～的存在

29.（ **A** ）W：My sister is having a baby next week.

M：Is she having a boy or a girl?

W：She didn't ask.　She wants to be surprised.

M：Is she going to have a natural birth or a C-section?

W：She's going to let her physician decide.

Question：What will the baby's gender be?

A.　Nobody knows yet.　　　B.　She hopes for a boy.

C.　She wants a healthy girl.　D.　It's up to the doctor.

* ***have a baby*** 生小孩

　　natural birth 自然生產（＝ *natural childbirth* ）

　　C-section〔'si͵sɛkʃən〕*n.* 剖腹生產（＝ *Caesarean section* ）

　　physician〔fə'zɪʃən〕*n.* 醫師　　gender〔'dʒɛndə〕*n.* 性別

　　yet〔jɛt〕*adv.* 尚（未）　　***be up to*** 由～決定

30.（ **A** ）M：Love has so many definitions.　How would you
　　　　define true love?

W：It's a mystery to me.　True love is like a puzzle.

M：Haven't you ever been in love?

Question：What's going on between the man and the
woman?

A. They're discussing love.

B. They're falling in love.

C. Romance is in the air.

D. They're trying to define a puzzle.

* definition〔͵dɛfə'nɪʃən〕*n.* 定義

   define〔dɪ'faɪn〕*v.* 爲～下定義

   mystery〔'mɪstərɪ〕*n.* 神秘的事物；謎   puzzle〔'pʌzḷ〕*n.* 謎

   be in love 在戀愛   ***go on*** 發生

   discuss〔dɪ'skʌs〕*v.* 討論   ***fall in love*** 戀愛

   romance〔ro'mæns〕*n.* 浪漫   ***in the air*** （氣氛等）瀰漫著

📂 PART **C**.

Questions 31-32 refer to the following announcement.

Greetings, guys and gals of all ages! Summer is coming
fast and that means it's time to join the City Summer
Program. Sign up and register for the C.S.P., which starts
next week. This summer we are offering over 70 different
activities and classes for both youths and adults. We have
everything from Japanese art to martial arts. This year we
have expanded on our popular computer camp. We've also
added an exciting sports camp. Learn new skills and
improve your swimming, basketball, volleyball, badminton
and ping-pong abilities. Have a fun summer. Get healthy
and fit! Give us a call right now.

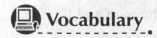

Vocabulary

greetings〔'gritɪŋz〕*n. pl.* 問候　　guy〔gaɪ〕*n.* 男子

gal〔gæl〕*n.* 女孩　　program〔'progræm〕*n.* 課程

sign up 報名　　register〔'rɛdʒɪstɚ〕*v.* 登記

register for 註冊　　offer〔'ɔfɚ〕*v.* 提供

adult〔ə'dʌlt〕*n.* 成人　　Japanese〔,dʒæpə'niz〕*adj.* 日本的

Japanese art 日本藝術

martial〔'marʃəl〕*adj.* 武術的　　***martial Art*** 武術

expand〔ɪk'spænd〕*v.* 擴大　　camp〔kæmp〕*n.* 營

add〔æd〕*v.* 增加　　volleyball〔'valɪ,bɔl〕*n.* 排球

badminton〔'bædmɪntən〕*n.* 羽毛球

ping-pong〔'pɪŋ,paŋ〕*n.* 乒乓球；桌球

fit〔fɪt〕*adj.* 健康的　　***give sb. a call*** 打電話給某人

31. (**D**) How many different activities are being offered?

　　A. Over seven hours every week.

　　B. It depends on the number of registrants.

　　C. Too many popular ones.

　　D. Over seventy all summer.

　　＊ ***depend on*** 視～而定

　　　register〔'rɛdʒɪstrənt〕*n.* 登記者

32. (**C**) This summer program is focused on what age groups?

　　A. Adults only.

　　B. Students on summer vacation.

　　C. Both young people and adults.

　　D. Young people only.

　　＊ ***be focused on*** 集中於；針對

Questions 33-35 refer to the following broadcast.

> Due to the outbreak of the highly infectious disease SARS, strict quarantine regulations are now in effect. All citizens must wear a surgical mask over their face when going out in public. Absolutely no unnecessary travel is advised. All public schools have cancelled classes until further notice. All government departments and agencies are also closed. If you feel dizzy, have a high fever, or experience any flu-like symptoms, please go to the nearest emergency room.

Vocabulary

broadcast〔'brɔd,kæst〕*n.* 廣播

due to 由於　　outbreak〔'aut,brek〕*n.* 爆發

highly〔'haɪlɪ〕*adv.* 高度地；非常

infectious〔ɪn'fɛkʃəs〕*adj.* 易傳染的

disease〔dɪ'ziz〕*n.* 疾病

SARS 嚴重急性呼吸道症候群（= *Severe Acute Respiratory Syndrome*）　　strict〔strɪkt〕*adj.* 嚴格的

quarantine〔'kwɔrən,tin〕*n.* 隔離

regulation〔,rɛgjə'leʃən〕*n.* 規定

in effect 在實施中；生效的　　citizen〔'sɪtəzn̩〕*n.* 公民；國民

surgical〔'sɝdʒɪkl̩〕*adj.* 手術用的

mask〔mæsk〕*n.* 口罩　　**in public** 在公共場所

absolutely〔'æbsə,lutlɪ〕*adv.* 絕對地

unnecessary (ʌn'nɛsə,sɛrɪ) adj. 不必要的

advise (əd'vaɪz) v. 建議　　**public school** 公立學校

cancel ('kænsl̩) v. 取消　　further ('fɝðə) adj. 更進一步的

notice ('notɪs) n. 通知　　government ('gʌvənmənt) n. 政府

department (dɪ'pɑrtmənt) n. 部門

agency ('edʒənsɪ) n. (政府) 機關

dizzy ('dɪzɪ) adj. 頭暈的　　fever ('fivə) n. 發燒

experience (ɪk'spɪrɪəns) v. 經歷

flu (flu) n. 流行性感冒　　**flu-like** 像流行性感冒的

symptom ('sɪmptəm) n. 症狀　　**emergency room** 急診室

33. (**B**) What is happening to the area?

    A. School officials are going on vacation.

    B. A contagious disease is spreading fast.

    C. Animals are spreading sickness.

    D. Many employees are quitting their jobs.

    * area ('ɛrɪə) n. 地區　　official (ə'fɪʃəl) n. 公務員

    go on vacation 去渡假

    contagious (kən'tedʒəs) adj. 接觸傳染的

    spread (sprɛd) v. 蔓延；散播　　sickness ('sɪknɪs) n. 疾病

    employee (,ɛmplɔɪ'i) n. 員工　　quit (kwɪt) v. 辭職

34. (**A**) Are people free to leave their homes?

    A. Yes, but they're advised not to.

    B. No, the police are locking doors.

    C. Only for unnecessary travel.

    D. Everyone is too nervous to go out.

    * free (fri) adj. 自由的；隨意的　　lock (lɑk) v. 鎖

    nervous ('nɝvəs) adj. 緊張的

35. (**D**) What facilities are not shutting down?

    A. Public schools.

    B. Government offices.

    C. Departments and agencies of the government.

    D. Hospitals and clinics.

    * facility〔fə'sɪlətɪ〕*n.* 場所　　*shut down* 關閉

    　clinic〔'klınık〕*n.* 診所

Questions 36-37 refer to the following article.

My little ones just love the Disney cartoon channel. Watching those wonderfully animated cartoons and movies are part of my family's regular routine. I trust this channel completely and I'm confident it has a positive influence on my precious little munchkins. The program content is always wholesome, moral and entertaining. The many fantasy stories really educate young minds about honesty, courage, good and evil.

🖥 Vocabulary

little ones 孩子（= *children*）　　cartoon〔kɑr'tun〕*n.* 卡通

channel〔'tʃænḷ〕*n.* 頻道

animated〔'ænə,metɪd〕*adj.* 動畫的；卡通影片的

animated cartoon 卡通　　regular〔'rɛgjələ〕*adj.* 固定的

routine〔ru'tin〕*n.* 例行公事；日常工作

trust〔trʌst〕*v.* 信任　　completely〔kəm'plitlı〕*adv.* 完全地

confident〔'kɑnfədənt〕*adj.* 有信心的

positive〔'pɑzətɪv〕*adj.* 正面的

influence〔'ɪnflʊəns〕*n.* 影響　　precious〔'prɛʃəs〕*adj.* 珍愛的

munchkin〔'mʌnkɪn〕*n.* 小孩（源於《綠野仙蹤》故事中負責任又討人

喜愛的小好人）

content〔'kɑntɛnt〕*n.* 內容

wholesome〔'holsəm〕*adj.*（在道德上）健全的；有益的

moral〔'mɔrəl〕*adj.* 有道德教育意義的

entertaining〔͵ɛntə'tenɪŋ〕*adj.* 有趣的

fantasy〔'fæntəsɪ〕*n.* 幻想　　mind〔maɪnd〕*n.* 心靈

courage〔'kɝɪdʒ〕*n.* 勇氣　　good〔gʊd〕*n.* 善　　evil〔'ivl̩〕*n.* 惡

36. (**C**) Who is recommending this channel?

 A. An older sibling.

 B. A nursery school administrator.

 C. A loving parent.

 D. A child psychologist.

 * recommend〔͵rɛkə'mɛnd〕*v.* 推薦

  sibling〔'sɪblɪŋ〕*n.* 兄弟姊妹

  nursery〔'nɝsərɪ〕*n.* 托兒所　　***nursery school*** 托兒所

  administrator〔əd'mɪnə͵stretə〕*n.* 管理人

  loving〔'lʌvɪŋ〕*adj.* 充滿著愛的；戀愛的

  psychologist〔saɪ'kɑlədʒɪst〕*n.* 心理學家

37. (**A**) According to the author, how often do "the little ones"

watch Disney?

 A. Just about every day.

 B. Several times a month.

 C. Just on the weekends.

 D. Almost all day long.

 * ***according to*** 根據　　author〔'ɔθɚ〕*n.* 作者

 all day long 整天

Questions 38-40 refer to the following recommendation.

You have to visit the new city zoo. It has been completely renovated and expanded into a modern animal wonderland. There are dozens of new animal habitats, exhibits, displays and hiking trails. The new zoo has over 1,000 fascinating animals. They have all the usual favorites like elephants, gorillas, penguins and tigers. They also have a new petting zoo just for kids. In addition, there's a new reptile house and a new museum with an incredible dinosaur section. Go to the zoo! Go early and plan to spend the whole day. There's a lot to see. Young or old, you'll have a ball!

🖥 Vocabulary

recommendation 〔,rɛkəmɛn'deʃən 〕 *n.* 口頭推薦

renovate 〔'rɛnə,vet 〕 *v.* 翻新

wonderland 〔'wʌndɚ,lænd 〕 *n.* 奇境;仙境;非常奇妙的地方

dozen 〔'dʌzn̩ 〕 *n.* 一打;十二個　　***dozens of*** 幾十個;許多的

habitat 〔'hæbə,tæt 〕 *n.* (動物的) 棲息地

exhibit 〔 ɪg'zɪbɪt 〕 *n.* 展覽　　display 〔 dɪ'sple 〕 *n.* 展出

hiking trail 步道　　fascinating 〔'fæsn̩,etɪŋ 〕 *adj.* 迷人的

favorite 〔'fevərɪt 〕 *n.* 特別喜愛的人或物

gorilla 〔 gə'rɪlə 〕 *n.* 大猩猩　　penguin 〔'pɛngwɪn 〕 *n.* 企鵝

petting 〔'pɛtɪŋ 〕 *adj.* 寵愛的;寵物的

petting zoo 寵物動物園 (裡面飼養溫和的小動物,可供兒童撫摸及餵養)

reptile 〔'rɛptl̩ 〕 *n.* 爬蟲類動物　　***a reptile house*** 爬行動物館

incredible 〔 ɪn'krɛdəbl̩ 〕 *adj.* 不可思議的

dinosaur 〔'daɪnə,sɔr 〕 *n.* 恐龍

section 〔'sɛkʃən 〕 *n.* 區域　　***have a ball*** 玩得開心

38. (**B**) How much is the zoo entrance fee?
 A. It's free for everyone.
 B. It's not mentioned in the article.
 C. Entrance is free on weekdays.
 D. The price depends on your age.

 * entrance〔'ɛntrəns〕*n.* 進入；入場　　fee〔fi〕*n.* 費用
 free〔fri〕*adj.* 免費的　　mention〔'mɛnʃən〕*v.* 提到
 weekday〔'wik,de〕*n.* 平日　　price〔praɪs〕*n.* 價格

39. (**D**) What's a new attraction especially for kids?
 A. Wild dinosaur statues.
 B. Excellent hiking trails.
 C. The new penguin house.
 D. The petting zoo area.

 * attraction〔ə'trækʃən〕*n.* 吸引人的事物
 especially〔ə'spɛʃəlɪ〕*adv.* 特別
 wild〔waɪld〕*adj.* 野生的；兇猛的　　statue〔'stætʃʊ〕*n.* 雕像
 excellent〔'ɛksḷənt〕*adj.* 極好的

40. (**C**) What does this writer recommend?
 A. Bring a ball to play with.
 B. Don't feed the animals.
 C. Go early and stay long.
 D. Take many photos.

 * feed〔fid〕*v.* 餵　　*take a photo* 拍照

Questions 41-42 refer to this story.

I live in a country in which many citizens are bilingual. There are two major languages that people speak. There is an official language that is used by the government, the media, and in schools. However, there is also another very popular language that most people speak at home. This situation often confuses foreign visitors and it also creates some misunderstandings in our society. There are also about ten other minority dialects and languages that people speak in my country. As our world turns into a global village, we must adapt and try to learn other languages whenever possible.

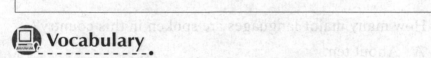 **Vocabulary**

bilingual〔baɪˈlɪŋgwəl〕*adj.* 精通兩種語言的
major〔ˈmedʒɚ〕*adj.* 主要的　　official〔əˈfɪʃəl〕*adj.* 官方的
media〔ˈmidɪə〕*n. pl.* 媒體（medium 的複數）
popular〔ˈpɑpjəlɚ〕*adj.* 普遍的　　confuse〔kənˈfjuz〕*v.* 使困惑
foreign〔ˈfɔrɪn〕*adj.* 外國的　　create〔krɪˈet〕*v.* 引起
misunderstanding〔ˌmɪsʌndɚˈstændɪŋ〕*n.* 誤會
minority〔maɪˈnɔrətɪ〕*adj.* 少數民族的
dialect〔ˈdaɪəlɛkt〕*n.* 方言
turn into 變成　　global〔ˈglobl̩〕*adj.* 全世界的
global village 地球村　　adapt〔əˈdæpt〕*v.* 適應

41. (**A**) What is the writer's tone or attitude?

    A. Objective and fair.

    B. Subjective and biased.

    C. Critical and tolerant.

    D. Informative and upset.

    * tone〔ton〕*n.* 語調　　attitude〔'ætə,tjud〕*n.* 態度

      objective〔əb'dʒɛktɪv〕*adj.* 客觀的

      fair〔fɛr〕*adj.* 公正的

      subjective〔səb'dʒɛktɪv〕*adj.* 主觀的

      biased〔'baɪəst〕*adj.* 有偏見的

      critical〔'krɪtɪkḷ〕*adj.* 批評的

      tolerant〔'tɑlərənt〕*adj.* 寬容的

      informative〔ɪn'fɔrmətɪv〕*adj.* 能增進知識的

      upset〔ʌp'sɛt〕*adj.* 不高興的

42. (**D**) How many major languages are spoken in this country?

    A. About ten.

    B. Over a dozen.

    C. Too many to count.

    D. Two main languages.

    * country〔'kʌntrɪ〕*n.* 國家

      over〔'ovɚ〕*prep.* 超過

      dozen〔'dʌzn̩〕*n.* 十二個

      count〔kaʊnt〕*v.* 計算

      main〔men〕*adj.* 主要的

Questions 43-45 are based on the following announcement.

Attention, please. To all passengers on Flight 007. This is your captain, Joe Incredible, speaking. I have a bit of bad news for everyone today. I have to report we're in for at least a two-hour delay. We had a little mix-up with our luggage check-in security system. All bags in our storage areas must be returned to the terminal to be checked with our passenger list. Each piece of luggage must be identified by a ticket holding passenger. Due to international regulations, we must all evacuate the plane. We're sorry for the delay. Free beverages and snacks will be available to you in our waiting lounge. Your safety is our number one priority. Thank you.

Vocabulary

announcement〔əˈnaʊnsmənt〕 _n._ 宣布
Attention, please. 請各位注意。　　passenger〔ˈpæsn̩dʒɚ〕 _n._ 乘客
flight〔flaɪt〕 _n._ 班機　　captain〔ˈkæptən〕 _n._ （飛機的）機長
a bit of 一點　　**_be in for_** 肯定會　　delay〔dɪˈle〕 _n._ 延誤
mix-up〔ˈmɪksˌʌp〕 _n._ 混亂　　luggage〔ˈlʌgɪdʒ〕 _n._ 行李
check-in〔ˈtʃɛkˌɪn〕 _n._ 登機手續　　security〔sɪˈkjʊrətɪ〕 _adj._ 安全的
storage〔ˈstorɪdʒ〕 _n._ 儲藏；保管　　terminal〔ˈtɝmənl̩〕 _n._ 航空站
check〔tʃɛk〕 _v._ 核對 <_with_>　　list〔lɪst〕 _n._ 名單
identify〔aɪˈdɛntəˌfaɪ〕 _v._ 確認　　regulation〔ˌrɛgjəˈleʃən〕 _n._ 規定
evacuate〔ɪˈvækjuˌet〕 _v._ 從～離去　　beverage〔ˈbɛvərɪdʒ〕 _n._ 飲料
available〔əˈveləbl̩〕 _adj._ 可獲得的　　lounge〔laʊndʒ〕 _n._ 休息室
priority〔praɪˈɔrətɪ〕 _n._ 優先考慮的事

43. (**C**) Why is the flight delayed?

　　　A.　Some bags were stolen.

　　　B.　Some passengers are stowaways.

　　　C.　There was a mix-up with baggage security.

　　　D.　There is mechanical difficulty in the storage section.

　　　* steal〔stil〕v. 偷走【三態變化為 steal-stole-stolen】
　　　　stowaway〔'stoə,we〕n. 偷渡客　baggage〔'bægɪdʒ〕n. 行李
　　　　mechanical〔mə'kænɪkl̩〕adj. 機械的
　　　　difficulty〔'dɪfə,kʌltɪ〕n. 故障
　　　　section〔'sɛkʃən〕n. 區域；部門

44. (**B**) How long will everyone have to wait?

　　　A.　Not more than four hours.

　　　B.　Probably about two hours.

　　　C.　Until the weather clears up.

　　　D.　It depends on the police.

　　　* *clear up* 放晴

45. (**A**) How will the passengers be compensated?

　　　A.　They'll receive free drinks and snacks.

　　　B.　They'll get free coupons.

　　　C.　A full refund is available.

　　　D.　Free mileage discounts will be offered.

　　　* compensate〔'kɑmpən,set〕v. 補償
　　　　coupon〔'kjupɑn〕n. 折價券　refund〔'ri,fʌnd〕n. 退錢
　　　　mileage〔'maɪlɪdʒ〕n. 哩程數
　　　　discount〔'dɪskaʊnt〕n. 折扣

中高級閱讀測驗詳解 ②

🖱 PART A : Sentence Completion

1. (**C**) The mayor was asked to <u>condense</u> his speech in order to allow time for his audience to raise questions.

市長被要求縮短演講，以便讓聽眾有時間提出問題。

(A) constrain〔kən'stren〕*v.* 壓抑；抑制

(B) conduct〔kən'dʌkt〕*v.* 引導；做

(C) *condense*〔kən'dɛns〕*v.* 濃縮；縮短

(D) contrast〔kən'træst〕*v.* 使對照；對比

* mayor〔'meɚ〕*n.* 市長　　allow〔ə'lau〕*v.* 給與
audience〔'ɔdɪəns〕*n.* 聽眾
raise〔rez〕*v.* 提出

2. (**B**) The morning newspaper says a school bus <u>collided</u> with a train and the police were sent to the scene immediately.

早報上說，有一輛校車和火車相撞，警方立即被派往現場。

(A) bump〔bʌmp〕*v.* 碰撞 < *into / against* >

(B) *collide*〔kə'laɪd〕*v.* 相撞 < *with* >

(C) crash〔kræʃ〕*v.* 撞碎 < *into* >；墜毀

(D) strike〔straɪk〕*v.* 打擊

* *morning newspaper* 早報　　say〔se〕*v.* (報紙、信等) 說
scene〔sin〕*n.* 現場　　immediately〔ɪ'midɪɪtlɪ〕*adv.* 立即

3. (**D**) Of the thousands of known volcanoes in the world, the <u>overwhelming</u> majority are inactive.

在全世界已知的數千座火山中，<u>絕大</u>多數是死火山。

(A) dogmatic〔dɔg'mætɪk〕*adj.* 武斷的

(B) merciful〔'mɜsɪfəl〕*adj.* 仁慈的

(C) impromptu〔ɪm'prɑmptju〕*adj.* 未事先準備的；即席的

(D) *overwhelming*〔͵ovɚ'hwɛlmɪŋ〕*adj.* 壓倒性的

* known〔non〕*adj.* 已知的　　volcano〔vɑl'keno〕*n.* 火山
　majority〔mə'dʒɔrətɪ〕*n.* 大多數
　inactive〔ɪn'æktɪv〕*adj.* 不活動的

4. (**C**) I want to get a <u>perm</u> so that I can have curly hair.

我想要去<u>燙髮</u>，這樣我才能擁有一頭捲髮。

(A) germ〔dʒɜm〕*n.* 細菌

(B) herb〔hɜb，ɜb〕*n.* 草藥

(C) *perm*〔pɜm〕*n. v.* 燙髮（為 permanent wave 之簡寫）

(D) term〔tɜm〕*n.* 名詞；用語

* curly〔'kɜlɪ〕*adj.* 捲的

5. (**B**) He was <u>tempted</u> to steal the money when he saw it lying on the table.

看到錢放在桌上，他<u>很想</u>把錢偷走。

(A) drag〔dræg〕*v.* 拖；拉

(B) *tempt*〔tɛmpt〕*v.* 引誘；使（人）想…
　　be tempted to V. 想要…

(C) inhale〔ɪn'hel〕*v.* 吸入（↔ exhale〔ɛks'hel〕*v.* 呼出）

(D) attract〔ə'trækt〕*v.* 吸引（= *appeal to*）

* lie〔laɪ〕*v.* 在；位於

6. (**A**) Although most dreams apparently happen <u>spontaneously</u>, dream activity may be provoked by external influences.

雖然大部分的夢表面上看起來是<u>自然產生的</u>，但外在的影響也會使人作夢。

(A) ***spontaneously*** 〔 spɑn'tenɪəslɪ 〕 *adv.* 自然地；自動自發地

(B) simultaneously 〔 ‚saɪml̩'tenɪəslɪ , ‚sɪml̩- 〕 *adv.* 同時地
  (= *at the same time*)

(C) contagiously 〔 kən'tedʒəslɪ 〕 *adv.* 易感染地

(D) instantaneously 〔 ‚ɪnstən'tenɪəslɪ 〕 *adv.* 即時地；同時地

* apparently 〔 ə'pærəntlɪ 〕 *adv.* 表面上看來；似乎
  provoke 〔 prə'vok 〕 *v.* 引起
  external 〔 ɪk'stɝnl̩ 〕 *adj.* 外在的
  influence 〔'ɪnfluəns 〕 *n.* 影響

7. (**A**) The insurance company paid him $10,000 in <u>compensation</u> after his accident. 保險公司在意外發生後，給他一萬元的<u>賠償</u>。

(A) ***compensation*** 〔‚kɑmpən'seʃən 〕 *n.* 賠償

(B) comparison 〔 kəm'pærəsn̩ 〕 *n.* 比較

(C) substitution 〔‚sʌbstə'tjuʃən 〕 *n.* 代替

(D) commission 〔 kə'mɪʃən 〕 *n.* 委託；佣金

* insurance 〔 ɪn'ʃurəns 〕 *n.* 保險

8. (**C**) Your excuse that an elephant fell on you and made you late is just <u>incredible</u>.

你說有頭大象攻擊你，你才遲到，這個藉口實在<u>令人難以置信</u>。

(A) inevitable 〔 ɪn'ɛvətəbl̩ 〕 *adj.* 不可避免的

(B) indispensable 〔‚ɪndɪs'pɛnsəbl̩ 〕 *adj.* 不可或缺的

(C) ***incredible*** 〔 ɪn'krɛdəbl̩ 〕 *adj.* 令人難以置信的

(D) incurable 〔 ɪn'kjurəbl̩ 〕 *adj.* 無可救藥的

* excuse 〔 ɪk'skjus 〕 *n.* 藉口   ***fall on*** 攻擊

9. (**B**) Iceland lies far north in the Atlantic, with its northernmost <u>tip</u> actually touching the Arctic Circle.

冰島位於大西洋極北的地區，其最北端實際上已與北極圈相接。

(A) oval〔'ovḷ〕n. 橢圓形

(B) *tip*〔tɪp〕n. 尖端；小費

(C) crust〔krʌst〕n. 地殼

(D) dome〔dom〕n. 圓頂

* Iceland〔'aɪslənd〕n. 冰島　　*the Atlantic* 大西洋
northernmost〔'nɔrðən,most〕adj. 最北端的
Arctic〔'ɑrktɪk〕adj. 北極的　　*the Arctic Circle* 北極圈

10. (**D**) A window in the kitchen was <u>smashed</u>, there was rubbish everywhere, and the curtains and carpets had been stolen.

廚房有個窗戶被打碎，滿地都是垃圾，窗簾和地毯都被偷走了。

(A) scatter〔'skætɚ〕v. 散布

(B) scrape〔skrep〕v. 刮

(C) scratch〔skrætʃ〕v. 搔；抓

(D) *smash*〔smæʃ〕v. 打碎

* rubbish〔'rʌbɪʃ〕n. 垃圾　　curtain〔'kɝtn̩〕n. 窗簾
carpet〔'kɑrpɪt〕n. 地毯

11. (**B**) If you <u>keep off</u> the bottle and cigarettes, you'll be much healthier.　如果你戒除菸酒，你會健康許多。

(A) take off 起飛（↔ *land* v. 降落）

(B) *keep off* 不接近；遠離；戒除（菸、酒）

(C) put off 拖延；延期（= *postpone*）

(D) set off 出發（= *set out*）

* *the bottle* 酒　　cigarette〔'sɪgə,rɛt〕n. 香菸

12. (**A**) They tossed your thoughts back and forth for over an hour, but still could not <u>make sense of</u> them. 他們反覆討論你的 想法，花了一個多鐘頭，仍然無法<u>理解</u>你的意思。

(A) ***make sense of*** 理解 (*= figure out = understand*)

(B) make the most of 充分利用 (*= make the best of*)

(C) make light of 輕視；忽視 (*= make little of*)
   (↔ *make much of* 重視)

(D) make fun of 取笑 (*= laugh at*)

* toss 〔 tɔs 〕 *v.* 討論   ***back and forth*** 來回地

13. (**D**) Though <u>by no means</u> rich, he was better off than at any other period in his life.
   儘管他<u>沒有</u>錢，他已比一生中其他任何時候都富有了。

(A) by any means 無論如何；以任何方法

(B) by some means (or other) 總得；想盡辦法

(C) by all means 務必；盡一切方法

(D) ***by no means*** 絕不；一點也不 (*= not at all*)

* ***be better off*** 更富裕；處境更好

14. (**A**) A large part of human activity, particularly that in relation to the environment, is <u>in response to</u> conditions or events.
   人類大部分的活動，尤其是和環境有關的活動，都是<u>對</u>各種情 況和事件<u>的反應</u>。

(A) ***in response to*** 對～的反應
   response 〔 rɪ'spɑns 〕 *n.* 反應

(B) in favor of 贊成；支持

(C) in contrast to 和～形成對比
   contrast 〔'kɑntræst 〕 *n.* 對比

(D) in excess of 超過   excess 〔 ɪk'sɛs 〕 *n.* 超過

* particularly 〔 pɚ'tɪkjələˈlɪ 〕 *adv.* 尤其   ***in relation to*** 關於

15. (**A**) Recycling waste <u>slows down</u> the rate at which we use up the Earth's finite resources.

回收利用廢物可以<u>減緩</u>我們消耗地球有限資源的速度。

(A) **slow down** 減緩　　(B) speed up 加速

(C) put away 收拾　　(D) cope with 應付；處理

* waste〔 west 〕n. 廢物　　**use up** 用完

finite〔'faɪnaɪt〕adj. 有限的

PART B：Cloze

Questions 16-22

　　Although interior design has existed since the beginning of architecture, its development <u>into</u> a specialized field is really quite
　　　　　　　　　　　　　　　　　　　　16
recent. Interior designers have become important partly because of the many facilities that might be <u>contained</u> in a single large building.
　　　　　　　　　　　　　　　　　　17

　　雖然自從有建築以來，室內設計就已經存在了，但是它發展成專門領域，其實是相當近代的事。室內設計師變得很重要，部分是因為同一棟大樓裡面，可能包含很多設備。

interior〔 ɪn'tɪrɪɚ 〕adj. 室內的　　design〔 dɪ'zaɪn 〕n. v. 設計
interior design 室內設計　　exist〔 ɪg'zɪst 〕v. 存在
beginning〔 bɪ'gɪnɪŋ 〕n. 開始；起源
architecture〔'ɑrkə,tɛktʃɚ〕n. 建築術；建築學
development〔 dɪ'vɛləpmənt 〕n. 發展
specialized〔'spɛʃəl,aɪzd〕adj. 專門的　　field〔 fild 〕n. 領域
recent〔'risṇt〕adj. 最近的　　designer〔 dɪ'zaɪnɚ 〕n. 設計師
facilities〔 fə'sɪlətɪz 〕n. pl. 設備　　single〔'sɪŋgḷ〕adj. 單一的

16. (**A**) development *into*… 發展成為…

17. (**B**) 依句意，選 (B) *contained*。　　contain〔kən'ten〕*v.* 包含
而 (A) consist 常加 of，作「由…組成」解，(C) compose
〔kəm'poz〕*v.* 組成，(D) compromise〔'kɑmprə,maɪz〕*v.* 妥
協，均不合句意。

The importance of interior design becomes evident when we
realize how much time we spend surrounded by four <u>walls</u>.　Being
　　　　　　　　　　　　　　　　　　　　　　　　18
indoors so much, we want our surroundings to be as attractive and
comfortable as possible.　We also expect each place to be appropriate
to its use.　You would be shocked if your bedroom were suddenly
changed to look like the inside of a restaurant.　And you wouldn't
feel <u>right</u> in an office that had the appearance of a school.
　19
　　當我們了解到，自己被四面牆壁所環繞的時間有多少時，室內設計的
重要性就變得很明顯了。因為我們在室內的時間是如此地長，所以就會希
望週遭的環境，能儘可能舒適且吸引人。我們也會期待，每個地方都能符
合其應有的用途。如果你的臥室突然間變得像是餐廳的內部，你一定會十
分震驚。而且在一間外觀像學校的辦公室裡，你也會覺得不對勁。

　　　　evident〔'ɛvədənt〕*adj.* 明顯的
　　　　realize〔'rɪə,laɪz〕*v.* 知道；了解
　　　　surround〔sə'raund〕*v.* 包圍；環繞
　　　　indoors〔'ɪn'dorz〕*adv.* 在室內
　　　　surroundings〔sə'raundɪŋz〕*n. pl.* 環境
　　　　as…*as possible* 儘可能…　　attractive〔ə'træktɪv〕*adj.* 吸引人的
　　　　expect〔ɪk'spɛkt〕*v.* 期待
　　　　appropriate〔ə'proprɪɪt〕*adj.* 適合…的 < *to* / *for* >
　　　　use〔jus〕*n.* 用途　　shocked〔ʃɑkt〕*adj.* 震驚的
　　　　suddenly〔'sʌdn̩lɪ〕*adv.* 突然地　　inside〔'ɪn'saɪd〕*n.* 內部
　　　　appearance〔ə'pɪrəns〕*n.* 外觀；樣子

18. (**D**)　(A) pillar〔ˈpɪlɚ〕*n.* 柱子

　　　　　(B) beam〔bim〕*n.* 橫樑

　　　　　(C) column〔ˈkɑləm〕*n.* 圓柱

　　　　　(D) ***walls***〔wɔlz〕*n. pl.* 牆壁

19. (**C**)　依句意，在一間外表像學校的辦公室裡，你會覺得不「對勁」，

　　　　　選 (C) ***right***。(A) correct「正確的」，(B) proper「適當的」，

　　　　　(D) suitable「適合的」，均不合句意。

It soon becomes clear that the interior designer's most important and basic concern is the function of the particular space. For example, a theater with poor lines of sight, poor sound quality, and too few entrances and <u>exits</u> will not work for its purpose, no
20
matter how beautifully it might be decorated. <u>Consequently</u>, for
21
any kind of space, the designer has to make many decisions. He or she must coordinate the shape, lighting and decoration of everything from <u>ceiling</u> to floor. In addition, the designer must
22
usually select furniture or design built-in furniture, according to the functions that need to be served.

　　顯而易見地，設計師最重要而且基本的考量，就是特定空間的功能。例如，一間視線差、音效不好，而且入口與出口都太少的戲院，無論裝潢得多美，都不符合其用途。因此，對於任何一種空間，設計師都必須做很多決定。他或她都必須讓形狀、燈光照明，以及從天花板到地板的每樣東西的裝潢都能互相搭配。此外，設計師通常必須選擇傢俱，或根據所須符合的功能，設計安裝固定的傢俱。

basic〔ˈbesɪk〕*adj.* 基本的

concern〔kənˈsɝn〕*n.* 關心的事   function〔ˈfʌŋkʃən〕*n.* 功能

particular〔pəˈtɪkjələ〕*adj.* 特定的

space〔spes〕*n.* 空間   poor〔pʊr〕*adj.* 不佳的

line of sight 視線   *sound quality* 音效

entrance〔ˈɛntrəns〕*n.* 入口

work〔wɝk〕*v.* 有效；行得通   purpose〔ˈpɝpəs〕*n.* 目的

decorate〔ˈdɛkəˌret〕*v.* 裝飾；裝潢   *no matter how* 無論怎麼樣

coordinate〔koˈordn̩ˌet〕*v.* 使協調；使搭配

lighting〔ˈlaɪtɪŋ〕*n.* 燈光；照明

decoration〔ˌdɛkəˈreʃən〕*n.* 裝飾；裝潢

in addition 此外   furniture〔ˈfɝnɪtʃə〕*n.* 傢俱

built-in〔ˈbɪltˈɪn〕*adj.* 內建的；安裝固定的

function〔ˈfʌŋkʃən〕*n.* 功能   serve〔sɝv〕*v.* 符合；適合

20. (**A**) (A) *exit*〔ˈɛgzɪt〕*n.* 出口

(B) exist〔ɪgˈzɪst〕*v.* 存在

(C) axis〔ˈæksɪs〕*n.* 軸心

(D) matrix〔ˈmætrɪks〕*n.* 矩陣；母體（組織）

21. (**B**) 依句意，選 (B) *Consequently*〔ˈkɑnsəˌkwɛntlɪ〕*adv.* 因此。
而 (A) on the contrary「相反地」，(C) nevertheless「然而」，
(D) namely「也就是」，均不合句意。

22. (**C**) 依句意，從「天花板」到地板的每樣東西，選 (C) *ceiling*〔ˈsilɪŋ〕
n. 天花板。而 (A) roof〔ruf〕*n.* 屋頂，(B) cabinet〔ˈkæbənɪt〕*n.*
櫥櫃；（有玻璃窗戶的）裝飾櫃，(D) cupboard〔ˈkʌbəd〕*n.* 碗
櫥，均不合句意。

Questions 23-30

When Winston Churchill retired for the second time from his post <u>as</u> prime minister of England, he was invited to <u>address</u> the
23　　　　　　　　　　　　　　　　　　　　　　　24
graduating class at Oxford University.　Sir Winston was seated at the head table, and was dressed in his formal wear, including his ever-present top hat, cane, and cigar.

當溫士頓・邱吉爾第二次從英國首相一職退休之後，他受邀到牛津大學，對即將畢業的班級演講。邱吉爾爵士坐在主桌，穿著正式的服裝，包括他那經常出現的高頂絲質禮帽、手杖，以及雪茄。

> ***Winston Churchill*** 〔ˈwɪnstən ˈtʃɝtʃɪl 〕 *n.* 溫士頓・邱吉爾
> 　【1874-1965，英國的政治家，兩度任首相（1940-1945, 1951-1955）】
> retire 〔 rɪˈtaɪr 〕 *v.* 退休；退職　　***for the second time*** 第二次
> post 〔 post 〕 *n.* 職位　　***prime minister*** 首相
> graduating 〔ˈgrædʒʊ͵etɪŋ 〕 *adj.* 快畢業的
> Oxford 〔ˈɑksfəd 〕 *n.* 牛津　　sir 〔 sə, sɝ 〕 *n.* 爵士
> ***be seated*** 坐　　***head table*** 主桌　　***be dressed in*** 穿著
> formal 〔ˈfɔrml̩ 〕 *adj.* 正式的
> wear 〔 wɛr 〕 *n.* 服裝（ = *clothes* ）
> ever-present 〔ˈɛvəˈprɛznt̩ 〕 *adj.* 一直出現的；經常出現的
> ***top hat*** 高頂絲質禮帽　　cane 〔 ken 〕 *n.* 手杖；拐杖
> cigar 〔 sɪˈgɑr 〕 *n.* 雪茄

23. (**B**)　「*as* + 身份」表「身為…；擔任…」。

24. (**C**)　依句意，選 (C) ***address*** 〔 əˈdrɛs 〕 *v.* 向…演說。而 (A) talk，
　　　　　　(B) speak，都必須加 to，才能接人，(D) speech 〔 spitʃ 〕 *n.* 演
　　　　　　講，是名詞，均用法不合。

After an <u>extended</u> and too-lengthy introduction, he walked to
25

the podium. <u>Grabbing</u> the lectern in both hands, he paused for a
26

number of seconds and looked at his audience. Then in that
Churchillian way that was <u>uniquely</u> his, he looked at them for a
27

full thirty seconds and said, "Never, never, never give up!" Then
another long pause, and with even greater emphasis and <u>eloquence</u>,
28

he repeated, "Never, never, never give up!" He looked at the
audience a few more seconds and sat down.

在詳細及過度冗長的介紹之後，他走向講台。他雙手緊抓著講台，停
頓了幾秒，注視著聽眾。他以他獨有，專屬於邱吉爾的方式，看著他們整
整三十秒，然後說：「絕對、絕對、絕對不要放棄！」接著又停頓很久之
後，以更強調的語氣，且更具說服力的方式重複說：「絕對、絕對、絕對
不要放棄！」他再看了聽眾幾秒後，就坐了下來。

> lengthy〔'lɛŋθɪ〕adj. 冗長的
> introduction〔,ɪntrə'dʌkʃən〕n. 介紹
> podium〔'podɪəm〕n. 講台　　lectern〔'lɛktən〕n. 演講台
> pause〔pɔz〕v. n. 停頓　　*a number of* 幾個
> second〔'sɛkənd〕n. 秒　　audience〔'ɔdɪəns〕n. 聽眾
> Churchillian〔'tʃɜtʃɪlɪən〕adj. 邱吉爾的
> full〔fʊl〕adj. 足足的；整整的　　*give up* 放棄
> emphasis〔'ɛmfəsɪs〕n. 強調　　repeat〔rɪ'pit〕v. 重複

25. (**C**)　(A) extension〔ɪk'stɛnʃən〕n. 延長；分機
　　　　　(B) extensible〔ɪk'stɛnsəbḷ〕adj. 可延伸的；伸縮的
　　　　　(C) *extended*〔ɪk'stɛndɪd〕adj. 長時間的；詳細的
　　　　　(D) extending 為 extend「延伸」的現在分詞或動名詞。

26.(D) 本句是由副詞子句：When he grabbed the lectern…簡化而來
的分詞構句。副詞子句改為分詞構句有三個步驟：①去連接詞
（When 去掉），②主詞相同可省略（he 省略），③動詞改為
現在分詞（grabbed 改成 grabbing），故選 (D) *Grabbing*。
grab〔græb〕v. 緊抓

27.(B) (A) universally〔‚junə'vɝslɪ〕adv. 一般地；普遍地
(B) *uniquely*〔ju'niklɪ〕adv. 獨特地；特有地
(C) ultimately〔'ʌltəmɪtlɪ〕adv. 最後；終於
(D) solemnly〔'sɑləmlɪ〕adv. 嚴肅地

28.(B) (A) hypocrisy〔hɪ'pɑkrəsɪ〕n. 偽善
(B) *eloquence*〔'ɛləkwəns〕n. 流利的口才；說服力
(C) prosperity〔prɑs'pɛrətɪ〕n. 繁榮
(D) vanity〔'vænətɪ〕n. 虛榮

　Undoubtedly, this presentation was the shortest major address
in history. It also was one of Churchill's most <u>memorable</u>.
                                                          29

　If you do <u>take</u> the advice of Winston Churchill, then I really will
            30
see you at the top!

　無疑地，這場演講是有史以來最短的重要演講，也是邱吉爾最令人難
忘的一場演講。

　如果你真的聽從邱吉爾的建議，那麼我真的就可以看見，你將會非常
成功！

undoubtedly〔ʌn'dautɪdlɪ〕adv. 無疑地
presentation〔‚prɛzn'teʃən〕n. 演講
major〔'medʒə〕adj. 重要的　　address〔ə'drɛs〕n. 演講
history〔'hɪstrɪ〕n. 歷史　　advice〔əd'vaɪs〕n. 勸告
top〔tɑp〕n. 頂點；最高處　　*at the top* 非常成功；高居首位

29. (**D**) (A) forgetful〔fəˋgɛtfəl〕*adj.* 健忘的

(B) scornful〔ˋskɔrnfəl〕*adj.* 輕蔑的；輕視的

(C) memorial〔məˋmorɪəl〕*adj.* 紀念的；追悼的

(D) *memorable*〔ˋmɛmərəbḷ〕*adj.* 令人難忘的

(= *unforgettable*)

30. (**A**) 依句意，選 (A) *take one's advice*「聽從某人的勸告」

(= *follow one's advice*)。而 (B) receive「收到」，

(C) grant〔grænt〕*v.* 答應；給予，(D) adapt〔əˋdæpt〕*v.*

使適應；改編，均不合句意。

📁 PART C : **Reading**

Questions 31-35

Although "lie detectors" are being used by governments, police departments, and businesses that all want guaranteed ways of detecting the truth, the results are not always accurate. Lie detectors are also called emotion detectors, for their aim is to measure bodily changes that indicate a contradiction in what a person says. The polygraph machine records changes in heart rate, breathing, blood pressure, and the electrical activity of the skin.

雖然「測謊器」被政府、警察局，及企業所使用，而且他們全都想要一個能測出真相的可靠方法，但測謊的結果，卻未必是準確的。測謊器又稱爲情緒偵測器，因爲其目標，是要測量身體的改變，而這些改變，就能顯示出一個人所說的話，是否有矛盾之處。測謊器會記錄心跳速率、呼吸、血壓，及皮膚電流活動的改變。

detector〔dɪˈtɛktɚ〕n. 偵測器　　**lie detector** 測謊器

police department 警察局

guaranteed〔ˌgærənˈtid〕adj. 有保證的；確定的；可靠的

detect〔dɪˈtɛkt〕v. 偵測

not always 未必；不一定　　accurate〔ˈækjərɪt〕adj. 準確的

emotion〔ɪˈmoʃən〕n. 情緒　　aim〔em〕n. 目的

measure〔ˈmɛʒɚ〕v. 測量　　bodily〔ˈbadɪlɪ〕adj. 身體的

indicate〔ˈɪndəˌket〕v. 顯示

contradiction〔ˌkantrəˈdɪkʃən〕n. 矛盾

polygraph〔ˈpalɪˌgræf〕n. 測謊器（= *lie detector*）

heart rate 心跳速率　　breathing〔ˈbriðɪŋ〕n. 呼吸

blood pressure 血壓　　electrical〔ɪˈlɛktrɪkl̩〕adj. 電的

electrical activity 電流活動　　skin〔skɪn〕n. 皮膚

In the first part of the polygraph test, you are electronically connected to the machine and asked a few neutral questions, like "What's your name?" or "Where do you live?". Your physical reactions serve as the standard for evaluating what comes next. Then you are asked a few critical questions among the neutral ones, like "When did you rob the bank?" The assumption is that if you are guilty, your body will reveal the truth, even if you try to deny it. Your heart rate and respiration will change quickly as you respond to the incriminating questions.

在測謊的第一部份，你會被用電子儀器連結到機器上，並被問一些較不敏感的問題，像是「你叫什麼名字？」或「你住在哪裡？」。你的身體反應會被當作是一項標準，用來評估你接下來的反應。然後在這些較不敏感的問題中，你會被問到一些重要的問題，像是「你何時搶銀行？」。其假設就是，如果你有罪，你的身體會透露真相，即使你想否認也一樣。當你回答那些會顯示你有罪的問題時，你的心跳速率和呼吸，會快速地改變。

electronically〔ɪˌlɛk'trɑnɪklɪ〕*adv.* 電子地

connect〔kə'nɛkt〕*v.* 連結

be electronically connected to 利用電子儀器連結到

neutral〔'njutrəl〕*adj.* 中性的；普通的；較不敏感的

physical〔'fɪzɪkl̩〕*adj.* 身體的

reaction〔rɪ'ækʃən〕*n.* 反應

serve as 充當；當作　　standard〔'stændə∂d〕*n.* 標準

evaluate〔ɪ'vælju͵et〕*v.* 評估

critical〔'krɪtɪkl̩〕*adj.* 決定性的；重要的

rob〔rɑb〕*v.* 搶　　assumption〔ə'sʌmpʃən〕*n.* 假定

guilty〔'gɪltɪ〕*adj.* 有罪的

reveal〔rɪ'vil〕*v.* 透露；洩露　　***even if*** 即使

deny〔dɪ'naɪ〕*v.* 否認　　respiration〔͵rɛspə'reʃən〕*n.* 呼吸

respond〔rɪ'spɑnd〕*v.* 回答；回應

incriminating〔ɪn'krɪmə͵netɪŋ〕*adj.* 顯示有罪的；使人有罪的

　　That is the theory, but psychologists have found that lie detectors are simply not reliable. Since most physical changes are the same across all emotions, machines cannot tell whether you are feeling guilty, angry, nervous, or thrilled. Innocent people may be nervous about the whole procedure. They may react greatly to a certain word ("bank") not because they robbed it, but because they recently bounced a check. In either case the machine will record a "lie." Besides, some practiced liars can lie without flinching, and others learn to beat the machine by tensing muscles or thinking about an exciting experience during neutral questions.

理論上就是那樣，但是心理學家已經發現，事實上測謊器並不可靠。因為所有的情緒所造成的身體變化，大部分都是相同的，機器無法分辨你是覺得有罪、生氣、緊張，還是興奮。無罪的人可能會對整個過程覺得緊張，他們可能會對某些字（如「銀行」）作出很大的反應，不是因為他們搶了銀行，而是因為最近支票跳票。不管是哪種情況，機器都會記錄他「說謊」。此外，有些經驗豐富的說謊者，能毫不畏懼地說謊，有些則是學會欺騙測謊器，藉由使肌肉拉緊，或在回答一些較不敏感的問題時，想某個刺激的經驗。

theory〔'θɪərɪ〕 *n.* 理論

psychologist〔saɪ'kɑlədʒɪst〕 *n.* 心理學家

simply〔'sɪmplɪ〕 *adv.* 事實上；實際上

reliable〔rɪ'laɪəbḷ〕 *adj.* 值得信賴的

across〔ə'krɔs〕 *prep.* 遍及　　tell〔tɛl〕 *v.* 知道；分辨

nervous〔'nɝvəs〕 *adj.* 緊張的　　thrilled〔'θrɪld〕 *adj.* 興奮的

innocent〔'ɪnəsṇt〕 *adj.* 清白的；無罪的

procedure〔prə'sidʒɚ〕 *n.* 程序；過程　　react〔rɪ'ækt〕 *v.* 反應

certain〔'sɝtṇ〕 *adj.* 某個　　recently〔'risṇtlɪ〕 *adv.* 最近

bounce〔baʊns〕 *v.* 使彈跳；因存款不足而拒絕兌現（支票）

check〔tʃɛk〕 *n.* 支票　　either〔'iðɚ〕 *adj.*（兩者）任一的

case〔kes〕 *n.* 情況　　besides〔bɪ'saɪdz〕 *adv.* 此外

practiced〔'præktɪst〕 *adj.* 經驗豐富的；熟練的

liar〔'laɪɚ〕 *n.* 說謊者　　flinch〔flɪntʃ〕 *v.* 退縮；畏縮；逃避

some…others~ 有些…有些~　　beat〔bit〕 *v.* 打敗；欺騙

tense〔tɛns〕 *v.* 拉緊；使緊張　　muscle〔'mʌsḷ〕 *n.* 肌肉

31.（**A**）根據本文，測謊器的測試

(A) 會記錄一個人的身體反應。

(B) 會測量一個人的想法。

(C) 一定能透露跟某個人有關的真相。

(D) 會使有罪的人生氣。

32.(**B**) 根據本文，測謊的第一部份會問什麼問題？

　　(A) 重要的。　　　　　(B) 不重要的。

　　(C) 會顯示有罪的。　　(D) 情緒化的。

　　* emotional〔ɪˋmoʃənḷ〕adj. 情緒化的；感人的

33.(**B**) 本文的主題是什麼？

　　(A) 身體的反應會顯示出有罪。

　　(B) 如何使用測謊器，以及它們是否可靠。

　　(C) 測謊器能分辨不同的情緒。

　　(D) 測謊器會使無罪的人緊張。

　　* guilt〔gɪlt〕n. 有罪；犯罪

　　reliability〔rɪ͵laɪəˋbɪlətɪ〕n. 可靠性

　　distinguish〔dɪˋstɪŋgwɪʃ〕v. 分辨

34.(**D**) 從本文可推論出下列何者？

　　(A) 測謊器非常可靠。　　(B) 無罪的人一定不會被判決有罪。

　　(C) 心理學家從不會為任何事爭執。

　　(D) 大部分的人無法控制其身體的反應。

　　* infer〔ɪnˋfɝ〕v. 推論　　find〔faɪnd〕v. 判決；判定

　　argue〔ˋɑrgju〕v. 爭論

35.(**D**) 從本文可斷定，測謊器的測試

　　(A) 是判定一個人是否有罪最好的方法。

　　(B) 可以看出一個人的想法。

　　(C) 是法庭上所需要的唯一證據。

　　(D) 原則上行得通，但實際上行不通。

　　* determine〔dɪˋtɝmɪn〕v. 判定；確定　　read〔rid〕v. 看出

　　evidence〔ˋɛvədəns〕n. 證據　　*court of law* 法庭（= *court*）

　　work〔wɝk〕v. 行得通　　principle〔ˋprɪnsəpḷ〕n. 原則

　　in principle 原則上　　*in practice* 實際上

Questions 36-37

One of the most serious respiratory diseases is influenza, for it is able to attack people of all ages throughout the world. Incidence frequently is highest in young adults. It is an example of a disease that has increased in virulence throughout the years, although since 1942 it seems to have become milder again. Influenza periodically has been epidemic in the United States from 1918 to the present time. Several tragic worldwide pandemics have occurred. One of the most dreadful was the 1918-1919 outbreak, in which there were some 20 million cases of influenza and pneumonia and approximately 850,000 deaths occurred.

流行性感冒是最嚴重的呼吸器官疾病之一，因爲它會侵襲全世界各個年齡層的人。通常年輕人的罹患率是最高的。它也是病毒會逐年增加毒性的一個例子，雖然自從一九四二年以來，其毒性似乎又變得比較溫和。從一九一八年到現在，美國定期會出現流行性感冒。全世界已經發生了好幾次可怕的流行病。其中最嚴重的，是在一九一八年到一九一九年之間爆發的流行病。當時大約有兩千萬人罹患流行性感冒及肺炎，有將近八十五萬人死亡。

respiratory (rɪ'spaɪrə͵torɪ) adj. 呼吸的
influenza (͵ɪnflu'ɛnzə) n. 流行性感冒
attack (ə'tæk) v. 攻擊；侵襲　　throughout (θru'aut) prep. 遍及
incidence ('ɪnsədəns) n. 發生率；罹患率
frequently ('frikwəntlɪ) adv. 經常　　virulence ('vɪrjələns) n. 毒性
milder ('maɪldə) adj. 較溫和的
periodically (͵pɪrɪ'adəkḷɪ) adv. 定期地
epidemic (͵ɛpə'dɛmɪk) adj. (疾病) 流行 (性) 的
the present time 目前　　tragic ('trædʒɪk) adj. 可怕的
pandemic (pæn'dɛmɪk) n. 世界性的流行病
occur (ə'kɝ) v. 發生　　dreadful ('drɛdfəl) adj. 可怕的；嚴重的
outbreak ('aut͵brek) n. 爆發　　some (sʌm) adv. 大約
case (kes) n. 病例；患者　　pneumonia (nju'monjə) n. 肺炎
approximately (ə'praksəmɪtlɪ) adv. 大約

Influenza is an acute disease of the respiratory tract that affects the whole body. It is characterized by a sudden onset, with chills, a fever of around 102 degrees that may rise to 104 degrees, headache, muscular pains, prostration, sore throat, and cough. Like the common cold, it paves the way for secondary infections such as hemolytic streptococci and pneumonia. Most deaths are due to complications from pneumonia. Recovery is usual in four or five days.

流行性感冒是一種會影響全身的呼吸道疾病。它的特色是會突然發病，身體發冷，發燒到大約 102 度，而且可能會上升到 104 度，頭痛、肌肉痛、疲勞、喉嚨痛，以及咳嗽。它就像普通的感冒，會為二度感染作準備，像是 B 型溶血性鏈球菌和肺炎。大部份的死亡都是因為肺炎引起的併發症。流行性感冒通常要四、五天才會康復。

acute〔ə'kjut〕*adj.* 急性的　　tract〔trækt〕*n.* 道

respiratory tract 呼吸道　　affect〔ə'fɛkt〕*v.* 影響

characterize〔'kærɪktə,raɪz〕*v.* 使成為⋯的特色

be characterized by 特色是　　sudden〔'sʌdn̩〕*adj.* 突然的

onset〔'ɑn,sɛt〕*n.* 攻擊；發病　　chill〔tʃɪl〕*n.* 發冷；顫抖

fever〔'fivɚ〕*n.* 發燒　　degree〔dɪ'gri〕*n.* 度

rise〔raɪz〕*v.* 上升　　headache〔'hɛd,ek〕*n.* 頭痛

muscular〔'mʌskjələ〕*adj.* 肌肉的

prostration〔prɑ'streʃən〕*n.* 疲勞；衰弱　　***sore throat*** 喉嚨痛

cough〔kɔf〕*n.* 咳嗽　　common〔'kɑmən〕*adj.* 普通的

pave the way for 為⋯鋪路；為⋯作準備

secondary〔'sɛkən,dɛrɪ〕*adj.*（重要性、順序等）第二位的

infection〔ɪn'fɛkʃən〕*n.* 感染

secondary infection 二度感染

hemolytic streptococci B 型溶血性鏈球菌　　***be due to*** 由於

complication〔,kɑmplə'keʃən〕*n.* 併發症

recovery〔rɪ'kʌvərɪ〕*n.* 康復

36. (**A**)　流行性感冒這種疾病，

　　　(A)　通常毒性會增強。　　　(B)　美國人並不知道。

　　　(C)　毒性會持續不變。　　　(D)　不難控制。

　　　＊ generally〔ˋdʒɛnərəlɪ〕 *adv.* 通常

　　　　remain〔rɪˋmen〕 *v.* 保持

　　　　constant〔ˋkɑnstənt〕 *adj.* 不變的

　　　　toxicity〔tɑksˋɪsətɪ〕 *n.* 毒性

37. (**C**)　大部分因流行性感冒而致死都是因為

　　　(A)　副流感病毒。　　　(B)　誤診。

　　　(C)　肺炎引起的併發症。　　　(D)　導致肝炎的併發症。

　　　＊ parainfluenza〔͵pærəɪnfluˋɛnzə〕 *n.* 副流感；副流感病毒

　　　　faulty〔ˋfɔltɪ〕 *adj.* 錯誤的

　　　　diagnosis〔͵daɪəgˋnosɪs〕 *n.* 診斷

　　　　lead to 導致　　hepatitis〔͵hɛpəˋtaɪtɪs〕 *n.* 肝炎

Questions　38-40

　　Fungi are seen as a diverse group of either single-celled or multicelluar organisms that obtain food by direct absorption of nutrients.　The food is dissolved by enzymes that the fungi excrete, is then absorbed through thin cell walls, and is distributed by simple circulation, or streaming, of the protoplasm.　Together with bacteria, fungi are responsible for the decay and decomposition of all organic matter and are found wherever other forms of life exist.　Some are parasitic on living matter and cause serious plant and animal diseases.　The study of fungi is called mycology.

黴菌被視爲是一個單細胞或多細胞生物的另類族群，它能藉由直接吸收養份，而獲得食物。食物會在黴菌分泌的酵素中分解，然後通過薄薄的細胞壁被吸收，再藉由原生質的簡單循環，也就是流動，分配到各處。黴菌和細菌一起負責讓所有的有機物腐爛與分解，而且在其他生物存在的地方，都可以找得到黴菌。有些黴菌會寄生在生物上，並導致嚴重的動植物疾病。研究黴菌的學問被稱爲黴菌學。

fungi〔'fʌndʒaɪ〕 n. pl. 黴菌；眞菌（包括黴菌、傘菌等）【單數是 fungus〔'fʌngəs〕】　diverse〔daɪ'vɝs〕 adj. 不同的

single-celled〔'sɪŋgl'sɛld〕 adj. 單細胞的

multicellular〔'mʌltɪ'sɛljələ〕 adj. 多細胞的

organism〔'ɔrgən,ɪzəm〕 n. 生物　obtain〔əb'ten〕 v. 獲得

absorption〔əb'sɔrpʃən〕 n. 吸收

nutrient〔'njutrɪənt〕 n. 營養　dissolve〔dɪ'zɑlv〕 v. 分解

enzyme〔'ɛnzaɪm〕 n. 酵素　excrete〔ɪk'skrit〕 v. 分泌

cell〔sɛl〕 n. 細胞　*cell wall* 細胞壁

distribute〔dɪ'strɪbjut〕 v. 分配；分發

circulation〔,sɝkjə'leʃən〕 n. 循環　stream〔strim〕 v. 流動

protoplasm〔'protə,plæzəm〕 n.（構成細胞的）原生質

together with 連同　bacteria〔bæk'tɪrɪə〕 n. pl. 細菌

be responsible for 負責　decay〔dɪ'ke〕 n. 腐爛

decomposition〔,dikampə'zɪʃən〕 n. 分解

organic matter 有機物　*form of life* 生物

parasitic〔,pærə'sɪtɪk〕 adj. 寄生的　*living matter* 生物

mycology〔maɪ'kɑlədʒɪ〕 n. 黴菌學；眞菌學

Fungi were traditionally classified as a division in the plant kingdom. They were thought of as plants that have no stems or leaves and that in the course of becoming food absorbers lost the pigment chlorophyll, which is needed for conducting photosynthesis.

Most scientists today, however, view them as an entirely separate group that evolved from unpigmented flagellates and place them either in the protist kingdom or in their own kingdom, according to the complexity of organization. Approximately 100,000 species of fungi are known. The more complex groups are believed to have derived from the primitive types, which have flagellated cells at some stage in their life cycle.

傳統上，黴菌被歸類為是植物界的一個分支。它們被認為是沒有莖或葉的植物，而且在汲取養料的過程中，失去了行光合作用所需要的葉綠素。然而，現在大部份的科學家，都把它們視為是從無葉綠素的鞭毛蟲演化成的，完全不同的族群，不是將它們歸類在原生生物，就是根據它們複雜的結構，讓它們自成一類。現在已知的黴菌約有十萬種。一般認為，比較複雜的黴菌，是源自於原始的黴菌，它們在生命週期的某個階段，擁有鞭狀的細胞。

traditionally〔trə'dɪʃənlɪ〕*adv.* 傳統上
classify〔'klæsə,faɪ〕*v.* 分類
division〔də'vɪʒən〕*n.*【生物學分類】門；分支；類
kingdom〔'kɪŋdəm〕*n.*【生物學分類】界　***plant kingdom*** 植物界
stem〔stɛm〕*n.* 莖　　leaves〔livz〕*n. pl.* 葉子【單數是 leaf】
course〔kors〕*n.* 過程　　food〔fud〕*n.* 食物；養料
absorber〔əb'sɔrbɚ〕*n.* 吸收者　　pigment〔'pɪgmənt〕*n.* 色素
chlorophyll〔'klorə,fɪl〕*n.* 葉綠素
conduct〔kən'dʌkt〕*v.* 進行
photosynthesis〔,fotə'sɪnθəsɪs〕*n.* 光合作用
view A ***as*** B 視 A 為 B　　entirely〔ɪn'taɪrlɪ〕*adv.* 完全地
separate〔'sɛpərɪt〕*adj.* 不同的　evolve〔ɪ'vɑlv〕*v.* 進化；演變
unpigmented〔ʌn'pɪgməntɪd〕*adj.* 無色素的；無葉綠素的
flagellate〔'flædʒə,let〕*n.* 鞭毛蟲　　place〔ples〕*v.* 放置
protist〔'protɪst〕*n.* 原生物

complexity〔kəm'plɛksətɪ〕 n. 複雜

organization〔,ɔrgənə'zeʃən〕 n. 結構

approximately〔ə'prɑksəmɪtlɪ〕 adv. 大約

species〔'spiʃɪz〕 n. 種　　complex〔'kɑmplɛks〕 adj. 複雜的

derive from 源自於　　primitive〔'prɪmətɪv〕 adj. 原始的

flagellated〔'flædʒə,letɪd〕 adj. 有鞭毛形的

cell〔sɛl〕 n. 細胞　　some〔sʌm〕 adj. 某個

stage〔stedʒ〕 n. 階段　　cycle〔'saɪkl̩〕 n. 週期

38. (**C**) 下列何者是本文最好的標題？

　　(A) 植物界　　　　　　　(B) 細菌界

　　(C) 自然界的分解者　　　(D) 光合作用的過程

　　* decomposer〔,dikəm'pozɚ〕 n. 分解者

　　　process〔'prɑsɛs〕 n. 過程

39. (**D**) 根據本文，下列何者正確？

　　(A) 黴菌是一種植物，它會利用吃下去的食物所產生的酵素。

　　(B) 黴菌是沒有莖或葉的植物。

　　(C) 黴菌無法汲取養料。

　　(D) 黴菌不是植物。

40. (**D**) 從本文可以推論出下列何者？

　　(A) 黴菌應該被消滅，因為它們會造成嚴重的動植物疾病。

　　(B) 在植物界，黴菌屬於很獨特的一門。

　　(C) 黴菌和植物唯一的不同點在於行光合作用所需要的葉綠素。

　　(D) 黴菌須依賴動植物才能生存。

　　* infer〔ɪn'fɝ〕 v. 推論　　exterminate〔ɪks'tɝmə,net〕 v. 滅絕

　　　unique〔ju'nik〕 adj. 獨特的　　*lie in* 在於

　　　survival〔sə'vaɪvl̩〕 n. 生存

Questions 41-43

Alexander, Caesar, Napoleon—they spent their lives fighting wars, defeating nations and building empires. We remember these men because they wanted the world and often came close to winning it. But none came as close as one man—Genghis Khan.

亞歷山大、凱撒，拿破崙——他們終生都在打仗、打敗其他國家，建立帝國。我們記得這些人，因為他們想要全世界，而且往往差一點就贏得全世界。但是沒有一個像這個人那麼靠近目標——那就是成吉思汗。

Alexander〔͵ælɪgˋzændɚ〕*n.* 亞歷山大【馬其頓國王】
Caesar〔ˋsizɚ〕*n.* 凱撒　　Napoleon〔nəˋpoljən〕*n.* 拿破崙
defeat〔dɪˋfit〕*v.* 打敗　　empire〔ˋɛmpaɪr〕*n.* 帝國
come close to 接近
Genghis Khan〔ˋdʒɛŋgɪzˋkɑn〕*n.* 成吉思汗

Genghis Khan had an outgoing personality, but even as a boy he was merciless. It is said that his half-brother Bekhter often stole the food Genghis Khan got by hunting and fishing. To repay these insults, Khan and his younger brother killed Bekhter by shooting him with an arrow.

成吉思汗性格外向，即使在小時候，他也是很冷酷無情的。據說他的同父異母兄弟別克帖兒，常會偷成吉思汗打獵或捕魚所獲得的食物。為了報復他的侮辱，成吉思汗和弟弟就用箭把別克帖兒射死。

outgoing〔ˋaʊt͵goɪŋ〕*adj.* 外向的
personality〔͵pɝsṇˋælətɪ〕*n.* 性格
merciless〔ˋmɝsɪlɪs〕*adj.* 冷酷的；無情的
It is said that … 據說…　　half-brother *n.* 同父異母的兄弟
repay〔rɪˋpe〕*v.* 回報　　insult〔ˋɪnsʌlt〕*n.* 侮辱
shoot〔ʃut〕*v.* 射殺　　arrow〔ˋæro〕*n.* 箭

Khan's strategy in gaining followers was straightforward and very effective. First, he realized that the best way to build a skillful army was by rewarding and promoting the most able warriors. Thus his officers gained power not because of which family they belonged to, but because they had served Khan well. Furthermore, to his enemies, Khan gave a very simple choice: Surrender or die.

成吉思汗獲得部下的方法，是直接而有效的。首先，他知道建立精銳部隊的最好方法，就是獎勵與拔擢最有能力的戰士。因此，他的軍官獲得權力，不是因為他們屬於什麼家族，而是因為他們效忠成吉思汗。此外，對於敵人，成吉思汗會給他們很簡單的選擇：投降或是死。

strategy (ˈstrætədʒɪ) *n.* 策略　　gain (gen) *v.* 獲得

follower (ˈfɑloə) *n.* 隨從；手下；部下

straightforward (ˌstretˈfɔrwəd) *adj.* 直接的

effective (əˈfɛktɪv) *adj.* 有效的　　realize (ˈriəˌlaɪz) *v.* 了解

skillful (ˈskɪlfəl) *adj.* 精湛的；熟練的

army (ˈɑrmɪ) *n.* 軍隊　　reward (rɪˈwɔrd) *v.* 獎賞

promote (prəˈmot) *v.* 拔擢；使升官

able (ˈebl̩) *adj.* 有能力的　　warrior (ˈwɔrɪə) *n.* 戰士

thus (ðʌs) *adv.* 因此　　officer (ˈɔfəsə) *n.* 軍官

serve (sɝv) *v.* 效忠　　furthermore (ˈfɝðəˌmor) *adv.* 此外

surrender (səˈrɛndə) *v.* 投降

Thus, Khan, who was not born into greatness or power, through a combination of strong leadership, personal courage and effective discouragement of resistance, was able to build an empire that reached from the Pacific Ocean to the Adriatic Sea.

因此，成吉思汗並非生來就偉大或有權勢，他是透過結合強大的領導能力、個人的勇氣，以及有效的制止反抗，才能夠建立一個勢力範圍從太平洋一直延伸到亞得里亞海的帝國。

greatness〔'gretnɪs〕 n. 偉大　　through〔θru〕prep. 透過；經由
combination〔͵kɑmbə'neʃən〕 n. 結合
leadership〔'lidə͵ʃɪp〕 n. 領導能力　　courage〔'kɝɪdʒ〕 n. 勇氣
discouragement〔dɪs'kɝɪdʒmənt〕 n. 制止；阻止
resistance〔rɪ'zɪstəns〕 n. 反抗　　*the Pacific Ocean* 太平洋
Adriatic〔͵edrɪ'ætɪk〕 n. 亞得里亞海
the Adriatic Sea 亞得里亞海

41. (**D**)　成吉思汗爲何殺死自己同父異母的弟弟？

 (A)　他偷了成吉思汗的錢。

 (B)　他向成吉思汗挑戰，想取得權力。

 (C)　他背叛成吉思汗。

 (D)　他偷了成吉思汗自己找到的食物。

 * betray〔bɪ'tre〕 v. 背叛；出賣

42. (**A**)　成吉思汗軍隊中的士兵是如何獲得升遷？

 (A)　非常效忠成吉思汗以及軍隊。

 (B)　付了大筆的錢。

 (C)　有良好的家族關係。

 (D)　在戰場上打敗成吉思汗。

 * connections〔kə'nɛkʃənz〕 n. pl. 人際關係
  battle〔'bætḷ〕 n. 戰役；戰鬥

43. (**C**)　根據本文，下列敘述何者爲非？

 (A)　當一提到征服世界，成吉思汗不會輸給任何人。

 (B)　對於被成吉思汗軍隊抓到的人而言，向成吉思汗投降是唯一的生存之道。

 (C)　雖然成吉思汗小時候就很冷酷無情，但他對身邊的人總是很溫和。

 (D)　成吉思汗並不是靠家世背景而成就他的偉大。

* ***be next to no one*** 不輸給任何人
  when it comes to 一提到　　capture〔'kæptʃɚ〕*v.* 捕捉
  alive〔ə'laɪv〕*adj.* 活的　　gentle〔'dʒɛntl̩〕*adj.* 溫和的
  on the strength of 依靠；憑藉
  background〔'bæk,graʊnd〕*n.* 背景

Questions 44-46

Attention
Vintage Volkswagen Enthusiasts

Do you like vintage Volkswagens ("bugs" or vans made before 1970)? The San Jose chapter of the International Volkswagen Fan Club is looking for you. The club is open to all who are interested in old Volkswagens and the era they represent. We welcome owners, previous owners or those who just like to talk about the cars. We meet on the 2nd and 4th Sundays of each month at the Elks Club on Grove Street at noon. Members who have one drive their Volkswagens to the club for everyone to see and take a ride in. Twice a year we organize a cross-country rally of over 50 "bugs" and vans. If interested in joining us, call Harry Anderson at 555-1234 after 5:00 p.m., or Richard Bailey at 555-4321 after 6:00 p.m. Richard can also be reached through our website at <u>www.volkswagenclub.com</u>. Or just stop by the club on Sundays when we're meeting. You'll find us to be the friendliest people on earth!

注　意
古典型的福斯汽車迷

　　你喜歡古典型的福斯汽車（「金龜車」，或是 1970 年以前製造的廂型車）嗎？「國際福斯汽車俱樂部」聖荷西分會正在找你。這個俱樂部開放給對舊型的福斯汽車，以及它們所代表的時代有興趣的人。我們歡迎車主或前車主，或是那些只是喜歡談論汽車的人。我們每個月的第二及第四個星期天中午，在樹叢街的麋鹿俱樂部聚會。有福斯汽車的會員，會把車開來俱樂部，給大家看看，並且搭乘。我們一年會舉辦兩次，五十幾輛的金龜車和廂型車的越野長途賽車。如果你有興趣，想加入我們，就在下午五點以後，打 555-1234 找哈利・安德森，或在下午六點以後，打 555-4321 找理察・貝利。也可利用我們的網址www.volkswagenclub.com 連絡理察。或是就在我們有聚會的星期天，順道拜訪我們的俱樂部。你會發現，我們是全世界最友善的人！

attention〔əˋtɛnʃən〕n. 注意　　vintage〔ˋvɪntɪdʒ〕adj. 古典型的
Volkswagen〔ˋfolks͵vɑgən〕n. 福斯汽車
enthusiast〔ɪnˋθjuzɪ͵æst〕n. 狂熱份子；迷　　bug〔bʌg〕n. 金龜車
van〔væn〕n. 廂型車　　San Jose〔͵sænhoˋze〕n. 聖荷西
chapter〔ˋtʃæptɚ〕n. 分會　　*fan club* 影、歌迷等的俱樂部
era〔ˋɪrə〕n. 時代　　represent〔͵rɛprɪˋzɛnt〕v. 代表
owner〔ˋonɚ〕n. 擁有者　　previous〔ˋprivɪəs〕adj. 之前的
elk〔ɛlk〕n. 麋鹿　　grove〔grov〕n. 小樹叢
member〔ˋmɛmbɚ〕n. 會員　　*take a ride* 搭乘
organize〔ˋɔrgən͵aɪz〕v. 發起
cross-country〔ˋkrɔs͵kʌntrɪ〕adj. 越野的
rally〔ˋrælɪ〕n. 長途賽車　　reach〔ritʃ〕v. 連絡
website〔ˋwɛb͵saɪt〕n. 網址　　*stop by* 順道拜訪
friendly〔ˋfrɛndlɪ〕adj. 友善的

44. (**C**) 這個俱樂部在找什麼？
    (A) 舊的福斯汽車。　　(B) 他們這次長途賽車的贊助者。
    (C) 新的會員。　　　　(D) 俱樂部的擁有者。

    * sponsor ('spɑnsə) n. 贊助者
      upcoming ('ʌp,kʌmɪŋ) adj. 即將來臨的；這次的

45. (**A**) 這個俱樂部的會員多久聚會一次？
    (A) 一個月兩次。　　(B) 一年兩次。
    (C) 每個星期天。　　(D) 一個月一次。

    * **get together** 聚在一起

46. (**C**) 下列何者正確？
    (A) 俱樂部有入會費。
    (B) 只有擁有金龜車的人，才准許加入俱樂部。
    (C) 俱樂部一年舉行兩次賽車。
    (D) 可以透過網路聯絡哈利和理察。

    * entry ('ɛntrɪ) n. 進入　　fee (fi) n. 費用
      entry fee 入會費　　hold (hold) v. 舉行　　**car race** 賽車

Questions 47-50

OBITUARY

BROWN, Nat Jackson—

Nat Jackson Brown was born in Selma, Alabama, on
April 22, 1916. He graduated from the Tuskegee Institute in
Tuskegee, Alabama in 1938 with a degree in elementary
education. In 1941 Mr. Brown received a master's degree in
education administration from Morehouse College in Atlanta,
Georgia.

After teaching for several years at George Washington Carver Elementary School in Atlanta, Mr. Brown moved to Savannah, Georgia. There he became an assistant principal at Du Bois Middle School in 1946. Mr. Brown remained assistant principal at Du Bois for eight years until he was promoted to principal, a position he held for the next ten years.

Mr. Brown so impressed the school board that they recommended him to the State Secretary of Education for the job of superintendent of schools for the whole of Harris County, Georgia in 1966.

Mr. Brown remained superintendent for 15 years—the longest in Georgia's history— until he retired in 1981 to Savannah, Georgia. However, he served on the board of education for a local elementary school in Savannah until his death. When asked why he chose to finish his career on the board of an elementary school, Mr. Brown replied, "because that's where it all begins."

訃　聞

布朗，奈特‧傑克森——

　　奈特‧傑克森‧布朗於一九一六年四月二十二日，出生於阿拉巴馬州的塞爾瑪。他在一九三八年，畢業於阿拉巴馬州塔斯奇基的塔斯奇基學院，並獲得初等教育的學位。布朗先生於一九四一年，在喬治亞州亞特蘭大的摩爾豪斯大學，取得教育行政的碩士學位。

布朗先生在亞特蘭大的喬治華盛頓卡佛小學教了幾年書之後,就搬到喬治亞州的薩維納。一九四六年,他成為杜柏伊斯中學的副校長。布朗先生在杜柏伊斯中學擔任八年的副校長,之後才被升為校長,其後的十年,他都一直擔任校長這個職位。

布朗先生令學校的董事會印象非常深刻,所以他們於一九六六年,向該州的教育部長推薦,讓他去擔任整個喬治亞州哈里斯郡所有學校的督學。

布朗先生擔任督學十五年,是喬治亞州有史以來最久的,直到他於一九八一年退休,回到喬治亞州的薩維納為止。然而,他直到去世之前,都一直擔任薩維納當地小學的教育委員會委員。當布朗先生被問到,為何他選擇以擔任小學委員會的委員,來作為事業的結束時,他回答說:「因為那是我一切事業的開始。」

obituary〔ə'bɪtʃʊˌɛrɪ〕n. 訃聞

Alabama〔ˌæləˈbæmə〕n. 阿拉巴馬州【美國東南部之一州】

graduate〔'grædʒʊˌet〕v. 畢業

institute〔'ɪnstəˌtjut〕n. 學院;研究所　　degree〔dɪ'gri〕n. 學位

elementary〔ˌɛlə'mɛntərɪ〕adj. 初等的　　***master's degree*** 碩士學位

administration〔ədˌmɪnə'streʃən〕n. 行政;管理

Atlanta〔æt'læntə〕n. 亞特蘭大【美國喬治亞州之首府】

Georgia〔'dʒɔrdʒə〕n. 喬治亞州　　move〔muv〕v. 搬家

assistant〔ə'sɪstənt〕adj. 副的;助理的

principal〔'prɪnsəpl̩〕n. 校長　　***assistant principal*** 副校長

middle school 中學　　remain〔rɪ'men〕v. 依然;繼續擔任

promote〔prə'mot〕v. 使升遷　　position〔pə'zɪʃən〕n. 職位

hold〔hold〕v. 擔任　　impress〔ɪm'prɛs〕v. 使印象深刻

board〔bord〕n. 理事會;董事會;委員會

recommend〔ˌrɛkə'mɛnd〕v. 推薦　　state〔stet〕adj. 州的

secretary〔'sɛkrəˌtɛrɪ〕n.(部會)首長

superintendent〔ˌsuprɪnˈtɛndənt〕*n.* 監督者；管理者；督學
county〔ˈkaʊntɪ〕*n.* 郡　　retire〔rɪˈtaɪr〕*v.* 退休
serve on 擔任…的委員　　local〔ˈlokl̩〕*adj.* 當地的
career〔kəˈrɪr〕*n.* 事業　　reply〔rɪˈplaɪ〕*v.* 回答

47.（ **C** ）訃聞是什麼？

(A) 一個人找工作時，所使用的學經歷書面說明。

(B) 其他人的行為與私生活的詳細報告。

(C) 一則印好的公告，發佈某人的死訊，上面附有簡短的生平敘述。

(D) 搶在競爭對手之前印好或廣播的刺激的新聞報導。

* written〔ˈrɪtn̩〕*adj.* 書面的
account〔əˈkaʊnt〕*n.* 說明；敘述　　past〔pæst〕*adj.* 過去的
employment〔ɪmˈplɔɪmənt〕*n.* 工作
detail〔ˈditel〕*n.* 細節　　private〔ˈpraɪvɪt〕*adj.* 私人的
printed〔ˈprɪntɪd〕*adj.* 印好的　　notice〔ˈnotɪs〕*n.* 公告
biographical〔ˌbaɪəˈgræfɪkl̩〕*adj.* 傳記的；有關某人一生的
broadcast〔ˈbrɔdˌkæst〕*v.* 廣播；播送
competitor〔kəmˈpɛtətɚ〕*n.* 競爭者；對手

48.（ **C** ）布朗先生當校長當多久？

(A) 五年。　　(B) 八年。　　(C) 十年。　　(D) 十五年。

49.（ **D** ）布朗先生拿到哪個領域的碩士學位？

(A) 特殊教育。　　　　　　(B) 初等教育。

(C) 企業管理。　　　　　　(D) 教育行政。

* field〔fild〕*n.* 領域　　receive〔rɪˈsiv〕*v.* 獲得

50.（ **B** ）布朗先生去世的時候，是做什麼工作？

(A) 校長。　　　　　　　　(B) 學校委員會的委員。

(C) 副校長。　　　　　　　(D) 學校的督學。

全民英語能力分級檢定測驗
GENERAL ENGLISH PROFICIENCY TEST
中高級聽力測驗
HIGH-INTERMEDIATE LISTENING COMPREHENSION TEST

This listening comprehension test will test your ability to understand spoken English. In this test, each conversation, short talk and question will be spoken JUST ONE TIME. They will not be written out for you. There are three parts to this test. Special instructions will be given to you at the beginning of each part.

Part A

In part A, you will hear 15 questions. After you hear a question, read the four choices in your test book and decide which one is the best answer to the question you have heard.

Example:

You will hear: Mary, can you tell me what time it is?

You will read: A. About two hours ago.
　　　　　　　　B. I used to be able to, but not now.
　　　　　　　　C. Sure, it's half past nine.
　　　　　　　　D. Today is October 22.

The best answer to the question "Mary, can you tell me what time it is?" is C: "Sure, it's half past nine." Therefore, you should choose answer C.

1. A. You ride the bus.
   B. I prefer to study.
   C. I want to find an ATM.
   D. Let's have a nice walk.

2. A. It sure is.
   B. I think you're marvelous.
   C. We all think you're terrific.
   D. It's fantastic to be with you.

3. A. Sorry, it's a secret.
   B. Neither did I.
   C. What did I say?
   D. Sorry about that.

4. A. He needs a new toothbrush.
   B. Thanks for the money.
   C. I'll buy some mouthwash.
   D. Thanks for buying that.

5. A. Is he married or single?
   B. Does he have a job?
   C. Why does he do that?
   D. What is her problem?

6. A. You should learn massage.
   B. Take some pain medicine.
   C. Violence never solves anything.
   D. I'll be back in a flash.

7. A. Yes, I could use your help.
   B. Do you need one or two?
   C. No problem. Help yourself.
   D. No problem. I'd be happy to help.

8. A. Check under the seat cushion.
   B. It's on TV.
   C. Sorry, I forgot to buy one.
   D. Check in the refrigerator.

9. A. You bet I am.
   B. No, I started counting calories.
   C. You need to lose weight.
   D. You're not overweight!

10. A. It hurts a lot.
    B. OK, I'll help you.
    C. OK, I'll do it right now.
    D. I bite them when I'm nervous.

Please turn to the next page. ▮⟹

11. A. Yes, I live in a house.
    B. Yes, I live in a ten-floor apartment.
    C. No, I'm not that tall.
    D. Yes, the temperature is high where I live.

12. A. Would you please help me?
    B. Yes, I will.
    C. No, it's complete.
    D. No, I still have to type it.

13. A. Yes, mom, right away.
    B. I use them to blow my nose.
    C. Is the garbage truck coming?
    D. Please keep them for me.

14. A. Yes, it's not so bad.
    B. I agree with you 100%.
    C. Don't argue with me.
    D. That's because he's so old.

15. A. Yes, we are alive.
    B. It's nice to live there.
    C. Yes, life is terrific!
    D. It's wonderful to have money.

Part B

In part B, you will hear 15 conversations between a man and a woman. After each conversation, you will hear a question about the conversation. After you hear the question, read the four choices in your test book and choose the best answer to the question you have heard.

Example:

<u>You will hear</u>: (Man) May I see your driver's license?

      (Woman) Yes, officer. Here it is. Was I speeding?

      (Man) Yes, ma'am. You were doing sixty in a forty-five-mile-an-hour zone.

      (Woman) No way! I don't believe you.

      (Man) Well, it is true and here is your ticket.

      Question: Why does the man ask for the woman's driver's license?

<u>You will read</u>: A. She was going too fast.

      B. To check its limitations.

      C. To check her age.

      D. She entered a restricted zone.

The best answer to the question "Why does the man ask for the woman's driver's license?" is A: "She was going too fast." Therefore, you should choose answer A.

Please turn to the next page. ⟹

16. A. A 747 jet was hijacked.
    B. There was an earthquake at the airport.
    C. A jet ran out of gas.
    D. Two planes crashed into each other.

17. A. Soft indoor slippers.
    B. Stylish boots.
    C. Sports shoes.
    D. Sexy nightclothes.

18. A. The party plans.
    B. The church plans.
    C. The money situation.
    D. The wedding dress.

19. A. Cook it in a pot.
    B. Fry it in a pan.
    C. Make it in a microwave oven.
    D. Bake it in an oven.

20. A. That he's dishonest.
    B. That he is naive.
    C. That he is a humorous guy.
    D. He might be a thief.

21. A. He gave some money.
    B. He volunteered his time.
    C. He helped her find a job.
    D. He helped her change her life.

22. A. A final pay check.
    B. A company stock report.
    C. A notice of job termination.
    D. A letter of recommendation.

23. A. She wants immediate training.
    B. She wants to evade the obligation.
    C. She wants to commit suicide.
    D. She wants to start the ball rolling.

24. A. Absolutely nothing.
    B. Have a physical examination.
    C. Get a personal background check.
    D. Avoid telling the truth.

25. A. That they might get promoted.
    B. That she might quit.
    C. Headquarters will expand.
    D. That her boss won't give credit to her and her colleagues.

26. A. He has become too important.
    B. He's a selfish official.
    C. He is changing his friends.
    D. He's acting too proud.

27. A. Maybe she should go away.
    B. It's too stressful there.
    C. The pay is too low.
    D. Maybe he should resign.

28. A. Starving and angry.
    B. Upset and thirsty.
    C. Rude and impolite.
    D. Hungry and impatient.

29. A. That he eats like a pig.
    B. That he isn't very smart.
    C. She feels that he's polite.
    D. He thinks she's too picky.

30. A. She's very thirsty.
    B. His feet hurt.
    C. The temperature is going up.
    D. The weather is changing fast.

Please turn to the next page. ⬜⟹

Part C

In part C, you will hear several short talks. After each talk, you will hear 2 to 3 questions about the talk. After you hear each question, read the four choices in your test book and choose the best answer to the question you have heard.

Example:

<u>You will hear</u>:

Thank you for coming to this, the first in a series of seminars on the use of computers in the classroom. As the brochure informed you, there will be a total of five seminars given in this room every Monday morning from 6:00 to 7:30. Our goal will be to show you, the teachers of our schoolchildren, how the changing technology of today can be applied to the unchanging lessons of yesterday to make your students' learning experience more interesting and relevant to the world they live in. By the end of the last seminar, you will not be computer literate, but you will be able to make sense of the hundreds of complex words and technical terms related to the field and be aware of the programs available for use in the classroom.

Question number 1: What is the subject of this seminar series?

<u>You will read</u>: A. Self-improvement.
B. Using computers to teach.
C. Technology.
D. Study habits of today's students.

The best answer to the question "What is the subject of this seminar series?" is B: "Using computers to teach." Therefore, you should choose answer B.

Now listen to another question based on the same talk.

<u>You will hear</u>:

Question number 2: What does the speaker say participants will be able to do after attending the seminars?

<u>You will read</u>: A. Understand today's students.
B. Understand computer terminology.
C. Motivate students.
D. Deal more confidently with people.

The best answer to the question "What does the speaker say participants will be able to do after attending the seminars?" is B: "Understand computer terminology." Therefore, you should choose answer B.

Please turn to the next page. ⇨

31. A. Press two.
    B. Press zero and wait.
    C. Press one and listen.
    D. Press three.

32. A. is a foreign visitor.
    B. has a visa question.
    C. is applying for a passport.
    D. is an American.

33. A. Students on vacation.
    B. Women who are overweight.
    C. Adults who feel tired and stressful.
    D. Those who have health problems.

34. A. A massage.
    B. A manicure.
    C. Exercise machines.
    D. Sauna baths.

35. A. Check out the classifieds.
    B. Request a video.
    C. Read the newspaper.
    D. Via the Internet.

36. A. Get to the basement.
    B. Get out of the building.
    C. Park all the cars away from the spill.
    D. Direct and help colleagues to the exits.

37. A. At an administration
       building.
    B. At a stock market
       company.
    C. At a plastics factory.
    D. On a university
       campus.

38. A. In the high 90s
       Fahrenheit.
    B. About 70 degrees
       Fahrenheit.
    C. Around 90 degrees
       Centigrade.
    D. Extremely hot.

39. A. Windy and hot.
    B. Humid and cloudy.
    C. Clear skies and light
       winds.
    D. Breezy with possible
       meteor showers.

40. A. The Italian Pizza
       Delight.
    B. The Royal Palace.
    C. The 12oz. T-bone
       steak.
    D. The Italian Combo
       Dish.

Please turn to the next page. ▯⟹

41. A. Alcoholic beverages.
    B. Desserts.
    C. Soups.
    D. Vegetables.

42. A. Bangkok.
    B. Hong Kong.
    C. Southeast.
    D. Manila.

43. A. That the traveler fly
       on Southeast Airlines.
    B. That the traveler wait
       a couple of days.
    C. That the traveler pay
       extra money.
    D. That the traveler fly
       on Thai Airlines.

44. A. machine operators
    B. regional sales agents
    C. dynamic leaders
    D. transportation
       experts

45. A. An employment
       application.
    B. School transcripts and
       recommendations.
    C. Past tax statements.
    D. An account of past
       work experience.

-The End-

中高級閱讀測驗

HIGH-INTERMEDIATE

READING COMPREHENSION TEST

This test has three parts, with 50 multiple-choice questions (each with four choices) in total. Special directions will be provided for each part. You will have 50 minutes to complete this test.

Part A: Sentence Completion

This part of the test has 15 incomplete sentences. Beneath each sentence, you will see four words or phrases, marked A, B, C and D. You are to choose the word or phrase that best completes the sentences. Then on your answer sheet, find the number of the question and mark your answer.

1. _____ among the troops has been low due to the enemy's continual victories.
   A. Moral
   B. Morale
   C. Mortal
   D. Morality

Please turn to the next page. ⟹

2. There were too many _____ words in your essay. I suggest that you make a long story short and rewrite it more concisely.

   A. reformatory

   B. refined

   C. rearmost

   D. redundant

3. He was feared by his enemies as a _____ conqueror, who showed no mercy for those who surrendered or were captured.

   A. ruthless

   B. heedless

   C. tactless

   D. listless

4. _____ is a primary factor in learning. Without it, you lack something to urge you by.

   A. Incinerator

   B. Inconsistency

   C. Incense

   D. Incentive

5. Everyone has his own _____ in mind on which to judge prospective friends.

   A. adaptation

   B. assumption

   C. criteria

   D. congeniality

6. There was a severe traffic jam on the _____ highway,
   and so we had no other choice but to take another road.
   A. accelerated
   B. elevated
   C. revised
   D. blockaded

7. After the strong typhoon, fallen trees _____ the streets
   and traffic was terribly congested.
   A. instructed
   B. constructed
   C. destructed
   D. obstructed

8. I _____ the smell of gasoline. It makes me sick and
   gives me a headache.
   A. wreathe
   B. loathe
   C. breathe
   D. soothe

Please turn to the next page. ▌⟹

9. He is very trustworthy. He is _____. Your secret is safe with him.
   A. as broad as it is long
   B. as clear as mud
   C. as right as rain
   D. as close as an oyster

10. The bad news came like _____. He was not in the least prepared for it and broke down.
    A. a drop in the bucket
    B. a frog in the throat
    C. a bolt out of the blue
    D. a fly in the ointment

11. As far as I can see, the machine only needs a minor adjustment: a turn of screw here, a little tightening up there, a drop of oil and it will be _____ new.
    A. as good as
    B. as soon as
    C. as well as
    D. as long as

12. Someone said, "Life is precious but love is more valuable. But I would rather give up both _____ freedom." That is, he would rather die _____ have no freedom.
    A. exchanging ; to
    B. in exchange for ; than
    C. changing for ; than
    D. to change ; than to

13. _____ hard the task may be, and _____ difficulty may come my way, I have decided to take on the challenge and will spare no effort to accomplish it.

    A. No matter ; however

    B. No matter how ; whatever

    C. Whatever ; whatever

    D. However ; however

14. She kept climbing up the mountain and ran out of breath, _____ beads of sweat _____ down her face.

    A. while ; running

    B. with ; ran

    C. with ; running

    D. when ; running

15. He is too ready to criticize others. (Choose the correct answer.)

    A. He is too careful to criticize others.

    B. He prepares too well to criticize others.

    C. He is not ready to find fault with others.

    D. He is fond of finding fault with others.

Please turn to the next page. ▯⟹

Part B: Cloze

This part of the test has two passages. Each passage contains seven or eight missing words or phrases. There is a total of 15 missing words or phrases. Beneath each passage, you will see seven or eight items with four choices, marked A, B, C and D. You are to choose the best answer for each missing word or phrase in the two passages. Then, on your answer sheet, find the number of the question and mark your answer.

Questions 16-23

A manuscript written by Mozart is to go on show at the British Library, its two halves reunited after a 170-year ___(16)___, the museum said on Wednesday. Written in 1773 when the composer was 17, the score was cut in two by his widow Constance and sold in 1835.

One side contains two new cadenzas Mozart envisaged for piano concertos he had already written, one ___(17)___ when he was eleven. The other has a short minuet for a string quartet which he later abandoned in a spirit of self-criticism for an ___(18)___ version.

"The manuscript ___(19)___ important light on the 17-year-old composer's development at a transitional ___(20)___ in his life," said Chris Banks, the British Library's head of music collections. "It speaks ___(21)___ about his maturity. Mozart was trying to make his mark as a serious composer. He was well known as a ___(22)___, but by 17 he couldn't really continue with that."

The library has owned since 1953 the lower half of the manuscript, which had been given to a minor functionary in Bavaria in southern Germany, probably in exchange for some service. But it acquired only recently the other half, ___(23)___ Constance initially sold to a court musician, Julius Leidke.

The manuscript will go on public display Saturday as part of a series of events to mark the 250th anniversary of the birth of Wolfgang Amadeus Mozart.

16. A. unification
    B. identification
    C. exploration
    D. separation

17. A. composed
    B. consisted
    C. comprised
    D. constituted

18. A. initiative
    B. imperative
    C. alternative
    D. affirmative

19. A. sheds
    B. strikes
    C. hides
    D. places

20. A. physics
    B. phobia
    C. phrase
    D. phase

21. A. a great amount
    B. a great deal
    C. quite a few
    D. a small number

22. A. child's play
    B. child prodigy
    C. childproof
    D. child minder

23. A. what
    B. to which
    C. which
    D. X

Please turn to the next page. ▢⇨

Questions 24-30

For many Chinese, the annual Ching Ming festival can be more ____(24)____ than harmonic, as people flock to cemeteries to sweep the graves of their ancestors. In an effort to beat the endless bottlenecks and lack of parking around burial grounds, Taiwan's Kinbaushan Cemetery now offers cyber-____(25)____ which can be ____(26)____ with a few mouse-clicks. On-line tomb-sweepers are treated to Buddhist music and images of candles when accessing cyber-plots ____(27)____, depending on their size, can cost up to US$1,000.

Many people sweeping graves in Taipei during the festival were ____(28)____. "You can't cut the grass of your father's grave using a computer," exclaimed one man. But a firefighter on hand to extinguish the frequent fires ____(29)____ careless burning of ghost money was more upbeat. ____(30)____ ceremonies, he said, "would make our jobs a lot easier."

24. A. organic
    B. chaotic
    C. elastic
    D. gigantic

25. A. gravesites
    B. gravestones
    C. gravel pits
    D. graveled paths

26. A. intended
    B. pretended
    C. extended
    D. tended

27. A. in which
    B. whose
    C. that
    D. what

28. A. ethical
    B. skeptical
    C. tactical
    D. physical

29. A. sparks
    B. sparking
    C. sparked
    D. sparked by

30. A. Ritual
    B. Visual
    C. Virtuous
    D. Virtual

Part C: Reading

In this part of the test, you will read several passages. Each passage is followed by several questions. There is a total of 20 questions. You are to choose the best answer, A, B, C or D, to each question on the basis of what is stated or implied in the passage. Then on your answer sheet, find the number of the question and mark your answer.

Questions 31-35

Britain's government is considering to tackle increasing levels of obesity by imposing a so-called "fatty food tax" on foodstuffs with poor nutritional value, according to a report Thursday. Other measures being considered include standardized labeling of fat and sugar contents in processed foods, The Times said.

Please turn to the next page. ⇒

According to the newspaper, Prime Minister Tony Blair's official think tank has drawn up proposals to tackle consumption of unhealthy items such as burgers, potato crisps and soft drinks. In an as-yet unpublished document seen by the newspaper, the Prime Minister's Strategy Unit admitted that a rising trend toward fatness among British people was "largely outside the direct influence" of the country's health service.

One plan could be to impose "improved regulated nutritional standards for common processed foods and drinks" to inform the public. "There might even be potential to consider fiscal measures—a 'fatty food tax' applied to food not people—or different VAT treatment for foods with poor nutritional standards," it said, referring to value added tax, a 17.5 percent sales tax imposed on certain goods in Britain. "This would be a signal to producers as well as consumers, and serve more broadly as a signal to society that nutritional content in food is important."

Earlier this month, British doctors' groups urged the government to take swift action over the "terrifying health consequences" of the nation's obesity problem. A joint report by three leading medical groups warned that if nothing was done, a third of all British adults would be clinically obese by 2020, as well as a similar proportion of girls and a fifth of all boys.

Also Thursday, a separate report said that Britain's government planned to place health warnings on alcoholic drinks later this year. Information about the number of units of alcohol contained within a drink as well as warnings about the effects of binge drinking will be introduced, the Daily Mirror said quoting unnamed health officials.

31. Which of the following would be the best theme of this article?
    A. The Brits have declared war on fatty foods.
    B. Imposing food taxes are a necessity.
    C. Brits are considering proposals to solve a health crisis.
    D. British health services can't control rising obesity levels.

32. All of the following qualify as anti-obesity measures EXCEPT
    A. implementing fiscal measures.
    B. better informing the public of nutritional values.
    C. establishing an easily understood labeling system.
    D. limiting binge drinking in public places.

33. Which of the following pairs or groups of words are most closely related?
    A. nutritional value—standardized labeling
    B. foodstuffs—processed foods
    C. strategy unit—think tank
    D. an unpublished document—a separate report

Please turn to the next page. ⇨

34. Which of the following ideas is NOT mentioned in this article?
    A. Fighting fat by raising fees.
    B. Taxing people who patronize fast food restaurants.
    C. Putting warning labels on alcoholic beverages.
    D. Implementing a uniform labeling system detailing food content.

35. Of the statements below, which is definitely true?
    A. By the year 2020, 20% of all English girls will be overweight.
    B. There is a rising trend of alcoholism in Great Britain.
    C. A significant number of British physicians are alarmed by the obesity dilemma.
    D. Major food producers are fighting the food taxes aimed at them.

Questions 36-40

Men in non-traditional jobs, such as stay-at-home dads, are at high risk of heart disease and their chances of dying of cardiovascular disease are greater, a study found out Wednesday.

The study presented to the American Heart Association's Asia Pacific Scientific Forum in Honolulu examined whether stress linked to certain jobs <u>translated into</u> increased heart attacks and death, though it stopped short of establishing a direct connection.

But researchers were surprised at finding a higher frequency of heart disease among those in non-traditional jobs.

Men who work in the home for the better part of their adulthood are 82 percent more likely to have a shorter life span than their <u>counterparts</u> who work outside the home, the study found.

Likewise, women who work in positions commanding a great deal of authority are three times likely to suffer from heart ailments than women who do not.

"These findings may indicate that people who perform work or social roles incongruent with what is socially expected suffer greater risk of heart disease and death during the 10-year study," said study author Elaine Eaker, of Wisconsin's Eaker Epidemiology Enterprises.

"Perhaps those men and women on the cutting edge of social roles and norms change with time, and it is hoped that the harmful effects of having jobs or social roles that are considered outside the norm will be diminished." Men holding jobs considered prestigious, such as physicians, lawyers, architects or engineers, have less risk of heart disease, the report said.

Please turn to the next page. ▯⟩

36. What does the phrase "translate into" in line 7 mean?
    A. to change words into another language
    B. to account for another effect
    C. to decipher some mysterious code
    D. to serve as an interpreter

37. Who does the word "counterparts" in line 14 refer to?
    A. specialists
    B. women
    C. men
    D. patients

38. According to the study, why are non-traditional jobholders at higher risk of heart disease?
    A. They earn less money and lead less happy lives.
    B. They are perfectionists and aim high in everything.
    C. They have lower social statuses and are often laughed at.
    D. Their jobs are considered outside the norm and so they are under a lot more stress.

39. According to the passage, which kind of job is likely to be considered non-traditional for a woman?
    A. a kindergarten teacher
    B. a bookkeeper at a company
    C. a bank teller
    D. the CEO of an enterprise

40. Which of the following statements is NOT true?
   A. The study was made public at a forum in Honolulu.
   B. Women holding managerial positions have less risk of
      heart disease than housewives.
   C. Researchers have not yet established a direct connection
      between stress coming from non-traditional jobs and
      cardiovascular disease.
   D. Traditionally, men are supposed to work outside the
      home.

Questions 41-45

    For Taipei animal lovers who want a salubrious final
resting place for the family pooch, help is at hand. The Peaceful
Pet Garden of Happiness provides funeral, cremation and ash
storage services of a kind normally reserved for humans,
complete with complimentary sticks of incense and stacks of
"ghost money" to finance the pet's after-life activities.

    In the facility's memorial room, more than 1,000 urns can
be found, each with a photograph of the animal in happier days.
Regal-looking <u>felines</u> recline on comfortable armchairs, while
dogs of a staggering variety of sizes and shapes romp on rare
pieces of Taipei green space. Many urns are also surrounded
with mementoes of the pet's corporeal existence; small
home-made tombstones and Buddhist icons compete with
collars and well-chewed tennis balls.

Please turn to the next page. ▮⟹

The services are not limited to dogs and cats. Rabbits, birds, several fish, three monkeys, a ferret and even a large iguana are pictured. "If it fits in the incinerator we'll accept it," says cemetery owner, Mr. Wu, who adds that some customers visit once or twice a week to honor their pets' remains.

There are two Buddhist shrines in the room. "Not all our customers are Buddhist, though," says Wu. "All kinds of people come here, including Japanese, Americans and Canadians. Taiwanese people have traditionally treated pets like a commodity, something you can buy and then just throw away," he says. "More and more Taiwanese are beginning to realize the value of animals."

The proof is in the billing. A year's storage at the cemetery costs around US$100, with special long-term storage plans available from US$1,000.

41. What kind of place is the Peaceful Pet Garden of Happiness?
   A. It is a funeral home for pets.
   B. It is a shrine for Buddhists.
   C. It is an incinerator for burning corpses.
   D. It is a peaceful garden for pets to run about in.

42. What does "felines" in line 9 mean?
   A. pets   B. cats
   C. monkeys   D. lizards

43. Which of the following services is NOT provided by the cemetery?
    A. Funeral directors to help handle everything.
    B. Storage space for ash urns.
    C. An incinerator for cremation.
    D. A large green place for picnics.

44. The cemetery will accept a pet
    A. as long as the owner promises to visit his pet sometimes.
    B. as long as the animal can be put into the incinerator.
    C. only if the owner agrees to burn "ghost money" for his pet.
    D. only if the owner is a Buddhist.

45. "The proof is in the billing." What does this sentence mean?
    A. Some people treat their pets as a commodity and sell them for a high price.
    B. People are willing to pay such a high price for their pets because they can benefit more.
    C. People are willing to pay such a high price for their pets because they realize the value of animals.
    D. Many people can't afford such a high price to have their pets cremated.

Please turn to the next page. ⟹

Questions 46-50

William Shakespeare set nearly half of his works in Italy. Now the city of Rome is honoring the playwright by building a faithful replica of the 16th century Globe Theater, where his most famous plays were shown.

Starting in October, spectators can lend their ears to the Bard's masterpieces in a round, wooden theater amid the crickets and greenery of the Villa Borghese, one of the city's public parks.

The setting couldn't be more appropriate: A few kilometers away is the Roman Forum, where Shakespeare's Mark Anthony pleaded "lend me your ears" to his fellow citizens as he spoke over Julius Caesar's murdered body.

"It's a great cultural initiative and, at the same time, a tribute to such an important structure," the theater's project manager, Giuseppe Viggiano, said Friday.

"We needed a theater like this in Italy," Viggiano added. "A theater of words, where actors will be able to express themselves only with their voice and acting, without sets, lights or microphones, just as the theater was in its origins."

The wooden structure will open Oct. 15 with Romeo and Juliet, the classic tale of doomed love set in the northern town of Verona.

　　Although it is not clear whether Shakespeare, who lived from 1564 to 1616, ever visited Italy, almost half his plays are set in cities and landscapes scattered throughout <u>the boot-shaped peninsula</u>. The original Globe is believed to have opened with a performance of Julius Caesar set in ancient Rome.

　　A faithful replica of the Bard's playhouse was opened in London in 1996 on the banks of the river Thames, just a few hundred meters from where the original stood.

46. Which of the following is NOT true about the new theater in Rome?
    A. It will be round in shape and be built of wood.
    B. There will be no lights and microphones on stage.
    C. The first play to be staged there will be Julius Caesar.
    D. It will be situated in a park near the Roman Forum.

47. What is a "playwright"?
    A. music composed for a film
    B. a publishing company
    C. an all-star cast of a film
    D. an author of a drama

Please turn to the next page. ⟹

48. The noun "the Bard" was mentioned twice in the passage.
    What does it refer to?
    A. the Globe Theater
    B. Italy
    C. William Shakespeare
    D. the city of Rome

49. What does "the boot-shaped peninsula" refer to?
    A. the town of Verona
    B. Italy
    C. the city of Rome
    D. Globe Theater

50. Which of the following is true?
    A. The original Globe Theater was located in London.
    B. Shakespeare came to Italy and fell in love with it at
       first glance. That's why nearly half of his plays are
       set in Italy.
    C. The people of Rome do not seem to welcome the
       construction of the new Globe Theater.
    D. The newly-built theater is the first replica of
       Shakespeare's Globe theater.

-The End-

中高級聽力測驗詳解 ③

PART A

1. (**D**) Do you want to walk or ride there?

   A. You ride the bus.

   B. I prefer to study.

   C. I want to find an ATM.

   D. Let's have a nice walk.

   * ride〔raɪd〕v. 乘車　　prefer〔prɪ'fɜ〕v. 寧願
     ATM 自動櫃員機 (= *automated teller machine*)

2. (**A**) Isn't the weather glorious?

   A. It sure is.

   B. I think you're marvelous.

   C. We all think you're terrific.

   D. It's fantastic to be with you.

   * glorious〔'glorɪəs〕*adj.* 燦爛的
     marvelous〔'mɑrvl̩əs〕*adj.* 極優秀的
     terrific〔tə'rɪfɪk〕*adj.* 極佳的
     fantastic〔fæn'tæstɪk〕*adj.* 極好的

3. (**A**) What are you thinking? A penny for your thoughts.

   A. Sorry, it's a secret.　　B. Neither did I.

   C. What did I say?　　　　D. Sorry about that.

   * *A penny for your thoughts.* 你呆呆地在想些什麼呢？
     secret〔'sikrɪt〕*n.* 祕密　　neither〔'niðɚ〕*adv.* 也不

4. (**C**) Sis, your breath smells terrible!

    A.　He needs a new toothbrush.

    B.　Thanks for the money.

    C.　I'll buy some mouthwash.

    D.　Thanks for buying that.

    * sis〔sɪs〕*n.* 小姐　　breath〔brɛθ〕*n.* 氣息；呼吸

      toothbrush〔'tuθ,brʌʃ〕*n.* 牙刷

      mouthwash〔'mauθ,waʃ〕*n.* 漱口藥水

5. (**C**) He nags us every day.

    A.　Is he married or single?

    B.　Does he have a job?

    C.　Why does he do that?

    D.　What is her problem?

    * nag〔næg〕*v.* 不斷嘮叨　　married〔'mærɪd〕*adj.* 已婚的

      single〔'sɪŋgl̩〕*adj.* 單身的　　problem〔'prɑbləm〕*n.* 問題

6. (**B**) My back is killing me.

    A.　You should learn massage.

    B.　Take some pain medicine.

    C.　Violence never solves anything.

    D.　I'll be back in a flash.

    * back〔bæk〕*n.* 背部

      kill〔kɪl〕*v.*（病痛部位）給人很大的苦痛

      massage〔mə'saʒ〕*n.* 按摩　　pain〔pen〕*n.* 疼痛

      violence〔'vaɪələns〕*n.* 暴力　　solve〔sɑlv〕*v.* 解決

      be back 回來　　***in a flash*** 立刻

7. (**D**) How about giving me a hand with these math equations?

    A. Yes, I could use your help.

    B. Do you need one or two?

    C. No problem. Help yourself.

    D. No problem. I'd be happy to help.

    * **give** *sb.* **a hand** 幫忙某人

      math〔mæθ〕 *n.* 數學（= *mathematics*）

      equation〔ɪ'kweʃən〕 *n.* 方程式　　***Help yourself.*** 自己來。

8. (**A**) Where's that darn remote control? Where did you put it?

    A. Check under the seat cushion.

    B. It's on TV.

    C. Sorry, I forgot to buy one.

    D. Check in the refrigerator.

    * darn〔dɑrn〕 *interj.* 該死（= *damn*）

      remote control 遙控器　　　check〔tʃɛk〕 *v.* 查看

      cushion〔'kuʃən〕 *n.* 椅墊　　***on TV*** 在電視螢幕上

      refrigerator〔rɪ'frɪdʒə,retə〕 *n.* 冰箱

9. (**A**) Are you still on that vegetarian diet?

    A. You bet I am.

    B. No, I started counting calories.

    C. You need to lose weight.

    D. You're not overweight!

    * ***You bet I am.*** 那當然。

      vegetarian〔,vɛdʒə'tɛrɪən〕 *adj.* 素食的

      diet〔'daɪət〕 *n.* 飲食　　count〔kaʊnt〕 *v.* 計算

      calorie〔'kælərɪ〕 *n.* 卡路里（= *calory*）（熱量單位）

      lose weight 減重　　overweight〔'ovə'wet〕 *adj.* 超重的

10. (**C**) Why don't you cut your fingernails?　They are too long.

　　　A.　It hurts a lot.

　　　B.　OK, I'll help you.

　　　C.　OK, I'll do it right now.

　　　D.　I bite them when I'm nervous.

　　　* fingernail〔'fɪŋgɚ,nel〕 n. 手指甲　　hurt〔hɝt〕 v. 疼痛

　　　　 bite〔baɪt〕 v. 咬　　nervous〔'nɝvəs〕 adj. 緊張的

11. (**B**) Do you live in a high-rise?

　　　A.　Yes, I live in a house.

　　　B.　Yes, I live in a ten-floor apartment.

　　　C.　No, I'm not that tall.

　　　D.　Yes, the temperature is high where I live.

　　　* high-rise〔'haɪ'raɪz〕 n. 高樓　　floor〔flor〕 n. 樓層

　　　　 apartment〔ə'partmənt〕 n. 公寓

　　　　 temperature〔'tɛmprətʃɚ〕 n. 溫度

12. (**D**) Did you finish that important report?

　　　A.　Would you please help me?

　　　B.　Yes, I will.

　　　C.　No, it's complete.

　　　D.　No, I still have to type it.

　　　* finish〔'fɪnɪʃ〕 v. 完成

　　　　 important〔ɪm'pɔrtn̩t〕 adj. 重要的

　　　　 report〔rɪ'port〕 n. 報告

　　　　 complete〔kəm'plit〕 adj. 完成的

　　　　 type〔taɪp〕 v. 打字

13. (**A**) Please throw your dirty tissues in the trash can.

    A. Yes, mom, right away.

    B. I use them to blow my nose.

    C. Is the garbage truck coming?

    D. Please keep them for me.

    * throw〔θro〕*v.* 丟（三態變化爲：throw-threw-thrown）

    dirty〔'dɜtɪ〕*adj.* 髒的

    tissue〔'tɪʃʊ〕*n.* 衛生紙   ***trash can*** 垃圾筒

    right away 立刻   ***blow*** *one's* ***nose*** 擤鼻涕

    garbage truck 垃圾車   keep〔kip〕*v.* 保存

14. (**B**) This is the slowest elevator in the world!

    A. Yes, it's not so bad.

    B. I agree with you 100%.

    C. Don't argue with me.

    D. That's because he's so old.

    * slow〔slo〕*adj.* 緩慢的   elevator〔'ɛlə,vetɚ〕*n.* 電梯

    agree〔ə'gri〕*v.* 同意   argue〔'ɑrgjʊ〕*v.* 爭執

15. (**C**) Isn't it wonderful to be alive?

    A. Yes, we are alive.

    B. It's nice to live there.

    C. Yes, life is terrific!

    D. It's wonderful to have money.

    * wonderful〔'wʌndəfəl〕*adj.* 很棒的

    alive〔ə'laɪv〕*adj.* 活著的

📄 **PART B**

16. (**D**) M：Did you see today's headlines?

W：No, I never read the paper.

M：Oh, there was a terrible accident.

W：What happened?

M：Two jumbo jets collided on a runway.

Question：What tragedy occurred?

A. A 747 jet was hijacked.

B. There was an earthquake at the airport.

C. A jet ran out of gas.

D. Two planes crashed into each other.

* headline〔'hɛd,laɪn〕*n.* 標題　　paper〔'pepɚ〕*n.* 報紙

accident〔'æksədənt〕*n.* 意外　　jet〔dʒɛt〕*n.* 噴射機

jumbo jet 巨無霸噴射客機　　collide〔kə'laɪd〕*v.* 碰撞

runway〔'rʌn,we〕*n.*（機場）跑道

tragedy〔'trædʒədɪ〕*n.* 悲劇　　occur〔ə'kɝ〕*v.* 發生

hijack〔'haɪ,dʒæk〕*v.* 劫機

earthquake〔'ɝθ,kwek〕*n.* 地震

airport〔'ɛr,port〕*n.* 機場　　***run out of*** 用光

gas〔gæs〕*n.* 汽油　　***crash into*** 撞到

17. (**C**) W：I love your sneakers.

M：Thanks, so do I.

W：That's a comfortable-looking style.

M：They are. I feel like I'm walking on air.

W：That's a good line for a commercial.

Question：What is the woman complimenting?

A. Soft indoor slippers.　　B. Stylish boots.

C. Sports shoes.　　　　　D. Sexy nightclothes.

* sneakers〔'snikəz〕 *n. pl.* 球鞋

comfortable-looking〔'kʌmfətəbḷ'lukɪŋ〕 *adj.* 看起來很舒服的

style〔staɪl〕 *n.* 樣式　　***feel like*** 感覺好像

walk on air 這個片語是形容一個人「很高興的樣子」，所以走起
路來輕飄飄的，在此是雙關語。　　　line〔laɪn〕 *n.* 台詞

commercial〔kə'mɝʃəl〕 *n.*（電視）廣告

compliment〔'kɑmpləˏmɛnt〕 *v.* 稱讚

indoor〔'ɪnˏdor〕 *adj.* 室內的　　slippers〔'slɪpəz〕 *n. pl.* 拖鞋

stylish〔'staɪlɪʃ〕 *adj.* 流行的　　boots〔buts〕 *n. pl.* 靴子

sports〔sports〕 *adj.* 運動的　　sexy〔'sɛksɪ〕 *adj.* 性感的

nightclothes〔'naɪtˏkloðz〕 *n.* 睡衣

18.（ **A** ）M：Are you ready for your wedding?

W：Things are getting crazy.

M：Stay cool and try to relax.

W：I can't. I'm worried about the reception and the
　　entertainment.

M：Everything will turn out just fine, you'll see.

Question：What is troubling the woman?

A. The party plans.　　　B. The church plans.

C. The money situation.　D. The wedding dress.

* wedding〔'wɛdɪŋ〕 *n.* 婚禮　　crazy〔'krezɪ〕 *adj.* 瘋狂的

stay cool 保持冷靜　　relax〔rɪ'læks〕 *v.* 放鬆

reception〔rɪ'sɛpʃən〕 *n.* 招待會；（婚禮）喜宴

entertainment〔ˏɛntə'tenmənt〕 *n.* 娛樂；款待；宴會

turn out 結果是～　　trouble〔'trʌbḷ〕 *v.* 使煩惱

situation〔ˏsɪtʃʊ'eʃən〕 *n.* 情況　　***wedding dress*** 結婚禮服

19. (**D**) W : How do you make a pizza?

M : Just bake some dough in an oven.

W : No, I mean what's the recipe? What are the ingredients?

M : Basically, it's just cheese, tomato sauce and toppings on the bread.

W : How long do you have to bake it?

Question : How do you prepare a pizza properly?

A. Cook it in a pot.

B. Fry it in a pan.

C. Make it in a microwave oven.

D. Bake it in an oven.

* bake〔bek〕v. 烤　　dough〔do〕n. 生麵糰
  oven〔ˋʌvən〕n. 烤箱　　recipe〔ˋrɛsəpɪ〕n. 食譜
  ingredient〔ɪnˋgridɪənt〕n. 原料
  basically〔ˋbesɪklɪ〕adv. 基本上　　sauce〔sɔs〕n. 醬
  topping〔ˋtɑpɪŋ〕n. 加在頂層之物（配料、裝飾等）
  prepare〔prɪˋpɛr〕v. 準備
  properly〔ˋprɑpəlɪ〕adv. 適當地　　pot〔pɑt〕n. 鍋子
  fry〔fraɪ〕v. 煎；炒　　pan〔pæn〕n. 平底鍋
  microwave oven 微波爐

20. (**B**) M : What a rip-off! This watch is fake.

W : Of course it is. Who are you kidding?

M : But the vendor said it was a genuine Rolex.

W : You can't buy a Rolex for ten bucks.

M : I thought it was stolen merchandise.

Question : How does the woman feel about the man?

A. That he's dishonest.

B. That he is naive.

C. That he is a humorous guy.

D. He might be a thief.

* rip-off〔'rɪp,ɔf〕*n.* 搶劫;詐騙

　　fake〔fek〕*adj.* 仿冒的

　　kid〔kɪd〕*v.* 欺騙　　vendor〔'vɛndɚ〕*n.* 小販

　　genuine〔'dʒɛnjuɪn〕*adj.* 眞的

　　Rolex〔'rolɛks〕*n.* 勞力士

　　buck〔bʌk〕*n.* 美金　　stolen〔'stolən〕*adj.* 偷來的

　　merchandise〔'mɝtʃən,daɪz〕*n.* 商品

　　dishonest〔dɪs'ɑnɪst〕*adj.* 不誠實的

　　naive〔nɑ'iv〕*adj.* 天眞的

　　humorous〔'hjumərəs〕*adj.* 幽默的

　　thief〔θif〕*n.* 小偷

21.(**A**) W：Thanks for your generous donation.

　　　 M：I'm more than happy to contribute.

　　　 W：I wish more people were like you.

　　　 M：I'm just an average Joe.　There are lots of people better than me.

　　　 W：My oh my, you're modest and humble, too.

　　　 Question：Why is the woman praising the man?

　　　 A. He gave some money.

　　　 B. He volunteered his time.

　　　 C. He helped her find a job.

　　　 D. He helped her change her life.

* generous〔'dʒɛnərəs〕adj. 慷慨的
  donation〔do'neʃən〕n. 捐款　　*more than* 非常地
  contribute〔kən'trɪbjut〕v. 捐款
  average〔'ævərɪdʒ〕adj. 普通的　　Joe〔dʒo〕n. 男人
  my〔maɪ〕interj. 哎呀（表驚奇）
  modest〔'mɑdɪst〕adj. 謙虛的
  humble〔'hʌmbl̩〕adj. 謙卑的　　praise〔prez〕v. 稱讚
  volunteer〔,vɑlən'tɪr〕v. 自願提供

22. (**C**) M: I heard that Joseph got fired.

W: Really? That's news to me!

M: Yeah, he got a pink slip yesterday.

W: What did he do to deserve that?

M: He accidentally borrowed some money from a safe.

Question: What is a pink slip?

A. A final pay check.

B. A company stock report.

C. A notice of job termination.

D. A letter of recommendation.

* ***get fired*** 被解僱　　***pink slip*** 解僱通知
  deserve〔dɪ'zɝv〕v. 應得
  accidentally〔,æksə'dɛntl̩ɪ〕adv. 偶然地
  borrow〔'bɑro〕v. 借（入）
  safe〔sef〕n. 保險箱　　final〔'faɪnl̩〕adj. 最後的
  pay check 薪水支票
  stock〔stɑk〕n. 股票　　notice〔'notɪs〕n. 通知
  termination〔,tɝmə'neʃən〕n. 期滿
  recommendation〔,rɛkəmɛn'deʃən〕n. 推薦

23. (**B**) W: Public speaking scares me to death.

M: Do you have to give an oral presentation?

W: Yes, and I want to avoid it more than anything in the world.

Question: What does the woman want to do?

A. She wants immediate training.

B. She wants to evade the obligation.

C. She wants to commit suicide.

D. She wants to start the ball rolling.

* *scare sb. to death* 把某人嚇得要死

oral〔'orəl〕*adj.* 口頭的

presentation〔,prɛzn̩'teʃən〕*n.* 陳述;介紹;報告

avoid〔ə'vɔɪd〕*v.* 避免

immediate〔ɪ'midɪɪt〕*adj.* 立即的

evade〔ɪ'ved〕*v.* 逃避

obligation〔,ablə'geʃən〕*n.* 義務

commit suicide 自殺

start the ball rolling 開始進行

24. (**A**) M: I hope you do well on your interview.

W: Thanks. Actually it's a security clearance examination.

M: What does that involve?

W: I have to answer questions while being hooked up to a lie detector machine.

M: That sounds a little frightening to me.

Question：What does the man have to do?

A. Absolutely nothing.

B. Have a physical examination.

C. Get a personal background check.

D. Avoid telling the truth.

* interview〔ˈɪntəˌvju〕*n.* 訪問

　actually〔ˈæktʃʊəlɪ〕*adv.* 實際上

　security〔sɪˈkjʊrətɪ〕*n.* 安全

　clearance〔ˈklɪrəns〕*n.* 參與機密工作的許可

　security clearance 忠貞審查（指在選派某人參加國家機密

　　工作前，對其是否忠貞所進行的審查）

　examination〔ɪɡˌzæməˈneʃən〕*n.* 測試；檢查

　involve〔ɪnˈvɑlv〕*v.* 含有　　***hook up*** 連接

　lie detector machine 測謊器

　frightening〔ˈfraɪtn̩ɪŋ〕*adj.* 令人恐懼的

　absolutely〔ˈæbsəˌlutlɪ〕*adv.* 完全地

　physical〔ˈfɪzɪkl̩〕*adj.* 身體的

　background〔ˈbækˌɡraʊnd〕*n.* 背景

25.（ **D** ）W：Welcome back, Tony. How was your trip to
　　　　Chicago?

　　　M：Freezing cold, but extremely successful. We got
　　　　the big contract.

　　　W：That's terrific. You're the man, the big man, TONY!

　　　M：The credit goes to you guys here at headquarters.
　　　　You did all the background work.

　　　W：Thanks for saying that, but management doesn't
　　　　see it that way.

Question : What does the woman imply?

A. That they might get promoted.

B. That she might quit.

C. Headquarters will expand.

D. That her boss won't give credit to her and her colleagues.

* freezing〔'frizɪŋ〕adv. 冰凍般地

extremely〔ɪk'strimlɪ〕adv. 極度地

contract〔'kɑntrækt〕n. 合約　　***the (very) man*** 正適合的人選

credit〔'krɛdɪt〕n. 功勞；榮譽

headquarters〔'hɛd'kwɔrtɚz〕n. pl. 總部

background〔'bæk,graund〕n. 幕後

management〔'mænɪdʒmənt〕n. 管理部門

imply〔ɪm'plaɪ〕v. 暗示　　　promote〔prə'mot〕v. 升遷

quit〔kwɪt〕v. 辭職　　expand〔ɪk'spænd〕v. 擴展

give credit to 歸功於～　　　colleague〔'kɑlig〕n. 同事

26. (**D**) M : Have you noticed that Tom has changed lately?

W : I know exactly what you're talking about.

M : Since he won the election, he seems like a different person.

W : The whole thing has gone to his head.

M : Yeah, he's acting snobbish and stuck-up.

Question : What's the matter with Tom?

A. He has become too important.

B. He's a selfish official.

C. He is changing his friends.

D. He's acting too proud.

* notice〔'notɪs〕 v. 注意　　change〔tʃendʒ〕 v. 改變

　lately〔'letlɪ〕 adv. 最近

　exactly〔ɪg'zæktlɪ〕 adv. 完全地

　election〔ɪ'lɛkʃən〕 n. 選舉

　go to one's ***head***（勝利等）使人興奮

　act〔ækt〕 v. 行為　　snobbish〔'snabɪʃ〕 adj. 勢利的

　stuck-up〔'stʌk'ʌp〕 adj. 高傲的

　selfish〔'sɛlfɪʃ〕 adj. 自私的　　proud〔praʊd〕 adj. 驕傲的

27.（ **D** ）W：How's your new job?

　　　　　M：It's a big challenge. It's too early to tell.

　　　　　W：What do you mean by that?

　　　　　M：I might be in over my head. The pressure is
　　　　　　　unbelievable.

　　　　　W：Maybe it's not worth the hassle and stress.

　　　　　Question：What is the woman suggesting?

　　　　　A. Maybe she should go away.

　　　　　B. It's too stressful there.

　　　　　C. The pay is too low.

　　　　　D. Maybe he should resign.

　　* challenge〔'tʃælɪndʒ〕 n. 挑戰

　　　over one's ***head*** 某人無法理解

　　　pressure〔'prɛʃɚ〕 n. 壓力

　　　unbelievable〔͵ʌnbɪ'livəbl̩〕 adj. 難以相信的

　　　worth〔wɝθ〕 adj. 值得的　　hassle〔'hæsl̩〕 n. 困難；麻煩

　　　stress〔strɛs〕 n. 壓力　　stressful〔'strɛsfəl〕 adj. 壓力大的

　　　low〔lo〕 adj. 低的　　resign〔rɪ'zaɪn〕 v. 辭職

28. (**C**)　M：Hey, what's for dinner? Anything delicious?

　　　　W：Yes, we're having leftovers from yesterday.

　　　　M：May I suggest McDonald's instead?

　　　　W：You sound like a spoiled brat. When I was little…

　　　　M：Please spare me the childhood poverty story. I've heard it a million times.

　　Question：How would you describe the boy's disposition?

　　A. Starving and angry.

　　B. Upset and thirsty.

　　C. Rude and impolite.

　　D. Hungry and impatient.

　　* leftover ('lɛft͵ovɚ) n. 剩飯

　　　instead (ɪn'stɛd) adv. 代替

　　　spoiled (spɔɪld) adj. 被寵壞的

　　　brat (bræt) n. 小孩；小鬼　　spare (spɛr) v. 使免去

　　　poverty ('pɑvɚtɪ) n. 貧窮　　describe (dɪ'skraɪb) v. 描述

　　　disposition (͵dɪspə'zɪʃən) n. 氣質；性情

　　　starving ('stɑrvɪŋ) adj. 飢餓的　　rude (rud) adj. 粗魯的

　　　impolite (͵ɪmpə'laɪt) adj. 無禮的

　　　impatient (ɪm'peʃənt) adj. 沒有耐心的

29. (**A**)　W：Please sit up straight and chew with your mouth closed.

　　　　M：Just let me eat in peace, OK?

　　　　W：Sorry, but I can't let you eat like a slob.

　　　　M：I'm starving and I'm in a hurry.

　　　　W：That's no excuse.

Question：What does the woman think?

A.　That he eats like a pig.

B.　That he isn't very smart.

C.　She feels that he's polite.

D.　He thinks she's too picky.

> * **sit up straight** 坐直　　chew〔tʃu〕v. 咀嚼
>
> **in peace** 安靜地　　slob〔slɑb〕n. 邋遢的人
>
> **in a hurry** 匆忙；趕時間
>
> excuse〔ɪk'skjus〕n. 藉口　　polite〔pə'laɪt〕adj. 有禮的
>
> picky〔'pɪkɪ〕adj. 挑剔的

30.（ **D** ）M：Wow, the temperature is dropping fast!

W：Yeah, it's getting chilly and my feet are cold.

M：OK, let's go home.　I'm cold, too.

W：Want to stop somewhere for a hot drink?

M：No, thanks.　Let's go straight home.

Question：What's happening to the couple at the park?

A.　She's very thirsty.

B.　His feet hurt.

C.　The temperature is going up.

D.　The weather is changing fast.

> * drop〔drɑp〕v. 下降
>
> chilly〔'tʃɪlɪ〕adj. 寒冷的　　drink〔drɪŋk〕n. 飲料
>
> straight〔stret〕adv. 直接地
>
> couple〔'kʌpl̩〕n. 一對男女；夫婦　　hurt〔hɜt〕v. 受傷
>
> **go up** 上升　　weather〔'wɛðɚ〕n. 天氣

PART C.

<u>Questions 31-32</u> refer to the following message.

Thank you for calling the U.S.I.N.S. We're the United States Immigration and Naturalization Service. This is our information service "hot line." Most general questions can be answered by simply following these instructions. Press one if you have a visa question. Press two if you are applying for a green card or a U.S. passport. Press three if you are an American citizen who has lost a passport. If you have an emergency or any other problem, please press zero and hold the line. An operator will be with you as soon as possible.

Vocabulary

U.S.I.N.S. 美國移民歸化局 (= *United States Immigration and Naturalization Service*)

immigration〔͵ɪmə'greʃən〕*n.* 移民

naturalization〔͵nætʃərələ'zeʃən〕*n.* 歸化

information〔͵ɪnfɚ'meʃən〕*n.* 資訊　　service〔'sɝvɪs〕*n.* 服務

hot line 熱線　　general〔'dʒɛnərəl〕*adj.* 一般的

simply〔'sɪmplɪ〕*adv.* 只　　instruction〔ɪn'strʌkʃən〕*n.* 指示

press〔prɛs〕*v.* 按　　visa〔'vizə〕*n.* 簽證

apply for 申請　　*green card* 綠卡

passport〔'pæs͵port〕*n.* 護照　　citizen〔'sɪtəzn̩〕*n.* 公民

emergency〔ɪ'mɝdʒənsɪ〕*n.* 緊急情況　　*hold the line* 不要掛電話

operator〔'ɑpə͵retɚ〕*n.* 總機　　*as soon as possible* 儘快

31. (**A**) What number should you press if you want a green card?
        A. Press two.   B. Press zero and wait.
        C. Press one and listen.   D. Press three.

32. (**D**) If a person presses the number three, that person _____.
        A. is a foreign visitor.
        B. has a visa question.
        C. is applying for a passport.
        D. is an American.
        * foreign〔ˈfɔrɪn〕adj. 外國的

Questions 33-35 refer to the following advertisement.

Do you feel depressed? Has the hustle and bustle of life got you down? Don't let all the pressure stress you out! Join the Hawaii Paradise Spa today and you'll feel like a new person in no time at all!

Our health facility has the most comprehensive treatment center in the area. We have multiple swimming pools, steam rooms, sauna baths, and massage rooms. We also have a top-flight modern fitness center with all the latest exercise equipment. Our professional trainers and expert staff are waiting to help you. Get healthy and fit! Change your life and feel great. Join us at Hawaii Paradise today. Call us now for more information at 1-800-567-1234 or visit us on the Internet at www.hawaiiparadise.com.

Vocabulary

advertisement（͵ædvɚˈtaɪzmənt）*n.* 廣告

depressed（dɪˈprɛst）*adj.* 沮喪的　　hustle（ˈhʌsḷ）*n.* 急忙

bustle（ˈbʌsḷ）*n.* 喧鬧　　***get sb. down*** 使某人無精打采

stress sb. out 使某人累壞了　　Hawaii（həˈwajə）*n.* 夏威夷島

paradise（ˈpærə͵daɪs）*n.* 天堂　　spa（spɑ）*n.* 溫泉浴場

in no time (at all) 立刻　　facility（fəˈsɪlətɪ）*n.* 設備

comprehensive（͵kɑmprɪˈhɛnsɪv）*adj.* 廣泛的；綜合的

treatment（ˈtritmənt）*n.* 治療　　center（ˈsɛntɚ）*n.* 中心

multiple（ˈmʌltəpḷ）*adj.* 由許多部份組成的　　***steam room*** 蒸汽室

sauna（ˈsɔnə）*n.* 三溫暖　　massage（məˈsɑdʒ）*n.* 按摩

top-flight（ˈtɑp͵flaɪt）*adj.* 一流的

modern（ˈmɑdɚn）*adj.* 現代的　　***fitness center*** 健身中心

latest（ˈletɪst）*adj.* 最新的

equipment（ɪˈkwɪpmənt）*n.* 設備

professional（prəˈfɛʃnḷ）*adj.* 專業的

trainer（ˈtrenɚ）*n.* 訓練師　　expert（ˈɛkspɝt）*adj.* 專家的

staff（stæf）*n.* 工作人員　　fit（fɪt）*adj.* 健康的

Internet（ˈɪntɚ͵nɛt）*n.* 網際網路

33. (**C**) For whom is the advertisement intended?

　　A. Students on vacation.

　　B. Women who are overweight.

　　C. Adults who feel tired and stressful.

　　D. Those who have health problems.

　　* intend（ɪnˈtɛnd）*v.* （為…而）準備　　***on vacation*** 渡假
　　overweight（ˈovɚˈwet）*adj.* 超重的

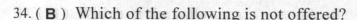

34. (**B**) Which of the following is not offered?

　　　A. A massage. 　　　　　B. A manicure.

　　　C. Exercise machines. 　　D. Sauna baths.

　　　* offer〔'ɔfɚ〕*v.* 提供　　manicure〔'mænɪ,kjʊr〕*n.* 修指甲

35. (**D**) How can one get more information?

　　　A. Check out the classifieds.

　　　B. Request a video.

　　　C. Read the newspaper.

　　　D. Via the Internet.

　　　* ***check out*** 查看　　***the classifieds*** 分類廣告

　　　　request〔rɪ'kwɛst〕*v.* 要求　　via〔'vaɪə〕*prep.* 經由

Questions 36-37 are based on the following announcement.

　　Attention, all employees, attention please. Due to a hazardous chemical spill in the basement, everyone must evacuate the building immediately. In accordance with state health and safety regulations, every person in this building must leave the premises. Please do so in a calm and orderly fashion. This is not a drill. Please walk directly to the nearest exit and proceed outside to the far parking lot by the picnic area. There, we'll wait for the fire department to give us permission to reenter the building. Once again, please hurry to the nearest exit.

Vocabulary

attention〔ə'tɛnʃən〕 interj. 注意

employee〔,ɛmplɔɪ'i〕 n. 員工

due to 由於　　hazardous〔'hæzədəs〕 adj. 危險的

chemical〔'kɛmɪkl̩〕 adj. 化學藥物的　　spill〔spɪl〕 n. 溢出

basement〔'besmənt〕 n. 地下室

evacuate〔ɪ'vækjuˌet〕 v. 撤退

immediately〔ɪ'midɪɪtlɪ〕 adv. 立刻

in accordance with 根據　　state〔stet〕 adj. 國家的

safety〔'seftɪ〕 n. 安全　　regulation〔,rɛgjə'leʃən〕 n. 規定

premise〔'prɛmɪs〕 n. 建築物　　calm〔kɑm〕 adj. 鎮定的

orderly〔'ɔrdəlɪ〕 adj. 有秩序的　　fashion〔'fæʃən〕 n. 方式

drill〔drɪl〕 n. 演習　　directly〔də'rɛktlɪ〕 adv. 直接地

exit〔'ɛgzɪt〕 n. 出口　　proceed〔prə'sid〕 v. 前進

far〔fɑr〕 adj. 較遠的　　**parking lot** 停車場

picnic area 野餐區　　**fire department** 消防局

permission〔pə'mɪʃən〕 n. 許可

reenter〔ri'ɛntə〕 v. 再進入　　hurry〔'hɝɪ〕 v. 趕往

36. (**B**) What is the main idea of this message?

　　A. Get to the basement.

　　B. Get out of the building.

　　C. Park all the cars away from the spill.

　　D. Direct and help colleagues to the exits.

　　* **main idea** 主旨　　park〔pɑrk〕 v. 停車
　　　direct〔də'rɛkt〕 v. 指揮

37. (**C**) Where is this accident probably taking place?
    A. At an administration building.
    B. At a stock market company.
    C. At a plastics factory.
    D. On a university campus.

    * probably〔ˈprɑbəblɪ〕*adv.* 可能　　*take place* 發生
    administration〔əd͵mɪnəˈstreʃən〕*n.* 管理
    stock market 股市　　*stock market company* 股票上市公司
    plastics〔ˈplæstɪks〕*adj.* 塑膠的
    factory〔ˈfæktrɪ〕*n.* 工廠
    university〔͵junəˈvɝsətɪ〕*n.* 大學
    campus〔ˈkæmpəs〕*n.* 校園

Questions 38-39 are based on the following weather forecast.

> Here's the CNBC forecast for the next twenty-four hours. It's gonna be another scorcher today with temperatures in the upper 90s. We'll have clear skies with zero chance of rain. Late tonight, things will cool down a bit, the temperature will drop to the low to mid 70s. We'll have very clear skies tonight — great for all you stargazers — and we'll have a light breeze coming in off the ocean. Stay tuned for sports at nine and highlights from today's championship game.

💻 Vocabulary

forecast〔ˋforˌkæst〕n. 預報　　scorcher〔ˋskɔrtʃə〕n. 酷熱的日子

upper〔ˋʌpə〕adj. 上方的；較高的

clear〔klɪr〕adj. 晴朗的；無雲的

cool down 變涼　　mid〔mɪd〕adj. 中間的

stargazer〔ˋstɑrˌgezə〕n. 天文學家；看星星的人

light〔laɪt〕adj. 輕微的　　breeze〔briz〕n. 微風

off〔ɔf〕prep. 在⋯的海上　　tuned〔tjund〕adj. 調好頻道的

stay tuned 繼續收聽；不要轉台　　highlight〔ˋhaɪˌlaɪt〕n. 精采部份

championship〔ˋtʃæmpɪənˌʃɪp〕n. 冠軍

38. (**A**) What will the daytime temperature be?

    A. In the high 90s Fahrenheit.

    B. About 70 degrees Fahrenheit.

    C. Around 90 degrees Centigrade.

    D. Extremely hot.

    * Fahrenheit〔ˋfærənˌhaɪt〕n. 華氏溫度

      degree〔dɪˋgri〕n. 度數

      Centigrade〔ˋsɛntəˌgred〕n. 攝氏溫度

39. (**C**) What's the forecast for tonight?

    A. Windy and hot.

    B. Humid and cloudy.

    C. Clear skies and light winds.

    D. Breezy with possible meteor showers.

    * windy〔ˋwɪndɪ〕adj. 有風的　　humid〔ˋhjumɪd〕adj. 潮濕的

      cloudy〔ˋklaudɪ〕adj. 多雲的　　breezy〔ˋbrizɪ〕adj. 有微風的

      meteor〔ˋmitɪə〕n. 隕石；流星

      shower〔ˋʃauə〕n. 陣雨　　**meteor shower** 流星雨

Questions 40-41 refer to the following talk.

Welcome to the Royal Palace, folks! My name is Adam and I have the pleasure of serving you this evening. Before you take a look at the menu, I'd like to tell you about our specials. The first special is the super twelve-ounce (12 oz.) T-bone steak. It's served with a baked potato or fries, a green salad, vegetables, onion soup, topped off with coffee and a slice of pie for dessert. Our second special is the Italian combination dish. It includes spaghetti with meatballs, lasagna with sausage, a bowl of pasta, and some garlic bread. Of course, this also comes with a salad. Any questions? Take your time to decide. I'll be back in a few minutes.

🖥️ Vocabulary

royal (ˈrɔɪəl) adj. 皇家的；王室的　　palace (ˈpælɪs) n. 宮殿

folks (fok) n. pl. 【用於親密的稱呼】各位

pleasure (ˈplɛʒə) n. 榮幸　　serve (sɝv) v. 上菜；供應；為…服務

take a look 看一眼　　menu (ˈmɛnju) n. 菜單

special (ˈspɛʃəl) n. 特餐　　ounce (auns) n. 盎司

T-bone steak 丁骨牛排　　bake (bek) v. 烤

salad (ˈsæləd) n. 沙拉　　onion (ˈʌnjən) n. 洋蔥

soup (sup) n. 湯　　**top off with** 以～作為結束

a slice of 一片　　dessert (dɪˈzɝt) n. 甜點

Italian (ɪˈtæljən) adj. 義大利的

combination (ˌkɑmbəˈneʃən) n. 組合

dish〔dɪʃ〕*n.* 菜餚   include〔ɪnˈklud〕*v.* 包括

spaghetti〔spəˈgɛtɪ〕*n.* 義大利麵

meatball〔ˈmit,bɔl〕*n.* 肉丸

lasagna〔ləˈzænjə〕*n.* 義大利式鹵汁麵條（形狀寬而扁，上澆
    肉末，乳酪和蕃茄汁）

sausage〔ˈsɔsɪdʒ〕*n.* 香腸   bowl〔bol〕*n.* 碗

pasta〔ˈpastə〕*n.* 麵食（義大利麵、通心粉等）

garlic〔ˈgarlɪk〕*n.* 大蒜   ***take your time*** 慢慢來

40. (**C**) Which of the two specials has the most items?

    A. The Italian Pizza Delight.

    B. The Royal Palace.

    C. The 12oz. T-bone steak.

    D. The Italian Combo Dish.

    * item〔ˈaɪtəm〕*n.* 項目

     delight〔dɪˈlaɪt〕*n.* 高興；樂事

     combo〔ˈkambo〕*n.* 組合（= *combination* ）

41. (**A**) What is an item that wasn't mentioned?

    A. Alcoholic beverages.

    B. Desserts.

    C. Soups.

    D. Vegetables.

    * mention〔ˈmɛnʃən〕*v.* 提到

     alcoholic〔,ælkəˈhɔlɪk〕*adj.* 含有酒精的

     beverage〔ˈbɛvərɪdʒ〕*n.* 飲料

Questions 42-43 refer to the following announcement.

> Hey buddy, I've got some bad news for you. I called Southeast Airlines and they have no flights from Bangkok to Hong Kong on Saturdays or Sundays. If you really want to fly on the weekend, your best option would be to fly on Thai Airlines. The only problem is you'll have to pay 20% more for switching airlines. I suggest that you extend your trip another three days. You can stay over at my beach bungalow. We can go snorkeling and have a great weekend together.

📺 Vocabulary

buddy〔ˈbʌdɪ〕*n.* 兄弟；夥伴（稱呼對方）

airlines〔ˈɛrˌlaɪnz〕*n. pl.* 航空公司　　flight〔flaɪt〕*n.* 班機

Bangkok〔ˈbæŋkak〕*n.* 曼谷（泰國首都）　　***Hong Kong*** 香港

option〔ˈapʃən〕*n.* 選擇　　Thai〔ˈta‧i〕*adj.* 泰國的

switch〔swɪtʃ〕*v.* 轉換　　suggest〔səˈdʒɛst〕*v.* 建議

extend〔ɪkˈstɛnd〕*v.* 延長　　***stay over*** 過夜

bungalow〔ˈbʌŋɡəˌlo〕*n.* 別墅（爲有陽台的木造平房，構造簡單
　　而簡潔舒適，通常用作避暑別墅）

snorkel〔ˈsɔrkl̩〕*v.* （潛水者）使用水下呼吸管潛游

go snorkeling 去浮潛

42. (**B**) Where does the traveler want to go?

    A. Bangkok.   B. Hong Kong.

    C. Southeast.   D. Manila.

    * Manila〔məˈnɪlə〕*n.* 馬尼拉（菲律賓首都）

43. (**B**) What is the speaker suggesting?

    A. That the traveler fly on Southeast Airlines.

    B. That the traveler wait a couple of days.

    C. That the traveler pay extra money.

    D. That the traveler fly on Thai Airlines.

    * ***a couple of*** 幾個的 (= *several* = *a few*)

      extra〔ˈɛkstrə〕*adj.* 額外的

Questions 44-45 refer to the following advertisement.

    Manager wanted for a Fortune 500 corporation in the transportation industry. We're looking for motivated, self-starting individuals who are not afraid of challenges and being a "hands-on" operator. We will train the selected applicant to be an integral part of our Southeast Asia management team. We offer an exciting career and a generous employment package. An attractive salary, fast promotions, partnership options, and complete benefits are all part of the package that we offer at GLOBAL International. Please send your resume to the address listed below.

💻 Vocabulary

manager〔'mænɪdʒɚ〕 n. 經理

wanted〔'wɑntɪd〕 adj. 徵求～的　　fortune〔'fɔrtʃən〕 n. 財富

corporation〔,kɔrpə'reʃən〕 n. 公司

Fortune 500 corporation 前 500 大企業（Fortune 雜誌專選）

transportation〔,trænspɚ'teʃən〕 n. 運輸

industry〔'ɪndəstrɪ〕 n. 工業；產業

motivated〔'motə,vetɪd〕 adj. 有動機的；積極的

self-starting〔'sɛlf'stɑrtɪŋ〕 adj. 自動的

individual〔,ɪndə'vɪdʒuəl〕 n. 個人　　***be afraid of*** 害怕

challenge〔'tʃælɪndʒ〕 n. 挑戰

hands-on〔'hændz'ɑn〕 adj. 親身實踐的

operator〔'ɑpə,retɚ〕 n. 操作者　　train〔tren〕 v. 訓練

selected〔sə'lɛktɪd〕 adj. 被挑選出來的

applicant〔'æpləkənt〕 n. 申請人

integral〔'ɪntəgrəl〕 adj. 不可缺的

southeast〔,sauθ'ist〕 adj. 東南的　　Asia〔'eʒə〕 n. 亞洲

management〔'mænɪdʒmənt〕 n. 管理　　team〔tim〕 n. 團隊

exciting〔ɪk'saɪtɪŋ〕 adj. 令人興奮的；有趣的

career〔kə'rɪr〕 n. 職業

generous〔'dʒɛnərəs〕 adj. 豐富的；慷慨的

employment〔ɪm'plɔɪmənt〕 n. 就業

package〔'pækɪdʒ〕 n. 所有利益

employment package 聘用條件；員工福利

attractive〔ə'træktɪv〕 adj. 吸引人的

salary〔'sælərɪ〕 n. 薪水　　promotion〔prə'moʃən〕 n. 升遷

partnership〔'pɑrtnɚ,ʃɪp〕 n. 合夥關係　　option〔'ɑpʃən〕 n. 選擇

complete〔kəm'plit〕*adj.* 完善的   benefit〔'bɛnəfɪt〕*n.* 利益

global〔'globl̩〕*adj.* 全球的

international〔ˌɪntə'næʃənl̩〕*n.* 國際性組織

resume〔ˌrɛzu'me〕*n.* 履歷

address〔'ædrɛs〕*n.* 地址   list〔lɪst〕*v.* 列出

44. (**C**) This company is looking for _____.

　　A. machine operators

　　B. regional sales agents

　　C. dynamic leaders

　　D. transportation experts

　　* regional〔'ridʒənl̩〕*adj.* 區域的

　　　sales agent 業務人員

　　　dynamic〔daɪ'næmɪk〕*adj.* 充滿活力的

　　　leader〔'lidə〕*n.* 領導人；主管

45. (**D**) What essential document must applicants send?

　　A. An employment application.

　　B. School transcripts and recommendations.

　　C. Past tax statements.

　　D. An account of past work experience.

　　* essential〔ə'sɛnʃəl〕*adj.* 基本的

　　　document〔'dɑkjəmənt〕*n.* 文件

　　　application〔ˌæplə'keʃən〕*n.* 申請

　　　transcript〔'træn,skrɪpt〕*n.* 成績單

　　　recommendation〔ˌrɛkəmɛn'deʃən〕*n.* 推薦書

　　　tax〔tæks〕*n.* 稅   statement〔'stetmənt〕*n.* 報告書

　　　account〔ə'kaunt〕*n.* 說明；報告

中高級閱讀測驗詳解 ③

PART A : Sentence Completion

1. (**B**) <u>Morale</u> among the troops has been low due to the enemy's continual victories.
由於敵人連續勝利，軍隊裡的<u>士氣</u>低落。

(A) moral〔'mɔrəl〕 n. 寓意；教訓（ = lesson ）　adj. 道德的
(B) ***morale***〔 mə'ræl , mo- 〕 n. 士氣
(C) mortal〔'mɔrtḷ〕 n. 凡人（ = human ）　adj. 會死的
(D) morality〔 mə'rælətɪ 〕 n. 道德；品行（ = ethics ）

* troop〔 trup 〕 n. 軍隊　　***due to*** 由於
　 enemy〔'ɛnəmɪ〕 n. 敵人
　 continual〔 kən'tɪnjuəl 〕 adj. 連續的
　 victory〔'vɪkt(ə)rɪ〕 n. 勝利

2. (**D**) There were too many <u>redundant</u> words in your essay. I suggest that you make a long story short and rewrite it more concisely. 你的文章裡<u>贅字</u>太多。我建議你長話短說，重新寫得更簡潔一點。

(A) reformatory〔 rɪ'fɔrmə,torɪ 〕 adj. 改革的；矯正的
　　 n. 感化院（ = reform school ）
(B) refined〔 rɪ'faɪnd 〕 adj. 精煉的；文雅的
(C) rearmost〔'rɪr,most 〕 adj. 最後面的
(D) ***redundant***〔 rɪ'dʌndənt 〕 adj. 冗長的；過多的
　　（ = unwanted ; unnecessary ）

* essay〔'ɛse〕 n. 文章
　 make a long story short 長話短說
　 concisely〔 kən'saɪslɪ 〕 adv. 簡潔地

3. (**A**) He was feared by his enemies as a <u>ruthless</u> conqueror, who showed no mercy for those who surrendered or were captured.

他的敵人都懼怕他，因爲他是個<u>無情的</u>征服者，對投降者和俘虜都沒有一點慈悲。

(A) **ruthless**〔ˈruθlɪs〕*adj.* 無情的；冷酷的
　　(= *merciless* ; *cruel*)

(B) heedless〔ˈhidlɪs〕*adj.* 不注意的 (↔ *heedful*) < *of* >

(C) tactless〔ˈtæktlɪs〕*adj.* 無機智的；不圓滑的 (↔ *tactful*)

(D) listless〔ˈlɪstlɪs〕*adj.* 沒有興致的；懶散的

* conqueror〔ˈkɑŋkərə〕*n.* 征服者
　mercy〔ˈmɝsɪ〕*n.* 慈悲
　surrender〔səˈrɛndə〕*v.* 投降
　capture〔ˈkæptʃə〕*v.* 擄獲

4. (**D**) <u>Incentive</u> is a primary factor in learning. Without it, you lack something to urge you by.

<u>動機</u>是學習的主要因素之一。沒有它，你就缺乏驅策的動力。

(A) incinerator〔ɪnˈsɪnəˌretə〕*n.* 焚化爐；火葬爐

(B) inconsistency〔ˌɪnkənˈsɪstənsɪ〕*n.* 不一致；矛盾
　　(= *contradiction*)

(C) incense〔ˈɪnsɛns〕*n.* (供神焚燒的) 香
　　a stick of incense 一柱香

(D) **incentive**〔ɪnˈsɛntɪv〕*n.* 動機；刺激 (= *motivation*)

* primary〔ˈpraɪˌmɛrɪ〕*adj.* 主要的
　factor〔ˈfæktə〕*n.* 因素
　urge〔ɝdʒ〕*v.* 驅策

5. (**C**) Everyone has his own <u>criteria</u> in mind on which to judge prospective friends.

每個人心中都有自己的<u>標準</u>，來評定可能適合當朋友的人。

(A) adaptation〔͵ædəp'teʃən〕*n.* 適應；改編

(B) assumption〔ə'sʌmpʃən〕*n.* 假定；擔任

(C) *criterion*〔kraɪ'tɪrɪən〕*n.*（判斷、批評的）標準
（*criteria* 爲複數型）

(D) congeniality〔kən͵dʒinɪ'æləti〕*n.* 意氣相投；（思想、興趣等）一致

* *in mind* 在心中

prospective〔prə'spɛktɪv〕*adj.* 未來的；有希望的

on which 相當於 on the criteria，介系詞 on 表示「根據」之意，其後的不定詞爲形容詞用法，來修飾名詞 criteria。

6. (**B**) There was a severe traffic jam on the <u>elevated</u> highway, and so we had no other choice but to take another road.

這條<u>高架</u>道路上嚴重塞車，所以我們只好走另一條路。

(A) accelerated〔æk'sɛlə͵retɪd〕*adj.* 加速的

(B) *elevated*〔'ɛlə͵vetɪd〕*adj.* 提高的；架高的
elevated highway 高架道路

(C) revised〔rɪ'vaɪzd〕*adj.* 修正過的

(D) blockaded〔blɑ'kedɪd〕*adj.* 被封鎖的

* severe〔sə'vɪr〕*adj.* 嚴重的

traffic jam 塞車；交通阻塞

have no (other) choice but to + V. 除了～外別無選擇；只好

7. (**D**) After the strong typhoon, fallen trees <u>obstructed</u> the streets and traffic was terribly congested.

強烈颱風過後，倒塌的樹木<u>阻礙</u>道路，交通嚴重壅塞。

(A) instruct〔ɪn'strʌkt〕*v.* 教導；指示

(B) construct〔kən'strʌkt〕*v.* 建設

(C) destruct〔dɪ'strʌkt〕*v.*（火箭、飛彈等）爆破；自毀

(D) ***obstruct***〔əb'strʌkt〕*v.* 阻礙；阻擋

* congest〔kən'dʒɛst〕*v.* 阻塞；<u>壅塞</u>

8. (**B**) I <u>loathe</u> the smell of gasoline. It makes me sick and gives me a headache.

我<u>非常討厭</u>汽油的味道，聞到會使我噁心想吐，還會頭痛。

(A) wreathe〔rið〕*v.* 做花圈、花環

wreath〔riθ〕*n.* 花圈；花環

(B) ***loathe***〔loð〕*v.* 極厭惡；討厭

loathsome〔'loðsəm〕*adj.* 討厭的；令人作嘔的

(C) breathe〔brið〕*v.* 呼吸　　breath〔brɛθ〕*n.* 呼吸

(D) soothe〔suð〕*v.* 撫慰；舒緩

soothing〔'suðɪŋ〕*adj.* 撫慰的

* smell〔smɛl〕*n.* 味道　　gasoline〔ˌgæsḷ'in〕*n.* 汽油

9. (**D**) He is very trustworthy. He is <u>as close as an oyster</u>. Your secret is safe with him.

他非常值得信任，他<u>守口如瓶</u>。他絕對能保守你的秘密。

(A) as broad as it is long 長寬相同；兩者都一樣

(B) as clear as mud 和泥巴一樣清楚；含糊不清的（反諷的説法）

(C) as right as rain 很順利

(D) ***as close as an oyster*** 像牡蠣一樣緊閉著；守口如瓶的

* trustworthy〔'trʌstˌwɜðɪ〕*adj.* 值得信任的（= *worthy of trust*）

10. (**C**) The bad news came like <u>a bolt out of the blue</u>. He was not in the least prepared for it and broke down.

這個壞消息來如<u>晴天霹靂</u>。他一點心理準備都沒有，所以就崩潰了。

(A) a drop in the bucket/ocean　滄海之一粟；九牛一毛

(B) a frog in the throat　喉嚨裡有青蛙；聲音嘶啞

(C) *a bolt out of the blue* (*sky*)　晴天霹靂

(D) a fly in the ointment　藥膏中的蒼蠅；美中不足

* *not in the least*　一點也不（= *not at all*）

　 prepared〔prɪˈpɛrd〕*adj.* 有準備的　　　*break down*　崩潰

11. (**A**) As far as I can see, the machine only needs a minor adjustment: a turn of screw here, a little tightening up there, a drop of oil and it will be <u>as good as</u> new.

就我所見，這台機器只需要一點輕微的調整：這裡螺絲旋一下，那裡調緊一點，再上點油，就會<u>像</u>新的<u>一樣</u>了。

(A) *as good as*　就像～一樣；等於是～（置於形容詞、動詞之前，做副詞用）

(B) as soon as　一～就（連接詞用法）

(C) as well as　和～一樣好；以及

(D) as long as　像～一樣久；只要

* *as far as*　就…（連接詞用法）

　 minor〔ˈmaɪnɚ〕*adj.* 輕微的

　 adjustment〔əˈdʒʌstmənt〕*n.* 調整

　 screw〔skru〕*n.* 螺絲

　 tighten〔ˈtaɪtn̩〕*v.* 變緊；變牢固　　 drop〔drɑp〕*n.* 滴

12. (**B**) Someone said, " Life is precious but love is more valuable. But I would rather give up both <u>in exchange for</u> freedom." That is, he would rather die <u>than</u> have no freedom.

有人說過：「生命誠可貴，愛情價更高。若爲自由故，兩者皆可拋。（我寧願拋棄這兩者以<u>交換</u>自由。）」換言之，他寧願死<u>也不願</u>沒有自由。

* precious〔'prɛʃəs〕*adj.* 珍貴的
  valuable〔'væljʊəbḷ〕*adj.* 寶貴的；重要的
  would rather V_A than V_B 寧願 A 也不願 B (= *prefer to V_A rather than V_B*)
  in exchange for 以交換～（若用動詞應寫成 *I would rather exchange* both *for freedom.* 或 *I would rather change* both *for freedom.*)
  that is (***to say***) 換言之；也就是說 (= *in other words*)

13. (**B**) <u>No matter how</u> hard the task may be, and <u>whatever</u> difficulty may come my way, I have decided to take on the challenge and will spare no effort to accomplish it.

無論這個工作可能<u>有多難</u>，也無論我會遭遇<u>什麼</u>困難，我已經決定接受這個挑戰，而且會不遺餘力完成這個工作。

* 引導副詞子句，前者爲複合關係副詞，no matter how 相當於 However，修飾 hard，後者爲複合關係形容詞，whatever 相當於 no matter what，形容 difficulty。
  task〔tæsk〕*n.* 工作
  come *one's* ***way*** （事情）發生在某人身上
  take on 接受　　challenge〔'tʃælɪndʒ〕*n.* 挑戰
  spare〔spɛr〕*v.* 吝惜　　***spare no effort*** 不遺餘力
  accomplish〔ə'kɑmplɪʃ〕*v.* 完成；達成

14. (**C**) She kept climbing up the mountain and ran out of breath, <u>with</u> beads of sweat <u>running</u> down her face.

她一直往山上爬，爬得上氣不接下氣，汗水一滴一滴從臉上流下來。

* 後半句表示「附帶狀態」，可用「*with* ＋受詞＋受詞補語」的用法，補語形容汗珠流下來，為主動，應用 *running*，故本題選 (C)。若選擇 (A) 和 (D)，皆有連接詞，就不必用分詞的形式，而用動詞 ran 即可。

out of breath 氣喘的；上氣不接下氣

bead〔bid〕*n.* 滴；珠子   sweat〔swɛt〕*n.* 汗水

15. (**D**) He is too ready to criticize others. (Choose the correct answer.) 他動輒批評他人。

(A) He is too careful to criticize others.

他太小心了，不會批評他人。

(B) He prepares too well to criticize others.

他準備得太好了，不會批評他人。

(C) He is not ready to find fault with others.

他還沒有準備好要批評他人。

(D) *He is fond of finding fault with others*.

他喜歡批評他人。

* *too ready to* ＋ *V.* 太容易～；傾向～；動輒～

criticize〔'krɪtə,saɪz〕*v.* 批評

find fault with 挑毛病；批評

be fond of 喜歡

PART B：Cloze

Questions 16-23

A manuscript written by Mozart is to go on show at the British Library, its two halves reunited after a 170-year <u>separation</u>, the museum said on Wednesday. Written in 1773 when the composer was 17, the score was cut in two by his widow Constance and sold in 1835.

莫札特的手稿將在大英圖書館展出，這份手稿被分成兩半，在分別一百七十年後，又重新結合，該博物館星期三表示。這份樂譜寫於一七七三年，當時莫札特十七歲，後來被他的遺孀康絲坦分成兩半，並在一八三五年出售。

> manuscript〔'mænjə,skrɪpt〕*n.* 手稿
> Mozart〔'mozɑrt〕*n.* 莫札特【1756-1791；奧地利作曲家】
> **be to V**. 即將　　**on show** 展覽；展示
> British〔'brɪtɪʃ〕*adj.* 英國的　　library〔'laɪ,brɛrɪ〕*n.* 圖書館
> **the British Library** 大英圖書館
> half〔hæf〕*n.* 一半【複數為 halves〔hævz〕】
> reunite〔,rijʊ'naɪt〕*v.* 再結合；重聚
> composer〔kəm'pozɚ〕*n.* 作曲家　　score〔skor〕*n.* 樂譜
> widow〔'wɪdo〕*n.* 遺孀

16. (**D**) (A) unification〔,junəfə'keʃən〕*n.* 統一
　　　　　　(B) identification〔aɪ,dɛntəfə'keʃən〕*n.* 身分確認
　　　　　　(C) exploration〔,ɛksplə'reʃən〕*n.* 探索；探險
　　　　　　(D) **separation**〔,sɛpə'reʃən〕*n.* 分開

One side contains two new cadenzas Mozart envisaged for piano concertos he had already written, one <u>composed</u> when he
17
was eleven. The other has a short minuet for a string quartet which he later abandoned in a spirit of self-criticism for an <u>alternative</u> version.
18

其中一半包含莫札特為他十一歲時作的鋼琴協奏曲，而寫的兩段新裝飾樂。另一半是為弦樂四重奏所寫的短篇小步舞曲，但莫札特後來本著自我批判的精神而放棄了那首小步舞曲，並寫了另一個替代的版本。

contain〔kənˈten〕v. 包括　　cadenza〔kəˈdɛnzə〕n. 裝飾樂

envisage〔ɛnˈvɪzɪdʒ〕v. 構想；設想

concerto〔kənˈtʃɛrto〕n. 協奏曲

minuet〔ˌmɪnjuˈɛt〕n. 小步舞曲

string〔strɪŋ〕n.（樂器的）弦；弦樂

quartet〔kwɔrˈtɛt〕n. 四重奏

abandon〔əˈbændən〕v. 放棄　　spirit〔ˈspɪrɪt〕n. 精神

self-criticism〔ˌsɛlfˈkrɪtəˌsɪzəm〕n. 自我批判

version〔ˈvɝʒən〕n. 版本

17. (**A**) (A) ***compose***〔kəmˈpoz〕v. 作曲；組成

(B) consist〔kənˈsɪst〕v. 組成

(C) comprise〔kəmˈpraɪz〕v. 組成

(D) constitute〔ˈkɑnstəˌtjut〕v. 組成

18. (**C**) (A) initiative〔ɪˈnɪʃɪˌetɪv〕n. 主動權

(B) imperative〔ɪmˈpɛrətɪv〕adj. 必要的

(C) ***alternative***〔ɔlˈtɝnətɪv〕adj. 替代的

(D) affirmative〔əˈfɝmətɪv〕adj. 肯定的

"The manuscript <u>shed</u> important light on the 17-year-old
      19
composer's development at a transitional <u>phase</u> in his life," said
                                          20
Chris Banks, the British Library's head of music collections.

"It speaks <u>a great deal</u> about his maturity. Mozart was trying to
           21
make his mark as a serious composer. He was well known as a

<u>child prodigy</u>, but by 17 he couldn't really continue with that."
      22

「這份手稿很重要，它說明了這位十七歲的作曲家，在人生過渡階段的發展，」克里斯‧班克斯說，他是大英圖書館的音樂收藏部負責人。
「這份手稿充分顯露出莫札特的成熟，他試著要以嚴謹的作曲家成名。他曾是著名的音樂神童，但到了十七歲時，他實在不能繼續當神童了。」

transitional〔træn'zɪʃənḷ〕*adj.* 過渡時期的
head〔hɛd〕*n.* 主管   collection〔kə'lɛkʃən〕*n.* 收藏品
maturity〔mə'tjurətɪ〕*n.* 成熟
make one's mark 成功；成名
serious〔'sɪrɪəs〕*adj.* 嚴肅的   ***be well known as*** 是有名的…
continue〔kən'tɪnju〕*v.* 繼續

19. (**A**) (A) ***shed***〔ʃɛd〕*v.* 放射；發出   ***shed light on*** 說明
      (B) strike〔straɪk〕*v.* 打
      (C) hide〔haɪd〕*v.* 隱藏
      (D) place〔ples〕*v.* 放置

20. (**D**) (A) physics〔'fɪzɪks〕*n.* 物理學
      (B) phobia〔'fobɪə〕*n.* 恐懼症
      (C) phrase〔frez〕*n.* 片語
      (D) ***phase***〔fez〕*n.* 階段

21. (**B**) 依句意，空格應填副詞片語，選 (B) ***a great deal*** 「很多；大量地」。而 (A) a great amount 常接 of，作「大量的」解，(C) quite a few 相當多的 (＝ *many*)，(D) a small number 常接 of，作「少數的」解，用法均不合。

22. (**B**) (A) child's play *n.* 輕而易舉的事

        (B) ***child prodigy*** *n.* 神童

                prodigy〔'prɑdədʒɪ〕*n.* 神童

        (C) childproof〔'tʃaɪld‚pruf〕*adj.* 保護兒童安全的

        (D) child minder *n.* 保姆

                minder〔'maɪndə〕*n.* 照顧者

      The library has owned since 1953 the lower half of the manuscript, which had been given to a minor functionary in Bavaria in southern Germany, probably in exchange for some service. But it acquired only recently the other half, <u>which</u> Constance initially
                                                          23
sold to a court musician, Julius Leidke.

      The manuscript will go on public display Saturday as part of a series of events to mark the 250th anniversary of the birth of Wolfgang Amadeus Mozart.

      大英圖書館從一九五三年開始擁有後半段的手稿，康絲坦當初可能是為了交換某些服務，而把它送給德國南部巴伐利亞的一個小公務員。但是到了最近，大英圖書館才得到另一半的手稿，康絲坦最初將這個部份賣給一位宮廷樂師 —— 朱力阿思・雷得克。

      這份手稿將在星期六公開展出，這是紀念莫札特兩百五十歲冥誕的一系列活動之一。

own〔on〕v. 擁有　　lower〔'loɚ〕adj.（上下一對之物中）下面的

minor〔'maɪnɚ〕adj. 較小的

functionary〔'fʌŋkʃən,ɛrɪ〕n. 公務員

Bavaria〔bə'vɛrɪə〕n. 巴伐利亞【德國南部一省，首府爲慕尼黑】

Germany〔'dʒɝmənɪ〕n. 德國

acquire〔ə'kwaɪr〕v. 得到　　recently〔'risn̩tlɪ〕adv. 最近

initially〔ɪ'nɪʃəlɪ〕adv. 最初

court〔kort〕adj. 宮廷的　　*go on display* 展示

a series of 一連串的　　event〔ɪ'vɛnt〕n. 事件；活動

mark〔mark〕v. 表示；紀念

anniversary〔,ænə'vɝsərɪ〕n. 周年紀念

23.（**C**）空格應填關係代名詞，代替先行詞 the other half，故選
　　（C）*which*。

Questions 24-30

　　For many Chinese, the annual Ching Ming festival can be more
<u>chaotic</u> than harmonic, as people flock to cemeteries to sweep the
　　24
graves of their ancestors.

　　對許多中國人來說，每年的清明節可能是混亂多於和諧，因爲人們會
聚集到墓地去替祖先掃墓。

annual〔'ænjʊəl〕adj. 每年的

festival〔'fɛstəvl̩〕n. 節慶

Ching Ming festival 清明節（ = *Tomb-Sweeping Festival*）

harmonic〔har'manɪk〕adj. 和諧的　　flock〔flak〕v. 聚集

cemetery〔'sɛmə,tɛrɪ〕n. 墓地；墓園

sweep〔swip〕v. 掃　　grave〔grev〕n. 墳墓（ = *tomb*）

ancestor〔'ænsɛstɚ〕n. 祖先

24. (**B**) (A) organic〔ɔr'gænɪk〕adj. 有機的

　　　　　(B) ***chaotic***〔ke'atɪk〕adj. 混亂的

　　　　　(C) elastic〔ɪ'læstɪk〕adj. 有彈性的

　　　　　(D) gigantic〔dʒaɪ'gæntɪk〕adj. 巨大的

In an effort to beat the endless bottlenecks and lack of parking around burial grounds, Taiwan's Kinbaushan Cemetery now offers cyber-<u>gravesites</u> which can be <u>tended</u> with a few mouse-clicks.
　　　　　　　　　　25　　　　　　　　　　　　　26

為了要戰勝無止盡的塞車問題，以及墓地附近停車位不足的問題，台灣的金寶山墓園現在提供網路墓地，只要按幾下滑鼠，就可以把墓地照顧好。

> effort〔'ɛfət〕n. 努力
>
> ***in an effort to*** + ***V.*** 為了要～
>
> beat〔bit〕v. 打敗；戰勝
>
> endless〔'ɛndlɪs〕adj. 無止盡的
>
> bottleneck〔'batḷ,nɛk〕n. 瓶頸；交通阻塞
>
> lack〔læk〕n. 缺乏；不足　　parking〔'parkɪŋ〕n. 停車
>
> burial〔'bɛrɪəl〕n. 埋葬　　***burial ground*** 墓地
>
> cyber〔'saɪbə〕adj. 網路的
>
> mouse〔maʊs〕n. 滑鼠　　click〔klɪk〕n. 按壓

25. (**A**) (A) ***gravesite***〔'grev,saɪt〕n. 墓地

　　　　　(B) gravestone〔'grev,ston〕n. 墓碑

　　　　　(C) gravel pit 砂石場　　gravel〔'grævḷ〕n. 砂石

　　　　　　　pit〔pɪt〕n. 採掘場

　　　　　(D) graveled path 碎石子路

26. (**D**)　(A)　intend〔ɪn'tɛnd〕v. 打算

　　　　　(B)　pretend〔prɪ'tɛnd〕v. 假裝

　　　　　(C)　extend〔ɪk'stɛnd〕v. 擴張

　　　　　(D)　***tend***〔tɛnd〕v. 照顧

On-line tomb-sweepers are treated to Buddhist music and images
of candles when accessing cyber-plots <u>that</u>, depending on their
　　　　　　　　　　　　　　　　　　　　27
size, can cost up to US$1,000.

線上掃墓者在進入網路墓地時，會聽到佛教音樂，並看到蠟燭的影像，
網路墓地依照大小來定價，有些價位高達美金一千元。

　　　　tomb〔tum〕n. 墳墓　　　sweeper〔'swipɚ〕n. 掃除者
　　　　treat〔trit〕v. 招待　　　Buddhist〔'budɪst〕adj. 佛教的
　　　　image〔'ɪmɪdʒ〕n. 影像　　candle〔'kændl〕n. 蠟燭
　　　　access〔'æksɛs〕v. 進入　　plot〔plɑt〕n. 一小塊土地
　　　　depend on 依照　　　size〔saɪz〕n. 大小
　　　　up to 高達

27. (**C**)　空格應填關係代名詞，代替先行詞 cyber-plots，故選 (C) ***that***。

　　Many people sweeping graves in Taipei during the festival
were <u>skeptical</u>. "You can't cut the grass of your father's grave
　　　　28
using a computer," exclaimed one man.

　　在清明節期間，許多在台北掃墓的人都感到很懷疑。「你不能用電
腦來替你父親的墓地除草，」有個人大聲說。

　　　　exclaim〔ɪk'sklem〕v. 大叫

28. (**B**) (A) ethical〔ˈɛθɪkḷ〕adj. 道德的

(B) ***skeptical***〔ˈskɛptɪkḷ〕adj. 懷疑的

(C) tactical〔ˈtæktɪkḷ〕adj. 戰術的

(D) physical〔ˈfɪzɪkḷ〕adj. 身體的

But a firefighter on hand to extinguish the frequent fires <u>sparked</u>
                                                                                                         29
<u>by</u> careless burning of ghost money was more upbeat. <u>Virtual</u>
                                                                                          30
ceremonies, he said, "would make our jobs a lot easier."

但在附近待命的一位消防隊員則比較樂觀，他是負責撲滅人們因燒紙錢不小心而經常引發的火災。他說：「虛擬儀式會讓我們的工作輕鬆一點」。

> firefighter〔ˈfaɪrˌfaɪtɚ〕n. 消防隊員　***on hand*** 在附近
>
> extinguish〔ɪkˈstɪŋgwɪʃ〕v. 撲滅
>
> frequent〔ˈfrikwənt〕adj. 經常的
>
> careless〔ˈkɛrlɪs〕adj. 粗心的；不小心的
>
> ghost〔gost〕n. 鬼
>
> ***ghost money*** 紙錢（ = *paper money* ）
>
> upbeat〔ˈʌpˌbit〕adj. 樂觀的
>
> ceremony〔ˈsɛrəˌmonɪ〕n. 儀式

29. (**D**) 空格原為 which were ***sparked by*** … ，which were 被省略，

故本題選 (D)。　spark〔spɑrk〕n. 火花　v. 引起

30. (**D**) (A) ritual〔ˈrɪtʃuəl〕adj. 儀式的

(B) visual〔ˈvɪʒuəl〕adj. 視覺的

(C) virtuous〔ˈvɝtʃuəs〕adj. 有品德的

(D) ***virtual***〔ˈvɝtʃuəl〕adj. 虛擬的

📁 PART C : **Reading**

Questions 31-35

Britain's government is considering to tackle increasing levels of obesity by imposing a so-called "fatty food tax" on foodstuffs with poor nutritional value, according to a report Thursday. Other measures being considered include standardized labeling of fat and sugar contents in processed foods, The Times said.

根據星期四的一份報告顯示，英國政府正考慮要對營養價值不高的食物，課徵所謂的「多脂肪食物稅」，以解決日益嚴重的肥胖問題。倫敦時報寫說，其他考慮實施的措施，包括在加工食品上，以標準化的方式標示脂肪和糖的含量。

consider〔kənˈsɪdɚ〕v. 考慮

tackle〔ˈtækl〕v. 處理；解決　　obesity〔oˈbisətɪ〕n. 肥胖

impose〔ɪmˈpoz〕v. 課徵；實行

so-called〔ˈsoˈkɔld〕adj. 所謂的

fatty〔ˈfætɪ〕adj. 脂肪的　　tax〔tæks〕n. 稅

foodstuff〔ˈfud,stʌf〕n. 食品

poor〔pʊr〕adj. 不好的；差的

nutritional〔njuˈtrɪʃənl〕adj. 營養的

value〔ˈvæljʊ〕n. 價值

measure〔ˈmɛʒɚ〕n. 措施　　include〔ɪnˈklud〕v. 包括

standardized〔ˈstændɚd,aɪzd〕adj. 標準化的

labeling〔ˈleblɪŋ〕n. 標示　　fat〔fæt〕n. 脂肪

content〔ˈkantɛnt〕n. 含量

processed〔ˈprasɛst〕adj. 加工的

The Times　（英國）倫敦時報　　say〔se〕v. 寫著

According to the newspaper, Prime Minister Tony Blair's official think tank has drawn up proposals to tackle consumption of unhealthy items such as burgers, potato crisps and soft drinks. In an as-yet unpublished document seen by the newspaper, the Prime Minister's Strategy Unit admitted that a rising trend toward fatness among British people was "largely outside the direct influence" of the country's health service.

根據報紙上的說法，英國首相東尼・布萊爾的官方智囊團，正在草擬一些提議，以解決攝取像是漢堡、洋芋片和清涼飲料，這些垃圾食品的問題。報上還提到，首相的策略小組在一篇至今尚未公開的文件中承認，英國人有愈來愈胖的趨勢，這已在政府衛生機構的直接影響之外。

> ***prime minister*** 首相
> official〔ə'fɪʃəl〕*adj.* 官方的　*n.* 官員
> ***think tank*** 智囊團　　***draw up*** 草擬
> proposal〔prə'pozḷ〕*n.* 提議
> consumption〔kən'sʌmpʃən〕*n.* 消耗；吃
> item〔'aɪtəm〕*n.* 項目；物品
> ***potato crisp*** 洋芋片（＝*potato chip*）
> ***soft drink*** 清涼飲料　　***as-yet*** 至今
> unpublished〔ʌn'pʌblɪʃt〕*adj.* 未公開的
> document〔'dɑkjəmənt〕*n.* 文件
> strategy〔'strætədʒɪ〕*n.* 策略
> unit〔'junɪt〕*n.* 小組；單位　　admit〔əd'mɪt〕*v.* 承認
> trend〔trɛnd〕*n.* 趨勢　　fatness〔'fætnɪs〕*n.* 肥胖
> outside〔aʊt'saɪd〕*prep.* 超出…的範圍
> direct〔də'rɛkt〕*adj.* 直接的
> ***health service*** 衛生機構

One plan could be to impose "improved regulated nutritional standards for common processed foods and drinks" to inform the public. "There might even be potential to consider fiscal measures —a 'fatty food tax' applied to food not people—or different VAT treatment for foods with poor nutritional standards," it said, referring to value added tax, a 17.5 percent sales tax imposed on certain goods in Britain. "This would be a signal to producers as well as consumers, and serve more broadly as a signal to society that nutritional content in food is important."

有個可能會實行的計畫是「改善一般加工食品及飲料的規定營養標準」，以告訴人民這些食品的營養成份。這份文件提到，「甚至也有可能會考慮施行財政措施──對食物而不是對人課徵的『多脂肪食物稅』──或是以不同的 VAT 來處理營養標準較低的食物，」VAT 指的是加值稅，英國有某些商品會多課徵百分之十七點五的貨物稅。「這對生產者和消費者而言，都是一個信號，而且在更廣的層面上，也可以作爲給社會的信號，讓人們知道，食物中的營養成分是很重要的。」

improved〔ɪm'pruvd〕*adj.* 改善的

regulated〔'rɛgjə,letɪd〕*adj.* 規定的

standard〔'stændəd〕*n.* 標準　　common〔'kɑmən〕*adj.* 一般的

inform〔ɪn'fɔrm〕*v.* 告知　　***the public*** 人民

potential〔pə'tɛnʃəl〕*n.* 可能性　　fiscal〔'fɪskḷ〕*adj.* 財政上的

apply〔ə'plaɪ〕*v.* 施用 *< to >*

VAT 加值稅（*= value added tax*）

treatment〔'tritmənt〕*n.* 處理　　refer〔rɪ'fɜ〕*v.* 指

percent〔pə'sɛnt〕*n.* 百分比　　***sales tax*** 貨物稅；銷售稅

certain〔'sɝtṇ〕*adj.* 某些的　　goods〔gudz〕*n. pl.* 商品

signal〔'sɪgnḷ〕*n.* 信號　　***as well as*** 和

consumer〔kən'sumə〕*n.* 消費者　　***serve as*** 作爲

broadly〔'brɔdlɪ〕*adv.* 寬廣地

Earlier this month, British doctors' groups urged the government to take swift action over the "terrifying health consequences" of the nation's obesity problem. A joint report by three leading medical groups warned that if nothing was done, a third of all British adults would be clinically obese by 2020, as well as a similar proportion of girls and a fifth of all boys.

在這個月月初時，英國醫師團體就催促政府，要針對全國因肥胖問題，而在「健康方面所造成的駭人結果」，採取迅速的行動。由三個主要的醫療團體所提出的聯合報告警告人們，如果再不採取任何行動，到了二〇二〇年，就有三分之一的英國成人、同樣比例的女孩，以及五分之一的男孩，在臨床上被判定是肥胖的。

urge〔ʒdʒ〕v. 催促　　swift〔swɪft〕adj. 快速的

terrifying〔'tɛrə,faɪɪŋ〕adj. 駭人的

consequence〔'kɑnsə,kwɛns〕n. 結果

joint〔dʒɔɪnt〕adj. 聯合的　　leading〔'lidɪŋ〕adj. 主要的

medical〔'mɛdɪkl̩〕adj. 醫學的　　warn〔wɔrn〕v. 警告

a third of 三分之一的～　　adult〔ə'dʌlt〕n. 成人

clinically〔'klɪnɪkl̩ɪ〕adv. 臨床上；醫學上

obese〔o'bis〕adj. 肥胖的　　similar〔'sɪmələ〕adj. 相同的

proportion〔prə'porʃən〕n. 比例　　***a fifth of*** 五分之一的～

Also Thursday, a separate report said that Britain's government planned to place health warnings on alcoholic drinks later this year. Information about the number of units of alcohol contained within a drink as well as warnings about the effects of binge drinking will be introduced, the Daily Mirror said quoting unnamed health officials.

　　同樣在星期四，另一份報告指出，英國政府計畫今年稍後，要在酒精飲料上放有關健康的警告。要標示的資訊包括酒精飲料中所含的酒精量，並警告人們狂飲作樂會帶來什麼結果，以上是每日鏡報引用不具名的衛生官員所說的話。

> separate〔'sɛpərɪt〕*adj.* 不同的
>
> place〔ples〕*v.* 放置　　warning〔'wɔrnɪŋ〕*n.* 警告
>
> alcoholic〔͵ælkə'hɑlɪk〕*adj.* 含酒精的
>
> alcohol〔'ælkə͵hɔl〕*n.* 酒精　　contain〔kən'ten〕*v.* 包含
>
> binge〔bɪndʒ〕*n.* 狂飲作樂
>
> introduce〔͵ɪntrə'djus〕*v.* 帶來；引起
>
> *the Daily Mirror* 每日鏡報　　quote〔kwot〕*v.* 引用
>
> unnamed〔ʌn'nemd〕*adj.* 不具名的

31. (**C**) 下列何者是最適合本文的主題？

    (A) 英國人向多脂肪食物宣戰了。

    (B) 課徵食物稅是必要的。

    (C) 英國正考慮一些提議來解決健康危機。

    (D) 英國衛生機構無法控制日益嚴重的肥胖程度。

    * theme〔θim〕*n.* 主題　　Brit〔brɪt〕*n.* 英國人

      declare〔dɪ'klɛr〕*v.* 宣布　　*declare war on* 宣戰

      necessity〔nə'sɛsətɪ〕*n.* 必要　　crisis〔'kraɪsɪs〕*n.* 危機

32. (**D**) 下列措施都適合用來對抗肥胖，除了

    (A) 實行財政措施。

    (B) 把營養價值更清楚地告訴人們。

    (C) 建立容易了解的標示制度。

    (D) 限制人們不能在公共場所狂飲作樂。

    * qualify〔'kwɑlə͵faɪ〕*v.* 適合　　anti- 對抗

      implement〔'ɪmplə͵mɛnt〕*v.* 實行

      establish〔ə'stæblɪʃ〕*v.* 建立

33. (**C**)　下列哪一組字最密切相關？

(A) 營養價值——標準化的標示。

(B) 食品——加工食品。

(C) 策略小組——智囊團。

(D) 尚未公開的文件——不同的報告。

* pair〔pɛr〕*n.* 一組　　related〔rɪ'letɪd〕*adj.* 相關的

34. (**B**)　本文沒有提到下列哪一個想法？

(A) 以提高費用的方式來對抗脂肪。

(B) 對光顧速食餐廳的人課稅。

(C) 在酒精飲料上放警告標語。

(D) 實行統一的標示制度，詳細說明食物的成分。

* mention〔'mɛnʃən〕*v.* 提到　　fee〔fi〕*n.* 費用

tax〔tæks〕*v.* 課稅　　patronize〔'petrən‚aɪz〕*v.* 光顧

beverage〔'bɛvərɪdʒ〕*n.* 飲料

uniform〔'junə‚fɔrm〕*adj.* 統一的　　detail〔dɪ'tel〕*v.* 詳述

35. (**C**)　下列敘述中，何者一定正確？

(A) 到了二〇二〇年，有百分之二十的英國女孩會超重。

(B) 英國的酗酒情況有日益嚴重的趨勢。

(C) 肥胖所引發的困境使許多英國醫生感到憂慮。

(D) 大型的食品製造商正在對抗針對他們而定的食物稅。

* statement〔'stetmənt〕*n.* 敘述

definitely〔'dɛfənɪtlɪ〕*adv.* 一定

overweight〔'ovə'wet〕*adj.* 超重的

alcoholism〔'ælkəhɔl‚ɪzəm〕*n.* 酗酒　　***Great Britain*** 英國

significant〔sɪg'nɪfəkənt〕*adj.* 相當數量的

physician〔fə'zɪʃən〕*n.* 醫師　　alarm〔ə'lɑrm〕*v.* 使憂慮

dilemma〔də'lɛmə〕*n.* 困境　　major〔'medʒə〕*adj.* 大型的

aim〔em〕*v.* 針對 < *at* >

Questions 36-40

Men in non-traditional jobs, such as stay-at-home dads,
are at high risk of heart disease and their chances of dying of
cardiovascular disease are greater, a study found out Wednesday.

從事非傳統職業的男性，像是家庭主夫，罹患心臟病的風險很高，
而且他們死於心血管疾病的可能性也較高，星期三揭露的報告指出。

> ***stay-at-home dad*** 家庭主夫
> risk〔rɪsk〕*n.* 風險　　***heart disease*** 心臟病
> cardiovascular〔͵kɑrdɪoˊvæskjulə〕*adj.* 心血管的
> ***find out*** 揭露；發現

The study presented to the American Heart Association's Asia
Pacific Scientific Forum in Honolulu examined whether stress
linked to certain jobs <u>translated into</u> increased heart attacks and
death, though it stopped short of establishing a direct connection.

這份報告是美國心臟協會在檀香山舉行的亞太科學論壇中所提出的，
該報告調查與某些工作有關的壓力，是否為增加心臟病發作和死亡的原
因，但該調查未能建立二者間直接的關聯。

> present〔prɪˊzɛnt〕*v.* 提出　　association〔ə͵soʃɪˊeʃən〕*n.* 協會
> Pacific〔pəˊsɪfɪk〕*adj.* 太平洋的
> scientific〔͵saɪənˊtɪfɪk〕*adj.* 科學的
> forum〔ˊforəm〕*n.* 討論會；論壇
> Honolulu〔͵hɑnəˊlulə〕*n.* 檀香山【美國夏威夷州的首府】
> examine〔ɪgˊzæmɪn〕*v.* 調查　　stress〔strɛs〕*n.* 壓力
> link〔lɪŋk〕*v.* 與…有關
> translate〔trænsˊlet〕*v.* 成為
> ***translate into*** 成為～的原因；引發（＝*cause*）
> ***heart attack*** 心臟病發作　　***stop short of Ving*** 未能～
> connection〔kəˊnɛkʃən〕*n.* 關聯

But researchers were surprised at finding a higher frequency of heart disease among those in non-traditional jobs.

Men who work in the home for the better part of their adulthood are 82 percent more likely to have a shorter life span than their <u>counterparts</u> who work outside the home, the study found.

但是研究人員感到很驚訝，因為他們發現那些從事非傳統職業的人，心臟病發作的頻率較高。

該研究發現，成年之後，大部份的時間都在家裡工作的男性，壽命較短的機率比出外工作的人高出百分之八十二。

> researcher〔rɪˈsɝtʃɚ〕n. 研究人員
> frequency〔ˈfrikwənsɪ〕n. 頻率
> ***the better part of*** …的大部份
> adulthood〔əˈdʌlthʊd〕n. 成年
> likely〔ˈlaɪklɪ〕adj. 可能的　***life span*** 壽命
> counterpart〔ˈkaʊntɚˌpart〕n. 相對應的人或物

Likewise, women who work in positions commanding a great deal of authority are three times likely to suffer from heart ailments than women who do not.

同樣地，在工作崗位上握有大權的女性，可能罹患心臟疾病的機率，比沒有握有權力的女性高出三倍。

> likewise〔ˈlaɪkˌwaɪz〕adv. 同樣地
> position〔pəˈzɪʃən〕n. 職位
> command〔kəˈmænd〕v. 要求；得到
> ***a great deal of*** 許多的
> authority〔əˈθɔrətɪ〕n. 權力　　time〔taɪm〕n. 倍
> suffer〔ˈsʌfɚ〕v. 罹患　　ailment〔ˈelmənt〕n. 疾病

"These findings may indicate that people who perform work
or social roles incongruent with what is socially expected suffer
greater risk of heart disease and death during the 10-year study,"
said study author Elaine Eaker, of Wisconsin's Eaker
Epidemiology Enterprises.

「這些發現顯示，在這十年的研究當中，那些工作或社會角色不符
合社會期望的人，罹患心臟病且死亡的機率較大，」研究發起人愛蓮・
伊克說，他來自威斯康辛州的伊克流行病學企業。

> indicate〔ˈɪndəˌket〕v. 顯示　　perform〔pɚˈfɔrm〕v. 執行；做
> role〔rol〕n. 角色　　incongruent〔ɪnˈkɑŋgruənt〕adj. 不合的
> expect〔ɪkˈspɛkt〕v. 期望　　author〔ˈɔθɚ〕n. 發起人
> epidemiology〔ˌɛpɪˌdimɪˈɑlədʒɪ〕n. 流行病學
> enterprise〔ˈɛntɚˌpraɪz〕n. 企業

"Perhaps those men and women on the cutting edge of social
roles and norms change with time, and it is hoped that the harmful
effects of having jobs or social roles that are considered outside
the norm will be diminished." Men holding jobs considered
prestigious, such as physicians, lawyers, architects or engineers,
have less risk of heart disease, the report said.

「或許那些在社會角色和標準上，具有領先優勢的男女，會隨著時
間改變，而且我們希望，那些因為被認為擁有不合標準的工作或社會角
色，而帶來的不良影響會減少。」該研究指出，從事有名望的工作的男
性，像是醫生、律師、建築師或工程師，患心臟病的風險較低。

> ***cutting edge*** 領先的優勢　　norm〔nɔrm〕n. 標準
> harmful〔ˈharmfəl〕adj. 有害的　　diminish〔dəˈmɪnɪʃ〕v. 減少
> hold〔hold〕v. 擁有　　prestigious〔prɛsˈtɪdʒɪəs〕adj. 有名望的
> lawyer〔ˈlɔjɚ〕n. 律師　　architect〔ˈɑrkəˌtɛkt〕n. 建築師
> engineer〔ˌɛndʒəˈnɪr〕n. 工程師

36. (**B**) 在第七行的 "translate into" 意思是？

(A) 把文字變成另一種語言。

(B) 導致另一種結果

(C) 解出某種神祕的密碼

(D) 擔任口譯者

* phrase〔frez〕 *n.* 片語

account for 說明；成為～之因；導致

effect〔ə'fɛkt〕 *n.* 結果　decipher〔dɪ'saɪfə〕 *v.* 解（碼）

mysterious〔mɪs'tɪrɪəs〕 *adj.* 神祕的

code〔kod〕 *n.* 密碼　interpreter〔ɪn'tɜprɪtə〕 *n.* 口譯者

37. (**C**) 第十四行的 "counterparts" 是指？

(A) specialist〔'spɛʃəlɪst〕 *n.* 專家

(B) 女性

(C) 男性

(D) patient〔'peʃənt〕 *n.* 病人

* refer〔rɪ'fɜ〕 *v.* 是指＜ *to* ＞

38. (**D**) 根據這份報告，為什麼從事非傳統職業的人，得心臟病的風險較高？

(A) 他們錢賺得少，生活過得比較不快樂。

(B) 他們是完美主義者，而且對每件事都胸懷大志。

(C) 他們的社會地位較低，而常被嘲笑。

(D) 他們的工作被認為是不合標準的，所以承受很大的壓力。

* jobholder〔'dʒɑb,holdə〕 *n.* 擁有固定工作的人

earn〔ɜn〕 *v.* 賺取　lead〔lid〕 *v.* 過（某種生活）

perfectionist〔pə'fɛkʃənɪst〕 *n.* 完美主義者

aim〔em〕 *v.* 以…為目標　status〔'stetəs〕 *n.* 地位

laugh at 嘲笑　***under pressure*** 承受壓力

39. (**D**) 根據本文，對女性來說，哪一種工作可能會被視爲非傳統的？

(A) 幼稚園老師。

(B) 公司的記帳員。

(C) 銀行出納員。

(D) 企業總裁。

* kindergarten〔ˈkɪndəˌgɑrtn̩〕*n.* 幼稚園
bookkeeper〔ˈbʊkˌkipə〕*n.* 記帳員
teller〔ˈtɛlə〕*n.* 出納員
CEO 總裁（*= chief executive officer*）

40. (**B**) 下列敘述，何者不正確？

(A) 這個研究在檀香山一場討論會中被公布。

(B) 擔任管理職位的女性，得心臟病的風險比家庭主婦來得低。

(C) 研究人員尚未建立，來自非傳統職業的壓力，和心血管疾
病之間的直接關聯。

(D) 傳統上，男性被認爲應該要出外工作。

* **make public** 公布
managerial〔ˌmænəˈdʒɪrɪəl〕*adj.* 管理的
suppose〔səˈpoz〕*v.* 認爲

Questions 41-45

For Taipei animal lovers who want a salubrious final resting
place for the family pooch, help is at hand. The Peaceful Pet
Garden of Happiness provides funeral, cremation and ash storage
services of a kind normally reserved for humans, complete with
complimentary sticks of incense and stacks of "ghost money" to
finance the pet's after-life activities.

對台北的動物愛好者而言，想要給家犬一個健康的墓地，幫手來了。和平寵物安樂園提供通常是專門留給人類的葬禮、火葬和骨灰保管等服務，還包括免費的香，以及支付寵物死後活動開支的大量「冥紙」。

salubrious〔sə'lubrɪəs〕adj. 有益健康的　　***resting place*** 墳墓
pooch〔putʃ〕n. 狗　　***at hand*** 在近處；即將到來
peaceful〔'pisfəl〕adj. 和平的　　pet〔pɛt〕n. 寵物
Garden of Happiness 安樂園　　provide〔prə'vaɪd〕v. 提供
funeral〔'fjunərəl〕n. 葬禮　　cremation〔krɪ'meʃən〕n. 火葬
ash〔æʃ〕n. 骨灰　　storage〔'storɪdʒ〕n. 儲存；保管
normally〔'nɔrml̩ɪ〕adv. 通常
reserve〔rɪ'zɝv〕v. 把⋯專門留給
complete with 包括（ = including ）
complimentary〔ˌkɑmplə'mɛntərɪ〕adj. 免費的
stick〔stɪk〕n. 一柱（香）
incense〔'ɪnsɛns〕n. （供神所焚燒的）香
stacks〔stæks〕n. pl. 大量
finance〔'faɪnæns〕v. 支付費用　　***after-life*** 死後的生活；來生

　　In the facility's memorial room, more than 1,000 urns can be found, each with a photograph of the animal in happier days. Regal-looking <u>felines</u> recline on comfortable armchairs, while dogs of a staggering variety of sizes and shapes romp on rare pieces of Taipei green space.　Many urns are also surrounded with mementoes of the pet's corporeal existence; small home-made tombstones and Buddhist icons compete with collars and well-chewed tennis balls.

　　在這座設施的追思堂，可以發現一千多個骨灰罈，每個骨灰罈上面都有一張寵物很快樂的照片。像帝王一樣的貓，橫躺在舒適的扶手椅上，還有大小外形種類多到驚人的狗，在台北少見的綠地上嬉戲。許多骨灰罈還被寵物生前的紀念品所環繞著；自製的小墓碑和佛像，對抗項圈和被咬爛的網球。

facility〔fə'sɪlətɪ〕*n.* 設施

memorial〔mə'morɪəl〕*adj.* 紀念的；追悼的

urn〔ɜn〕*n.* 骨灰罈   regal〔'rigl〕*adj.* 似王者的；帝王的

feline〔'filaɪn〕*n.* 貓   recline〔rɪ'klaɪn〕*v.* 橫躺

armchair〔'arm,tʃɛr〕*n.* 扶手椅

staggering〔'stægərɪŋ〕*adj.* 驚人的

variety〔və'raɪətɪ〕*n.* 種類   shape〔ʃep〕*n.* 外形

romp〔ramp〕*v.* 嬉戲   rare〔rɛr〕*adj.* 少見的

piece〔pis〕*n.* 片；塊   surround〔sə'raund〕*v.* 環繞

memento〔mɪ'mɛnto〕*n.* 紀念品；遺物

corporeal〔kɔr'porɪəl〕*adj.* 有形的

existence〔ɪg'zɪstəns〕*n.* 存在

homemade〔'hom'med〕*adj.* 自製的

tombstone〔'tum,ston〕*n.* 墓碑

icon〔'aɪkan〕*n.* 肖像   ***compete with*** 與～競爭；對抗

collar〔'kalə〕*n.* 項圈   well-chewed〔'wɛl'tʃud〕*adj.* 被咬爛的

The services are not limited to dogs and cats. Rabbits, birds, several fish, three monkeys, a ferret and even a large iguana are pictured. "If it fits in the incinerator we'll accept it," says cemetery owner, Mr. Wu, who adds that some customers visit once or twice a week to honor their pets' remains.

這些服務不限於狗和貓。照片裡還有兔子、鳥、一些魚，以及三隻猴子、一隻雪貂，甚至還有一隻大鬣蜥。「只要能裝進焚化爐裡的，我們就會接受，」墓園所有者吳先生說，他還說，有些顧客一週會來一兩次，向寵物的遺體致意。

ferret〔'fɛrɪt〕*n.* 雪貂   iguana〔ɪ'gwanə〕*n.* 鬣蜥

picture〔'pɪktʃə〕*v.* 畫；拍攝   fit〔fɪt〕*v.* 把…放入

incinerator〔ɪn'sɪnə,retə〕*n.* 焚化爐   add〔æd〕*v.* 又說

honor〔'anə〕*v.* 致敬   remains〔rɪ'menz〕*n. pl.* 遺體

There are two Buddhist shrines in the room. "Not all our customers are Buddhist, though," says Wu. "All kinds of people come here, including Japanese, Americans and Canadians. Taiwanese people have traditionally treated pets like a commodity, something you can buy and then just throw away," he says. "More and more Taiwanese are beginning to realize the value of animals."

在追思堂裡有兩座佛堂。「不過我們的顧客並非全是佛教徒。」吳先生說。「各式各樣的人都會來到這裡，包括日本人、美國人和加拿大人。台灣人傳統上把寵物視為一種商品，你可以買下來，然後再丟掉，」他說。「有愈來愈多的台灣人開始了解動物的價值了。」

> shrine〔ʃraɪn〕n. 聖殿　　Japanese〔ˌdʒæpəˈniz〕n. 日本人
> Canadian〔kəˈnedɪən〕n. 加拿大人
> Taiwanese〔ˌtaɪwɑˈniz〕adj. 台灣的　n. 台灣人
> treat〔trit〕v. 把…看成；對待
> commodity〔kəˈmɑdətɪ〕n. 商品

The proof is in the billing. A year's storage at the cemetery costs around US$100, with special long-term storage plans available from US$1,000.

證據就在收費。墓園一年的保管費就要美金一百元左右，特殊的長期保管計畫也有，美金一千元起跳。

> proof〔pruf〕n. 證據　　billing〔ˈbɪlɪŋ〕n. 收費
> long-term〔ˈlɔŋˌtɝm〕adj. 長期的
> available〔əˈveləbḷ〕adj. 可買到的；可獲得的

41. (**A**) 和平寵物安樂園是什麼樣的地方？

　　(A) 是寵物的殯儀館。　　　(B) 是佛堂。

　　(C) 是焚燒屍體的焚化爐。

　　(D) 是讓動物在裡面到處跑的平靜庭園。

　　* **funeral home** 殯儀館　　corpse〔kɔrps〕n. 屍體

42. (**B**) 第九行的 "felines" 是什麼意思？

    (A) 寵物   (B) 貓

    (C) 猴子   (D) 蜥蜴

    * lizard〔'lɪzəd〕*n.* 蜥蜴

43. (**D**) 下列哪一項服務不是墓園所提供的？

    (A) 可以幫你處理一切的喪葬業者。

    (B) 骨灰罈的保管場所。

    (C) 火葬用的焚化爐。

    (D) 供野餐用的大片綠地。

    * *funeral director* 承辦喪葬者   handle〔'hændḷ〕*v.* 處理

44. (**B**) 墓園會接受一隻寵物

    (A) 只要寵物的主人保證，有時候會來看他的寵物。

    (B) 只要這隻動物可以被放進焚化爐裡。

    (C) 只要寵物的主人同意要燒「冥紙」給他的寵物。

    (D) 只要寵物的主人是佛教徒。

    * *as long as* 只要   promise〔'prɑmɪs〕*v.* 保證

    only if 只要   agree〔ə'gri〕*v.* 同意

45. (**C**) 「證據就在收費。」這句話是什麼意思？

    (A) 有些人把寵物看成一種商品，並高價出售寵物。

    (B) 人們會願意替寵物付這麼高的價錢，因為他們能獲得更多利益。

    (C) 人們會願意替寵物付這麼高的價錢，因為他們知道動物的價值。

    (D) 許多人付不起這麼高的價錢，來讓寵物火葬。

    * willing〔'wɪlɪŋ〕*adj.* 願意的   benefit〔'bɛnəfɪt〕*v.* 獲益

    afford〔ə'ford〕*v.* 負擔得起   cremate〔'krimet〕*v.* 火葬

Questions 46-50

　　William Shakespeare set nearly half of his works in Italy. Now the city of Rome is honoring the playwright by building a faithful replica of the 16th century Globe Theater, where his most famous plays were shown.

　　威廉・莎士比亞的著作中，有將近一半的背景設定在義大利。現在，羅馬城爲了向這位劇作家致敬，建造了一座十六世紀的環球戲院的逼眞複製品，莎士比亞最有名的作品都是在那裡上演的。

> William Shakespeare〔ˈwɪljəm ˈʃekˌspɪr〕n. 莎士比亞【英國
> 　劇作家、詩人】　　set〔sɛt〕v. 設定背景　n. 佈景
> work〔wɝk〕n. 作品　　playwright〔ˈpleˌraɪt〕n. 劇作家
> faithful〔ˈfeθfəl〕adj. 如實的；逼眞的
> replica〔ˈrɛplɪkə〕n. 複製品　　play〔ple〕n. 戲劇
> show〔ʃo〕v. 上演

　　Starting in October, spectators can lend their ears to the Bard's masterpieces in a round, wooden theater amid the crickets and greenery of the Villa Borghese, one of the city's public parks.

　　從十月開始，觀衆們可以在圓形的木造戲院中，聆聽莎士比亞的傑作，而且同時還置身於蟋蟀的叫聲和綠葉中，這座戲院位於波各塞莊園，是羅馬的公園之一。

> spectator〔ˈspɛktetɚ〕n. 觀衆　　***lend** one's **ears to*** 聆聽
> ***the Bard** (**of Avon**)* 阿文河畔的詩人【指莎士比亞】
> masterpiece〔ˈmæstɚˌpis〕n. 傑作　　round〔raʊnd〕adj. 圓的
> wooden〔ˈwʊdn̩〕adj. 木造的　　amid〔əˈmɪd〕prep. 在…中
> cricket〔ˈkrɪkɪt〕n. 蟋蟀　　greenery〔ˈgrinərɪ〕n. 綠葉
> villa〔ˈvɪlə〕n. 莊園

The setting couldn't be more appropriate: A few kilometers away is the Roman Forum, where Shakespeare's Mark Anthony pleaded "lend me your ears" to his fellow citizens as he spoke over Julius Caesar's murdered body.

這個背景再適合不過了：幾公里外就是羅馬廣場，莎士比亞筆下的馬克・安東尼，就是在那裡跨過凱撒被謀殺的屍體，懇求他的同胞們「仔細聽我說」。

> setting〔'sɛtɪŋ〕*n.* 佈景；背景
> appropriate〔ə'proprɪɪt〕*adj.* 適合的
> forum〔'forəm〕*n.* 廣場
> plead〔plid〕*v.* 懇求　　***lend me your ears*** 仔細聽我說
> fellow〔'fɛlo〕*adj.* 同伴的；同類的
> citizen〔'sɪtəzn̩〕*n.* 人民　　***fellow citizen*** 同胞
> Julius Caesar〔'dʒuljəs'sizɚ〕*n.* 凱撒大帝【西元前 100-44 年，
> 　　羅馬專制君主】　　murdered〔'mɝdɚd〕*adj.* 被謀殺的
> body〔'badɪ〕*n.* 屍體

"It's a great cultural initiative and, at the same time, a tribute to such an important structure," the theater's project manager, Giuseppe Viggiano, said Friday.

「這是一項偉大的文化創舉，同時對這麼重要的建築物來說，也是一種讚許。」該戲院的企劃經理 Giuseppe Viggiano 星期五這樣說。

> initiative〔ɪ'nɪʃɪˌetɪv〕*n.* 創舉
> tribute〔'trɪbjut〕*n.* 貢品；讚許
> structure〔'strʌktʃɚ〕*n.* 建築物
> project〔'pradʒɛkt〕*n.* 企劃

"We needed a theater like this in Italy," Viggiano added. "A theater of words, where actors will be able to express themselves only with their voice and acting, without sets, lights or microphones, just as the theater was in its origins."

「我們在義大利需要有這樣一座戲院，」Viggiano 又說。「這是一座全靠台詞的戲院，演員們只能透過聲音和演技來表達，沒有佈景、燈光或麥克風，就像這座戲院原本的樣子。」

words〔wɜdz〕 *n. pl.* 台詞　　express〔ɪk'sprɛs〕 *v.* 表達
***express** oneself* 表達自己的意思　　acting〔'æktɪŋ〕 *n.* 演技
microphone〔'maɪkrə,fon〕 *n.* 麥克風
origin〔'ɔrədʒɪn〕 *n.* 開始；起源

The wooden structure will open Oct. 15 with Romeo and Juliet, the classic tale of doomed love set in the northern town of Verona.

這座木造建築將在十月十五日開演，戲碼是「羅密歐與茱麗葉」，這是一齣經典的愛情悲劇，背景在義大利北部的維羅納這個城市。

Romeo and Juliet 羅密歐與茱麗葉【莎士比亞戲劇】
classic〔'klæsɪk〕 *adj.* 經典的　　tale〔tel〕 *n.* 故事
doomed〔dumd〕 *adj.* 不幸的

Although it is not clear whether Shakespeare, who lived from 1564 to 1616, ever visited Italy, almost half his plays are set in cities and landscapes scattered throughout <u>the boot-shaped peninsula</u>. The original Globe is believed to have opened with a performance of Julius Caesar set in ancient Rome.

　　雖然不是很確定活在一五六四年到一六一六年間的莎士比亞，是否曾經去過義大利，但是他有一半的劇作，背景是設定在散佈於這座馬靴型半島上的城市和風景。一般相信，原本的環球戲院開演的戲碼是「凱撒大帝」，該齣戲的背景是設定在古羅馬。

> landscape〔'lænskep〕*n.* 風景
> scatter〔'skætɚ〕*v.* 分散
> throughout〔θru'aʊt〕*prep.* 遍及
> boot-shaped〔'but'ʃept〕*adj.* 馬靴型的
> peninsula〔pə'nɪnsələ〕*n.* 半島
> original〔ə'rɪdʒənḷ〕*adj.* 原本的
> performance〔pɚ'fɔrməns〕*n.* 上演

A faithful replica of the Bard's playhouse was opened in London in 1996 on the banks of the river Thames, just a few hundred meters from where the original stood.

　　一九九六年時，在倫敦的泰晤士河畔，有一座莎士比亞戲院的逼真複製品開張，它離原本的莎士比亞戲院只有幾百公尺遠。

> **the Bard's playhouse** 莎士比亞戲院【即十六世紀的環球戲院】
> playhouse〔'ple,haʊs〕*n.* 戲院　　bank〔bæŋk〕*n.* 河岸
> Thames〔tɛmz〕*n.* 泰晤士河

46.（ **C** ）關於羅馬這座新戲院，下列何者不正確？

(A) 它的形狀是圓的，而且是木造的。

(B) 舞台上沒有燈光和麥克風。

(C) 第一部上演的劇作將是凱撒大帝。

(D) 它將坐落於羅馬廣場附近的一座公園裡。

> * stage〔stedʒ〕*n.* 舞台　*v.* 上演
> 　 situated〔'sɪtʃu,etɪd〕*adj.* 坐落於…的

47. (**D**) 何謂 "playwright"？

(A) 爲一部影片所作的音樂

(B) 一家出版公司

(C) 一部影片的大卡司

(D) <u>一位劇作家</u>

* compose〔kəmˊpoz〕v. 作曲

publish〔ˊpʌblɪʃ〕v. 出版

cast〔kæst〕n. 卡司；演員陣容　　***all-star cast***　大卡司

drama〔ˊdrɑmə , ˊdræmə〕n. 戲劇

author〔ˊɔθɚ〕n. 作家

48. (**C**) 本文提到 "the Bard" 這個名詞兩次。它是指？

(A) 環球戲院　　　　　　(B) 義大利

(C) <u>威廉・莎士比亞</u>　　(D) 羅馬城

49. (**B**) 「馬靴型半島」指的是？

(A) 維羅納城　　　　　　(B) <u>義大利</u>

(C) 羅馬城　　　　　　　(D) 環球戲院

50. (**A**) 下列何者正確？

(A) <u>原本的環球戲院位於倫敦。</u>

(B) 莎士比亞來過義大利，而且第一眼就愛上它。這就是他把
　　將近一半的劇作背景設定在義大利的原因。

(C) 羅馬人似乎不歡迎興建新環球戲院。

(D) 新建的戲院是莎士比亞的環球戲院的第一個複製品。

* located〔loˊketɪd〕adj. 位於…的

glance〔glæns〕n. 一瞥　　***at first glance***　第一眼

construction〔kənˊstrʌkʃən〕n. 建築

newly〔ˊnjulɪ〕adv. 最近

全民英語能力分級檢定測驗
GENERAL ENGLISH PROFICIENCY TEST
中高級聽力測驗
HIGH-INTERMEDIATE LISTENING COMPREHENSION TEST

This listening comprehension test will test your ability to understand spoken English. In this test, each conversation, short talk and question will be spoken JUST ONE TIME. They will not be written out for you. There are three parts to this test. Special instructions will be given to you at the beginning of each part.

Part A

In part A, you will hear 15 questions. After you hear a question, read the four choices in your test book and decide which one is the best answer to the question you have heard.

Example:

You will hear: Mary, can you tell me what time it is?

You will read: A. About two hours ago.

             B. I used to be able to, but not now.

             C. Sure, it's half past nine.

             D. Today is October 22.

The best answer to the question "Mary, can you tell me what time it is?" is C: "Sure, it's half past nine." Therefore, you should choose answer C.

1. A. Their birthdays are coming soon.
   B. My grandparents are very old.
   C. Grandma and grandpa are close in age.
   D. They're both in their seventies.

2. A. The time is not accurate.
   B. I need a new watch, too.
   C. By all means, return it.
   D. Buy some more medicine.

3. A. No, I know how to drive.
   B. It sure does.
   C. Fast drivers are dangerous.
   D. It doesn't. I never drink and drive.

4. A. You are too careless.
   B. I guess I need new shoes.
   C. I guess I'm forgetful.
   D. You can never be too cautious.

5. A. I prefer low-fat ice cream.
   B. I love vanilla.
   C. I prefer candy.
   D. Everyone enjoys sweet flavors.

6. A. I have a sore throat.

   B. I have a fever today.

   C. Talk softly, please.

   D. Slow down; I can't understand you.

7. A. I don't like Chinese food.

   B. I like to prepare my own.

   C. I am a vegetarian.

   D. I don't like them.

8. A. Our store has a big sale.

   B. Would you like a magazine?

   C. I'm a new customer, too.

   D. I'm a representative. How can I help you?

9. A. No problem. I can lend you twenty.

   B. I can't borrow from the bank.

   C. Sorry, I have no spare time.

   D. Yes, I can go with you.

10. A. All my classes are filled up.

   B. I signed up for English.

   C. I'm taking five.

   D. I want to teach a few.

Please turn to the next page. ⇒

11. A. Congratulations!
    B. That's a shame.
    C. I believe in them, too.
    D. I'm sorry to say that.

12. A. Sure thing.
    B. Yes, but I can't.
    C. Sorry, I already sold it.
    D. I already have yours.

13. A. Just press the remote control.
    B. Yes, he makes me sad.
    C. That's awful news.
    D. Yes, it's very gloomy.

14. A. She is strong and courageous.
    B. I think women are clever.
    C. I think it's perfectly OK.
    D. Some people are dangerous.

15. A. Since I was ten years old.
    B. I plan to study English forever.
    C. It takes years to be fluent.
    D. Since the day after I was born.

Part B

In part B, you will hear 15 conversations between a man and a woman. After each conversation, you will hear a question about the conversation. After you hear the question, read the four choices in your test book and choose the best answer to the question you have heard.

Example:

You will hear: (Man)　　May I see your driver's license?

(Woman) Yes, officer. Here it is. Was I speeding?

(Man)　　Yes, ma'am. You were doing sixty in a forty-five-mile-an-hour zone.

(Woman) No way! I don't believe you.

(Man)　　Well, it is true and here is your ticket.

Question: Why does the man ask for the woman's driver's license?

You will read: A.　She was going too fast.

B.　To check its limitations.

C.　To check her age.

D.　She entered a restricted zone.

The best answer to the question "Why does the man ask for the woman's driver's license?" is A: "She was going too fast." Therefore, you should choose answer A.

Please turn to the next page. ⏩

16. A. Forgive his debt.
    B. Give him more time to repay.
    C. Forget about his repaying.
    D. Give him one more day.

17. A. She's disappointed, too.
    B. She is bummed out about him.
    C. She is impressed by his dedication.
    D. She is surprised by the cancellation.

18. A. Impolite and humorous.
    B. Patient and calm.
    C. Rude and diligent.
    D. Embarrassed and apologetic.

19. A. Basketball.
    B. The long jump
    C. Track and field.
    D. Swimming.

20. A. She plans to teach a course.
    B. She wants to take an "on-line" class.
    C. She wants to attend a class.
    D. She's still not sure.

21. A. He's an architect.
    B. He's a businessman.
    C. He is a foot doctor.
    D. He's an engineer.

22. A. He stayed up all night.
    B. He did research for weeks.
    C. He met a deadline.
    D. He almost ran out of time.

23. A. She's a flatterer.
    B. She looks great in what she wears.
    C. She's a businesswoman.
    D. She's in love with a flatterer.

24. A. He's agreeing with
       the woman.
    B. He's criticizing
       women.
    C. He's trying to defend
       Kevin.
    D. He's idolizing
       Kevin.

25. A. He's a difficult
       person to deal with.
    B. He's not believable.
    C. He's both stubborn
       and trusting.
    D. He's an old
       fashioned person.

26. A. Outside the car.
    B. Inside the house.
    C. In the backyard.
    D. In the garage.

27. A. $12,000 U.S. dollars.
    B. Twelve thousand dollars.
    C. Around $1,200 U.S.
       dollars.
    D. $2,000 U.S. dollars.

28. A. He's getting upset.
    B. He's uncertain about
       ghosts.
    C. To talk about something
       else.
    D. She is being impolite.

29. A. Husband – wife.
    B. Boss – secretary.
    C. Father – daughter.
    D. Intern – student.

30. A. Accelerate.
    B. Put on his seat belt.
    C. Reduce his mileage.
    D. Slow down his speed.

Please turn to the next page. ▮⟹

Part C

In part C, you will hear several short talks. After each talk, you will hear 2 to 3 questions about the talk. After you hear each question, read the four choices in your test book and choose the best answer to the question you have heard.

Example:

<u>You will hear</u>:

Thank you for coming to this, the first in a series of seminars on the use of computers in the classroom. As the brochure informed you, there will be a total of five seminars given in this room every Monday morning from 6:00 to 7:30. Our goal will be to show you, the teachers of our schoolchildren, how the changing technology of today can be applied to the unchanging lessons of yesterday to make your students' learning experience more interesting and relevant to the world they live in. By the end of the last seminar, you will not be computer literate, but you will be able to make sense of the hundreds of complex words and technical terms related to the field and be aware of the programs available for use in the classroom.

Question number 1: What is the subject of this seminar series?

You will read: A. Self-improvement.
              B. Using computers to teach.
              C. Technology.
              D. Study habits of today's students.

The best answer to the question "What is the subject of this seminar series?" is B: "Using computers to teach." Therefore, you should choose answer B.

Now listen to another question based on the same talk.

You will hear:

Question number 2: What does the speaker say participants will be able to do after attending the seminars?

You will read: A. Understand today's students.
              B. Understand computer terminology.
              C. Motivate students.
              D. Deal more confidently with people.

The best answer to the question "What does the speaker say participants will be able to do after attending the seminars?" is B: "Understand computer terminology." Therefore, you should choose answer B.

Please turn to the next page. ⇨

31. A. Adults feeling sad or blue.
    B. Students or anyone away from home.
    C. All adults with nutrient problems.
    D. Anyone with physical symptoms.

32. A. Financial assistance.
    B. Fitness classes.
    C. Anger management courses.
    D. Counseling services.

33. A. secret and confidential.
    B. absolutely free.
    C. brief and successful.
    D. very inexpensive.

34. A. It's about one hundred U.S. dollars.
    B. This article doesn't mention a price.
    C. The cost varies.
    D. The price depends on the installation level.

35. A. Service repair men.
    B. Electricians.
    C. Company engineers.
    D. Customer service representatives.

36. A. A weekly magazine.
    B. A cable T.V. channel.
    C. A newspaper.
    D. An international radio station.

37. A. They are all native.
    B. All have journalism
       degrees.
    C. They also subscribe to
       Asia News.
    D. They have won awards.

38. A. A water machine.
    B. A beverage machine.
    C. A coffee machine.
    D. A hot cocoa machine.

39. A. Someone dispensing the
       machine.
    B. Someone might get
       burned or scalded.
    C. Employees breaking the
       machine.
    D. Employees were psyched.

40. A. Stand under a solid
       doorway.
    B. Take the stairway,
       and flee the
       building.
    C. Get under a
       well-built table.
    D. Stay put, and seek
       sturdy protection.

41. A. In elevators.
    B. Outside next to
       buildings.
    C. Near electrical
       appliances.
    D. In a car in a tunnel.

Please turn to the next page. ⏩

42. A. They help you switch jobs.
    B. They help you to tow your car.
    C. They provide travel and health insurance.
    D. They pack and transport households.

43. A. From the front door to the back door.
    B. From door to door in each room.
    C. From the old location to the new location.
    D. From east to west or from north to south.

44. A. Eat right to stay healthy.
    B. You eat only what you like to eat.
    C. Eat junk and you'll be junk.
    D. Be responsible and avoid candy.

45. A. A vegetable salad.
    B. A fish sandwich.
    C. A slice of chocolate cake.
    D. Whole wheat bread.

-The End-

中高級閱讀測驗

HIGH-INTERMEDIATE

READING COMPREHENSION TEST

This test has three parts, with 50 multiple-choice questions (each with four choices) in total. Special directions will be provided for each part. You will have 50 minutes to complete this test.

Part A: Sentence Completion

This part of the test has 15 incomplete sentences. Beneath each sentence, you will see four words or phrases, marked A, B, C and D. You are to choose the word or phrase that best completes the sentences. Then on your answer sheet, find the number of the question and mark your answer.

1. Going on someone else's property without permission is considered _____ and is punishable by law.
   A. harassment
   B. trespassing
   C. embezzlement
   D. plagiarism

Please turn to the next page. ▯⟹

2. Our school held a seminar on environmental conservation and invited several _____ scholars to deliver lectures concerning this topic.
   A. expedient
   B. disinfected
   C. extinguished
   D. distinguished

3. According to a postmortem examination, the victim was _____ to death.
   A. strangled
   B. straightened
   C. stranded
   D. strengthened

4. In the story, the woman had lived in the neighborhood from the _____ to the grave. All her life, she had never left her hometown.
   A. shrine
   B. cradle
   C. canyon
   D. sanctuary

5. Chameleons are good at _____ their surroundings by changing the color of their skins.
   A. mirroring
   B. minimizing
   C. mimicking
   D. mingling

6. The more renowned he became, the lower _____ he presented. He didn't want to create a commotion.
   A. profile
   B. document
   C. transcript
   D. presentation

7. I was _____ grateful for your kind and generous help.
   A. profoundly
   B. profitably
   C. progressively
   D. prolifically

8. The plan he proposed sounded too perfect to be _____ to me.
   A. feverish
   B. feeble
   C. fictional
   D. feasible

Please turn to the next page. ⟹

9. After the war, a new city _____ of the old.
   A. rose to the bait
   B. rose with the lark
   C. rose from the ashes
   D. rose from the dust

10. You've got to _____ your own responsibility. Nobody will take it for you.
   A. lead up to
   B. face up to
   C. fire up
   D. roll up

11. " _____ in this town?" "I think Mr. Lin is the richest man in town."
   A. Whom do you think is the richest man
   B. Who do you think is the richest man
   C. Do you think who is the richest man
   D. Who you think is the richest man

12. About three-fourths of the group agreed to join the hike, and the remainder _____ stay at the hotel.
   A. were going to
   B. have been to
   C. was going to
   D. is have to

13. Doctoral students who are preparing to take their qualifying examinations have been studying in the library every night _____ the last three months.

   A. since

   B. for

   C. ago

   D. before

14. _____ are fed into a tape recorder, they magnetize the particles on the tape in varying patterns.

   A. Electric waves

   B. Electric waves that

   C. Because of electric waves

   D. When electric waves

15. She has been suffering from a kind of disease, _____.

   A. the cure for which is now possible

   B. whose cure is a recent recovery

   C. whose cure is unable

   D. the cure which is now be done

Please turn to the next page. ⇨

Part B: Cloze

This part of the test has two passages. Each passage contains five or ten missing words or phrases. There is a total of 15 missing words or phrases. Beneath each passage, you will see five or ten items with four choices, marked A, B, C and D. You are to choose the best answer for each missing word or phrase in the two passages. Then, on your answer sheet, find the number of the question and mark your answer.

<u>Questions 16-20</u>

The groundbreaking movie "Brokeback Mountain" will break even more ground, coming out for sale as a digital file online on the same day it's ___(16)___ on DVD, part of a move announced by half a dozen studios to sell movies online.

Twentieth Century Fox and the joint owners of Movielink— MGM, ___(17)___ Pictures, Sony Pictures, Universal and Warner Bros.—will offer their movies through Movielink. Sony also announced a deal with CinemaNow. The sites have traditionally allowed consumers to download movies for viewing over a 24-hour ___(18)___.

The move comes amid a slowdown of DVD sales and greater ease of illegal movie down-loading on high-speed Internet connections. But consumers could end up paying US$20 to US$30, in some cases more than the price of a DVD, and won't be able to burn discs for viewing on DVD players.

R

Movie executives said they're ___(19)___ consumers' demand by offering the service. "Basically what we're trying to do is to allow a consumer to build a digital library for the first time," said Jim Ramo, chief executive of Movielink, in a teleconference call Monday. "You can imagine now that a customer can have ___(20)___ 50 movies." Rick Finkelstein, president and chief operating officer of Universal Pictures, said, "It furthers our goal of providing consumers with our content whenever, however, and wherever they want it."

16. A. relieved
    B. released
    C. retreated
    D. recruited

17. A. Paramount
    B. Paradise
    C. Parachute
    D. Parallel

18. A. interval
    B. series
    C. period
    D. channel

19. A. subscribing to
    B. contributing to
    C. sticking to
    D. responding to

20. A. on a laptop
    B. a laptop of
    C. a laptop
    D. a laptop on

Please turn to the next page. ⟹

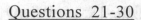

Questions 21-30

Thirty-three people were injured as they ___(21)___ a simulated emergency on Airbus' new A380 jetliner. The company said one man broke his leg and 32 other people suffered minor injuries during the exercise ___(22)___ 853 passengers and 20 crew exited the plane on slides in a darkened hangar. Some of the injured suffered friction burns from ___(23)___ the escape ramps, Airbus spokesman Tore Prang said.

___(24)___ the injuries, Airbus said the plane passed its test, with everybody out of the super-jumbo in about 80 seconds. "That was a very great success," Airbus manager Gustav Humbert said after the test at its factory in the north German city of Hamburg. The company had said that ___(25)___ 650 people out of the plane within 90 seconds would have been enough to meet safety ___(26)___.

Construction problems have delayed the introduction of the double-deck A380, the largest passenger plane in the world. ___(27)___, 16 customers have ordered 159 of the planes, and the first samples are to go to Singapore Airlines at the end of the year. ___(28)___ the plane's 16 exits, only eight were used in the drill, which was ___(29)___ in order for the A380 to receive its safety certification, Prang said.

Though the simulation was conducted inside a hangar, he said, Airbus sought to make it as realistic as possible, strewing debris in the aisles. Air safety officials were ___(30)___ to observe the simulation.

21. A. took notice of
    B. took hold of
    C. went in for
    D. went back on

22. A. which
    B. that
    C. what
    D. in which

23. A. sliding down
    B. leaping over
    C. scrambling over
    D. strolling around

24. A. Since
    B. Through
    C. Despite
    D. Though

25. A. brought
    B. bringing
    C. bring
    D. having bringing

26. A. inquiries
    B. requirements
    C. acquisitions
    D. equations

27. A. So far
    B. By and by
    C. Before long
    D. As yet

28. A. For
    B. On
    C. Of
    D. By

29. A. marginal
    B. magnetic
    C. mandatory
    D. manageable

30. A. by hand
    B. off hand
    C. out of hand
    D. on hand

Please turn to the next page. ▐◻⟹

Part C: Reading

In this part of the test, you will read several passages. Each passage is followed by several questions. There is a total of 20 questions. You are to choose the best answer, A, B, C or D, to each question on the basis of what is stated or implied in the passage. Then on your answer sheet, find the number of the question and mark your answer.

<u>Questions 31-36</u>

Golf is a game, a game of skill and patience. One that frustrates great athletes like Michael Jordan and very good athletes like my son and formerly mediocre athletes like myself. It is written that one-third of new golfers give it up after three years. Golf even frustrates Tiger Woods. Watch him <u>shake his head and mutter all day</u> on his way to another championship.

So what kind of fatal attraction does it have? What draws these tens of millions of people? What attracts Bill Clinton and Celine Dion and Kenny G.? Many things. It is the only sport with carts and cocktails. I'd still play basketball if you could use carts. When you're young, you compete in football, baseball, basketball and other games where the ball moves and so do you. As you get older you either choose doubles tennis, where you don't move, or golf, where the ball doesn't. Or you sit back and watch other people play these games on television. I predict that sumo wrestling will become the next big sport for aging baby boomers because it actually requires participants to be fat and each bout usually lasts about three seconds.

Friends always ask me to play with them, saying, incorrectly, that I couldn't possibly be as bad as I claim to be. They contend it doesn't even matter if I'm bad, so long as I just keep hitting the ball and don't hold them up. They speak of the fragrance of freshly mown grass, the sparkle of the morning dew, animals scampering across the fairways, the exhilaration of hitting even one fine shot, the relaxation and serenity and, perhaps most of all, the camaraderie.

I can't argue with any of that. I've had terrific times out on golf courses on beautiful days with partners who could hit bad shots and laugh about them. It's just the frustrating, maddening, impossible, merciless game I hate. But I want to see my friends, and about the only place to do that any more is on a golf course. So, steeling myself for humiliation and fearing addiction, I guess I'll have to give it a shot.

Please turn to the next page. ⟹

31. According to the author, why does golf have such a huge attraction?
    A. It frustrates athletes of all levels, whether you are great, good, or mediocre.
    B. Even older people can play it because they can ride a cart on the golf course and save much energy without having to walk.
    C. Friends always ask the author to join them in golf.
    D. The author thinks himself not energetic enough for other sports.

32. When might Tiger Woods "shake his head and mutter all day"?
    A. when he made a lousy shot
    B. when he made an excellent shot
    C. when he won a championship
    D. when he played a winning game

33. When you're young, you compete in football, baseball, basketball and other games where the ball moves and so do you. Which of the following about this sentence is NOT true?
    A. Young men enjoy running and chasing the ball.
    B. Young men like to take part in competitive ball games.
    C. Young men tend to be vigorous enough to run with the ball.
    D. Strenuous ball games like football, baseball and basketball are suitable for young men.

34. What doesn't the author say about "sumo wrestling"?
    A. The participants have to be fat.
    B. Most rounds last three seconds.
    C. It is appropriate for aging and fat people.
    D. The participants don't have to move.

35. Which of the following is NOT an argument mentioned by the author's friends for golf?
    A. the elation of hitting a nice shot
    B. the leisure and serene atmosphere on the freshly mown green
    C. the frustration of hitting lousy shots and being mocked
    D. the sparkle of the morning dew and the company of friends

36. What does the last sentence "steeling myself for humiliation" mean?
    A. strengthening myself to be prepared to be humiliated
    B. making myself stonyhearted against compassion and patience
    C. causing myself to become terribly humiliated
    D. making myself scared of facing humiliation

Please turn to the next page.

Questions 37-41

Taiwan baseball fans and observers were shocked to see their team being easily beaten by historic rivals from Korea and Japan at the preliminary round in Tokyo. They were awed by the Korean nine's flawless performance in defeating Japan's dream team twice in a row at Tokyo and Anaheim. But Team Japan's fighting spirit, perseverance and skills that enabled it to crush the once "unbeatable Cubans" and win the first championship of the 2006 World Baseball Classic were the most admirable and inspiring.

The WBC served as a mirror to Taiwan baseball, which has ceased to improve since a dozen years ago when gambling and game fixing became rampant and the baseball leadership was undermined by <u>mercantilism</u>. Once there were two professional leagues, each with six teams, but the island's annual crop of qualified new players numbered less than 10, and few of them had much international experience. Gone were the days when there was at least one international little league tournament every summer and an invitation championship journey every winter; six to eight teams from top baseball countries came to show skills.

Taiwan has big-name players in America's MLB and Japan's Central and Pacific Leagues. Sadaharu Oh, manager of the victorious Japanese Team, still carries a Republic of China passport. But Taiwan couldn't form a dream team. Why?

37. How did baseball fans in Taiwan feel about the performance of Team Chinese Taipei in the 2006 World Baseball Classic?
   A. They were overwhelming.
   B. They were impressed.
   C. They were inspired.
   D. They were disappointed.

38. What does the author think of the development of baseball in Taiwan?
   A. It remains very competitive in international games.
   B. It has made no further progress after scandals happened years ago.
   C. Every year top teams come from abroad to show skills.
   D. It is well qualified to participate in any kind of big tournament in the world.

39. What does "mercantilism" in line 13 probably mean?
   A. commercialism
   B. materialism
   C. enthusiasm
   D. skepticism

Please turn to the next page. ⟹

40. What adverse news concerning baseball in Taiwan is mentioned in the article?

   A. The Japanese Team won the championship in the 2006 WBC.

   B. The scandal of gambling and game fixing happened among the baseball leagues.

   C. At least one international game is held in Taiwan every year.

   D. Mr. Oh, despite being manager of the Team Japan, is still Taiwanese by nationality.

41. Which of the following is NOT a reason why Taiwan can't form a dream team?

   A. Famous players from Taiwan in overseas professional baseball teams.

   B. Insufficient international experience.

   C. Lack of excellent leadership.

   D. A limited number of well-qualified players.

Questions 42-46

   Believe in the healing power of touch. A friendly embrace. A backrub. The ways we show affection can also keep us healthy. Sure, a massage is relaxing, and always feels great— it's also good for you. Massage has been shown to relieve pain and anxiety, ease depression and speed recovery from medical treatment.

"The benefits of touch show up at almost every age," says psychologist Tiffany Field, who directs the Touch Research Institute at the University of Miami School of Medicine. Premature infants who are held often develop faster than those left alone, and healthy babies who get lots of physical contact cry less and sleep better.

How touch delivers such benefits is unclear, though researchers have documented its ability to slow heart rate, lower blood pressure and increase levels of serotonin, the brain chemical that's linked to a feeling of well-being. It also decreases levels of the stress hormone cortisol, which can boost immunity.

Massage can even hasten healing. At the University of Colorado Health Sciences Center, bone-marrow transplant patients given massages had better neurological function than those in a control group. And researchers in Sweden reported that massage reduced pain by 37 percent in patients with fibromyalgia, a condition characterized by chronic muscle aches.

Giving may be as good as receiving: A study at England's Queen Charlotte's and Chelsea Hospital found that mothers suffering from postpartum depression who massaged their infants related better to them. In another study, elderly

Please turn to the next page.

volunteers who massaged infants reported feeling less anxious and depressed. It even works when you do it yourself: A 1999 study found that smokers who were taught self-massage while trying to quit felt less anxiety and smoked less. A study by Italian researchers found that 43 percent of patients with tension headaches reported massaging their temples and necks to get relief. To try it, apply moderate pressure to your temples, hands, feet or the back of your neck.

42. What is a "premature baby"?
    A. a baby who cries a lot
    B. a baby who is born in due course
    C. a baby who is born too early
    D. a baby who is touched and held often

43. What will happen if the levels of serotonin are increased?
    A. A person's immunity will be boosted.
    B. A person's muscle aches will decrease.
    C. A person will feel more stressed-out.
    D. A person will be happier and feel better about himself.

44. Which of the following belongs to a control group?
    A. one who is treated in the experiment
    B. one who is left untreated in the experiment
    C. one who conducts the experiment
    D. one who finances the experiment

45. According to the passage, which of the following is NOT a benefit of massage?
    A. It can relieve pain and anxiety.
    B. It can ease depression.
    C. It can bring about a feeling of well-being.
    D. It can increase your desire to smoke.

46. Which of the following is NOT true according to the article?
    A. Massage is good no matter whether you receive it, give it or even do it yourself.
    B. The healing power of touch is effective for young and old.
    C. The stress hormone cortisol can heighten one's immunity.
    D. Self-massage can also help to relieve tension.

Questions 47-50

A Mediterranean diet, rich in olive oil, fish, poultry, and fruit and vegetables, can relieve the symptoms of rheumatoid arthritis, scientists said.

Although a Mediterranean diet is usually recommended to reduce the risk of heart disease, Dr. Lars Skoldstam, of Visby Hospital in Sweden, found it reduced the pain and improved the physical function of people with rheumatoid arthritis (RA). After three months on the diet, RA patients lost about three kg

Please turn to the next page. ⟹

(6.6 lb) in weight, had lower cholesterol levels and less pain in their joints than a control group of patients who did not change their eating habits.

"The treated group felt significantly improved compared to the controls after three months with this diet," Skoldstam told Reuters.

Rheumatoid arthritis is an autoimmune disease in which the body's immune system attacks cartilage in the joints. It affects about two percent of the population but more women suffer from it than men.

Skoldstam, who reported his findings in the Annals of the Rheumatic Diseases, believes that there are connections between rheumatoid arthritis and heart disease.

47. Which of the following is NOT true about rheumatoid arthritis?
   A. The percentage of men who suffer from it is larger than that of women who do by two percent.
   B. It is a disease in which the patients are affected in the joints.
   C. Among the two percent of those suffering from it, there are more women than men.
   D. It is reported that RA is likely to be connected with heart disease.

48. How did a Mediterranean diet help the RA patients?

   A. They lost some weight.

   B. Their cholesterol levels fell.

   C. They felt less pain in their joints.

   D. All of the above.

49. What is the chief finding of this experiment?

   A. A Mediterranean diet reduces the risk of heart disease.

   B. A Mediterranean diet lessens arthritis pain.

   C. A Mediterranean diet reduces cholesterol.

   D. A Mediterranean diet reduces the risk of developing RA.

50. What is true about the experiment mentioned?

   A. The control group changed their diet and nothing happened.

   B. The experiment was carried out in Stockholm in Switzerland.

   C. The experiment lasted for about half a year.

   D. The findings were published in a journal about rheumatic disease.

-The End-

中高級聽力測驗詳解 ④

PART A

1. (**D**) How old are your grandparents?
   A. Their birthdays are coming soon.
   B. My grandparents are very old.
   C. Grandma and grandpa are close in age.
   D. They're both in their seventies.

   * grandparents〔'grænd,pɛrənts〕n. pl. 祖父母
     close〔klos〕adj. 接近的
     in one's seventies 在某人七十多歲時

2. (**C**) This new watch really itches my wrist!
   A. The time is not accurate.
   B. I need a new watch, too.
   C. By all means, return it.
   D. Buy some more medicine.

   * itch〔ɪtʃ〕v. 使發癢   wrist〔rɪst〕n. 手腕
     accurate〔'ækjərɪt〕adj. 精確的
     by all means 無論如何   return〔rɪ'tɝn〕v. 退還

3. (**B**) Does my fast driving make you uncomfortable?
   A. No, I know how to drive.
   B. It sure does.   C. Fast drivers are dangerous.
   D. It doesn't. I never drink and drive.

   * uncomfortable〔ʌn'kʌmfətəbl〕adj. 不舒服的
     dangerous〔'dendʒərəs〕adj. 危險的
     drink and drive 酒後開車

4. (**C**) Your shoelaces are always untied.

    A. You are too careless.

    B. I guess I need new shoes.

    C. I guess I'm forgetful.

    D. You can never be too cautious.

    * shoelace (ˈʃuˌles) *n.* 鞋帶
      untied (ʌnˈtaɪd) *adj.* 沒有綁起來的
      forgetful (fɚˈgɛtfəl) *adj.* 健忘的
      cautious (ˈkɔʃəs) *adj.* 謹慎的
      can never be too~ 再~也不爲過

5. (**B**) Do you prefer chocolate, vanilla, or strawberry?

    A. I prefer low-fat ice cream.

    B. I love vanilla.

    C. I prefer candy.

    D. Everyone enjoys sweet flavors.

    * prefer (prɪˈfɝ) *v.* 較喜歡   vanilla (vəˈnɪlə) *n.* 香草
      low-fat (ˈloˈfæt) *adj.* 低脂的
      flavor (ˈflevɚ) *n.* 味道

6. (**A**) What's the matter with your voice?

    A. I have a sore throat.

    B. I have a fever today.

    C. Talk softly, please.

    D. Slow down; I can't understand you.

    * ***have a sore throat*** 喉嚨痛   ***have a fever*** 發燒
      softly (ˈsɔftlɪ) *adv.* 輕聲地
      slow down 減慢 (速度)

7. (**D**) How do you feel about hot and spicy food?

    A. I don't like Chinese food.

    B. I like to prepare my own.

    C. I am a vegetarian.

    D. I don't like them.

    * spicy (ˈspaɪsɪ) *adj.* 辣的   prepare (prɪˈpɛr) *v.* 煮（菜）

    vegetarian (ˌvɛdʒəˈtɛrɪən) *n.* 素食者

8. (**D**) Hello, I'd like to talk with a customer service

    representative, please.

    A. Our store has a big sale.

    B. Would you like a magazine?

    C. I'm a new customer, too.

    D. I'm a representative. How can I help you?

    * customer (ˈkʌstəmɚ) *n.* 顧客

    service (ˈsɝvɪs) *n.* 服務

    representative (ˌrɛprɪˈzɛntətɪv) *n.* 代表

    magazine (ˌmægəˈzin) *n.* 雜誌

9. (**A**) Can you spare me twenty dollars for the weekend?

    A. No problem. I can lend you twenty.

    B. I can't borrow from the bank.

    C. Sorry, I have no spare time.

    D. Yes, I can go with you.

    * spare (spɛr) *v.* 分讓（東西）

    lend (lɛnd) *v.* 借（出）

    borrow (ˈbaro) *v.* 借（入）   ***spare time*** 休閒時間

10. (**C**) How many courses are you taking next semester?

    A. All my classes are filled up.

    B. I signed up for English.

    C. I'm taking five.

    D. I want to teach a few.

    * course〔kors〕*n.* 課程

      take〔tek〕*v.* 修（課）

      semester〔sə'mɛstə〕*n.* 學期

      fill up 填滿　　***sign up for*** 報名參加

11. (**B**) I can't believe my uncle and aunt are getting a divorce!

    A. Congratulations!

    B. That's a shame.

    C. I believe in them, too.

    D. I'm sorry to say that.

    * divorce〔də'vors〕*n.* 離婚

      congratulations〔kən,grætʃə'leʃənz〕*n. pl.* 恭喜

      shame〔ʃem〕*n.* 憾事

12. (**A**) Can you please give me your e-mail address?

    A. Sure thing.

    B. Yes, but I can't.

    C. Sorry, I already sold it.

    D. I already have yours.

    * ***e-mail address*** 電子郵件網址

      Sure thing. 當然。（ = *Of course.*）

13. (**D**) Isn't all the recent news depressing?

    A.　Just press the remote control.

    B.　Yes, he makes me sad.

    C.　That's awful news.

    D.　Yes, it's very gloomy.

    * recent (ˋrisn̩t) adj. 最近的

       depressing (dɪˋprɛsɪŋ) adj. 令人沮喪的

       press (prɛs) v. 按；壓　　***remote control*** 遙控

       awful (ˋɔfʊl) adj. 糟糕的

       gloomy (ˋglumɪ) adj. 令人沮喪的；憂鬱的

14. (**C**) What's your opinion of women in the military?

    A.　She is strong and courageous.

    B.　I think women are clever.

    C.　I think it's perfectly OK.

    D.　Some people are dangerous.

    * opinion (əˋpɪnjən) n. 意見　　military (ˋmɪlə͵tɛrɪ) n. 軍隊

       courageous (kəˋredʒəs) adj. 勇敢的

       clever (ˋklɛvɚ) adj. 聰明的

       perfectly (ˋpɝfɪktlɪ) adv. 完全地

15. (**A**) How many years have you studied English?

    A.　Since I was ten years old.

    B.　I plan to study English forever.

    C.　It takes years to be fluent.

    D.　Since the day after I was born.

    * ***plan to*** 打算～　　forever (fɚˋɛvɚ) adv. 永遠地

       fluent (ˋfluənt) adj. 流利的

PART **B**

16. (**B**) M : Hey Jenny, about the money I owe you…

　　　　 W : Oh, I thought you had forgotten.

　　　　 M : No, I haven't.　My finances have really been tight!

　　　　 W : Would you like an extension?

　　　　 M : That would really make my day!

　　　　 Question : What is the woman going to do?

　　　　 A.　Forgive his debt.

　　　　 B.　Give him more time to repay.

　　　　 C.　Forget about his repaying.

　　　　 D.　Give him one more day.

　　　　 * owe〔 o 〕 *v.* 欠　　　 finance〔 'faɪnæns 〕 *n.* 財務情況
　　　　 tight〔 taɪt 〕 *adj.* 吃緊的　　 extension〔 ɪk'stɛnʃən 〕 *n.* 延期
　　　　 make** one's **day 使成爲 (某人) 最高興的一天
　　　　 forgive〔 fɚ'gɪv 〕 *v.* 原諒　　 debt〔 dɛt 〕 *n.* 負債
　　　　 repay〔 rɪ'pe 〕 *v.* 償還

17. (**C**) W : Have you heard the meeting has been cancelled?

　　　　 M : Oh, what a bummer!　I've been looking forward to it.

　　　　 W : We'll have it next week.　Don't fret.

　　　　 M : I'm just disappointed.　The cancellation is a letdown.

　　　　 W : You really are a dedicated member.

　　　　 Question : How does the woman feel about the man?

　　　　 A.　She's disappointed, too.

　　　　 B.　She is bummed out about him.

　　　　 C.　She is impressed by his dedication.

　　　　 D.　She is surprised by the cancellation.

* cancel〔ˈkænsḷ〕v. 取消
bummer〔ˈbʌmə〕n. 令人不愉快的事物
look forward to 期待　　fret〔frɛt〕v. 使苦惱
disappointed〔͵dɪsəˈpɔɪntɪd〕adj. 失望的
cancellation〔͵kænsḷˈeʃən〕n. 取消
letdown〔ˈlɛt͵daʊn〕n. 失望
dedicated〔ˈdɛdə͵ketɪd〕adj. 專注的；奉獻的
be bummed out 灰心喪氣的
be impressed by 對～印象深刻
dedication〔͵dɛdəˈkeʃən〕n. 奉獻

18. (**D**) M : You're over an hour late. That's unacceptable!
　　　　 It's rude.

　　　　 W : Wait a minute! I can explain.

　　　　 M : I have a cell phone. Why didn't you call me?

　　　　 W : My battery was dead, and I was caught in a traffic jam.

　　　　 M : Hmmm… maybe I'm overreacting but I just hate
　　　　　 to wait for people who are late.

　　　　 Question : How would you describe the man?

　　　　 A. Impolite and humorous.

　　　　 B. Patient and calm.

　　　　 C. Rude and diligent.

　　　　 D. Embarrassed and apologetic.

　　 * unacceptable〔͵ʌnəkˈsɛptəbḷ〕adj. 不能接受的
　　　 rude〔rud〕adj. 粗魯的　　explain〔ɪkˈsplen〕v. 解釋
　　　 battery〔ˈbætərɪ〕n. 電池　　dead〔dɛd〕adj.（電池）沒電的
　　　 be caught in 遇到　　***traffic jam*** 交通阻塞
　　　 overreact〔͵ovərɪˈækt〕v. 反應過度
　　　 describe〔dɪˈskraɪb〕v. 描述

impolite〔,ɪmpə'laɪt〕adj. 無禮的
humorous〔'hjumərəs〕adj. 有幽默感的
patient〔'peʃənt〕adj. 有耐心的　　calm〔kɑm〕adj. 鎮定的
embarrassed〔ɪm'bærəst〕adj. 感到不好意思的
apologetic〔ə,pɑlə'dʒɛtɪk〕adj. 認錯的

19. (**A**) W：Did you see the game last night?

M：Oh, wasn't it amazing? It was unbelievable!

W：Yeah, that last second shot in overtime was tremendous!

M：The coach called a great play. The players executed it perfectly.

W：I'm sure the owners will renew his contract.

Question：What sport are they probably talking about?

A.　Basketball.

B.　The long jump.

C.　Track and field.

D.　Swimming.

* amazing〔ə'mezɪŋ〕adj. 令人驚奇的
unbelievable〔,ʌnbɪ'livəbl〕adj. 難以置信的
shot〔ʃɑt〕n. 投球
overtime〔'ovɚ,taɪm〕n. (比賽和局後的) 延長時間
tremendous〔trɪ'mɛndəs〕adj. 很棒的
coach〔kotʃ〕n. 教練　　call〔kɔl〕v. 發號施令
execute〔'ɛksɪ,kjut〕v. 實行
renew〔rɪ'nju〕v. 更新
contract〔'kɑntrækt〕n. 契約
the long jump 跳遠　　*track and field* 田徑

20. (**C**)　W：How do I register for classes by phone?

　　　　　M：To be honest, I have no idea.

　　　　　W：I wonder how I can find out?

　　　　　M：Why don't you call the Registrar's Office or better yet, check their website?

　　　　　W：That's excellent advice, thanks.

　　　　　Question：What is the woman's future plan?

　　　　　A.　She plans to teach a course.

　　　　　B.　She wants to take an "on-line" class.

　　　　　C.　She wants to attend a class.

　　　　　D.　She's still not sure.

　　　*　register (ˈrɛdʒɪstə) v. 登記　　***to be honest** 老實說

　　　　wonder (ˈwʌndə) v. 想知道

　　　　registrar (ˈrɛdʒɪˌstrɑr) n. 註冊組長

　　　　***the Registrar's Office** 註冊組

　　　　yet (jɛt) adv.【與比較級或最高級連用，加強語氣】甚至

　　　　excellent (ˈɛkslənt) adj. 很棒的

　　　　advice (ədˈvaɪs) n. 建議　　attend (əˈtɛnd) v. 上學；上課

21. (**D**)　M：Why did you turn down the scholarship offer?

　　　　　W：It was an engineering school. I want a career in business.

　　　　　M：Really? I thought you'd follow in your father's footsteps.

　　　　　W：Nope, I like international trade and marketing. That's where my passion lies.

　　　　　M：Wow, I wish I were as focused as you.

Question：What does the woman's father do?

A. He's an architect.

B. He's a businessman.

C. He is a foot doctor.

D. He's an engineer.

* ***turn down*** 拒絕

scholarship〔'skɑlə,ʃɪp〕*n.* 獎學金

offer〔'ɔfə〕*n.* 提供；提議

engineering〔,ɛndʒə'nɪrɪŋ〕*n.* 工程學

career〔kə'rɪr〕*n.* 職業

business〔'bɪznɪs〕*n.* 商業

follow in *one's* ***footsteps*** 繼承（某人的）志向；效法

（= *walk in one's footsteps*）

nope〔nop〕*adv.* 不

international trade 國際貿易

marketing〔'mɑrkɪtɪŋ〕*n.* 行銷

passion〔'pæʃən〕*n.* 熱情；愛好

lie〔laɪ〕*v.* 在於   focused〔'fokəst〕*adj.* 專心的

architect〔'ɑrkə,tɛkt〕*n.* 建築師

engineer〔,ɛndʒə'nɪr〕*n.* 工程師

22. (**A**) W：Did you finish up your research paper?

M：Yes, I pulled an "all-nighter," but I did it!

W：So you beat the deadline.

M：Just in the nick of time, thank God.

W：I bet you are exhausted and elated!

Question：Why is the man extremely tired?

A. He stayed up all night.

B. He did research for weeks.

C. He met a deadline.

D. He almost ran out of time.

* **finish up** 完成　　research〔ˈrisɜtʃ〕n. 研究
  pull〔pul〕v. 實行　　all-nighter〔ˈɔlˈnaɪtɚ〕n. 通宵工作
  beat〔bit〕v. 搶在～之前　　deadline〔ˈdɛdˌlaɪn〕n. 截止期限
  in the nick of time 及時
  exhausted〔ɪgˈzɔstɪd〕adj. 精疲力竭的
  elated〔ɪˈletɪd〕adj. 得意洋洋的
  extremely〔ɪkˈstrimlɪ〕adv. 極度地　　**stay up** 熬夜
  meet a deadline 趕上截止時間　　**run out of** 用完

23. (**B**) M：You're such a nice dresser. I really like your style.

W：You flatter me. What a nice compliment!

M：It's true. You always look so elegant and sharp.

W：I try to look professional.

M：That's you to a T. You should be in a magazine.

Question：What can we say about the woman?

A. She's a flatterer.

B. She looks great in what she wears.

C. She's a businesswoman.

D. She's in love with a flatterer.

* dresser〔ˈdrɛsɚ〕n. 穿著講究的人
  flatter〔ˈflætɚ〕v. 諂媚；奉承
  compliment〔ˈkɑmpləmənt〕n. 恭維
  elegant〔ˈɛləgənt〕adj. 優雅的　　sharp〔ʃɑrp〕adj. 時髦的
  professional〔prəˈfɛʃənḷ〕adj. 專業的　　**to a T** 恰好地
  flatterer〔ˈflætərɚ〕n. 奉承者　　**be in love with** 愛著

24. (**C**)　W：Kevin is such a playboy.　He's a cad.

M：I disagree.　It's women who throw themselves
at him!

W：Do you think he respects women?

M：It's not his fault he looks like Brad Pitt!　Women
are attracted to him like sharks to meat!

W：Oh brother, now I've heard everything!

Question：What is the man trying to do?

A.　He's agreeing with the woman.

B.　He's criticizing women.

C.　He's trying to defend Kevin.

D.　He's idolizing Kevin.

* playboy〔'ple,bɔɪ〕*n.* 花花公子

cad〔kæd〕*n.* 無賴；下流的男人

disagree〔,dɪsə'gri〕*v.* 不同意

***throw** oneself **at** sb.* 拼命討好某人

respect〔rɪ'spɛkt〕*v.* 尊敬　　fault〔fɔlt〕*n.* 過錯

Brad Pitt 布萊德彼特 (知名電影明星)

attract〔ə'trækt〕*v.* 吸引　　shark〔ʃɑrk〕*n.* 鯊魚

brother〔'brʌðɚ〕*n.* 老兄；朋友

Now I've heard everything. 字面上的意思是「現在我已經聽
過所有說法了。」在此有諷刺的味道，表示聽者感到很驚訝，
而且難以相信。也可說成 I don't believe it. (我不相信。)
或是 You can't mean that. (你是在開玩笑吧！)

criticize〔'krɪtə,saɪz〕*v.* 批評　　defend〔dɪ'fɛnd〕*v.* 保護

idolize〔'aɪdḷ,aɪz〕*v.* 把 (某人) 當偶像崇拜

25. (**A**)　M: Why did you skip the exam? Are you crazy?

W: No, I overslept! My alarm didn't go off.

M: You'd better hustle over to the professor's office right now.

W: I know, I hope he believes me.

M: Good luck. He's a tough nut to crack!

Question: What does the man say about the teacher?

A. He's a difficult person to deal with.

B. He's not believable.

C. He's both stubborn and trusting.

D. He's an old fashioned person.

* skip〔skɪp〕v. 不參加　crazy〔'krezɪ〕adj. 瘋狂的
oversleep〔'ovɚ'slip〕v. 睡過頭
alarm〔ə'lɑrm〕n. 鬧鐘　*go off* 響起
hustle〔'hʌsl̩〕v. 趕忙
a tough nut to crack 不好應付的人　*deal with* 對付
believable〔bɪ'livəbl̩〕adj. 值得信任的
stubborn〔'stʌbɚn〕adj. 頑固的
trusting〔'trʌstɪŋ〕adj. 輕易信任別人的
old-fashioned〔'old'fæʃənd〕adj. 跟不上時代的

26. (**B**)　W: Oh no! John, do you have the keys?

M: No, don't you?

W: Oh great! We just locked ourselves out!

M: What are we going to do?

W: Either break a window or call the locksmith.

Question: Where are the keys?

A. Outside the car.

B. Inside the house.

C. In the backyard.

D. In the garage.

* lock〔lɑk〕v. 鎖上

  either A ***or*** B 不是 A，就是 B

  locksmith〔'lɑk,smɪθ〕n. 鎖匠

  backyard〔'bæk'jɑrd〕n. 後院

  garage〔gə'rɑʒ〕n. 車庫

27. (**C**) M：Your new laptop looks awesome.

   W：Thanks, I do love it, but it cost an arm and a leg.

   M：Do you mind if I ask how much?

   W：Close to twelve hundred U.S. with all the accessories.

   M：How many years warranty do you have?

   Question：How much did the computer cost?

   A. $12,000 U.S. dollars.

   B. Twelve thousand dollars.

   C. Around $1,200 U.S. dollars.

   D. $2,000 U.S. dollars.

* laptop〔'læp,tɑp〕n. 筆記型電腦

  awesome〔'ɔsəm〕adj. 嘆為觀止的；很棒的

  cost an arm and a leg 使（人）花很多錢的

  mind〔maɪnd〕v. 介意

  close to 接近　　accessory〔æk'sɛsərɪ〕n. 配件

  warranty〔'wɔrəntɪ〕n. 保證；保固

28. (**C**)　W：Hey, do you believe in life after death?

　　　　　M：I think I do, but I'm not 100% sure.

　　　　　W：I feel the same way. It's hard to imagine.

　　　　　M：Let's change the subject, OK?

　　　　　W：Are you too superstitious to discuss it?

　　　　　Question：What is the man suggesting?

　　　　　A.　He's getting upset.

　　　　　B.　He's uncertain about ghosts.

　　　　　C.　To talk about something else.

　　　　　D.　She is being impolite.

　　　　　* imagine〔 ɪ'mædʒɪn 〕v. 想像　　subject〔'sʌbdʒɪkt 〕n. 話題
　　　　　　superstitious〔,supə'stɪʃəs 〕adj. 迷信的
　　　　　　discuss〔 dɪ'skʌs 〕v. 討論
　　　　　　uncertain〔 ʌn's3tn 〕adj. 不確定的

29. (**B**)　M：Have you seen my box full of computer disks?

　　　　　W：Yes, I filed them in computer cabinet for you.

　　　　　M：Next time, please don't do that.

　　　　　W：But you told me to label and organize them.

　　　　　M：You're right, I did. I'm just nervous about all the
　　　　　　　financial records.

　　　　　Question：What is the probable relationship here?

　　　　　A.　Husband－wife.　　　　B.　Boss－secretary.

　　　　　C.　Father－daughter.　　　D.　Intern－student.

　　　　　* disk〔 dɪsk 〕n. 磁片　　file〔 faɪl 〕v. 把～歸檔
　　　　　　cabinet〔'kæbənɪt 〕n. 櫃子　　label〔'lebl̩ 〕v. 貼標籤
　　　　　　organize〔'ɔrgə,naɪz 〕v. 整理
　　　　　　financial〔 faɪ'nænʃəl 〕adj. 財務的　　record〔'rɛkə-d 〕n. 記錄
　　　　　　relationship〔 rɪ'leʃən,ʃɪp 〕n. 關係
　　　　　　intern〔'ɪnt3n 〕n. 實習老師

30. (**D**) W：Please slow down. It's awful slippery tonight.

M：I'm only doing twenty-five, relax.

W：With these icy conditions, I'd feel better at fifteen.

M：Maybe you're right. It's really slick.

W：Thank you, darling, safety first.

Question：What is the man going to do?

A. Accelerate.

B. Put on his seat belt.

C. Reduce his mileage.

D. Slow down his speed.

* ***slow down*** 減慢   awful〔'ɔfḷ〕*adv.* 十分地

slippery〔'slɪpərɪ〕*adj.* 滑的

do〔du〕*v.* 行駛   relax〔rɪ'læks〕*v.* 放鬆

I'm only doing twenty-five, relax. 我的時速只有二十五

公里，放輕鬆。

icy〔'aɪsɪ〕*adj.* 結冰的

condition〔kən'dɪʃən〕*n.* 狀況

slick〔slɪk〕*adj.* 滑的   darling〔'dɑrlɪŋ〕*n.* 親愛的人

safety〔'seftɪ〕*n.* 安全   ***safety first*** 安全第一

accelerate〔æk'sɛlə,ret〕*v.* 加速

put on 繫上   belt〔bɛlt〕*n.* 安全帶；扣帶

seat belt 安全帶   reduce〔rɪ'djus〕*v.* 減少

mileage〔'maɪlɪdʒ〕*n.* 總英里數

speed〔spid〕*n.* 速度

📁 PART C.

Questions 31-33 are based on the following advertisement.

When you need help, Center Counseling Service is for you. At times, each of us lives through stressful periods that make us feel depressed, anxious, uncomfortable or unable to make a decision. Being away from home, far from family and friends can make these concerns even more upsetting.

The Community Services Center offers counseling services to anyone and everyone. We are open and available to all. Professional counselors provide, in strict confidence, assistance to help you deal with problems and frustrations. For more information or an appointment, contact the center.

🖥 Vocabulary.

counseling〔'kaʊnslɪŋ〕 n. 心理諮詢　　*at times* 有時候

live through 經歷　　stressful〔'strɛsfəl〕 adj. 緊張的

period〔'pɪrɪəd〕 n. 期間　　depressed〔dɪ'prɛst〕 adj. 沮喪的

anxious〔'æŋkʃəs〕 adj. 焦慮的　　*make a decision* 做決定

concerns〔kən'sɝnz〕 n. pl. 事務　　upset〔ʌp'sɛt〕 v. 使心煩

community〔kə'mjunətɪ〕 n. 社區　　offer〔'ɔfɚ〕 v. 提供

open〔'opən〕 adj. 開放的　　available〔ə'veləbḷ〕 adj. 可利用的

counselor〔'kaʊnslɚ〕 n. 顧問　　provide〔prə'vaɪd〕 v. 提供

strict〔strɪkt〕 adj. 絕對的　　confidence〔'kɑnfədəns〕 n. 秘密

in strict confidence 極機密地　　assistance〔ə'sɪstəns〕 n. 協助

deal with 處理　　frustration〔frʌs'treʃən〕 n. 挫折

appointment〔ə'pɔɪntmənt〕 n. 約會

contact〔kɑn'tækt〕 v. 與～接觸

31. (**A**) Whom does this advertisement apply to?

    A. Adults feeling sad or blue.

    B. Students or anyone away from home.

    C. All adults with nutrient problems.

    D. Anyone with physical symptoms.

    * *apply to* 適用於   blue (blu) adj. 憂鬱的

    nutrient ('njutrɪənt) adj. 營養的

    physical ('fɪzɪkḷ) adj. 身體的

    symptom ('sɪmptəm) n. 症狀

32. (**D**) What does the center offer?

    A. Financial assistance.

    B. Fitness classes.

    C. Anger management courses.

    D. Counseling services.

    * fitness ('fɪtnɪs) n. 健康   anger ('æŋgɚ) n. 生氣

    management ('mænɪdʒmənt) n. 管理

    course (kors) n. 課程

33. (**A**) The center guarantees your visit will be

    A. secret and confidential.

    B. absolutely free.

    C. brief and successful.

    D. very inexpensive.

    * guarantee (ˌgærən'ti) v. 保證   secret ('sikrɪt) adj. 祕密的

    confidential (ˌkɑnfə'dɛnʃəl) adj. 機密的

    absolutely ('æbsəˌlutlɪ) adv. 絕對地

    brief (brif) adj. 簡短的

    inexpensive (ˌɪnɪk'spɛnsɪv) adj. 便宜的

Questions 34-35 refer to these tips on how to obtain a telephone line.

To obtain a new phone or fax line is very easy. First, you must contact a local telephone office, complete their application form, produce your I.D., and any signature chop you might have. Then, you must pay an installation fee, plus a refundable deposit for the equipment. Finally, just arrange an appointment for the telephone company engineers to install the wiring or the telephone. That's all you have to do; it's as easy as one, two, three!

💻 **Vocabulary**

refer〔rɪˋfɝ〕v. 參照；有關 <to>   tip〔tɪp〕n. 建議；情報

obtain〔əbˋten〕v. 獲得   fax〔fæks〕n. 傳眞

contact〔kɑnˋtækt〕v. 聯絡   local〔ˋlokl̩〕adj. 當地的

complete〔kəmˋplit〕v. 完成

application〔͵æpləˋkeʃən〕n. 申請

form〔fɔrm〕n. 表格   produce〔prəˋdjus〕v. 出示

I.D. 身分證（= *Identification*）

signature〔ˋsɪgnətʃ͏ɚ〕n. 簽名   chop〔tʃɑp〕n. 圖章

installation〔͵ɪnstəˋleʃən〕n. 安裝

fee〔fi〕n. 費用   plus〔plʌs〕prep. 加上

refundable〔rɪˋfʌndəbl̩〕adj. 可退還的

deposit〔dɪˋpɑzɪt〕n. 保證金

equipment〔ɪˋkwɪpmənt〕n. 設備

arrange〔əˈrendʒ〕*v.* 安排

appointment〔əˈpɔɪntmənt〕*n.* 約定

engineer〔ˌɛndʒəˈnɪr〕*n.* 工程師

install〔ɪnˈstɔl〕*v.* 安裝

wiring〔ˈwaɪrɪŋ〕*n.* 線路

as easy as one, two, three 很容易

34. (**B**) How much does it cost to install a phone?

    A. It's about one hundred U.S. dollars.

    B. This article doesn't mention a price.

    C. The cost varies.

    D. The price depends on the installation level.

    * mention〔ˈmɛnʃən〕*v.* 提到

      vary〔ˈvɛrɪ〕*v.* 改變

      depend on 視～而定   level〔ˈlɛvḷ〕*n.* 程度

35. (**C**) Who installs the telephone or fax line?

    A. Service repair men.

    B. Electricians.

    C. Company engineers.

    D. Customer service representatives.

    * *repair man* 修理工人

      electrician〔ɪˌlɛkˈtrɪʃən〕*n.* 電工

      customer〔ˈkʌstəmə〕*n.* 顧客

      representative〔ˌrɛprɪˈzɛntətɪv〕*n.* 代表

Questions 36-37 refer to the following advertisement.

Read Asia News to get all the news. Every day Asia News keeps you up-to-date with late-breaking, up-to-the-minute news. Our reporters are on the beat 24 hours a day, 7 days a week. Our award-winning staff is the most accurate, progressive and professional in all of Asia. Our reputation is known worldwide. No matter what information you need, financial, economic, political, entertainment, sports or just expert opinions and analysis, look to Asia News. We help you stay ahead all the time. Subscribe to Asia News today.

Vocabulary

Asia〔'eʃə〕 *n.* 亞洲　　up-to-date〔ˌʌptə'det〕 *adj.* 最新的
late-breaking〔'let'brekɪŋ〕 *adj.* 剛收到的
up-to-the-minute〔ˌʌptəðə'mɪnɪt〕 *adj.* 直到現在的；最新的
reporter〔rɪ'portɚ〕 *n.* 記者　　beat〔bit〕 *n.* 崗位
award-winning〔ə'wɔrd'wɪnɪŋ〕 *adj.* 獲獎的
staff〔stæf〕 *n.* 工作人員　　accurate〔'ækjərɪt〕 *adj.* 準確的
progressive〔prə'grɛsɪv〕 *adj.* 進步的
professional〔prə'fɛʃən̩l〕 *adj.* 專業的
reputation〔ˌrɛpjə'teʃən〕 *n.* 名聲　　known〔non〕 *adj.* 聞名的
worldwide〔'wɝld,waɪd〕 *adv.* 全世界　　***no matter what*** 無論什麼
financial〔fə'nænʃəl〕 *adj.* 財政的
economic〔ˌikə'nɑmɪk〕 *adj.* 經濟的

political〔pə'lɪtɪkḷ〕*adj.* 政治的

entertainment〔ˌɛntɚ'tenmənt〕*n.* 娛樂

sports〔sports〕*adj.* 運動的　　expert〔'ɛkspɝt〕*adj.* 專家的

opinion〔ə'pɪnjən〕*n.* 意見　　analysis〔ə'næləsɪs〕*n.* 分析

stay ahead 保持領先　　*all the time* 一直；經常

subscribe〔səb'skraɪb〕*v.* 訂閱

36. (**C**) What type of media outlet is Asia News?

　　A. A weekly magazine.

　　B. A cable T.V. channel.

　　C. A newspaper.

　　D. An international radio station.

　　* type〔taɪp〕*n.* 型態　　media〔'midɪə〕*n. pl.* 媒體

　　　outlet〔'aʊtˌlɛt〕*n.* 商店

　　　weekly〔'wiklɪ〕*adj.* 週刊的　　cable〔'kebḷ〕*n.* 有線電視

　　　channel〔'tʃænḷ〕*n.* 頻道

　　　international〔ˌɪntɚ'næʃənḷ〕*adj.* 國際的

　　　radio station 廣播電台

37. (**D**) What does this ad say about the staff?

　　A. They are all native.

　　B. All have journalism degrees.

　　C. They also subscribe to Asia News.

　　D. They have won awards.

　　* native〔'netɪv〕*adj.* 本國的

　　　journalism〔'dʒɝnḷˌɪzəm〕*n.* 新聞學

　　　degree〔dɪ'gri〕*n.* 學位　　award〔ə'wɔrd〕*n.* 獎

Questions 38-39 refer to this office announcement.

A new water cooler will be installed in our snack lounge on Friday. Please use caution and follow the directions when dispensing the water. The hot button is actually boiling hot, so extreme caution must be used. No plastic or thin beverage glasses are allowed. The lukewarm button is just that, moderately warm. The cool and cold buttons, of course, are less dangerous and need no special warning.

This machine guarantees 99.9% pure water and we hope to enjoy it for many years, so please once again pay attention and be careful. Thanks.

—— the Management

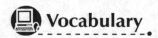 **Vocabulary**

cooler〔ˈkulɚ〕*n.* 冰箱；儲水機　　snack〔snæk〕*n.* 點心
lounge〔laʊndʒ〕*n.* 休息室　　caution〔ˈkɔʃən〕*n.* 謹慎
directions〔dəˈrɛkʃənz〕*n. pl.* 說明
dispense〔dɪˈspɛns〕*v.* 配；給　　button〔ˈbʌtn̩〕*n.* 按鈕
boiling〔ˈbɔɪlɪŋ〕*adv.* 沸騰般地；極度地
extreme〔ɪkˈstrim〕*adj.* 極度的　　plastic〔ˈplæstɪk〕*adj.* 塑膠的
thin〔θɪn〕*adj.* 薄的　　beverage〔ˈbɛvərɪdʒ〕*n.* 飲料
allow〔əˈlaʊ〕*v.* 允許　　lukewarm〔ˈlukˈwɔrm〕*adj.* 微溫的
moderately〔ˈmɑdərɪtlɪ〕*adv.* 適中地
warning〔ˈwɔrnɪŋ〕*n.* 警告　　guarantee〔͵gærənˈti〕*v.* 保證
pure〔pjʊr〕*adj.* 純淨的　　***pay attention*** 注意

38. (**A**) What kind of machine is being installed?

    A. A water machine.   B. A beverage machine.

    C. A coffee machine.   D. A hot cocoa machine.

    * cocoa (ˈkoko) *n.* 可可

39. (**B**) What is the management afraid of?

    A. Someone dispensing the machine.

    B. Someone might get burned or scalded.

    C. Employees breaking the machine.

    D. Employees were psyched.

    * ***get burned*** 被燙傷   ***get scalded*** 被燙傷

    employee (ˌɛmplɔɪˈi) *n.* 員工

    psyched (saɪkt) *adj.* 興奮的

Questions 40-41 refer to the following earthquake safety tips.

When an earthquake occurs, stay where you are! Most accidents or injuries happen to people as they try to flee or leave buildings. Falling objects near doorways or buildings are the greatest danger. Stay inside and take the best available cover you can. Get under a sturdy desk, stand under a strong doorway or brace yourself in an inside corner of a room. Some people say lying down in an empty bathtub is the safest spot. No matter what, turn off all electricity and gas, and don't use elevators or stairways. Also, stay away from windows and bookshelves.

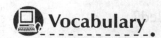 **Vocabulary**

occur〔ə'kɝ〕v. 發生　　injury〔'ɪndʒərɪ〕n. 傷害

flee〔fli〕v. 逃走　　object〔'abdʒɪkt〕n. 物體

doorway〔'dɔr,we〕n. 出入口　　danger〔'dendʒɚ〕n. 危險

available〔ə'veləbl〕adj. 可用的　　cover〔'kʌvɚ〕n. 遮蔽物

sturdy〔'stɝdɪ〕adj. 堅固的　　*brace oneself* 做好防備

corner〔'kɔrnɚ〕n. 轉角　　*lie down* 躺下

empty〔'ɛmptɪ〕adj. 空的　　bathtub〔'bæθ,tʌb〕n. 浴缸

spot〔spat〕n. 地點　　*turn off* 關掉（電源、瓦斯）

electricity〔ɪ,lɛk'trɪsətɪ〕n. 電　　gas〔gæs〕n. 瓦斯

elevator〔'ɛlə,vetɚ〕n. 電梯　　stairway〔'stɛr,we〕n. 樓梯

stay away from 遠離　　bookshelf〔'bʊk,ʃɛlf〕n. 書架

40. (**B**) What shouldn't you do when an earthquake occurs?

　　A. Stand under a solid doorway.

　　B. Take the stairway, and flee the building.

　　C. Get under a well-built table.

　　D. Stay put, and seek sturdy protection.

　　* solid〔'salɪd〕adj. 堅固的　　well-built〔'wɛl'bɪlt〕adj. 牢固的
　　stay put 不要動　　seek〔sik〕v. 尋找
　　protection〔prə'tɛkʃən〕n. 保護

41. (**B**) Where do most earthquake accidents happen?

　　A. In elevators.

　　B. Outside next to buildings.

　　C. Near electrical appliances.

　　D. In a car in a tunnel.

　　* appliance〔ə'plaɪəns〕n. 設備
　　electrical appliance 家電用品　　tunnel〔'tʌnl〕n. 隧道

Questions 42-43 refer to the following advertisement.

> If you have to move, call us — Asian Tigers. We're the moving specialists. We offer outstanding door to door service for both local and international moves. Our moving professionals pack, secure and move your valuables with the utmost care and efficiency. You can relax because we have that caring touch. Your precious items are even more precious to us. We also offer 100% door to door insurance coverage. Our record and our reputation is impeccable! Try us and you'll see. Move with Asian Tigers — it will be the best move you've ever made.

Vocabulary

move〔muv〕*v. n.* 搬家   specialist〔'spɛʃəlɪst〕*n.* 專家
offer〔'ɔfɚ〕*v.* 提供
outstanding〔'aʊt'stændɪŋ〕*adj.* 傑出的
door to door 挨家挨戶的   service〔'sɝvɪs〕*n.* 服務
local〔'lokḷ〕*adj.* 當地的
international〔,ɪntɚ'næʃənḷ〕*adj.* 國際的
professional〔prə'fɛʃənḷ〕*n.* 專家
pack〔pæk〕*v.* 打包   secure〔sɪ'kjur〕*v.* 保護
valuables〔'væljuəbḷz〕*n. pl.* 貴重物品
utmost〔'ʌt,most〕*adj.* 最大的   efficiency〔ɪ'fɪʃənsɪ〕*n.* 效率

caring〔'kɛrɪŋ〕 adj. 細心的　　touch〔tʌtʃ〕 n. 手法

precious〔'prɛʃəs〕 adj. 珍貴的

insurance〔ɪn'ʃurəns〕 n. 保險

coverage〔'kʌvərɪdʒ〕 n. 賠償　　record〔'rɛkəd〕 n. 記錄

reputation〔ˌrɛpjə'teʃən〕 n. 名聲

impeccable〔ɪm'pɛkəbḷ〕 adj. 無懈可擊的

make a move 採取行動（此處是雙關語，意指搬家）

42. (**D**) What does this company do?

　　A. They help you switch jobs.

　　B. They help you to tow your car.

　　C. They provide travel and health insurance.

　　D. They pack and transport households.

　　* switch〔swɪtʃ〕 v. 轉換　　tow〔to〕 v. 拖吊

　　　provide〔prə'vaɪd〕 v. 提供

　　　travel insurance 旅遊保險

　　　health insurance 健康保險

　　　transport〔træns'port〕 v. 運輸

　　　household〔'haʊsˌhold〕 n. 家庭

43. (**C**) What does the term "door to door" mean?

　　A. From the front door to the back door.

　　B. From door to door in each room.

　　C. From the old location to the new location.

　　D. From east to west or from north to south.

　　* term〔tɝm〕 n. 術語；用語

　　　location〔lo'keʃən〕 n. 位置

Questions 44-45 refer to the following information.

Always watch what you eat because you are what you eat. What you put into your mouth determines how well you perform every day. Food is like a fuel and our bodies are like engines or machines. Eat a healthy diet and always be conscious of good nutrition. Eat lots of fresh fruits, vegetables, whole grain foods and drink water like a fish! Also, take a multiple vitamin supplement every day. Avoid high calorie processed foods with lots of sugar. Also, stay away from fatty and greasy foods. Do all that and you'll live a healthy life.

Vocabulary

watch〔watʃ〕*v.* 注意
You are what you eat. 你吃什麼就會像什麼。
put into 放進　　mouth〔mauθ〕*n.* 嘴
determine〔dɪˈtɜmɪn〕*v.* 決定
perform〔pəˈfɔrm〕*v.* 做 (工作)　　fuel〔ˈfjuəl〕*n.* 燃料
engine〔ˈɛndʒən〕*n.* 引擎　　machine〔məˈʃin〕*n.* 機器
healthy〔ˈhɛlθɪ〕*adj.* 健康的　　diet〔ˈdaɪət〕*n.* 飲食
conscious〔ˈkɑnʃəs〕*adj.* 有意識的
be conscious of 意識到　　nutrition〔njuˈtrɪʃən〕*n.* 營養
fresh〔frɛʃ〕*adj.* 新鮮的　　grain〔gren〕*n.* 穀類
whole grain food 全穀類食品　　***drink like a fish*** 牛飲

multiple（'mʌltəpḷ）*adj.* 綜合的

vitamin（'vaɪtəmɪn）*n.* 維他命

supplement（'sʌpləmənt）*n.* 補充物　　avoid（ə'vɔɪd）*v.* 避免

calorie（'kælərɪ）*n.* 卡路里（熱量單位）

processed（'prɑsɛst）*adj.* 加工的

sugar（'ʃugɚ）*n.* 糖　　fatty（'fætɪ）*adj.* 油膩的

greasy（'grizɪ, -sɪ）*adj.* 油膩的

44.（ **A** ）What is the main idea here?

　　A. Eat right to stay healthy.

　　B. You eat only what you like to eat.

　　C. Eat junk and you'll be junk.

　　D. Be responsible and avoid candy.

　　* ***main idea*** 主旨　　stay（ste）*v.* 保持

　　　junk（dʒʌŋk）*n.* 垃圾（食物）

　　　responsible（rɪ'spɑnsəbḷ）*adj.* 負責的

45.（ **C** ）Which of the following would be a high calorie food?

　　A. A vegetable salad.

　　B. A fish sandwich.

　　C. A slice of chocolate cake.

　　D. Whole wheat bread.

　　* salad（'sæləd）*n.* 沙拉

　　　sandwich（'sændwɪtʃ）*n.* 三明治

　　　slice（slaɪs）*n.* 片　　wheat（hwit）*n.* 小麥

　　　whole wheat bread 全麥麵包

中高級閱讀測驗詳解 4

PART A : Sentence Completion

1. (**B**) Going on someone else's property without permission is considered <u>trespassing</u> and is punishable by law.
未經許可進入私人土地被認為是<u>侵入</u>，而且應該受到法律的懲罰。

  (A) harassment〔hə'ræsmənt〕*n.* 騷擾
  (B) ***trespass***〔'trɛspəs〕*v.* 侵入
  (C) embezzlement〔ɪm'bɛzḷmənt〕*n.* 侵吞；盜用
  (D) plagiarism〔'pledʒə,rɪzəm〕*n.* 剽竊

  * property〔'prɑpətɪ〕*n.* 房地產
    permission〔pə'mɪʃən〕*n.* 允許
    punishable〔'pʌnɪʃəbḷ〕*adj.* 可以處罰的；該罰的

2. (**D**) Our school held a seminar on environmental conservation and invited several <u>distinguished</u> scholars to deliver lectures concerning this topic. 本校辦了一場關於環境保育的研討會，並邀請數位<u>知名</u>學者針對此項主題發表演講。

  (A) expedient〔ɪk'spidɪənt〕*adj.* 方便的；權宜的 *n.* 權宜之計
  (B) disinfected〔,dɪsɪn'fɛktɪd〕*adj.* 已消毒的
  (C) extinguish〔ɪk'stɪŋgwɪʃ〕*v.* 熄滅 (= *put out*)
  (D) ***distinguished***〔dɪ'stɪŋgwɪʃt〕*adj.* 有名的；卓越的

  * seminar〔'sɛmə,nɑr〕*n.* 研討會
    conservation〔,kɑnsə'veʃən〕*n.* 保育
    scholar〔'skɑlə〕*n.* 學者   deliver〔dɪ'lɪvə〕*v.* 發表
    lecture〔'lɛktʃə〕*n.* 演講
    concerning〔kən'sɜnɪŋ〕*prep.* 與～有關

3. (**A**) According to a postmortem examination, the victim was
   <u>strangled</u> to death.　根據驗屍報告指出，被害人是被<u>勒斃</u>的。

   (A) **strangle**〔'stræŋgl̩〕v. 勒死

   (B) straighten〔'stretn̩〕v. 變直；整理＜ *up* ＞

   (C) strand〔strænd〕v. 擱淺；使進退兩難

   (D) strengthen〔'strɛŋθən〕v. 加強

   ＊ postmortem〔post'mɔrtəm〕adj. 死後的

   　　victim〔'vɪktɪm〕n. 受害者

4. (**B**) In the story, the woman had lived in the neighborhood
   from the <u>cradle</u> to the grave.　All her life, she had never
   left her hometown.　故事中，這位女士從<u>出生</u>到死亡都住
   在這個地區。她終其一生從未離開她的家鄉。

   (A) shrine〔ʃraɪn〕n. 神廟；神殿

   (B) **cradle**〔'kredl̩〕n. 搖籃　　　**the cradle** 幼年時代
   　　　from the cradle to the grave 從出生到死亡

   (C) canyon〔'kænjən〕n. 峽谷

   (D) sanctuary〔'sæŋktʃʊˌɛrɪ〕n. 神殿；庇護所

   ＊ grave〔grev〕n. 墳墓　　**the grave** 死亡

5. (**C**) Chameleons are good at <u>mimicking</u> their surroundings
   by changing the color of their skins.
   變色龍擅長藉由改變皮膚的顏色來<u>模擬</u>牠們的週遭環境。

   (A) mirror〔'mɪrɚ〕n. 鏡子　　v. 反射；反映

   (B) minimize〔'mɪnəˌmaɪz〕v. 減至最小、最少

   (C) **mimic**〔'mɪmɪk〕v. 模仿；模擬

   (D) mingle〔'mɪŋgl̩〕v. 混合

   ＊ chameleon〔kə'milɪən〕n. 變色龍　　**be good at** 擅長
   　　surroundings〔sə'raundɪŋz〕n. pl. 週遭環境

6. (**A**) The more renowned he became, the lower <u>profile</u> he presented. He didn't want to create a commotion.

他名氣越大，<u>姿態</u>就越低。他不想要引起騷動。

(A) **profile** (ˈprofaɪl) *n.* 側面；輪廓；外形

   present/keep a low profile 採取低姿態；保持低調

(B) document (ˈdɑkjəmənt) *n.* 文件

(C) transcript (ˈtræn͵skrɪpt) *n.* 成績單

(D) presentation (͵prɛznˈteʃən) *n.* 呈現；報告；發表

* renowned (rɪˈnaʊnd) *adj.* 有名的

  commotion (kəˈmoʃən) *n.* 騷動；暴動

7. (**A**) I was <u>profoundly</u> grateful for your kind and generous help.

我對你仁慈慷慨的幫助<u>深深</u>感激。

(A) **profoundly** (prəˈfaʊndlɪ) *adv.* 深深地

(B) profitably (ˈprɑfɪtəblɪ) *adv.* 有利地；有益地

(C) progressively (prəˈgrɛsɪvlɪ) *adv.* 進步地；有進展地；漸進地

(D) prolifically (prəˈlɪfɪklɪ) *adv.* 多產地；豐富地

* grateful (ˈgretfəl) *adj.* 感激的

  generous (ˈdʒɛnərəs) *adj.* 慷慨的

8. (**D**) The plan he proposed sounded too perfect to be <u>feasible</u> to me. 對我而言，他所提的計畫聽起來完美的不<u>合理</u>。

(A) feverish (ˈfivərɪʃ) *adj.* 發燒的；狂熱的

(B) feeble (ˈfibl̩) *adj.* 虛弱的 (= *frail* ; *weak*)

(C) fictional (ˈfɪkʃənl̩) *adj.* 小說的；虛構的

(D) **feasible** (ˈfizəbl̩) *adj.* 可能的；合理的

* propose (prəˈpoz) *v.* 提議 (= *suggest* ; *put forward*)

  sound (saʊnd) *v.* 聽起來   **too ~ to** + **V.** 太~而不…

  perfect (ˈpɝfɪkt) *adj.* 完美的

9. (**C**) After the war, a new city <u>rose from the ashes</u> of the old.

在戰後，<u>從舊城的廢墟中誕生</u>了一座新的城市。

(A) rise to the bait （魚）咬餌；上鉤；（人）被引誘

(B) rise with the lark 早起　　lark〔lɑrk〕*n.* 雲雀

(C) ***rise from the ashes*** 從灰燼中復原；復興

ashes〔'æʃɪz〕*n. pl.* 灰燼

(D) rise from the dust 從屈辱中重新站起

10. (**B**) You've got to <u>face up to</u> your own responsibility. Nobody will take it for you.

你必須<u>面對</u>你自己的責任，沒有人能夠替你<u>承擔</u>。

(A) lead up to 逐漸進入（ = *approach* ）

(B) ***face up to*** 面對（ = *face* ; *confront* ）

(C) fire up 生火；添加燃料；突然發怒

(D) roll up 捲起；增加（ = *accumulate* ）

11. (**B**) "<u>Who do you think is the richest man</u> in this town?" "I think Mr. Lin is the richest man in town."

「<u>你認為誰是本鎮最有錢的人</u>？」「我認為林先生是鎮上最有錢的人。」

* 這個問句中文和英文結構是不同的，主要的問題在於 Who is the richest man in this town，故 Who 應用主格，故 (A) 不合。而 do you think 必須放在疑問詞和子句中間，故本題選 (B) ***Who*** do you think <u>is the richest man in this town</u>? 名詞子句如果按照中文直接翻成英文，問句寫成 *Do you think who* is the richest man in this town?，這樣的寫法是 Yes/No 問句，但是回答 Yes 或 No 是個無意義的句子，故 (C) 不合。

12. (**A**) About three-fourths of the group agreed to join the hike, and the remainder <u>were going to</u> stay at the hotel.

這群人中大約有四分之三同意要參加健行，而其餘的人<u>將會</u>留在飯店裡。

* the remainder 之後省略了 of the group，the group 在此為一個集合，指這群人的組成分子時，為複數用法，而這群人中其餘的四分之一，應仍然為複數，故動詞亦用複數，故本題選 (A) *were going to*。

three-fourths 四分之三　　agree〔ə'gri〕v. 同意
hike〔haɪk〕n. 健行
remainder〔rɪ'mendɚ〕n. 其餘的人或物

13. (**B**) Doctoral students who are preparing to take their qualifying examinations have been studying in the library every night <u>for</u> the last three months.

正在準備資格考試的博士班學生，過去三個月<u>以來</u>，每晚都在圖書館裡苦讀。

* 現在完成式或完成進行式與時間副詞「*for* + 一段時間」連用，表示動作從過去到現在已經持續了一段時間，故本題選 (B)。since 不可接一段時間，而是接某個時刻，表示動作的起點時間，在此不合。「一段時間 + ago」通常用於過去式。

doctoral〔'dɑktərəl〕adj. 博士的
prepare〔prɪ'pɛr〕v. 準備
qualify〔'kwɑlə,faɪ〕v. 合格
examination〔ɪg,zæmə'neʃən〕n. 考試
qualifying examination 資格考試

14. (**D**) <u>When electric waves</u> are fed into a tape recorder, they magnetize the particles on the tape in varying patterns.

當電波被送入錄音機時，它們會以不停變化的模式，將錄音帶上的小分子磁化。

＊ 根據結構，前句為副詞子句，需要連接詞和主詞，故選 (D) **When electric waves**。(A) 缺乏連接詞，(B) 用 that 為關代用法，是形容詞子句，(C) because of 要接名詞，不接子句，均不合。

electric〔ɪˈlɛktrɪk〕*adj.* 電的　　***electric wave*** 電波
feed into 注入；送入　　***tape recorder*** 錄音機
magnetize〔ˈmægnəˌtaɪz〕*v.* 使磁化
particle〔ˈpɑrtɪkl〕*n.* 分子；粒子
tape〔tep〕*n.* 錄音帶；帶子
varying〔ˈvɛrɪɪŋ〕*adj.* 不停變化的
pattern〔ˈpætən〕*n.* 模式

15. (**A**) She has been suffering from a kind of disease, <u>the cure for which is now possible</u>.

她罹患了一種疾病，<u>那種病現在可能已經有辦法治療了</u>。

＊ 根據結構，後句為形容詞子句，而形容詞子句中的主詞是 the cure for the disease，與先行詞 disease 之前的關係，為所有格用法，可寫成 the cure for which 或是 whose cure，故本題選 (A) **the cure for which is now possible**。(B) 用 recovery 句意錯誤，應用 discovery「發現」才對，(C) unable 要用於人做主詞的情況，(D) the cure which 缺少介系詞，均不合。

cure〔kjur〕*n.* 治療　　recovery〔rɪˈkʌvərɪ〕*n.* 恢復

PART B：**Cloze**

Questions 16-20

　　The groundbreaking movie "Brokeback Mountain" will break even more ground, coming out for sale as a digital file online on the same day it's <u>released</u> on DVD, part of a move announced
　　　　　　　　　　16
by half a dozen studios to sell movies online.

　　「斷背山」這部具有開創性的電影,將開創更多新局面,在它發行 DVD 的同一天,也會在網路上發行數位檔案,這是六家電影公司宣布採取的行動之一,他們要在網路上賣電影。

　　groundbreaking (ˈgraʊnd͵brekɪŋ) *adj.* 開創性的
　　Brokeback Mountain 斷背山【李安導演的同性戀故事片,榮獲
　　　　奧斯卡最佳影片、最佳導演,以及最佳女配角三項大獎】
　　break (brek) *v.* 開拓;打開
　　ground (graʊnd) *n.* 領域;範圍
　　come out 發行　　***for sale*** 出售的
　　digital (ˈdɪdʒɪtḷ) *adj.* 數位的
　　online (ˈɑn͵laɪn) *adv.* 線上地
　　move (muv) *n.* 舉動;行動
　　announce (əˈnaʊns) *v.* 宣布　　dozen (ˈdʌzn̩) *n.* 十二個
　　studio (ˈstjudɪ͵o) *n.* 電影公司;製片廠

16. (**B**)　(A) relieve (rɪˈliv) *v.* 減輕
　　　　　　(B) ***release*** (rɪˈlis) *v.* 發行
　　　　　　(C) retreat (rɪˈtrit) *v.* 撤退
　　　　　　(D) recruit (rɪˈkrut) *v.* 招募

Twentieth Century Fox and the joint owners of Movielink —
MGM, <u>Paramount</u> Pictures, Sony Pictures, Universal and Warner
     17
Bros.—will offer their movies through Movielink. Sony also
announced a deal with CinemaNow. The sites have traditionally
allowed consumers to download movies for viewing over a 24-hour
<u>period</u>.
 18

二十世紀福斯電影公司，以及另外五家電影公司——米高梅、派拉蒙影業、新力影業、環球電影公司和華納兄弟影業，共同擁有的 Movielink 電影下載網站，將透過這個網站來出售他們的電影。新力還宣布要和「即時電影」簽約。這些網站原本就是讓顧客下載要觀賞的影片，但期限是二十四小時。

joint〔dʒɔɪnt〕*adj.* 聯合的 pictures〔'pɪktʃəz〕*n.* 電影業
universal〔ˌjunə'vɝsḷ〕*adj.* 環球的；全世界的
offer〔'ɔfə〕*v.* 出售；提供 deal〔dil〕*n.* 契約
site〔saɪt〕*n.* 網站（= *website*）
traditionally〔trə'dɪʃənḷɪ〕*adv.* 傳統上
allow〔ə'laʊ〕*v.* 讓；允許 consumer〔kən'sjumə〕*n.* 消費者
download〔'daʊnˌlod〕*v.* 下載 view〔vju〕*v.* 觀看

17. (**A**) (A) ***paramount***〔'pærəˌmaʊnt〕*adj.* 最高的
           n. 派拉蒙【電影公司名稱】
      (B) paradise〔'pærəˌdaɪs〕*n.* 天堂
      (C) parachute〔'pærəˌʃut〕*n.* 降落傘
      (D) parallel〔'pærəˌlɛl〕*n.* 平行線

18. (**C**) (A) interval〔'ɪntəvḷ〕*n.* 間隔
      (B) series〔'sɪrɪz〕*n.* 一系列
      (C) ***period***〔'pɪrɪəd〕*n.* 期間
      (D) channel〔'tʃænḷ〕*n.* 頻道

The move comes amid a slowdown of DVD sales and greater ease of illegal movie down-loading on high-speed Internet connections. But consumers could end up paying US$20 to US$30, in some cases more than the price of a DVD, and won't be able to burn discs for viewing on DVD players.

這個舉動是源自於 DVD 的銷售量衰退，還有人們愈來愈容易透過高速網路連結，來非法下載電影。但是顧客最後可能會付美金二十到三十元的代價，在某些情況下，付出去的錢甚至比 DVD 的價格還高，而且也不能燒成光碟，再用 DVD 播放裝置觀賞。

amid〔ə'mɪd〕prep. 在…中　slowdown〔'slo͵daʊn〕n. 衰退
ease〔iz〕n. 容易　illegal〔ɪ'ligḷ〕adj. 非法的
connection〔kə'nɛkʃən〕n. 連結　**end up** 最後
case〔kes〕n. 情況；事例　burn〔bɝn〕v. 燒錄
disc〔dɪsk〕n. 光碟

Movie executives said they're <u>responding to</u> consumers'
19
demand by offering the service. "Basically what we're trying to do is to allow a consumer to build a digital library for the first time," said Jim Ramo, chief executive of Movielink, in a teleconference call Monday.

電影業者說他們是為了回應顧客的需求，才提供這項服務的。「基本上，我們是第一次想試著讓顧客能建立自己的數位電影館。」吉姆・瑞蒙在星期一召開的視訊會議上說，他是 Movielink 電影下載網站的執行長。

executive〔ɪg'zɛkjʊtɪv〕n. 業者；長官
demand〔dɪ'mænd〕n. 需求
chief〔tʃif〕adj. 最高位的　**chief executive** 執行長
teleconference〔'tɛlə͵kɑnfərəns〕n. 視訊會議

19. (**D**) (A) subscribe 〔səb'skraɪb〕 *v.* 訂閱 < *to* >

        (B) contribute 〔kən'trɪbjut〕 *v.* 貢獻 < *to* >

        (C) stick 〔stɪk〕 *v.* 堅持 < *to* >

        (D) ***respond*** 〔rɪ'spɑnd〕 *v.* 回應 < *to* >

"You can imagine now that a customer can have <u>on a laptop</u> 50

　　　　　　　　　　　　　　　　　　　　　　　　　　　20
movies." Rick Finkelstein, president and chief operating officer
of Universal Pictures, said, "It furthers our goal of providing
consumers with our content whenever, however, and wherever
they want it."

「你現在可以想像，顧客可以在筆記型電腦中存放五十部電影，」里克‧
芬可斯坦說，他是環球電影公司的總裁兼營運長，「這種情況使我們的目
標推進到，只要顧客想要，我們將隨時隨地，並以任何方法，把我們的電
影內容提供給顧客。」

      imagine 〔ɪ'mædʒɪn〕 *v.* 想像

      president 〔'prɛzədənt〕 *n.* 總裁

      operating 〔'ɑpəretɪŋ〕 *adj.* 營運的

      chief operating officer 營運長

      further 〔'fɝðɚ〕 *v.* 推進　　goal 〔gol〕 *n.* 目標

      provide 〔prə'vaɪd〕 *v.* 提供

      content 〔'kɑntɛnt〕 *n.* 內容

20. (**A**) 空格應填表地點的副詞片語，依句意，選 (A) ***on a laptop*** 「在
        筆記型電腦中」。

        laptop 〔'læp,tɑp〕 *n.* 筆記型電腦

Questions 21-30

Thirty-three people were injured as they <u>went in for</u> a simulated
21

emergency on Airbus' new A380 jetliner. The company said one

man broke his leg and 32 other people suffered minor injuries

during the exercise <u>in which</u> 853 passengers and 20 crew exited
22

the plane on slides in a darkened hangar. Some of the injured

suffered friction burns from <u>sliding down</u> the escape ramps, Airbus
23

spokesman Tore Prang said.

　　有三十三個人在參加空中巴士公司的 A380 噴射客機的緊急情況模擬
時受傷。該公司表示，在演習中，有一個人摔斷腿，另外有三十二個人受
到輕傷，當時有八百五十三位乘客和二十位機組人員，要從位於陰暗停機
棚的滑坡下飛機。有些傷者在從避難滑行道滑下來時，受到了擦傷，空中
巴士的發言人陶爾‧布朗格先生說。

　　injured〔'ɪndʒəd〕adj. 受傷的
　　simulated〔'sɪmjə,letɪd〕adj. 模擬的
　　emergency〔ɪ'mɝdʒənsɪ〕n. 緊急情況
　　jetliner〔'dʒɛt,laɪnə〕n. 噴射客機　　suffer〔'sʌfə〕v. 遭受
　　minor〔'maɪnə〕adj. 輕微的　　injury〔'ɪndʒərɪ〕n. 損傷
　　exercise〔'ɛksə,saɪz〕n. 演習
　　passenger〔'pæsndʒə〕n. 乘客
　　crew〔kru〕n. 機組人員　　exit〔'ɛgzɪt〕v. 離開　n. 出口
　　slide〔slaɪd〕n. 滑坡　　darkened〔'dɑrkənd〕adj. 陰暗的
　　hangar〔'hæŋə〕n. 停機棚　　friction〔'frɪkʃən〕n. 摩擦
　　burn〔bɝn〕n. 擦傷；灼燒　　escape〔ə'skep〕n. 逃走
　　ramp〔ræmp〕n. 斜坡道　　*escape ramp* 避難；避難滑行道
　　spokesman〔'spoksmən〕n. 發言人

21. (**C**) (A) take notice of 注意到
(B) take hold of 抓住
(C) ***go in for*** 參加（ = *take part in* ）
(D) go back on 毀（約）

22. (**D**) 依句意，「在這場演習中」，故選 (D) ***in which***。關代 which 代替先行詞 the exercise。

23. (**A**) (A) ***slide*** 〔 slaɪd 〕 *v.* 滑下　　(B) leap 〔 lip 〕 *v.* 跳
(C) scramble 〔'skræmbḷ 〕 *v.* 爬行
(D) stroll 〔 strol 〕 *v.* 閒逛

Despite the injuries, Airbus said the plane passed its test, with
  24
everybody out of the super-jumbo in about 80 seconds. "That was a
very great success," Airbus manager Gustav Humbert said after the
test at its factory in the north German city of Hamburg. The
company had said that bringing 650 people out of the plane within
  25
90 seconds would have been enough to meet safety requirements.
  26

　　儘管有人受傷，空中巴士說這架飛機通過了測試，因為大家都在八十秒內離開了這架噴射客機。在這次的測試之後，空中巴士的經理居斯塔夫‧安貝爾說：「那是個大成功」，該測試是在德國北部的一個城市——漢堡的工廠所舉行的。該公司表示，在九十秒內把六百五十位乘客帶離飛機，就足以符合安全條件了。

　　　jumbo 〔'dʒʌmbo 〕 *n.* 巨無霸噴射客機
　　　success 〔 sək'sɛs 〕 *n.* 成功　　manager 〔'mænɪdʒɚ 〕 *n.* 經理
　　　German 〔'dʒɝmən 〕 *adj.* 德國的
　　　Hamburg 〔'hæmbɝg 〕 *n.* 漢堡【德國北部一城市】
　　　meet 〔 mit 〕 *v.* 符合　　safety 〔'seftɪ 〕 *adj.* 保障安全的

24. (**C**)　由於空格後是名詞，故須填介系詞，且依句意，選 (C) *Despite*
　　　　〔dɪ'spaɪt〕*prep.* 儘管。而 (A) since「由於；既然」是連接詞；
　　　　(B) through〔θru〕*prep.* 透過；藉由，不合句意，(D) though
　　　　「雖然」是連接詞，在此用法不合。

25. (**B**)　空格應填動名詞做子句的主詞，故選 (B) *bringing*。

26. (**B**)　(A)　inquiry〔ɪn'kwaɪrɪ , 'ɪnkwərɪ〕*n.* 詢問
　　　　　　(B)　*requirement*〔rɪ'kwaɪrmənt〕*n.* 必要條件
　　　　　　(C)　acquisition〔͵ækwə'zɪʃən〕*n.* 獲得
　　　　　　(D)　equation〔ɪ'kweʃən〕*n.* 相等

　　　Construction problems have delayed the introduction of the
double-deck A380, the largest passenger plane in the world. So far,
　　　　　　　　　　　　　　　　　　　　　　　　　　　　　　　　　27
16 customers have ordered 159 of the planes, and the first samples
are to go to Singapore Airlines at the end of the year. Of the plane's
　　　　　　　　　　　　　　　　　　　　　　　　　　　　　　　28
16 exits, only eight were used in the drill, which was mandatory in
　　　　　　　　　　　　　　　　　　　　　　　　　　　　　　29
order for the A380 to receive its safety certification, Prang said.

　　由於建造上的問題，使得雙層客機 A380 的引進受到延誤，A380 是世
界上最大的客機。至今，有十六個顧客訂了一百五十九架這種飛機，而第
一批樣品飛機將在年底前往新加坡航空公司。演習時，這架飛機的十六個
出口中只用到八個，這對於 A380 要拿到安全證書而言，是必要的，布朗
格說。

　　　　construction〔kən'strʌkʃən〕*n.* 建造　　delay〔dɪ'le〕*v.* 延誤
　　　　introduction〔͵ɪntrə'dʌkʃən〕*n.* 引進　　deck〔dɛk〕*n.* 層
　　　　passenger plane 客機　　sample〔'sæmpḷ〕*n.* 樣本
　　　　be to V. 即將⋯　　Singapore〔'sɪŋgə͵por〕*n.* 新加坡
　　　　airlines〔'ɛr͵laɪnz〕*n.* 航空公司　　drill〔drɪl〕*n.* 演習
　　　　certification〔͵sɜtəfə'keʃən〕*n.* 證明書

27. (**A**) (A) **so far** 至今　　　(B) by and by 不久

　　　　　(C) before long 不久　　(D) as yet 至今尚未

28. (**C**) 依句意，表「在…當中」，選(C) **Of**。

29. (**C**) (A) marginal〔ˈmɑrdʒɪnḷ〕adj. 邊緣的

　　　　　(B) magnetic〔mægˈnɛtɪk〕adj. 磁性的

　　　　　(C) **mandatory**〔ˈmændəˌtorɪ〕adj. 必要的

　　　　　(D) manageable〔ˈmænɪdʒəbḷ〕adj. 容易處理的

Though the simulation was conducted inside a hangar, he said, Airbus sought to make it as realistic as possible, strewing debris in the aisles. Air safety officials were <u>on hand</u> to observe the

30

simulation.

　　雖然模擬測試是在停機棚內進行的，他說，空中巴士仍試著要讓測試儘量逼眞，他們在走道上灑碎石。空安人員也在場觀看這場測試。

　　　　simulation〔ˌsɪmjəˈleʃən〕n. 模擬測試
　　　　conduct〔kənˈdʌkt〕v. 進行
　　　　seek〔sik〕v. 試圖【三態變化爲 seek-sought-sought】
　　　　realistic〔ˌriəˈlɪstɪk〕adj. 眞實的　　**as…as possible** 儘量
　　　　strew〔stru〕v. 撒　　debris〔dəˈbri〕n. 碎石
　　　　aisle〔aɪl〕n. 走道　　official〔əˈfɪʃəl〕n. 人員
　　　　observe〔əbˈzɝv〕v. 觀察；注意看

30. (**D**) (A) by hand 用手工

　　　　　(B) off hand 立刻

　　　　　(C) out of hand 即時

　　　　　(D) **on hand** 在附近；出席；在場

📁 PART C : Reading

Questions 31-36

Golf is a game, a game of skill and patience. One that frustrates great athletes like Michael Jordan and very good athletes like my son and formerly mediocre athletes like myself. It is written that one-third of new golfers give it up after three years. Golf even frustrates Tiger Woods. Watch him <u>shake his head and mutter all day</u> on his way to another championship.

高爾夫球是一種比賽，一種需要技巧和耐心的比賽。這個比賽讓像麥克・喬丹這樣偉大的運動員受挫，而且也讓我兒子這樣出色的運動員，以及像我這樣以前就很平庸的運動員吃驚。根據記載，有三分之一的高爾夫球新手，會在三年之後放棄高爾夫球。高爾夫球甚至曾讓老虎伍茲受挫。看他在前往另一場冠軍賽的途中，一整天都邊搖頭邊發牢騷就知道。

golf〔gɔlf〕n. 高爾夫球　　patience〔ˈpeʃəns〕n. 耐心
frustrate〔ˈfrʌstret〕v. 使受挫　　athlete〔ˈæθlit〕n. 運動員
formerly〔ˈfɔrməlɪ〕adv. 從前
mediocre〔ˈmidɪˌokə〕adj. 平庸的　　*It is written* 根據記載
one-third of 三分之一的　　golfer〔ˈgɔlfə〕n. 打高爾夫球的人
give up 放棄　　even〔ˈivən〕adv. 甚至
shake〔ʃek〕v. 搖頭　　mutter〔ˈmʌtə〕v. 喃喃自語；發牢騷
on one's way to 在～途中
championship〔ˈtʃæmpɪənˌʃɪp〕n. 冠軍賽

So what kind of fatal attraction does it have? What draws these tens of millions of people? What attracts Bill Clinton and Celine Dion and Kenny G.? Many things. It is the only sport with carts and cocktails. I'd still play basketball if you could use carts. When you're young, you compete in football, baseball, basketball and other games where the ball moves and so do you.

那麼高爾夫球有什麼致命的吸引力呢？是什麼吸引了數千萬人？是什麼吸引了比爾・克林頓、席琳狄翁和肯尼基？有很多地方吸引他們。高爾夫球是唯一一個有車子和雞尾酒的運動。如果有車可以開的話，我會繼續打籃球。當你年輕時，你可以參加足球、棒球、籃球比賽，以及其他球動你也要動的比賽。

fatal〔ˋfetḷ〕adj. 致命的	attraction〔əˋtrækʃən〕n. 吸引力
draw〔drɔ〕v. 吸引	*tens of millions of* 數千萬的～
attract〔əˋtrækt〕v. 吸引	cart〔kɑrt〕n. 高爾夫球車
cocktail〔ˋkɑkˌtel〕n. 雞尾酒	compete〔kəmˋpit〕v. 比賽

As you get older you either choose doubles tennis, where you don't move, or golf, where the ball doesn't. Or you sit back and watch other people play these games on television. I predict that sumo wrestling will become the next big sport for aging baby boomers because it actually requires participants to be fat and each bout usually lasts about three seconds.

當你漸漸變老，你要不是選不用動的網球雙打，就是選球不會動的高爾夫球。或者你也可以坐著看其他人在電視上比賽。我預測對於在嬰兒潮時出生，且漸漸變老的人而言，相撲將會成為下一個受歡迎的運動，因為事實上參加的人必須是胖子，而且每一回合的比賽只持續三秒鐘左右。

either A *or* B　不是 A 就是 B　　doubles〔ˋdʌbḷz〕n. 雙打
sit back　（靠椅背而）坐　　predict〔prɪˋdɪkt〕v. 預測
sumo〔ˋsumo〕n. 相撲　　wrestling〔ˋrɛsḷɪŋ〕n. 摔角
big〔bɪg〕adj. 受歡迎的　　aging〔ˋedʒɪŋ〕adj. 逐漸變老的
baby boomer　戰後嬰兒潮出生者【指 1945 年的二次世界大戰】
actually〔ˋæktʃuəlɪ〕adv. 實際上
require〔rɪˋkwaɪr〕v. 需要
participant〔pəˋtɪsəpənt〕n. 參加者
bout〔baut〕n. 一回合　　last〔læst〕v. 持續

Friends always ask me to play with them, saying, incorrectly, that I couldn't possibly be as bad as I claim to be. They contend it doesn't even matter if I'm bad, so long as I just keep hitting the ball and don't hold them up. They speak of the fragrance of freshly mown grass, the sparkle of the morning dew, animals scampering across the fairways, the exhilaration of hitting even one fine shot, the relaxation and serenity and, perhaps most of all, the camaraderie.

朋友總是要我跟他們一起玩，而且他們說，我不可能打得像我講得那樣糟，而那是不正確的。他們堅決認為，我打得糟不糟甚至可以說不重要，只要我繼續打球，然後不要妨礙他們就好。他們談論著剛割完草的香味、閃亮的朝露、跳過球道的動物，甚至是打一桿好球的興奮感，打球時的放鬆與寧靜，而最重要的，可能是友情。

incorrectly〔ˌɪnkəˈrɛktlɪ〕 adv. 不正確地

possibly〔ˈpɑsəblɪ〕 adv. 可能

claim〔klem〕 v. 主張；宣稱

contend〔kənˈtɛnd〕 v. 堅決認為

matter〔ˈmætɚ〕 v. 關係重要

so long as 只要　　*hold up* 妨礙

fragrance〔ˈfregrəns〕 n. 香味　　freshly〔ˈfrɛʃlɪ〕 adv. 最近

mow〔mo〕 v. 割草　　sparkle〔ˈspɑrkḷ〕 n. 閃耀

dew〔dju〕 n. 露　　scamper〔ˈskæmpɚ〕 v. 蹦蹦跳跳

fairway〔ˈfɛrˌwe〕 n. 球道

exhilaration〔ɪgˌzɪləˈreʃən〕 n. 興奮

shot〔ʃɑt〕 n. 揮桿　　relaxation〔ˌrilæksˈeʃən〕 n. 放鬆

serenity〔səˈrɛnətɪ〕 n. 平靜

perhaps〔pɚˈhæps〕 adv. 或許　　*most of all* 最重要的是

camaraderie〔ˌkɑməˈrɑdərɪ〕 n. 友情

I can't argue with any of that. I've had terrific times out on golf courses on beautiful days with partners who could hit bad shots and laugh about them. It's just the frustrating, maddening, impossible, merciless game I hate. But I want to see my friends, and about the only place to do that any more is on a golf course. So, steeling myself for humiliation and fearing addiction, I guess I'll have to give it a shot.

我無法反駁任何一點。我在高爾夫球場上度過許多美好的時光,在晴朗的日子裡,和打得不好的夥伴一起打球,並且嘲笑他們。我討厭這個遊戲,因為它是如此令人受挫、令人瘋狂、難以應付且冷酷的遊戲。但是我想見到我的朋友,而唯一可以見到他們的地方,就是高爾夫球場。所以,我只好堅強一點忍受羞辱,並抱著害怕上癮的心情。我想我必須要試一試。

argue〔'ɑrgjʊ〕v. 辯駁　　terrific〔tə'rɪfɪk〕adj. 極好的

course〔kors〕n. 球場

beautiful〔'bjutəfəl〕adj. 很好的;晴朗宜人的

partner〔'pɑrtnɚ〕n. 同伴

hit〔hɪt〕v. 打　　***laugh about*** 嘲笑

frustrating〔'frʌstretɪŋ〕adj. 令人受挫的

maddening〔'mædn̩ɪŋ〕adj. 使人瘋狂的

impossible〔ɪm'pɑsəbl̩〕adj. 難應付的

merciless〔'mɝsɪlɪs〕adj. 無情的　　***any more*** 再

steel〔stil〕v. 使硬起心腸;使堅強

humiliation〔hju,mɪlɪ'eʃən〕n. 羞辱

fear〔fɪr〕v. 害怕　　addiction〔ə'dɪkʃən〕n. 上癮

guess〔gɛs〕v. 猜想　　***give it a shot*** 嘗試;揮桿

31. (**B**) 根據作者的看法，高爾夫球爲什麼會有這麼大的吸引力？

   (A) 它使各種程度的運動員受挫，不論你是很厲害、很不錯，或是平庸的運動員。

   (B) <u>連老人都可以打高爾夫球，因爲他們可以在高爾夫球場上開車，不用走路可以省下很多精力。</u>

   (C) 朋友總是要求作者和他們一起打高爾夫球。

   (D) 作者認爲自己沒有足夠的精力來做其他運動。

   * author〔ˋɔθɚ〕n. 作者

   huge〔hjudʒ〕adj. 巨大的　　level〔ˋlɛvḷ〕n. 程度

   join〔dʒɔɪn〕v. 和…一起做同樣的事

   energetic〔ˌɛnɚˋdʒɛtɪk〕adj. 精力充沛的

32. (**A**) 老虎伍茲可能會在什麼時候「一整天邊搖頭邊發牢騷」？

   (A) <u>當他打得很差時</u>　　　(B) 當他打得很好時

   (C) 當他贏得冠軍賽時　　　(D) 當他打贏一場比賽時

   * lousy〔ˋlaʊzɪ〕adj. 差勁的

   excellent〔ˋɛksḷənt〕adj. 優秀的

33. (**B**) 當你年輕時，你可以參加足球、棒球、籃球比賽，以及其他球動你也要動的比賽。關於這句話，下列何者不正確？

   (A) 年輕人喜歡邊跑邊追球。

   (B) <u>年輕人喜歡參加競爭激烈的球賽。</u>

   (C) 年輕人比較容易有充足的精力和球一起跑。

   (D) 耗費力氣的球賽，像是足球、棒球和籃球，適合年輕人。

   * chase〔tʃes〕v. 追逐　　***take part in*** 參加

   competitive〔kəmˋpɛtətɪv〕adj. 競爭的

   tend to* + *V. 傾向；易於

   vigorous〔ˋvɪgərəs〕adj. 精力充沛的

   strenuous〔ˋstrɛnjʊəs〕adj. 耗費力氣的

   suitable〔ˋsutəbḷ〕adj. 適當的

34. (**D**) 作者沒有提到哪件關於「相撲」的事？

    (A) 參加者必須是胖子。

    (B) 大多數的回合是持續三秒鐘。

    (C) 它適合老人和胖子。

    (D) <u>參加的人不需要動。</u>

35. (**C**) 下列哪一項不是作者的朋友支持高爾夫球提出的論點？

    (A) 打出一記好球的興奮感

    (B) 在剛割過草的草皮上，有悠閒而寧靜的氣氛

    (C) <u>打得很差，還有被嘲笑的挫折感</u>

    (D) 閃耀的朝露，以及朋友的陪伴

    * argument〔ˋɑrgjəmənt〕v. 論點
      elation〔ıˋleʃən〕n. 興高采烈
      leisure〔ˋliʒɚ〕adj. 悠閒的　　serene〔səˋrin〕adj. 寧靜的
      mock〔mɑk〕v. 嘲笑　　company〔ˋkʌmpənı〕n. 陪伴

36. (**A**) 最後一句話「堅強一點忍受羞辱」意思是？

    (A) <u>使自己變得堅強，好準備忍受羞辱</u>

    (B) 讓自己變得鐵石心腸，以對抗同情和耐心

    (C) 使自己受到很大的羞辱

    (D) 使自己害怕面對羞辱

    * strengthen〔ˋstrɛŋθən〕v. 使堅強
      humiliate〔hjuˋmılıˏet〕v. 羞辱
      stonyhearted〔ˋstonıˋhɑrtıd〕adj. 鐵石心腸的
      compassion〔kəmˋpæʃən〕n. 同情
      terribly〔ˋtɛrəblı〕adv. 極度地
      scare〔skɛr〕v. 使害怕　　face〔fes〕v. 面對

Questions 37-41

Taiwan baseball fans and observers were shocked to see their team being easily beaten by historic rivals from Korea and Japan at the preliminary round in Tokyo. They were awed by the Korean nine's flawless performance in defeating Japan's dream team twice in a row at Tokyo and Anaheim.

台灣的棒球迷和觀察員對於他們的球隊，在東京的預賽中，輕易地被宿敵日韓打敗，感到很震驚。他們對韓國隊的完美表現心生敬畏，韓國隊連續在東京和阿納罕姆市，打敗日本的夢幻球隊兩次。

fan〔fæn〕*n.* 迷　　observer〔əb'zɝvɚ〕*n.* 觀察員
shocked〔ʃɑkt〕*adj.* 震驚的　　beat〔bit〕*v.* 打敗
historic〔hɪs'tɔrɪk〕*adj.* 歷史上的
rival〔'raɪvl̩〕*n.* 敵手
preliminary〔prɪ'lɪmə͵nɛrɪ〕*adj.* 預備的；初賽的
round〔raʊnd〕*n.* 一次比賽　　awe〔ɔ〕*v.* 心生敬畏
nine〔naɪn〕*n.*（九人一組的）棒球隊
flawless〔'flɔlɪs〕*adj.* 完美的
performance〔pɚ'fɔrməns〕*n.* 表現
defeat〔dɪ'fit〕*v.* 打敗
dream team 夢幻球隊　　***in a row*** 連續地
Anaheim〔'ænə͵haɪm〕*n.* 阿納罕姆市【位於美國南加州】

But Team Japan's fighting spirit, perseverance and skills that enabled it to crush the once "unbeatable Cubans" and win the first championship of the 2006 World Baseball Classic were the most admirable and inspiring.

但是日本隊的奮戰精神、毅力和技巧是最令人欽佩，且具有啟發性的，那些特質使他們擊敗了曾經「不敗的古巴隊」，贏得了二〇〇六年世界棒球經典賽的冠軍。

> fighting〔ˈfaɪtɪŋ〕*adj.* 奮戰的　　spirit〔ˈspɪrɪt〕*n.* 精神
> perseverance〔ˌpɝsəˈvɪrəns〕*n.* 毅力
> enable〔ɪnˈebḷ〕*v.* 使能夠　　crush〔krʌʃ〕*v.* 擊敗
> unbeatable〔ʌnˈbitəbḷ〕*adj.* 不敗的
> Cuban〔ˈkjubən〕*n.* 古巴人
> classic〔ˈklæsɪk〕*n.* 經典的事物
> admirable〔ˈædmərəbḷ〕*adj.* 令人欽佩的
> inspiring〔ɪnˈspaɪrɪŋ〕*adj.* 具有啟發性的

The WBC served as a mirror to Taiwan baseball, which has ceased to improve since a dozen years ago when gambling and game fixing became rampant and the baseball leadership was undermined by <u>mercantilism</u>.

世界棒球經典賽可以作為台灣棒球的借鏡，台灣棒球從十二年前就停止進步了，當時球賽簽賭和作弊的情形猖獗，棒球領導階層逐漸受到重商主義的損害。

> ***serve as*** 作為　　mirror〔ˈmɪrɚ〕*n.* 鏡子
> cease〔sis〕*v.* 停止　　improve〔ɪmˈpruv〕*v.* 進步
> gambling〔ˈgæmblɪŋ〕*n.* 賭博
> fixing〔ˈfɪksɪŋ〕*n.* 作弊【安排球局】
> rampant〔ˈræmpənt〕*adj.* 猖獗的
> leadership〔ˈlidɚˌʃɪp〕*n.* 領導階層
> undermine〔ˌʌndɚˈmaɪn〕*v.* 逐漸損害
> mercantilism〔ˈmɝkənˌtaɪlɪzṃ〕*n.* 重商主義

Once there were two professional leagues, each with six teams, but the island's annual crop of qualified new players numbered less than 10, and few of them had much international experience.

台灣曾有兩個職棒聯盟，每個聯盟有六支球隊，但是這個島上每年出現不到十個合格的新選手，而且他們很少人有豐富的國際賽經驗。

professional〔prəˋfɛʃənḷ〕 *adj.* 職業的
league〔lig〕 *n.* 聯盟
annual〔ˋænjʊəl〕 *adj.* 每年的　　crop〔krɑp〕 *n.* 產量
qualified〔ˋkwɑləˏfaɪd〕 *adj.* 合格的
number〔ˋnʌmbɚ〕 *v.* 數目達到

Gone were the days when there was at least one international little league tournament every summer and an invitation championship journey every winter; six to eight teams from top baseball countries came to show skills.

以前每年夏天至少都會舉辦一場國際少棒錦標賽，每年冬天都會有棒球邀請賽的行程；當時會有六到八隊來自頂尖棒球國家的隊伍，到台灣來展示技巧，這些日子都過去了。

gone〔gɔn〕 *adj.* 過去的
at least 至少　　*little league* 少棒聯盟
tournament〔ˋtɝnəmənt〕 *n.* 錦標賽
invitation〔ˏɪnvəˋteʃən〕 *n.* 邀請　　journey〔ˋdʒɝnɪ〕 *n.* 行程

Taiwan has big-name players in America's MLB and Japan's Central and Pacific Leagues. Sadaharu Oh, manager of the victorious Japanese Team, still carries a Republic of China passport. But Taiwan couldn't form a dream team. Why?

台灣在美國職棒大聯盟、日本中央聯盟，以及太平洋聯盟都有一流的選手。王貞治是日本這個優勝隊伍的總教練，他還是拿中華民國的護照。但是台灣為什麼無法組一支夢幻球隊呢？

> big-name〔'bɪg'nem〕*adj.* 有名的；一流的
> **MLB** 美國職棒大聯盟（= *Major League Baseball*）
> central〔'sɛntrəl〕*adj.* 中央的
> Pacific〔pə'sɪfɪk〕*adj.* 太平洋的
> manager〔'mænɪdʒə〕*n.* 經理；總教練
> victorious〔vɪk'toriəs〕*adj.* 優勝的　　carry〔'kærɪ〕*v.* 帶著
> **Republic of China** 中華民國　　passport〔'pæs,port〕*n.* 護照

37. (**D**) 台灣的棒球迷，對中華台北隊在二〇〇六年世界經典棒球賽中的表現，有什麼感受？

(A) 他們覺得難以抗拒。　　(B) 他們大受感動。

(C) 他們覺得受到鼓勵。　　(D) 他們覺得很失望。

* overwhelming〔,ovə'hwɛlmɪŋ〕*adj.* 無法抵抗的
  impressed〔ɪm'prɛst〕*adj.* 深受感動的
  inspire〔ɪn'spaɪr〕*v.* 鼓勵
  disappointed〔,dɪsə'pɔɪntɪd〕*adj.* 失望的

38. (**B**) 作者認為台灣的棒球發展如何？

(A) 在國際比賽中仍然很有競爭力。

(B) 在多年前的醜聞發生之後，就沒有任何進步。

(C) 每年都有來自國外的頂尖球隊來展示技巧。

(D) 有資格參加世界上的任何大型錦標賽。

* remain〔rɪ'men〕*v.* 仍然　　further〔'fɜðə〕*adj.* 進一步的
  progress〔'pragrɛs〕*n.* 進步　　scandal〔'skændl〕*n.* 醜聞
  abroad〔ə'brɔd〕*adv.* 在外國
  participate〔par'tɪsə,pet〕*v.* 參加

39. (**A**) 第十三行的 "mercantilism" 可能是什麼意思?

(A) **commercialism** 〔 kə'mɝʃəl,ɪzəm 〕 *n.* 商業主義

(B) materialism 〔 mə'tɪrɪəl,ɪzəm 〕 *n.* 物質主義

(C) enthusiasm 〔 ɪn'θjuzɪ,æzəm 〕 *n.* 熱忱

(D) skepticism 〔'skɛptə,sɪzəm 〕 *n.* 懷疑論

40. (**B**) 關於台灣的棒球,本文提到什麼不利的消息?

(A) 日本隊贏得了二○○六年世界棒球經典賽的冠軍。

(B) 棒球聯盟發生簽賭和作弊的醜聞。

(C) 台灣每年至少會舉辦一場國際賽事。

(D) 雖然王貞治是日本隊的總教練,他的國籍仍然是台灣。

* adverse 〔 əd'vɝs 〕 *adj.* 不利的

concerning 〔 kən'sɝnɪŋ 〕 *prep.* 有關

mention 〔'mɛnʃən 〕 *v.* 提到

despite 〔 dɪ'spaɪt 〕 *prep.* 儘管

Taiwanese 〔,taɪwɑ'niz 〕 *adj.* 台灣人的

nationality 〔,næʃən'ælətɪ 〕 *n.* 國籍

41. (**A**) 下列何者不是台灣無法組成夢幻球隊的原因?

(A) 台灣有名的選手都加入外國的職棒球隊了。

(B) 國際經驗不足。

(C) 缺乏優秀的領導階層。

(D) 合格的選手數目有限。

* overseas 〔'ovə'siz 〕 *adj.* 外國的

insufficient 〔,ɪnsə'fɪʃənt 〕 *adj.* 不足的

lack 〔 læk 〕 *n.* 缺乏   limited 〔'lɪmɪtɪd 〕 *adj.* 有限的

well-qualified 〔'wɛl'kwɑlə,faɪd 〕 *adj.* 夠資格的;合格的

Questions 42-46

Believe in the healing power of touch. A friendly embrace. A backrub. The ways we show affection can also keep us healthy. Sure, a massage is relaxing, and always feels great—it's also good for you. Massage has been shown to relieve pain and anxiety, ease depression and speed recovery from medical treatment.

你要相信接觸有治療的能力。一個友善的擁抱。揉一揉背。我們表達情感的方式也能使我們保持健康。當然，按摩令人放鬆，而且感覺總是很棒 —— 按摩也對你有益。人們已經證實，按摩有減輕疼痛及焦慮的效果，它還可以減輕憂鬱，並使人們更快從醫療中復原。

heal〔hil〕n. 治療　　embrace〔ɪm'bres〕n. 擁抱
backrub〔'bæk,rʌb〕n. 揉背　　affection〔ə'fɛkʃən〕n. 情感
massage〔mə'sɑʒ〕n.,v. 按摩
relaxing〔rɪ'læksɪŋ〕adj. 令人輕鬆的
relieve〔rɪ'liv〕v. 減輕　　anxiety〔æŋ'zaɪətɪ〕n. 憂慮
ease〔iz〕v. 減輕　　depression〔dɪ'prɛʃən〕n. 沮喪；憂鬱症
speed〔spid〕v. 加速　　recovery〔rɪ'kʌvərɪ〕n. 復原
medical〔'mɛdɪkḷ〕adj. 醫學的
treatment〔'tritmənt〕n. 治療

"The benefits of touch show up at almost every age," says psychologist Tiffany Field, who directs the Touch Research Institute at the University of Miami School of Medicine. Premature infants who are held often develop faster than those left alone, and healthy babies who get lots of physical contact cry less and sleep better.

「接觸的好處幾乎可以在各個年齡層看到。」心理學家蒂芬妮·菲爾特說，她掌管邁阿密大學醫學院的接觸研究機構。常被抱著的早產兒，發育速度比那些沒人理的快，還有常獲得肢體接觸的健康嬰兒，比較少哭，而且睡得比較好。

benefit〔'bɛnəfɪt〕*n.* 好處　　***show up*** 顯現

psychologist〔saɪ'kɑlədʒɪst〕*n.* 心理學家

direct〔də'rɛkt〕*v.* 指導；掌管　　research〔rɪ's₃tʃ〕*n.* 研究

institute〔'ɪnstə,tjut〕*n.* 機構　　university〔,junə'v₃sətɪ〕*n.* 大學

school〔skul〕*n.* 學院　　medicine〔'mɛdəsn̩〕*n.* 醫學

premature〔,prɪmə'tjur〕*adj.* 早產的

infant〔'ɪnfənt〕*n.* 嬰兒　　hold〔hold〕*v.* 抱

develop〔dɪ'vɛləp〕*v.* 發育　　***leave~alone*** 任由；不管

physical〔'fɪzɪkl̩〕*adj.* 身體的　　contact〔'kɑntækt〕*n.* 接觸

How touch delivers such benefits is unclear, though researchers have documented its ability to slow heart rate, lower blood pressure and increase levels of serotonin, the brain chemical that's linked to a feeling of well-being. It also decreases levels of the stress hormone cortisol, which can boost immunity.

我們還不清楚接觸如何傳達這些益處，不過研究人員已經記錄到，接觸可以減緩心跳速率、降低血壓，並提高血清素的含量，而這種腦化學物和幸福的感覺是有關係的。接觸還可以降低壓力賀爾蒙腎上腺素的含量，使免疫力提升。

deliver〔dɪ'lɪvɚ〕*v.* 傳達　　researcher〔rɪ's₃tʃɚ〕*n.* 研究人員

document〔'dɑkjə,mɛnt〕*v.* 記錄　　rate〔ret〕*n.* 速率

lower〔'loɚ〕*v.* 降低　　blood〔blʌd〕*n.* 血液

pressure〔'prɛʃɚ〕*n.* 壓力　　level〔'lɛvl̩〕*n.* 含量

serotonin〔,sɛrə'tonɪn〕*n.* 血清素

brain〔bren〕n. 大腦　　chemical〔ˈkɛmɪk!〕n. 化學物質
linked〔lɪŋkt〕adj. 連結的；有關的
well-being〔ˈwɛlˈbiɪŋ〕n. 幸福　　decrease〔dɪˈkris〕v. 降低
stress〔strɛs〕n. 壓力　　hormone〔ˈhɔrmon〕n. 賀爾蒙
cortisol〔ˈkɔrtɪsɑl〕n. 腎上腺皮質素
boost〔bust〕v. 提升　　immunity〔ɪˈmjunətɪ〕n. 免疫力

Massage can even hasten healing. At the University of Colorado Health Sciences Center, bone-marrow transplant patients given massages had better neurological function than those in a control group. And researchers in Sweden reported that massage reduced pain by 37 percent in patients with fibromyalgia, a condition characterized by chronic muscle aches.

按摩甚至可以使復原的速度加快。在科羅拉多大學的健康科學中心，接受按摩的骨髓移植病患，其神經功能會比對照組的人好。瑞典的研究人員說，按摩可以減少纖維肌痛患者百分之三十七的疼痛，這種病的特徵是肌肉長期疼痛。

hasten〔ˈhesn̩〕v. 加速　　healing〔ˈhilɪŋ〕n. 復原
bone〔bon〕n. 骨頭　　marrow〔ˈmæro〕n. 骨髓
bone-marrow 骨髓　　transplant〔ˈtræns͵plænt〕n. 移植
patient〔ˈpeʃənt〕n. 病患
neurological〔͵njurəˈlɑdʒɪkəl〕adj. 神經的
function〔ˈfʌŋkʃən〕n. 功能　　***control group*** 對照組
Sweden〔ˈswidn̩〕n. 瑞典　　report〔rɪˈpɔrt〕v. 報告；傳達說
fibromyalgia〔͵faɪbrəmaɪˈældʒɪə〕n. 纖維肌痛
condition〔kənˈdɪʃən〕n. 疾病；異常
characterize〔ˈkærɪktə͵raɪz〕v. 特徵是
chronic〔ˈkrɑnɪk〕adj. 長期的　　muscle〔ˈmʌs!〕n. 肌肉
ache〔ek〕n. 疼痛

Giving may be as good as receiving: A study at England's Queen Charlotte's and Chelsea Hospital found that mothers suffering from postpartum depression who massaged their infants related better to them. In another study, elderly volunteers who massaged infants reported feeling less anxious and depressed. It even works when you do it yourself:

施與受同樣有福：在英國的夏樂蒂皇后與雀兒喜醫院的研究發現，患有產後憂鬱症的母親，多替嬰兒按摩，會使親子間的相處更融洽。另一個研究發現，替嬰兒按摩的年長義工，比較不會覺得憂鬱和沮喪。甚至連幫自己按摩都是有效的：

suffer (ˈsʌfɚ) v. 罹患
postpartum (ˌpostˈpɑrtəm) adj. 產後的
relate (rɪˈlet) v. 有關；相處 < to >
volunteer (ˌvɑlənˈtɪr) n. 義工
anxious (ˈæŋkʃəs) adj. 憂慮的
depressed (dɪˈprɛst) adj. 沮喪的   work (wɝk) v. 有效

A 1999 study found that smokers who were taught self-massage while trying to quit felt less anxiety and smoked less. A study by Italian researchers found that 43 percent of patients with tension headaches reported massaging their temples and necks to get relief. To try it, apply moderate pressure to your temples, hands, feet or the back of your neck.

一九九九年的研究發現，在吸煙者試圖要戒煙時，教他們替自己按摩，會使他們比較不會覺得憂鬱，而且也會少抽點煙。由義大利研究人員所從事的研究發現，百分之四十三患有緊張性頭痛的病患說，藉由按摩太陽穴和脖子，可以減輕他們的症狀。試試看，用適當的力量來按摩你的太陽穴、手、腳，或是頸背。

quit〔kwɪt〕v. 停止；戒掉　　Italian〔ɪˋtæljən〕adj. 義大利的

tension〔ˋtɛnʃən〕n. 緊張　　***tension headache*** 緊張性頭痛

temple〔ˋtɛmpl̩〕n. 太陽穴　　neck〔nɛk〕n. 脖子

relief〔rɪˋlif〕n. 減輕　　apply〔əˋplaɪ〕v. 運用

moderate〔ˋmɑdərɪt〕adj. 適當的

pressure〔ˋprɛʃɚ〕n. 力量

42. (**C**) 何謂 "premature baby"？

(A) 常哭的嬰兒　　　　(B) 足月出生的嬰兒

(C) 太早出生的嬰兒　　(D) 常常被觸摸和擁抱的嬰兒

* ***in due course*** 在適當的時候

43. (**D**) 如果血清素的含量增加，會發生什麼事？

(A) 一個人的免疫力會提高。

(B) 一個人的肌肉酸痛會減輕。

(C) 一個人會覺得壓力比較大。

(D) 一個人會更快樂，而且感覺更好。

* stressed-out〔ˋstrɛst͵aʊt〕adj. 感到有壓力的

44. (**B**) 下列哪一項屬於對照組？

(A) 在實驗中接受治療的人。

(B) 在實驗中未接受治療的人。

(C) 做實驗的人。

(D) 出錢做實驗的人。

* belong〔bəˋlɔŋ〕v. 屬於　　treat〔trit〕v. 治療

experiment〔ɪkˋspɛrəmənt〕n. 實驗

leave〔liv〕v. 使維持某種狀態

conduct〔kənˋdʌkt〕v. 進行

finance〔fəˋnæns〕v. 資助；出錢

45. (**D**) 根據本文，下列哪一項不是按摩的好處？
 (A) 可以減輕疼痛和憂慮。
 (B) 可以減少憂慮。
 (C) 可以帶來幸福的感覺。
 (D) 可以提高你想抽煙的慾望。

 * **bring about** 引起；帶來　　desire〔dɪˈzaɪr〕n. 慾望

46. (**C**) 根據本文，下列何者不正確？
 (A) 無論你是被別人按摩、幫別人按摩，或者甚至是幫自己
　　按摩，對你都有好處。
 (B) 接觸的治療能力對老少都有效。
 (C) 壓力賀爾蒙腎上腺素可以提高免疫力。
 (D) 替自己按摩也有助於舒緩緊張。

 * **no matter** 無論　　effective〔əˈfɛktɪv〕adj. 有效的
　　heighten〔ˈhaɪtn̩〕v. 提高

Questions 47-50

　　A Mediterranean diet, rich in olive oil, fish, poultry, and fruit and vegetables, can relieve the symptoms of rheumatoid arthritis, scientists said.

　　科學家說，地中海式飲食富含橄欖油、魚肉、家禽肉、以及蔬菜水果，可以舒緩風濕性關節炎的症狀。

　　Mediterranean〔ˌmɛdətəˈrenɪən〕adj. 地中海的
　　diet〔ˈdaɪət〕n. 飲食　　rich〔rɪtʃ〕adj. 豐富的
　　olive oil〔ˈɑlɪvˈɔɪl〕n. 橄欖油　　poultry〔ˈpoltrɪ〕n. 家禽的肉
　　symptom〔ˈsɪmptəm〕n. 症狀
　　rheumatoid〔ˈrumə,tɔɪd〕adj. 風濕性的
　　arthritis〔ɑrˈθraɪtɪs〕n. 關節炎

Although a Mediterranean diet is usually recommended to reduce the risk of heart disease, Dr. Lars Skoldstam, of Visby Hospital in Sweden, found it reduced the pain and improved the physical function of people with rheumatoid arthritis (RA).

雖然地中海式飲食常被建議用來降低罹患心臟病的風險，但是瑞典維斯比醫院的醫生拉斯・史考德史丹發現，它還可以減輕風濕性關節炎患者的疼痛，並改善他們的身體機能。

> recommend〔͵rɛkə′mɛnd〕v. 推薦；建議
> disease〔dɪ′ziz〕n. 疾病

After three months on the diet, RA patients lost about three kg (6.6 lb) in weight, had lower cholesterol levels and less pain in their joints than a control group of patients who did not change their eating habits.

食用三個月的地中海飲食後，和沒有改變飲食習慣的對照組比較，風濕性關節炎患者的體重會減輕三公斤左右（6.6 磅），而且體內的膽固醇指數會減少，關節也比較不痛了。

> lose〔luz〕v. 減少
> lb （重量的）磅（＝ libra〔′laɪbrə〕）
> weight〔wet〕n. 體重
> cholesterol〔kə′lɛstə͵rol〕n. 膽固醇
> joint〔dʒɔɪnt〕n. 關節　　habit〔′hæbɪt〕n. 習慣

"The treated group felt significantly improved compared to the controls after three months with this diet," Skoldstam told Reuters.

「在吃三個月的地中海飲食之後,和對照組相較之下,治療組的人覺得病情大有起色。」史考德史丹告訴路透社說。

> treat〔trit〕v. 治療
> significantly〔sɪgˈnɪfəkəntlɪ〕adv. 大大地
> compare〔kəmˈpɛr〕v. 比較
> control〔kənˈtrol〕n. 對照組的人
> Reuters〔ˈrɔɪtəz〕n. 路透通訊社 (= *Reuter's News Agency*)

Rheumatoid arthritis is an autoimmune disease in which the body's immune system attacks cartilage in the joints. It affects about two percent of the population but more women suffer from it than men.

　　風濕性關節炎是一種自體免疫疾病,患者的免疫系統會攻擊關節的軟骨。大約有百分之二的人會受到這種疾病的侵襲,而且女性患者比男性患者多。

> autoimmune〔ˌɔtoɪˈmjun〕adj. 自體免疫的
> attack〔əˈtæk〕v. 攻擊
> cartilage〔ˈkɑrtḷɪdʒ〕n. 軟骨　　affect〔əˈfɛkt〕v. 侵襲
> population〔ˌpɑpjəˈleʃən〕n. 人口　　suffer〔ˈsʌfə〕v. 罹患

Skoldstam, who reported his findings in the Annals of the Rheumatic Diseases, believes that there are connections between rheumatoid arthritis and heart disease.

　　史考德史丹把他的研究結果發表在風濕性關節炎年報上,他認為風濕性關節炎和心臟病有關。

> report〔rɪˈport〕v. 公開發表;報導
> Annals〔ˈænḷz〕n. 年報;年刊
> connection〔kəˈnɛkʃən〕n. 關連

47. (**A**) 關於風濕性關節炎，下列何者不正確？
    (A) 有百分之二的女性罹患風濕性關節炎，而男性罹患這種疾病的百分比較女性高。
    (B) 這種疾病是患者的關節受到侵襲。
    (C) 在罹患風濕性關節炎的百分之二人口中，女性多於男性。
    (D) 報導說，風濕性關節炎可能跟心臟病有關。

    * percentage〔pə'sɛntɪdʒ〕*n.* 百分比
      likely〔'laɪklɪ〕*adj.* 可能的
      connected〔kə'nɛktɪd〕*adj.* 有關的

48. (**D**) 地中海式飲食對風濕性關節炎患者有何幫助？
    (A) 他們的體重減輕一些。　　(B) 他們的膽固醇指數降低了。
    (C) 他們的關節比較不痛了。　(D) 以上皆是。

49. (**B**) 這個實驗的主要發現是？
    (A) 地中海式飲食可以減少得心臟病的風險。
    (B) 地中海式飲食可以減輕關節炎的疼痛。
    (C) 地中海式飲食可以降低膽固醇。
    (D) 地中海式飲食可以減少罹患風濕性關節炎的風險。

    * chief〔tʃif〕*adj.* 主要的　　lessen〔'lɛsn̩〕*v.* 減輕
      develop〔dɪ'vɛləp〕*v.* 患（病）；顯出（疾病）的症狀

50. (**D**) 關於文中所提到的實驗，何者正確？
    (A) 對照組改變了他們的飲食，但是沒有發生任何事。
    (B) 這個實驗是在瑞士的斯德哥爾摩進行的。
    (C) 這個實驗持續了半年左右。
    (D) 研究結果被刊登在和風濕症有關的期刊上。

    * *carry out* 實行
      Stockholm〔'stɑk͵hom〕*n.* 斯德哥爾摩（瑞典首都）
      Switzerland〔'swɪtsələnd〕*n.* 瑞士（首都是伯恩 Bern）
      last〔læst〕*v.* 持續　　publish〔'pʌblɪʃ〕*v.* 出版；刊登
      journal〔'dʒɝnl̩〕*n.* 期刊